LIGHT

BOLT SAGA: VOLUME SIX
PARTS 16 - 17 - 18

ANGEL PAYNE

D1371726

LIGHT

BOLT SAGA: VOLUME SIX
PARTS 16 - 17 - 18

ANGEL PAYNE

WATERHOUSE PRESS

TABLE OF CONTENTS

To the two who have given up more than
anyone for this to happen:

Thomas and Jessica,
you are my heroes, my heart, my home, my fire,
my everlasting lights, my eternal inspirations.

You are my Excelsior.

LIGHT

PART 16

CHAPTER ONE

REECE

"Someone's been keeping a secret."

Faline Garand flings the singsong words at me with an insolent toss of her head. My human reaction of rage mixes with the inhuman energy of my blood, nearly driving me to stretch out my fingers until lightning ropes unfurl from their tips. I envision the lassos whipping around her bony neck. Searing into her ghost-white skin. Wrapping so tight, her coy nod becomes a prelude for the fast snap that will end her life.

That will end her command over *my* life.

One cinch. One yank. One twist. And then she's done.

Not going to happen.

Because I won't do it.

I *can't* do it.

Not when the bitch has my baby boy cradled in one arm and my woman's neck in a vise grip with the other.

Not when a simple snap ignited by her superpowers could end their lives before I have the chance to blink.

No. Jesus God. No!

Terror burns my gut and my veins, transforming them into impotent fury. "If you hurt one fucking hair on either of them..." I dissolve the rest of the sentiment into a growl, because truthfully, the growl is all I have. The bitch with the slicked black hair and the cutting feline eyes knows it too. The slow curve at the corner of her mouth tells me so. As her insolence intensifies, Emma's breathing quickens—and my heart screams louder.

Emmalina.

My flare. My light. My love.

My goddess has been shoved to her knees and is held by her hair, stark blue terror in her eyes and trembling rage across her lips. Her composure crumples as Faline twists her hair tighter. The bitch *tsks* smoothly into the murky, foggy air.

What the fuck is going on? Is all of this even real? I consider the questions harder while peering around, fighting to pierce the murk with fingers I've fired into light sticks. But the brighter I amp them, the thicker the fog gets. Where the *hell* are we? And do I really care? My only focus—the only reason I continue to breathe—is getting my little boy and my heart's beloved away from this witch and her sick addiction to my agony. Especially if she's the one causing it.

"Oh, all of their precious hairs are just fine, *cariño*," the woman soothes. "Most especially, *this* sweet little one's..." She brushes her bloodred lips across my baby's forehead—gashing deeper into my soul with every inch she covers. The edges of my vision turn a matching shade of red but are quickly taken over by blinding flashes of hot silver.

A harsh growl pours from me. I lurch forward but check my momentum when the bitch wrenches Emma's hair. Though my wife grits back the scream that clearly rises in her throat, tears seep from the corners of her huge eyes.

"Such a beautiful boy. Such a magnificent miracle."

Despite Faline's abject reverence, Emma bares her teeth and hisses through them before spewing, "If you hurt him, I swear to God, I'll—"

"Hurt him?" The witch eclipses her adoration with an insulted huff. "*Hurt* him?" She turns the huff into a snarl and sends a burst of electricity to her hand. At once, small puffs of smoke erupt from Emma's hair—and then undoubtedly from her scalp—as Faline embosses her fingerprints along the top of my wife's head. "For a *puta* smart enough to ensnare Reece Richards, you are truly a stupid peasant." She releases Emma with a violent shove, only to secure her prisoner again by planting a boot against Emma's throat. "Oh, I do not plan on *hurting* him, little *idiota*. You have my promise about that." As she looks down again at my boy, her tone takes on the same fierce adoration that takes over her face. "He will know he is a miracle, enhanced and exquisite, every day of his life. He will know that because I will make sure of it."

I'm not sure what chills me deeper: the possessiveness in the bitch's voice or the matching twines of it through her posture as she curls her upper body around the innocent form of my son.

Who reaches a tiny hand up to her face.

Who grabs at her cheek, as if recognizing her...and trusting her.

Who smiles as another hand moves in and cups Faline's face with the same open adoration.

A hand that's sneaked in from below. Belonging to my wife.

Who now rises, slowly sliding herself up Faline's form, her sweet smile lifting with every inch she climbs.

A smile no longer meant for me.

She's beaming it into the bitch's welcoming face. Trusting Faline exactly as my baby boy does. And finally, parting her lips to speak again.

Aha. Here's where she'll make it right. Where she'll tell that filthy harpy to get her goddamned hands off our son, and if she doesn't—

"She'll make sure of it, Reece." Without lowering her hand from Faline's pale cheek, Emma tilts her head to capture my gaze with the splendor of her own. Except that turquoise glory is no longer saved for me. Or even focused on me. Her dazzling blues are shrouded in unseeing mists. She stares right through me despite how she keeps speaking to me. "You heard her, didn't you? She's got this, baby. She'll make sure our bean is safe, okay? She'll make sure all is well."

"There, now." Faline's lips flow with a wider smirk. "It is all settled. You will have no more worries about this, my darling."

"I'm not your fucking darling," I seethe. "And this is *not* all settled! Emma. *Emma.*" But while I keep reaching to my wife, she doesn't respond. Her gaze becomes more vacant. More and more, she slips into a trance like the one her mother was in after Faline kidnapped the woman and then returned her to us eight hours later as a new member of the "Faline is Goddess of all" cult. Jesus. *No.* Emma would gash her wrists before signing up to drink that bitch's Kool-Aid. "Damn it! Emma, wake the hell up! She wants to take our boy! *Our son!*"

"And hers too." Emma weaves her head through the air as if following the sway of a tree in the wind. "He's special, Reece. He needs her special care and guidance."

"He needs *our* care and guidance!" My senses seize and blaze before exploding and then freezing. My terror is so immense, my body doesn't know what to do about its force. I don't give a shit. The implosion of my soul is all-consuming— and beyond devastating. How can Faline be doing this? How can Emmalina be *letting* her? What the living *fuck* is going on? "Emma, listen to what you're saying. This isn't right. Wake *up!*"

"Hmmm." She rocks her head again—before stopping her motions to pin me with the blue tranquility of her gaze. "I'm afraid not."

I plummet to my knees. "Jesus." Then utter beneath my breath, "No." Then whisper down at my clenched fists, "*No!*"

"*You're* the one who needs to wake up, baby." Her voice is also just a rasp. Soft but husky, like moss growing on a rusty gate that she's locked up tight and refuses to open. "Reece. *Reece.* Wake up..."

I can barely hear her.

Though she's standing right there, with her mist-covered gaze and her sweet swaying form, it sounds as if she's run off to an enchanted glade and is playing hide-and-seek in the trees with my addled psyche.

"Reece. Oh, baby. *Wake up.*"

But I stand my ground. Root myself in with the remaining strength left in my bones. "No, goddamnit. I'm not going to let you do this. I'm not going to let *her* do it!"

"Her who?"

"Huh?" Why is she fucking with me like this? She's pawing at Faline like a smitten disciple, and she dares ask me that? What the hell is wrong with her? What the hell has that bitch done to her?

"Reece. *Hey.* Zeus Man. Come on, now. Open your eyes and look at me."

Open my—

What the fuck? My eyes *are* open. Aren't they?

I funnel all my efforts toward my face, consciously blinking my eyes. *Well, holy shit.*

Faline is nowhere in sight.

What I *do* see are the familiar outlines of furniture in the master bedroom of the Newport Beach safe house in which Emmalina and I have been living for a little over two months. Though to get technical, I'm not sure the word "safe" will ever fully apply to my existence—or that the word "house" can really stand in for the oceanfront complex I secured in case we ever needed to really vanish from the Consortium's radar. All right, so it's an oxymoron—"disappearing" in a three-story Craftsman with a dozen bedrooms and panoramic ocean views—but the new digs and our Bohemian disguises have so far accomplished the trick.

Now if my subconscious would only read that memo. And believe it.

A cause my *conscious* mind has a few choice opinions about.

"Fuck." I swallow the end of the utterance while gathering Emma's hand tighter against my sweat-covered chest. "I...I was..."

"Dreaming." She soothes the word into the plane of my pectoral before trailing her lips up to the side of my neck, brushing her cool breath into my system along the way. "Just a dream, my love."

No. A nightmare.

But I keep the words to myself, not wanting to burden her with the disturbing shit that just dominated my mind. It's enough for me that none of it is true. That she's right here, free from that mist in her eyes, gazing at me with clarity and love, the sweet curves of her face defined by the perfect midnight glow filtering in through the windows.

"You want to talk about it?"

"*No*." The answer spills out way too fast and much too urgently—and neither tidbit escapes her attention.

"You sure?" she prods. "Baby, this is the third night in a row now, and—"

"I can count, Emma." At once regretting my snarl, I sift my fingers into her hair and gently rub her scalp. "It's really nothing, okay?" I shift a little, coaxing her body closer while dipping my lips toward hers. "Sorry I woke you."

"You didn't." Her smile is forgiving. "Well, not really, because your son already did the job." While guiding my hand across the prominence of her belly, she adds, "He's been playing 'Team Bolt Supersonic Obstacle Course' in there all night."

The second a robust little kick thuds against my palm, I chuckle. "No shit."

"Maybe you're just on the same wavelength with him again."

I mellow my laugh into a proud smile. "You think?"

Her expression turns enigmatic. "I wouldn't be surprised, Papa Richards. The bean is already very fond of his daddy."

Cynical chuff. "Or maybe it's the enchilada you had for dinner."

"It was a freaking *fine* enchilada."

Another chuff—though I'm darker about it this time. "Ohhhh, hell." And I weather her answering giggle in return, knowing that *she* knows the conclusion *I've* already jumped to.

"Awwww, come on!" she protests. "Can I help it if everything goes better with supersized pregnancy hormones?"

And damn, does the woman mean *everything*. Including garlic ice cream and Cheez-It toppings, classic Krispy Kremes dipped in cottage cheese, and pepperoni pizza slathered in squeeze-style frosting. Fortunately, I've got all of those stocked in the house by now—but the woman's been throwing some craving curve balls at me lately.

"All right," I finally grumble. "I might as well just get this over with." And then push up to one elbow, gently clearing some stray strands away from her cheek. "What'll it be for tonight's midnight snack, m'lady?"

At first, she just pulls her bottom lip in under her top teeth—but the impish glints in her eyes already warn me to expect the curve ball. "All I want is a giant dose of you, my lord."

Well, that *is* a curve ball.

One I'm completely ready to turn into a home run.

Yeah, despite the disturbing nightmare. Probably *because* of the damn thing. What would wash away Faline's stink from my mind better than burying my cock inside the sugar-and-cream goodness of my wife?

The possibility is so damn good, I have to reconfirm it. "Are you really saying you don't want *any* of the odd but awesome snacks I've stocked downstairs for you?"

"Oh, I want odd but awesome." Her touch is as steady as her gleaming, confident gaze—as she rolls to her side and reaches for the flesh that's already jumping between my legs. As she skims over my lower abs and then rubs me through my sleep pants, the friction of the fabric only stokes the energy of my arousal that much faster. Holy *fuck*, that's good. *So damn good.* "But my 'snack' of preference isn't downstairs."

I attempt to summon a glib comeback to my lips—but that shit isn't happening for my head, let alone my mouth. Instead, I tell her what she needs to know via the breath I finally let out, as staticky as it is, while the temptress of my dreams heats her palm enough to fry away the crotch of my sleep pants.

For a second, I'm too astonished to speak. Who the hell am I kidding? I'm not shocked; I'm turned way the fuck on. Just the idea of what damage she could've dealt to my cock with her tactile flare gun—but didn't—injects my bloodstream with the same demented sensation I get before taking down criminals. I guess it's true what they say. Danger and fear *are* a heady aphrodisiac.

I regain enough composure to glance down. Sure enough, the blackened threads of my sleep pants mingle with the copious precome seeping along the length of my throbbing cock. I'm already swollen with need but getting bigger and harder by the second. The sight of Emma's huge baby bump, even beneath her roomy sleep shirt, only adds to the lust transforming my erection into a glowing blue sex toy.

"Holy...*shit*," I grate.

"Sorry," Emma rushes out in a rough rasp. "About the... pants."

I glower with deliberate darkness. "No, you're not."

"All right, I'm not." She jogs her chin up. God*damn*it, the woman is breathtaking when she's feisty. "I'm just too hungry for my snack."

I tug at the hem of her shirt. Lift it until I can view the fullness of our baby beneath her naked skin. She hasn't bothered to put on panties with the ensemble. *Yesssss.*

I lean in, caressing her stomach with my fingers and her throat with my mouth. "You're too hungry...for me?" I snarl softly into her ear.

She trembles from head to toe, and I feel every perfect tremor of it. "*Yes.*" Her whisper is a wobble on the air, instantly surging my senses with the heady knowledge of my power over her. I love doing this to her. Unleashing the force of my electric field on the air and knowing what I'm doing to her with it. And anticipating everything I'm *about* to do, as well...

"What part is starving more, sweet bunny?" I roll my touch upward until I'm palming the fullness of her right breast. And then tugging and rolling at her nipple. And then reveling in the urgent gasp of need she gives in return. "Your wet, perfect pussy...or your hot, succulent mouth?"

She gulps hard. I almost give her a little reassurance. There's really no wrong answer here...

"My...my mouth."

But that definitely feels like the more *right* answer at this moment.

My perverted mind takes the idea and runs like hell with it. My willing dick is dragged along for the sprint. At once, my cockhead is drenched with scalding drops, and my pulse jacks to a marathon-level cadence. I'm so fucking ready for this. To burn away the revulsion from my dream with the fire of my beautiful Flare. To forget what her mouth declared in my subconscious by rendering her incapable of words. With my cock consuming her mouth—and then with the climax I'll rock her with from the inside out. That's always the best part: watching as my essence pours down through her, taking over every part of her until she can't stand the fire and finally gives in to the exquisite implosion.

Holy hell.

I can't fucking wait.

I *won't* fucking wait.

With that resolve, I pull far enough away so I'm not tempted to keep playing with her luscious tits. Christ, her breasts have always been the most entrancing things in my world, but that magic bean in her belly clearly saved some sorcery to enhance them more. From experience, I already know that if I suck them long enough, her nipples will glow for me like iridescent fairies.

But they're going to do that for me anyway...

As soon as I make her come like the horny little bunny she is.

"Well," I drawl while sliding my hands under her buttocks and helping her scoot back until she's leaning against the headboard. "You know what they say about keeping an expectant goddess from her midnight snack for too long."

After she settles into place, she flashes me a flirty, dirty smirk. "Oh, what *do* they say?"

"No fucking idea." I shrug, basking in her giggle. "I was hoping my smart-as-hell wife had that answer for me."

She waggles her brows. "You're in luck, mister. Turns out that she does."

Bantering with the woman, from blatant porn-worthy lines to these kind of cute back-and-forths, is always as big a turn-on as a twist to the balls, but tonight it means even more. Heals me even deeper. Takes me further away from the darkness of my dream. "Enlighten me, teacher." *My goddess. My deliverance. My miracle. My superheroine.*

Emma doesn't respond right away. She reaches out and takes command, tugging on me until I'm straddling her upper body. If my cock were flaccid, it'd be dangling directly between her breasts—but I'm positive my dick and flaccid haven't been acquainted since the day I met this woman. Just knowing she's in the world—in *my* world—has injected the thing with a constant charge, ready to zap into action from the second she needs me. Every minute of every day, I'm ready for her. Sometimes, it's every *second*.

Like right now.

I watch, feeling like a crackhead about to get his best high, as my wife reaches back and grabs the headboard, making her shirt stretch tight across her stiff nipples. When she adds a seductive stare through her dusky lashes, I'm nearly undone. Neither of us misses the milk that oozes from the slit atop my rock-hard length—or the way the whole stalk bobs on the air, my instinct already guiding it closer toward her full, pink mouth.

All she has to do is open.

Dear fuck, baby. Please open...

But she doesn't.

Instead, she purses those gorgeous pillows, rivaling any screen sex goddess that Hollywood ever created, and then unfurls a mystical little smile. "So. You *really* want to know the secret about goddesses and their snacks?"

The question alone has my dick jerking again, a zealous dog straining at its tether. "That depends," I growl.

Her expression turns inquisitive. "On what?"

"On whether you're going to make me go down to the kitchen and fetch Funyuns and hummus for you."

Her giggle is a musical cadence on the air. "Nope. No Funyuns." She punctuates it in the best way possible, splaying a hand around my ass and jerking me closer with clear command. "Only this. Only you." With her other hand now clutching its corresponding ass cheek, she yanks me in closer. I grunt in pleasure, moving close enough to feel her rapid breaths along my throbbing length, and steady my balance by bracing one hand to the top of the headboard. "You see, goddesses don't like to wait long for their cravings."

I chuckle. Okay, try to. "Ah. So *that's* the big secret, hmmm?"

She's not laughing anymore. She's intent and focused, her eyes glazed with gorgeous lust, as she homes in on the dark-red bulb before her face, still dripping with the arousal I can't control any longer. The need I can no longer hide—or restrain. "When a goddess wants something, Zeus, a goddess gets it any way she can."

The husk in her voice is enough incentive for a thousand new filaments of lust through my body. On top of that, there's the heat of her breaths, the fire in her gaze...

And at last, the opening of her gorgeous lips.

"Well." I'm so fixated on her welcoming beauty, I'm stunned I can talk. But I manage to complete my sentence by husking out, "Don't let it be said that I disappointed *my* goddess."

"Never." She whispers it while urging me closer by another inch—until she's able to suckle my shaft. When she closes her eyes, tilts her head back, and swallows my juice with a mewl of wonder, it takes the effort of every muscle in my frame not to push forward and sheath myself to the balls down her throat.

But I've got to release a fraction of my tension—so I do so by indulging in some filthy bedroom talk. "Christ on fucking high. You're the best goddamned thing that's ever happened to my cock, woman."

She drags her eyes open—at least enough to unleash the mesmerizing power of her blues on me once more. "And you're the best snack I've ever devoured, mister."

I grab myself by the base of my shaft. It's heaven and hell, since I'm now able to squeeze back the searing surge from my balls while guiding myself right toward the target of her waiting orifice. "But you're *not* devouring." I nudge my cockhead back between her soft, sweet lips. "Maybe it's time to change that."

"Mmmmm." Her moan is also heaven and hell—in all the best ways of both. "Mmmm-hmmm."

And then, at fucking *last*, she's giving me relief. Sucking me in. Taking me down. Surrounding my bulging, hammering shaft with her cushioning, caressing softness. Moaning around me, just to make it better. All the while gazing up at me, just to make it perfect.

"Yessssss," I hiss. "Oh, fuck me...*yes*, my goddess."

She swallows me down deeper. Then a little more. Possessing me with her heat. Branding me with her tongue...

Healing me with her hold.

"God*damn*it, Emma. The way you do that...oh fuck, *just like that*..." And my own long, tortured groan is my interruption as she curls in the tip of her tongue and uses it to trace the veins along the underside of my cock, starting at the heated sack at the base. *My* cock? There's the joke that's thoroughly on me. No way does this thing belong to *me* anymore. My sex has officially abandoned any control from my mind or instincts, declaring fealty to the goddess who has claimed its every clamoring inch and simmering drop...

Juice that continues to escape, making me growl and groan, as she swallows and undulates around me. Still, I yearn to be deeper. I lust to be the beast that fucks her throat until she can think of nothing but my cock and can't breathe without inhaling the dominating essence of my body.

"More." I slide my hand from her cheek, delving fingers into her hair, until I can control her angle with the force of my grip. "Take me more, Velvet. Deeper. Harder. Yes. *Yes*. I'm going to fuck this beautiful mouth until you take every drop from me. Every...damn...oh, holy *damn*."

And I'm my own interruption again, as even the dirty

words escape me because of the incredible sight beneath me.

As my precome works its way through my wife's beautiful body, she starts glowing. And I mean *glowing*. Her skin, at first pulsing with a faint amber hue, shines brighter and brighter every time I thrust my aching cock into her gorgeous body. The primal call of giving her my come this way has always been the wildest of turn-ons, but now that I see what it's doing for her—the way it's surging her with light from within—I can't help but pump even deeper into her mouth, letting her take more and more of my flesh with every new lunge...

Which turns her amber into gold and then her gold into light.

A thousand points of perfect effulgence, now beaming like the sun itself has taken over every inch of her succulent body.

As she screams out around my cock.

And quakes with the magnificent, sparkling spasms of her perfect, consuming orgasm.

"Ride it out, my love." I issue the command for her good *and* for mine. Not only does her carnal pleasure bring me complete joy, but I already know there's more of it in store for her. I just want the bridge there to be equally as good for her. No, better than good. I want her to never forget this—because I sure as hell know I never will. "*Fuck*, Emmalina. You're so glorious, baby. If you could see yourself..."

"Mmmm!" I'm not sure exactly what her wet little gurgle is meant to convey, but there's enough eager energy beneath the sound that I know she's having fun. *A lot* of it. And back in the day, I *was* known as the guy who kept the fun rolling. As much as I look back on my debauched living and want to cringe, there are other times that I'm grateful for all the wicked pro tips I've picked up over the years. Like making it okay for a woman to fulfill her own fantasies—by ordering her to do just that.

"*Ride. It. Out*, Emmalina." I get her renewed attention with the strict delivery. "That's not a suggestion, sweetheart. Do you need to help me out here? Then do it. Your fingers on your pussy, baby. Right now. Rub in that heat. Rub it in good."

I release a taut grunt as she complies without a hitch, spreading her thighs so I can see her slender fingers working against her glistening petals. At once, my cock is ten degrees hotter—and as much as I want to stretch out the moment, that means only one thing. I'm going to blow. Hard and hot and fast.

"Damn," I rasp out. "Oh, god*damn*."

My thighs burn. My ass clenches. My balls constrict, clamping down hard on the electrons racing through them.

Electrons that become heat.

Heat that shoots up my cock.

My cock, which bursts into the back of my woman's welcoming throat.

"Fuck!" The word falls out of me at least a dozen more times, through every new pump I give her mouth, every new scream she gives in return, and every new wave of fire and fulfillment that takes over us both...

Until we collapse onto the pillows together, limbs flopping like frayed electric cords.

Even our fingertips betray similar exhaustion, their tips like dying embers as we thread our hands together atop the sweat-soaked sheets. I don't allow that space to be a permanent thing, though. I already crave her nearness and show her so by rolling to my side and twining a calf around one of hers. My cock, still covered in electric come, is compressed between our bodies until we can feel the residual rhythm of our joining from it. Though the pulse is gentle and subtle, it resounds in my senses like a spiritual hammer. A reminder, loud and strong and mighty, of the fact that we haven't just shared bodily fluids.

We've woven our spirits.

Tangled our passion. Resealed our connection. Reaffirmed our love. Renewed our light.

And yeah...left behind the nightmares.

But even that's not as perfect a gift as the one I get from this dream of a moment—as steady thumps emanate from inside my wife's belly. Responding, with awestriking coordination, to the energy that still resonates from between our bodies.

Together, we gasp and then laugh.

At once, our bean kicks with twice his gusto.

"Holy shit." My mutter is answered by Emma's tinkling giggle and my son's dancing footsteps. I swear, as I observe the pattern across the stretch of her belly, the little dude is doing a Texas two-step—or a bad grapevine. Hard to tell when I've got only my dimming fingertips and the filtered moonlight as illumination.

"Well." She chuckles. "Holy *something*."

"I'm not sure whether to be proud and fascinated or stunned and freaked out."

Her laughter hitches. "Why freaked?" And then turns into a chiding huff. "What, because the beat our baby's dancing to is all over your cock and not flowing in your veins?" Since I have no decent answer and she knows it, she charges on. "What's the difference, really? It's your life force, no matter how you look at it. The stuff that created him."

I follow the path of my hand with a trail of reverent kisses. "But our love brought him to life." Yeah, her matter-of-fact side always brings out the mush in me—but can I be blamed?

The woman's mind is even more enticing than her breasts and surges me with the most sickening need to compose greeting card lines.

"Yes," she whispers. "He was created in love, and he'll live in a world filled with as much of it that we can give."

"Working on it every day, beautiful little bunny."

"I know, incredible hunky man."

Well, damn. While her voice is coated with sincerity, I'm just as aware of what she's *not* conveying aloud. There's something about the woman—some kind of frequency or vibration—that I alone have always been able to hear, since the night we first shook hands. From that moment on, I knew I wasn't alone in our magnetic attraction—and right now, that insight is running on its highest setting. Alerting me that everything she speaks isn't everything she's *saying*...

"Velvet." I sigh. "Listen. I'm—"

"Fine?" Her skeptical sneer proves the intuition isn't always one-sided. "Sure you are. You're having dreams so violent, I sometimes think you might rip the bed apart."

I lean up and then in, sealing the deal with a gavel pound of a kiss. "Just my brain burning off some residual tension, which is completely gone now." I go gentle with the amendment as well as my kisses, feathering her cheek with tiny circles until I get to the graceful shell of her ear. "So the solution here is simple..."

Emma snort-chuffs. "A blow job before bed every night?"

"And you thought *I* was the mind reader in the relationship."

"Husband, a *mosquito* could've pulled that one out of you."

"You're evading the subject."

"No, *you're* evading the subject." Her twist on my hair, pulling my sights back around to her, is a Little League bunt compared to the line drive of her voice. "*Zeus.* Talk to me." She curls the fingertips of her other hand into the stubble along my jaw. "You were threatening Faline in ways I've never heard before."

I scowl through a grunt. "Who says it was her in the dream?"

"Is there somebody *else's* brain you want to open like a can of beans and remove spoonful by spoonful?"

"Huh." I seesaw my head, thanking my joints for a couple of effective electrical cracks. "I said that? Well, that's got to score me creativity points."

She takes her turn at the scowl. "You really *are* going for that evasion gold medal, aren't you?"

The woman always gives me the best reasons to change glowers into grins. But sometimes—like now—it's an easier feat than usual. "Baby, I was grabbing gold from the second you came for me."

She rolls her eyes before shoving away and leaving the bed. As she pushes to her feet, she stabs her arms into her robe. "Fine. If we're really going to joke this away, for the third night in a row, maybe I *do* need some garlic ice cream."

As her footsteps grow fainter down the hall and then the stairway, I entertain a caveman urge to go after her. To not stop until I've got her back in here and under me again, screaming twice as loud for me. But eventually, that would land us right back in this position. Her, demanding I spill more than my come for her. Me, going after the gold medal in evasion. Because one time a night to live through Faline's soul evisceration, even subconsciously, is more than enough.

Especially with the day and night still ahead of us.

Which, God help me, will really be as boring as the plans look on paper.

I allow myself a below-the-breath chuckle of the F-word. Saying it any louder will only make the sentiment—and the disbelief beneath it—more real.

But yeah, this is really me, really thinking this. The guy who, just four years ago, was ringing in the new year with coke-spiked champagne and some willing Amsterdam beauties, who is now craving to be in *one* bed, with *one* woman, well before midnight.

Dear God, I can only hope.

Surged with that hope, I kick the covers back and hoist out of bed. Five minutes later, with a pair of workout shorts covering my junk in all the right places, I head out the door, down the hill, and toward the shoreline. Hopefully a predawn run will clarify shit in my psyche again—and rebuild the thin wall I'm fighting to keep erect between my reality and my imagination.

Emmalina and Bean and the love that binds us? *Reality.*

Faline and her obsessive power trip fuckery? *Not* my reality.

Nor will it ever be again.

I have to keep believing that. I have to keep choosing that. Even if it takes living *this* "reality" a little while longer. And even if that means I've got to get through a few hours tonight in disguise as a science nerd with a hard-on for UFO debates, escorting my equally "nerdy" wife to an intimate New Year's Eve "party-gathering-semi-fundraiser thing" with the neighbors.

Okay, so seventy people could technically still be

"intimate"—and if not, in the grand scheme of things, it could still be worse. Mel and Maddie Makra, our eccentric and energetic hosts, have confirmed that Emma's parents, who always ring in the new year from someplace exotic and expensive, won't be attending, thank God. That means that though we're attending the soirée as fabricated people, we'll get the chance to quietly bid on some silent auction packages benefiting our very real charity, Richards Reaches Out. And yeah, I do mean *quietly*. At this point, I'm even wondering if "Steve and Sophie's" attendance will be noticed, considering how Maddie and Mel have made it pretty damn clear the fundraising element of the evening is a blatant bid to score the first post-wedding appearance of *Reece and Emma Richards*.

Yeah, I'm completely serious.

And no, Merriam-Webster isn't accepting new submissions for their "Irony" listing.

At any rate, this is going to make things interesting.

So bring on the interesting. I'm ready. I can do this. It's just a couple of hours and only with seventy people. What could possibly go wrong?

The charge resonates through me as I pause atop the berm to catch a breath and watch the first tendrils of dawn sneak over my shoulders on their way to the water. But like the light on the ocean, my thoughts are illuminated by murky hues. There's no depth to those waves, still rolling beneath the sky as gray masses, crashing quietly against the sand to punctuate my instinct's response to its challenge.

What could possibly go wrong?
Plenty.
Plenty.
Plenty.

CHAPTER TWO

EMMA

In terms of everything Reece and I have faced together, the leftover strain from our morning tiff is nothing more than a semicolon in the narrative. Which is why I'm tempted to check myself into therapy for continuing to obsess over it. Yes, on New Year's Eve. Yes, in the crazy-ass sequined dress into which I've just changed for the Makras' party tonight. Go big or go home, right? And since home isn't an option right now, I'm diving all-in for big. Besides, I can definitely say this will be the first—and *only*—time I'll attend a Newport Beach society party clad in a gold-sequined maternity tent—errrr, dress.

Okay, so technically, I'm not really the one in the dress. Thank you, Sophie Sarsgard, alter-ego extraordinaire, for saving a little of my real-life dignity. So there *are* some upsides to the whole "total incognito" game besides not fearing for mine or my baby's life every other minute. And now that my sister has decided the "Sophie the nerd" look can withstand a few stylish choices between the hideous jumpers and mom-to-be jeans, I'm not as testy about having to appear in the knocked-up-Solid-Gold-dancer look for a few hours either.

But the thing I *am* still testy about?

How my husband let things stand between us this morning.

Not real walls, though they might as well have been. Walls I *thought* we'd already toppled between other things like kidnappings, explosions, family betrayals, friends dying, the destruction of half our city, and a "little" thing like my surprise pregnancy. Through it all, we always pushed our way back to each other. Forged a new path *with* each other. Leaned on and cried with and loved each other, at last arriving at the truth that we couldn't do it without each other. No noble heroics. No it's-for-the-best secrets.

No "it was nothing" nightmares.

A nothing that's been gnawing at me all day.

No. That's been eating away at me for *three* days. The seventy-two full hours in which my life *partner* has been slowly, subtly veiling himself from me. Oh, not all of it—but just enough, tucking back a little more each day, that I haven't noticed just how murky our connection has become until now.

And people think veils are only good devices for *women*.

Though as soon as Reece reenters the bedroom, fresh from his shower, it's not his "veils" that spike my disquiet.

It's his damn bath towel.

And the way he's cinched it so low on his beautifully muscled hips, his "happy V" is dangerously close to being an erotic exclamation point.

And the way I wish I could take full advantage of that observation—not to mention the bulging flesh below that declares *his* thoughts on the matter—but we have to stop dancing around his tricky secrecy. For the last three days, we've been handling his evasion with humor and sex. While both factors have been *very* nice, they're still exactly what I've just called them. *Evasions*.

"Hey, beautiful." His interjection is music on the air, a

harmony of sensuality and practicality that directly impacts *my* body's happy V. Just like that, I'm even "happier" down there—a state I fight with every synapse in my brain and force of my composure. "If you like what you see, I think I can talk the manager into letting you have a test drive."

Dear God. He's *not* making this easy. But after a self-reprimand of a terse head shake, I retort, "We're practically late for the party as it is."

Reece turns, hands braced at the top points of his V, a smirk already dancing across his formidable lips. "And that's a problem...why?"

I plop down on the seat at the lighted vanity. "Because the event is honoring *our* charity, remember?"

"And we'll be the only ones there who really know it."

"And *that's* a problem...why?" The retaliation is harsher than I intended, but maybe that's not a shitty thing. Reece drops his hands and jumps his brows, bringing a surge of satisfaction for me. No, that's not it. I'm not gratified; I'm grateful. For the first time in three days, we're cutting through our congenial surfaces and digging to what we really mean here. What we truly *need* to say. "RRO isn't something we simply started for the optics, remember?"

Reece draws in air through his nostrils. "Of course I remember."

He's peeved and it's obvious. Good. *Damn* good. I want his truth; not the I-am-Bolt-hear-me-roar PR kit. "Then let's enjoy the chance to support our team and their efforts without having to do it from a stage with a thousand flashbulbs popping in our face."

The sincerity I expect from him, in response to my own, doesn't manifest. My husband continues to stand there, still looking like he's going to be Mr. January for the "Hot Billionaires in the Shower" calendar, but also like he's not one damn bit comfortable with it.

Or any other word I've just said.

"What?" I finally prompt. "You saying you *miss* the stage and the flashbulbs?"

He folds his arms. Mentally, I slot him into the calendar as Mr. February—because the fewer days I have to share those burnished pecs, those rugged forearms, and that low towel line with the rest of the world, the better. "I'm saying that I'm not sure this will be the simple flight beneath the radar we want it to be."

"Huh?" He's thrown out the statement so casually, I wipe my hands on my thighs just for a break to reprocess. "Wh-What the hell are you saying? Have you noticed anything? Did someone recognize you up at the cupcake place this morning?" Because despite the man's field practice with his veils, he took time out of his morning run to grab me a pistachio special with cream cheese frosting while returning from his jog. "Or has the team learned something? Heard something?" I charge to my feet, ignoring Bean's protest as my heartrate triples. "Has Faline finally figured it all out?" I raise both hands. "Baby, I swear that when I FaceTimed with Mom last week, I had the blond wig secured and that beanie on tight. And she saw nothing lower than my shoulders—"

"Sssshhh." He steps over and gathers me close, his clutch as forceful as his admonition. "You're fine; you did nothing wrong. And I know that it's tearing you up, keeping Bean a secret from her."

"Not as much as it would if Faline learned about him." As soon as I utter it into his chest, which tightens from the texture of a brick wall into a titanium shield, comprehension slams me. "Holy shit." I pull back far enough to get a full stare at his face—and the fresh tension through his jaw. "That's what's been haunting you too," I assert. "In your dreams." As soon as he averts his gaze, I wrap my hands around the back of his head. "Oh, baby. Why didn't you just tell me?"

"Because it would have helped you *how*?" he counters.

"Because I'm your *wife*, damn it, and that's what I'm here for."

"To babysit my wussy nightmares?" It's obvious he doesn't want a response to that, so I abstain as he pulls away. He keeps his head dropped while sliding his long, sure fingers across my stomach. "You've got a more important guy to worry about these days, I think."

"You want to know what *I* think?" I drape my hand across his, meshing our fingers together. "That there's enough room in my mind and heart for *both* my guys."

His expression softens, despite the fierce silver glints in his gaze. As he grazes his grip upward and cups one of my breasts through my dress, he husks, "And what about your delectable goddess body?"

A reprimanding breath. Well, at least that's my intention. What comes out instead is a clutching choke, courtesy of the million zings between my legs. The fire caused by his simple touch. His adamant possession. The effect he alone wields over my desperate, electrified senses.

Damn it. *Damn it.*

"My body says that if you don't stop, we're going to be *really* late to the party."

His rough velvet hum does nothing to turn down the wattage in my blood. He worsens things by rolling his caresses across my chest, to the nipple already hardening for him. "My body says it likes how yours thinks."

"Who says I'm thinking anymore?" A truth if I've ever uttered one, especially as he teases my distended nub with his thumb.

"Who says that's a problem?"

I don't even try to concoct a quip at that. Not when the man puts actions to his words, jerking at the cinch of his towel so it puddles at our feet.

The *shoosh* of the material on the floor coincides with my dazed sigh. *Holy God.* This man and his flawless penis. Will I ever get over my amazement at him—and *it*? No wonder he's always had girls fighting like rabid spider monkeys to have it just for a night.

Not anymore.

This god is *mine,* for always and forever. I indulge one more moment of feminine victory about that, using the excuse to admire him more. He's long and proud but with a girth that promises ultimate satisfaction, especially with the mighty veins standing out against the burnished hardness. Veins that pulse with a mesmerizing cobalt hue from the moment I stroke him, starting at his taut balls and ending at the searing bulb at his tip.

"Bunny," he rasps, rolling his hips to shuttle that stunning length in and out of my grip. "Holy *fuck*."

I press closer, working him over with taunting little twists. "That a threat or a promise, Bolt Man?"

"Neither." He punctuates with a short smash of his lips to mine. "Too much thinking required."

I find the presence for a flirty pout. "So no holy fucking?"

Taking out my inner coquette has clearly unlocked the

cage on his inner Cro-Magnon. And damn, does the caveman look go well with this man's dark gorgeousness. With his nostrils flaring and his cheekbones harsh slashes beneath his skin, he seizes me by the hand and drags me across the bedroom. But he doesn't take me to the bed. Within a few steps, we're in front of the arched window that overlooks the back garden. I smile as I look down to the sturdy hammock swing hanging from the tree—and the illicit way we used it when "christening" the garden during our first week in the house.

But the smile doesn't stay in place long.

It's replaced by my stunned gape, courtesy of my tantalizing troglodyte and his horny impatience, who reaches from behind me to unlatch the window. In the same motion, he swings out the dual panes. In the next second, he's planting my hands atop the small ledge and then pushing the insides of my feet with his.

He spreads me wide until I'm secured and braced at both edges of the indention. Inside another second, he's shoved my dress up to my waist. Inside the third, he twists his other hand into the waistband of my lace panties, causing my pussy to clench and gush. *Oh, gawd.* It's such a clichéd reaction to a seduction stereotype, but for a guy who can—and has, many times—fry away that waistband like a torch through butter, this grabbing-the-undies thing is new for him—and thus, for me.

And it's exciting as hell.

A new color to the fireworks. A new amplitude to the electric box. Which definitely means the sexy beast is going to get what he damn well wants from *my* sweet box.

And yeah, I just went for *that* cliché, as well.

And yeah, do I mean every syllable.

God.

Yes.

Anything.

Not that I'm capable of knowing what a syllable even is as soon as the man leans in while torqueing my underwear tighter. I moan deeply, reacting to the delicious pain as the lace slices into the skin above my mons. I tense a little, waiting for the inevitable rip, but damn it if the man isn't aware of everything his torment is doing to me—so instead of destroying the panties, he starts *using* them. Yes, just as they are. Yes, without any extra voltage from his fingertips. Just that strip of lace, transformed into a stiff blade, and his artistry with it as a weapon of erotic intent.

Which, at the moment, involves sliding the material along my most sensitive flesh. And then again. And then—despite how I buck and gasp and wriggle as my clit shivers and shudders and pulses—yet again.

At last, he dips in closer. Fits his mouth against my ear while giving my pussy a reprieve from his wicked treatment. But it's not the enormous relief it seems, with his breath coming in torrid gusts along with the carnal words he brings in between.

"You're completely right, my beautiful bunny. No holy fucking right now." He wields his teeth too, sinking them into the flesh beneath my ear. "Only rutting." Then bites me harder. "Claiming. Burning. Owning."

Somehow, I force my lips around a word of response.

"Yes."

Then shove my hips back, offering more of my intimacy to his deeper invasion.

"*Yes.*"

Then gyrate against him, all but demanding him to finally

set my crotch free—so it can fully service his.

"Yes!"

The eruption of my cry is joined by the brutal *zwip* of the lace he finally severs. As my panties brush my inner thighs during their descent to the floor, I practically come from that naughty sensation. But damn it, Reece is in his finest mind-reading form, and his growl zaps me away from that precipice with as much command as his new digs into my hips. "Remember that part about owning you, Mrs. Richards?"

I tremble because it feels like my only viable choice. "Y-Yes, Mr. Richards." The words, equally undeniable. I don't need to be commanded into the formality; his stark snarl has already made that part clear. Just like this morning, he doesn't plan on sealing this connection with raindrops on roses, whiskers on kittens, and a Hallmark Channel cuddle. And like this morning, I comprehend the reason why—with even greater clarity. Faline doesn't have him shackled to a lab table anymore, but she's still violating him all the same. Her evil lives on, infiltrating the warrens of his imagination. But in the safe space that is thoroughly us, he can gain that control back. Get *himself* back.

And I'll do anything to help him.

Though as soon as the proclamation rings through my mind, I have to stifle a giggle at myself. I'm not exactly the village virgin sacrificing myself in the dragon's dungeon here. This restoration is just as much mine as his. I'm certain the man can already tell by feeling the pebbles along my skin and listening to the needy gasps from my lips—which pitch higher as he curls his hands around the top of my hips. He locks my body in place as he works his wet, throbbing cockhead between the swollen, soaked lips at my most intimate core.

"That means *I* tell your body what it can and cannot do." His growl is low and lava thick, a perfect match to the steady rolls of his hips behind mine. He sounds even better as he fits his glorious penis into my shivering tunnel. "Do you understand?" As I manage a frantic nod, he dictates, "No. In words. With those gorgeous, nasty lips of yours. Do. You. Understand?"

"Y-Yes. I understand."

"Perfect. Now do you understand that your beautiful cunt will take every inch of my cock, no matter how deep or hard I fuck it?"

I swallow with purpose, needing to regain some of the control he's robbed with his magical, filthy words. "Y-Yes," I finally manage. "I'll take all of your cock, no matter how hard or deep."

A truth he enforces the very next second—by gripping me ruthlessly and hauling my body back until he's buried to the balls inside me. At once, my limbs are golden fire and my body is a sparkling sun. Holy *shit*, he feels good. I close my eyes as my pores open, flowing with arousal and warmth and energy. I'm stretched and seared and stimulated, consumed by his strength until an exigent cry explodes from my lips.

Though my outburst layers over his dark moan, the man states with complete composure, "No coming, Bunny. Not until I tell you to. Understood?" When my dry throat only gives a croak of response, the man brings me back online by seizing his hold around my buttocks—arranging his thumbs dangerously close to the pucker that separates them. "Do. You. Understand?"

"Yes!" I damn near shriek. "Yes, I understand. No coming unless you—*aaahhh*!"

Though he's going to make the effort as hellacious as

possible, after wetting my asshole with some spittle and then teasing the aperture with those talented thumbs of his.

"Repeat yourself." His order is more arousing than that caress, raw sex mixed with pure sin, a carnal threat blended with erotic promise. And all he's asking for are a few words in return—but the idea of them feels so impossible because thought itself has become a bizarre concept. Surely the man himself must know that, simply from how my body clenches beneath him and my wet walls squeeze around him. "*All* the words this time. Repeat yourself."

"No...no coming...*oh!*" I grit my teeth as he shoves his thumbs in deeper, setting off another firestorm through my senses. *Words.* I have to remember the words. Well, the ones besides the choice labels I'm wanting to rage all over *him* at the moment. "N-No coming, unless you tell me I can."

His pleased hum is worth the price my senses paid for it. And yes, even the cost of being egregiously late to the Makras' fundraiser. It's more than just sound on the air. It's the timbre in his throat as he emits it, the fresh strength in his hold around me, and the brighter force in every finger he grips me with—including the thumbs he keeps working into my tender backside. And yes, the breathtaking boldness in every roll of his hips, resulting in every steady slide of his steely cock into my tremoring body. The body I order into submission by clenching my fists and stabbing fingernails into my palms as he swirls me into a fuzzy fugue state because of my spiraling lust and heat and need.

"Hang on, baby." He croons it because he can. Because he's no longer the one beyond control here...who's all but begging for release every time he surges his body back into mine. Who's ready to fall apart in a thousand ways, especially as he works his thumbs even deeper into my other entrance, tantalizing me from *that* direction...

"Reece!"

"No, Velvet."

"Reece, *please*!"

"Not. Yet."

"But...I can't hold on..."

"You will. Repeat it. Tell me you will."

"I—I—*oh*!" The last of it erupts on a startled scream as he grips my body brutally enough to change the angle of his lunges—ensuring his length teases along that special ridge of sensitivity along my inner walls. "Oh, *God*." At the same time, the bastard turns the two digits in my ass into a full lightsaber duel. Not that I can see any of it, with my eyes squeezed as tightly as my fists—but I sure as hell can feel every enticing degree of the battle, joining his strokes to my G spot to turn me into a puddle of erotic mush.

"Damn." The awe in his growl makes me want to gloat in glee—if only I wasn't so obsessed with holding back my orgasm just to please him. "*Damn it*, Velvet. You're going to break me in half."

"Is that a *complaint*?" I snap. "After this hell you've put me through?"

The ass has the nerve to chuckle low, tucking his face deeper into the crook of my neck while working my pussy deeper onto his ruthless iron length. "Then why don't we turn it into heaven instead?" Before I can summon so much as a gasp of reaction, he bites the base of my ear while pushing his thumbs all the way inside my ass. The sharp pain from one and invasive throb from the other have an instant effect on my pussy, making me clench his cock that much tighter. "Yes," he snarls. "Fuck *yes*, Emmalina."

As my name escapes his lips, his electric seed leaves his slit. At once, my body is an answering lightning storm, washed in the perfect, pounding brilliance of his climax. He groans, lost in the ecstasy of his release, inspiring me to break out a little turnabout-is-fair-play.

"Tell me," I direct, clamping my inner walls to keep his cock trapped inside me. "Tell me to do it, Mr. Richards. *Please.*"

He indulges me with half of a protesting growl, but after composing himself with a harsh breath, he grits out, "Come for me, Velvet. Come hard. *Now!*"

The slice of his voice cuts back the last tendrils of my composure. As the owner of my body, he sets free my passion. As the lover of my soul, he gives flight to my senses. While I'm physically shaking, I'm spiritually recentered. While my sex explodes from lust, my heart is flooded with love. Once again, this man brings me not only to a place of lusty magic but a mountaintop of emotional completion—and empowerment.

It's going to be all right.

The expression isn't just a hokey line from a Blake Shelton and Gwen Stefani duet. It's the vow of my heart and the core of my being—because it's never been my deeper truth. And as I turn around, a move that unseats his body from mine, it's nevertheless what keeps him close as his gaze stays locked to mine...

Betraying that he's come to the same conviction.

It's going to be all right.

We're *going to be all right.*

I lift a hand, pressing my palm to his cheek, unable to stop my cheesy sigh when he covers my fingers with the determined spread of his own. We continue gazing at each other, lingering through our last few moments of total honesty and completion with each other. All right, we know the inner connection isn't going anywhere—it hasn't even during the times when we've been halfway around the world from each other—but for the rest of tonight, our outward truth has to be our version of a New Year's Eve performance. "Steve" and "Sophie" are on center stage tonight, in all their nerd-tastic glory.

Ready and waiting is the beaded half jacket made to accompany "Sophie's" sequined tent dress, and hanging from the valet stand across the room are "Steve's" checked wool trousers, sports coat, sweater vest, and button-down scholar's shirt. Nearby are his polished loafers—or are those the "sensible" tan things that Reece ordered me to wear in place of the shiny kitten heels I'd already picked out for the ensemble? Doesn't really matter. My cover identity could be a nun named Gertrude, and I'd still refuse to leave the house in the clodhoppers.

Though at the moment, as my man buttons up his shirt, I get the impression he'd love nothing more than accepting my refusal to leave the house all night. When he maintains the not-so-subtle brood as he strides to the bathroom for his toiletry regime, I follow and stab right into his personal space by hiking one hip to the bathroom counter. I don't bother using the mirror to look at him, instead using my new vantage point to spear him directly with my challenging glower. "All right, mister. I thought we just went through this."

He abandons the contact lens prep to swing a puzzled gaze in return. "Through what?"

"Reclassifying this relationship as a no-sulk zone." I cross my arms with deliberation. "With keeping secrets subject to additional fines. *Stiff* ones."

As soon as the words leave my mouth, I want to kiss *and* punch myself for them. On one hand, they encourage the man to straighten and face me, his trademark smirk forming across his lips. On the other hand, *that damn smirk.*

Ohhhh, I'm in trouble.

"Well, I'm just fine with stiff penalties if you are, little bunny."

Yep. Trouble.

No, no, no, *no.*

"An option I'd be thrilled to take you up on, mister"— my breath clutches as he swoops over, hitching me up to the bathroom counter as if Bean and I weigh only five pounds instead of thirty times that much—"just as soon as we get home from the Makras'."

He slouches his shoulders and twists his lips though doesn't shift from his looming position over me. With his forehead dropped to mine, he grumbles, "You're determined to do this thing, aren't you?"

I fire back an equally determined scowl. "And why are you so determined *not* to?"

Like this whole situation, the question is fair and unfair at the same time. I know it, and so does he. The conflict storms through his gaze, in which I can see reflections of the same strife across my face. We're in hiding to escape the cage of Faline's evil again, but the shelter itself has become a prison. And right now, I need just a little peek outside. An assurance that my life is still actually here and waiting for me to return to it.

I need just a tiny taste of hope.

"I'm sorry, Velvet." Reece's grate betrays how he's already plucked that thought out of my head. "I know that living this way isn't really living. And I also know that you didn't sign up for any of this—"

"The hell I didn't." I make a V out of one hand and clamp his chin in the resulting vise. "Look at me," I order. "I signed up for loving *you*, Mr. Richards. Those weren't just corny, canned words that I randomly spoke at that altar to you. 'For better, for worse, for richer, for poorer, in sickness and in health.'" I cock my head and narrow my gaze. "Funny how there's no mention of an 'only in cases when I call you Reece instead of Steven' clause."

He answers my half grin with another glare, though this time there's a teasing glint to it. "I love you so much." He punctuates the murmur with a succinct but tender kiss.

"I know you do." It's easy to readjust my hand, tracing up the line of his jaw until my fingertips are burrowed into the dark waves along his nape. "Which is why *you* already know how truly important this thing is for me. To see that despite everything, up to and including the insanity of the Bolt and Flare traveling adventure show, we've managed to keep doing at least one cool thing for the world. This not-so-little thing called Richards Reaches Out."

Not-so-little. It's damn near an understatement, and I don't disguise my elation about that, either. A year and a half ago, we were helping Calvin Neves repair his house, get back into college, and support his little sisters, Tosca and Jina. Now, with international reach and offices in five cities across the globe, we're helping close to twenty new candidates each month: people like Cal, from all different backgrounds and circumstances, to receive the extra leg up they need to climb the ladders of their dreams. When counting my blessings about becoming Flare—despite the harrowing way she was outed to the world—one of the largest is that she'll help bring new awareness to the vital work that RRO is accomplishing.

"Yeah." There's awe in Reece's interjection, but there's also the verbal version of a mega perma-pen, soaking the air with his thick conviction. "But it's just the start, baby." He emulates my grip, sifting his hands back into my hair. "You do believe that, right? You *know* that once we deal with Faline for good—"

"*If* we deal with her."

"*When* we deal with her." His torso muscles stiffen, and his fingers tighten against my scalp. "We're going to change the whole world, my love." He dips his head until he can press a fervent kiss on the top curve of my stomach. "And this superstar is going to help us. Every damn step of the way."

His declaration does more than warm the plane of my belly. The man, truly my Zeus come to life, fills my soul like a thousand lightning bolts striking at once.

Or like destiny confirming how right she's really been all along.

Despite my bubbling emotions, I manage to quip back, "Oh? And did the superstar tell you that himself?"

Reece raises his head—with an expression committed to pure earnestness. "If I said yes, would you doubt it?"

I retangle a hand into his damp, thick strands. "Not for a second."

My husband catches his lower lip with his upper teeth. The move, usually my exclusive ploy, looks damn fine on his fresh-shaven features—and bloody hell if the man isn't distinctly aware of that fact. But he only indulges his adorable insolence for an instant, shoving it away for a fresh dose of gravity. "All right, so we're going to the damn party," he concedes. "But baby, this isn't just a dash up to Gelson's for soy milk or a quick walk on the beach at sunset. We're not 'just running into' Mel and Maddie in passing. Staying in character is going to require some intense concentration."

I'm beyond tempted to roll my eyes. Instead, I reply as diplomatically as possible, "I've taken Sophie Sarsgard out for a lot of test drives by now, okay? She's second skin for me." I bump his thigh with mine, signaling that pin-the-wife-to-the-bathroom-counter time is over. "Which, unbelievably, I'm going to count as a win for now."

But only for now.

I keep the amendment to myself, knowing he's just as weary of the identity pretenses as I am, despite how neutral he maintains his expression while helping me off the counter. I actually start wondering about his surreal Zen levels, until he turns and continues prepping his look for the night. After grooming his soul patch with stabbing motions, he scoops up some hair product and works it in so vigorously his cock swings like a banana on a rubber band. "You just need to let me know if things get even a little bumpy or you think your cover's being blown. You need to fucking *promise* me, okay?"

Aha. *There's* the stressed-out guy I know and love. Subsequently, it comes as an oddly weird reassurance, making my answering quip possible. "Ten-four," I croon back. "Roger-dodger. Copy and print. Cool beans 'n' hot fries."

"Damn it," he spits out, spinning back toward me. "I'm *serious*, Emma." He's so adamant, even his penis stops the banana gymnastics. Now it's just there in its normal capacity as a breath-stealing work of art. *"Don't* fuck around. If someone starts to recognize you, no witty one-liner is going to conveniently throw them off. That bullshit only works for people in TV and movies."

"But real-life superheroes...?" I add a smirk to the challenge.

"*Not* pregnant ones."

I revert back to a scowl. To Reece's credit, he's genuinely remorseful but stands his ground while spreading his arms.

"You demanded the no-secrets zone, lady. So here we are." He steps back into the bedroom to slip on a pair of tight black briefs, negating the good-thing bad-thing distraction of his cock. "As much as I wish I could help you carry our baby"— he scowls at my bark of a laugh—"the truth is, I can't. So you'll have to deal with the overbearing ox husband instead."

"Oh, whee." I slide on another pair of underwear for myself, figuring he can take care of the ruined pair on the floor. "Lucky me."

"Hey." He grunts while stepping over and yanking me close again. "That's *my* line."

But fifteen minutes later, as soon as we get to the Makras' place, I'm damn sure it's legitimately mine. Even play-acting as a nerd space scientist with a nasal problem, the man has a presence that wallops the air as forcefully as the first night I met him—meaning, of course, that half the crowd wants to run from him, and the other half wants to lick him. As we make our way through the spacious but packed living room, across an atrium that's outfitted in matching Nantucket décor, and then into the sprawling kitchen where Maddie and Mel are holding court, it doesn't escape my attention that the majority of the "lick him" contingent are women. Also not getting past me is my own onset of Zen about that. I may really be the size of a small house, but I'm also on the arm of the stud who supplied the cornerstone of that house—as well as its magical, incredible occupant.

But as we enter the kitchen together, I also recognize the huge step my mind is taking at the same time. Accepting its epiphany that my confidence has nothing to do with the baby in my belly, the wedding ring on my finger, or the possessive grip my man maintains around my hand. It has everything to do with *us*—with the invisible but invincible connection between us, which I now believe in more than the air in this room, the gravity keeping us in it, and the orbital pull of the globe that's responsible for it all. Why the hell has it taken me until now to recognize that? And why the hell has fate picked *here* for it to happen?

But most importantly, how have I forgotten that fate doesn't give a crap about timing?

And that it loves to laugh its ass off when someone's caught in the crosshairs of that truth?

In moments like right now.

Walking into the kitchen to greet Mel and Maddie with friendly hugs.

And then turning to see the small crowd they've been entertaining with stories from their summer trip to France.

A crowd consisting of the entire administrative team from the LA office of Richards Reaches Out.

And the New York office.

And Calvin Neves.

Yes, it's really all of them. And yes, it's really Cal, who has always held a special place in my heart as the inaugural RRO grant recipient. Helping him out had provided the seed we germinated into the whole concept for the organization— carried out with such passion and commitment by all twelve of the people now gathered in this space. I take in each of their faces, gulping back fresh tears with each visage I reach. Each name I know by heart. Every special soul who has turned my vision into their guiding goal as well.

It's so special. So surreal. And nearly too much to handle. Under other circumstances, I'd be flashing a stunned stare up at Reece, positive he'd had a hand in gathering everyone into one place like this as his idea of a unique holiday surprise—and he'd have been right. Every one of these people is a precious entity to me. I know about their backgrounds, their families, all the things that make them a unique treasure for what RRO has accomplished. In return, they all know a lot about me.

Except that right now, it's not *me* they've all stopped to stare at.

Holy God, I hope not.

You're Sophie Sarsgard. You're Sophie Sarsgard. You're Sophie Sarsgard.

My brain pounds me with the mantra despite how my pulse rate quadruples and my heart begs to burst from raw emotion. Everyone in here has been with RRO since our days as a fledgling nonprofit, working with me to convince the world that we truly wanted to change it.

But you don't recognize any of them. You can't *recognize them. They're complete strangers to you right now. That* has *to be your truth, damn it. They're just a sea of curious but friendly faces...*

"Well, hey-ho! It's Sophie and Steve-o!" For once, Mel's dorky humor is a welcome interjection. Despite the fact that I still have to grit out a smile in return, it's a grateful one. Nothing like one's fake name being turned into a lame rhyme to convince everyone how authentic it must really be. So thanks, Mel Baby, for flying that douchebag flag high and proud—and not showing any sign of letting it drop anytime soon either. "Come here, little space strawberry"—the guy thinks his awful nickname for "Sophie" gives him the right to yank me in for a hug that would send most bears into therapy—"and hello to you too, baby berry!" And then to yell at my stomach with the same scary familiarity.

I look up to see I'm pretty accurate with the "scary" label. Though everyone's good about masking their discomfort, I'm at least able to silently flash them with mine. Their resulting round of laughs is also given discretion. Thank God for Reece, who tosses enough of a gawky flair into his possessive grab to not only rescue me from Mel but increase the authenticity of our cover in front of the gang still stabbing us with their curious gawks.

"That's *Mister* Baby Berry to you, Mel," he drawls, managing to diffuse the awkward moment by giving everyone permission to openly chuckle. No one does so more than our party host, who adds a wry shake of his head while shaking Reece's free hand.

"Says the cat that got dragged in, eh, man?" he returns. "And maybe I do mean *dragged*." He waggles his brows at me. "Did this wanker make you pull him the *entire* way?"

Reece whips back his hand under the pretense of scratching his grimacing jaw. "Uh, yeah." He tightens the expression until it borders on a snarl. "Sorry about that. Thought I saw something unusual in the Cetus spiral galaxy, and I lost track of time."

I tilt my head, angling a gaze up at my husband with no pretense about its admiration. Between all the strategy meetings with the team, including their countless and fruitless searches for Faline's new hiding spot, he's been actually opening the books in "Steven's" vast space creature library. Clearly—and alluringly—it's been rubbing off.

"And I didn't have the heart to disturb him." My murmur coincides with the smoldering lock of our gazes. From his side, there are the memories of how we actually made ourselves late. And from mine, there's the message that I'd like to create some more—especially with what his space guy talk is doing to my geeky lady loins.

"Now I'm not sure whether to introduce you two or make sure you know where the spare bedroom is."

This time, Mel's the only one chortling at his one-liner. But my hero husband proves he doesn't possess the knack for just finessing lightning bolts. He saves the moment from transforming from an ice breaker into a glacier with his easy grin. "Well, sticking to the introductions means you can keep mixing the cocktails."

"*Excellent* idea." The volley comes from a new arrival to the little circle: a redhead who could seriously be a descendant of Rita Hayworth, with voluptuous boobs to match. Additionally, her full lips and sculptured profile are absolutely created for any camera lens—as she shows us all when tucking her nose against the side of Calvin's neck. "That *is* a super idea, right, Calzie palzie?"

Calzie palzie? Baby Hayworth looks like much more than a "palzie" with Calvin, snaking a hand toward his beltline with the determination of a woman familiar with the area. Cal grabs her wrist in time to redirect her hold around his waist, but not without a noticeable blush stealing up his face.

I watch the exchange with teeth firmly embedded into the inside of my lip. Oh hell, how I yearn to demand an explanation from "Calzie" along with an introduction to his new "palzie."

Ever since the first day we helped Cal and his little sisters, there's been a special protectiveness in my heart for the guy—and now, the fact that he has a "special friend" in his world is a stunner I can only experience on the inside, turning my gut into an aching knot and my head into a throbbing mess. Holding back tears is a *lot* freaking harder when I have to paste on a fake pleasant smile.

"Okay, then." Mel sweeps an empty blender over and tosses in some crushed ice. "Another round of Bolt-inis, coming right up!"

"*What*-inis?" Reece beats me to the punch on getting to siphon off some of his shock through the query, though his finesse with a mildly amused gape is better than my acting game.

"Oh, *yes*. Bolt-inis!" Surprisingly, Baby Hayworth isn't the source of burst. The exclamation comes from Yuli, a member of the New York RRO team. She's as petite as Cal's girl but bigger with her fashion statement. She's wearing a black leather pencil skirt that laces up the sides, with dark-green ties that match her high-heeled patent boots. Her black knit tank has *Wicked* spelled out across the front in sparkly green rivets, and the tips of her spiky updo are accented with similar hardware. Since I hired her for her creativity with RRO's marketing pieces, she's a perfect fit for the look. "Mel got to inventing it about an hour ago, as a tribute to our favorite superhero," she explains. "Like him, it zaps you before you know it."

"Zap, zap, zap, zap!" The cheeky chant grows as the whole group catches on, with Calvin's date adding a shimmy worthy of a Rio Carnival parade line. The look across Cal's face is a familiar one, making me long to hug him. That's the scowl he gets before having to break up a tiff between Tosca and Jina.

Reece steps in for the rescue yet again. "What's in it?" he asks Mel, tripping up the group's rhythm.

"Seeeecret ingredients," Mel jokes, starting to douse the ice in the blender with vodka. *A lot* of vodka. "Designed for loosening its victims' inhibitions—*and* checkbooks."

"Completely valid." Chester, our hipster PR guru from the LA office, arcs a finger into the air. "I think I'll be taking out a second on my condo to pay for the Bora Bora package."

"Unless I snap it up instead," cracks Clark, one of our awesome case management specialists. Like his comics canon namesake, Clark is boyish and charming on the outside but dogged and driven when given a *no* when he needs a *yes*. Or when he's hell-bent on going to Bora Bora.

"I think I wanna snap *you* up, baby." Though Cal's girl declares it to the whole group, she only has eyes for her guy. While I get it—Calvin is a drop-dead gorgeous mix of three different races—I can also see, along with everyone else, that the last thing on the guy's mind right now is getting "snapped up."

"Juliet." Once more he halts her wandering hand before she cups it all the way around his crotch. Past his well-trimmed beard and mustache, I can tell he's blushing worse than a Disney deer in a *Deadpool* plot. "This isn't the time or the—"

"Oh, *yaaayyy!*" Juliet herself cuts him off, jumping forward for a Bolt-ini refill along with everyone else. "More blue zaps."

"What are we drinking to this time?" Yuli asks.

"No better reason than welcoming our new party guests." Mel hands Reece a large glass of the magic blue libation, which seriously does look to be glowing now. I glance to the countertop and see that the man had the chance to add a number of blue liqueur components to the concoction when

I was more focused on whether Juliet would succeed at her hand job efforts with Cal or not. After Mel gives me a glass of ice water, he raises his glasses and shouts, "Everyone, please say hello to Dr. Steven Sarsgard and his lovely wife, Sophie."

After the group toasts us in a round of boisterous greetings, I summon "Sophie's" subtle Brit lilt, along with my most open and innocent smile, and reply, "And who all do we get to thank for this rousing huzzah?"

Mel's too busy strutting out from behind the blender to notice the eye flare I get from Reece, answered by my sheepish shrug. Okay, so maybe the nerves are getting to me. Borrowing British-isms from my Renaissance Faire days wasn't likely the best call, though everyone smiles as if I'm the hip Londoner in the room with new slang they've yet to learn. Not that Mel goes that far in caring. After puffing his chest and tossing his hair, the guy raises his martini glass yet again.

"Another toast!" he proclaims. "As I proudly introduce the LA and New York teams from the Richards Reaches Out organization."

"LA *and* New York?" Reece inflects it with the perfect amount of authentic interest.

"Both offices took the week off for the holidays, so Maddie and I invited the New York gang out for a few days of R and R, as well as the party." He leans in to add, just as I'm about to give him new props for being a bizarre but benevolent soul, "Besides, having them all here means there's a better chance of the *bigger* faces coming out for the night."

Luckily, Mel's too dense to notice the tension beneath Reece's "confused" smile. "Bigger...names? What do you m—"

"Oh, come *on*." Mel smacks Reece on the back with the force of a grizzly giving CPR. "The big 'R' in RRO, man.

Reece Richards himself! And as we all know by now, that little spitfire of his wife is sure to add some 'sunshine' to this chilly night. Am I right? Sunshine! Haaaaa!"

I struggle to catch Reece's eye as Mel gives new meaning to the concept of sunshine itself for ten minutes, including a hey-I-used-to-sing-in-high-school version of "You are My Sunshine" that has me seriously but silently exhorting my husband, over and over again, *Please don't kill him. Please don't kill him. Please don't kill him.*

"And hey, hey, hey." Fresh out of sunshine references, Mel seems to mellow out—or at least what his version of the stuff is. "At the very least, you know this charity shit is great for press optics."

Somehow, Reece rustles together a fake smile of commiseration and replies, "Oh, sure. And what *does* the press love more than their 'optics'?"

"Not a hell of a lot, I can tell you that." Mel's crack, while beyond irritating, is also beyond right. Even Bean jumps into my act, his pissed-off kicks matching the ire I fight to hide away—though likely for unnecessary reasons. Though it might chafe me that the RRO staffers are being used for better press coverage, I'm sure all of them knew exactly what they were doing when coming to the party—and exactly what the end result would be, as well. More exposure for our cause. More money with which to accomplish it.

There's a superhero life lesson in there somewhere—*worthy cause versus stupid attention for the day's meditation subject, anyone?*—but I'm yanked out of that mental mire by everyone's favorite attention magnet for the evening. All right, maybe everyone except Cal, who's bypassed vexated blushes in favor of full-on scorn for his date—which might have a little to do with the Bolt-ini she just downed in a gulp to rival Reece's fastest finger zap for speed.

We're all still watching in stunned silence as the first hit of the new alcohol hits her, and she swings her head aloft while letting her whole arm plummet. Fortunately, the martini glass that slips from her fingers is deftly caught by Clark, not that the girl notices enough to thank him. "Woohoooo!" she shouts as if she's dangling out of a limousine sunroof, waving to the tourists down Sunset Boulevard. "All the kisses for the optics! All of themmmm!"

There's a round of softly amused laughs from the women, at least—who among us hasn't been *that* girl at a party at one time or another?—but I feel awful for poor Cal, who tries to drag Juliet from her stool with calm but firm reprimands.

"Heeeeyyy!" she whines it into the guy's face, making Cal grimace. Her breath is probably a hundred proof by now. "I don't *wanna* go. It's finally getting funnnnn."

Calvin's jaw resembles a bronze box with its fresh tension. "I said you've had *enough*, Juliet, and I mean it."

"Fuck off!"

Our collective, uncomfortable silence is probably the last thing Cal wants, though the first thing instinct dictates to us. Reece, feeling for the guy, moves forward and murmurs, "Allow me to hel—"

"I said fuck *off*!"

Nothing's so silent anymore. At least not to me. After the round of stunned gasps have died out on the air, logical reactions to the *Exorcist*-style growl that's taken over Juliet's larynx, my head is filled with terrified thunder, and my chest is a solid beat of comprehension.

Juliet doesn't sound like herself—because she *isn't* herself.

Not even the next moment, as she visibly "collects" herself to "appear" more like the charming thing who arrived here on Calvin's arm, I can still feel the additional force in the room—the extra presence who's unmistakably swept into this atmosphere.

Holy. Shit.

Faline?

I'm so certain about it, I slam both hands across my stomach—not just in a mode of protection but in *de*tection. My boy, already so advanced beyond his embryonic state, must have something to tell me about all this. But damn it, he's fallen just as silent and still as everyone else in the room.

Too damn still.

"This...this isn't good." My rasp is heard only by my husband, but that's exactly my intention. The second Reece sweeps his stunned stare to mine, I know he's seen and felt the change too—and is just as tormented about what to about it as I am. There's a chance, however slim, that we've both just let our paranoia run away with our imaginations. But even if that's not the case, he can't just rush up, grab the woman, and force a confrontation. No matter how Faline's controlling the woman—whether it's full remote control or simple "Faline's Disciples Army" mode—there's still a damn good chance *our* cover hasn't been blown all the way open yet.

Yet.

So far, Juliet is simply regarding us as Mel and Maddie's eccentric neighbors. She continues doing so while hopping off her barstool and downing the rest of *Cal's* Bolt-ini, only to giggle at her date as if he's just let her chop off his dick instead. "Stupid, *stupid* boy," she spits. "Or am *I* the stupid one for letting you drag me to this ridiculously rank party?"

"Excuse *me*?" The objection comes from Maddie, newly arrived to the kitchen area with a stack of empty hors d'oeuvres plates. But her withering glare is given a serene smirk from Juliet—who's probably continuing to fool everyone that she *is* Juliet, except for Reece and me—before she rocks back on one heel and cocks one hand to her opposite hip.

"Not sure I can do that," she snips across the kitchen.

"Huh?" Maddie retorts.

"Excuse you," Juliet—or whoever the hell she is—counters. "Sorry but not sorry—I am completely certain that I cannot excuse you."

"*Jesus.*" Calvin really does cross himself this time—before grabbing the girl by the elbow and pulling her back. "Juliet. That's completely *enough*!"

"Is it, now?" She wrenches from him, which propels her around and then right up against the kitchen counter, into the spot Reece occupied until moving to try and help Cal. But as soon as Juliet sweeps herself this direction, my husband is by my side with speed that might baffle a few in the room. But at the moment, I don't care how he got here; merely that his hand is back in mine and we're together again.

Facing off against another antagonist again.

Because that's all Juliet can be categorized as at this point.

Gone is the saucy little flirt we first met at Calvin's side. Equally gone is the sloshed party girl, emulating her pretend sunset limo ride. What's left is a creature taken over by bright-eyed malice and open contempt, a demoness sheathed inside a beauty queen—especially as she quirks a demure smile just like a contender for some pageant crown. "Is it all ever *enough*?" she croons to us both. "What do *you* think, Dr. Sarsgard? Mrs. Sarsgard?" She draws out the pronunciation of our names as if they're in a foreign language and she wants to take care about getting them right. But the next second, she's back to the demeanor of not giving a shit—like the beauty queen who's already secured her crown.

Or the super-mutant bitch who's just found her prey.

"What's wrong?" She bites out the prompt after Reece and I give her nothing but silence in response. I keep praying Calvin will come to his damn senses and come grab her again, but even he looks stalled in the moment, as if he's still breathing but his limbs are encased in ice—an analogy *not* helping my careening, screaming senses or cracking the ice that's encased my baby in silence. "Cat caught your tongues, then?" Juliet spits, leaning over to examine both our faces more closely. "Or are you two simply waiting, just like me?"

I want to cheer *and* punch Reece as he pushes in, angling Juliet away from me by shooting his hand across the counter and then around her bent elbow. The tension in his jaw and the blazes in his eyes tell me that he's obeyed instinct more than intelligence for the move, which could be his hugest help or hindrance within the next few seconds. Fortunately, as the girl wrests away from him faster than she yanked free from Cal, I'm thinking the former.

Until Juliet smiles again.

Only the expression doesn't belong to *Juliet*.

It's the smile of someone else. A creature who moves her lips apart just enough to expose her sweet but feral smile...her patient but predatory glee.

"Oh, you *are* waiting," she drawls out—her feline inflection all too intimate...all too knowing. "Just like me. You want to know when she'll be here again...don't you? You want her back as badly as we *all* do...don't you? *Don't you*, you sneaky Sarsgards?"

Just like before, she's back to overembellishing the words—as if making sure she's projecting to the back of some unseen theater or getting the syllables right in order to file a report. I don't care *why* she's doing it; only that like before, every pore on my body is flooded with raw fear as she does.

But unlike before, my body is dealing with *another* reaction now.

Sensations I've never felt before.

Ice and flames. Cold pain mixed with hot agony. Sharp movements, kicking and blasting at the entirety of my belly. Surging and growing, a rebellion that's not just bursting in my soul but clamoring at my whole being.

Until I'm screaming.

At least I think I am.

My own voice is nothing but a hollow sound in the background of my senses, relegated to a distant horizon as one unmistakable outcry consumes nearly all of my consciousness. But despite the pain it brings, I welcome the intruder. I gasp in tearful awe of him. Yes, *him*. The little person who's been my passenger for so many months. The magnificent miracle I've carried, now shouting at me over and over again, repeating a sole phrase of desperate instruction.

Run, Mama. Run, Mama.

Now.

Now.

Run, Mama.

CHAPTER THREE

REECE

"Run!"

It's at least the thousandth time she's rasped it since seizing my hand, tearing us out of the party without any goodbyes and then racing back up the street as if the Makras' place is about to explode. At the moment, I'd prefer that over *her* exploding—a terror too damn close to possibility as her breath turns choppier and her steps fumble on the dark, uneven sidewalk.

"Emma. *Emmalina.* You've got to calm the hell—"

"Ah! Oh!"

My exhortation barely pierces her, but a crash of waves against the beach has her flinching like a horror movie ingénue fleeing a haunted forest. When she identifies the noise, she's hardly relieved. It's right back to the breathless and desperate rush, digging her nails into my forearm as she gouges my heart with her renewed litany. The same desperate repetition. The same rasping fear.

The same chunk of my psyche that understands every note of it.

"Emma." I try to slow her again. If she goes down on this cracked concrete, even my lightning reflexes won't be fast enough for the save. "Velvet, I know you're freaked. I am too."

"This isn't freaked," she rebuts. "This is terror, husband. To be clear, a lot of it. Plain, unfiltered terror."

"All right, I get that too."

"No." She quickens the pace despite having to grab at her back, looking like she's literally shoving herself forward. "I'm not sure you do."

"I was there, damn it. I heard every word that came out of that girl's mouth and exactly how it came out."

"And you're still telling me to stay *calm* about it?"

"I'm *begging* you to be *careful* about it." I manage to stop her long enough to circle around for a resolute stare. "Even if she's one of Faline's converts—"

"*If?*"

"So you're going to sacrifice our child to that terrorist, then?" I snarl. "Because that's what you're on the verge of doing—"

"I'm trying to *save* him, damn it!" Her tear-brimmed eyes catch the moon glow, and now I feel like the world's biggest douche—but only for a second. At this moment, there's only room for one of us to be taking the terrified and morose path. I'm more than willing to let that be her. "I'm trying to save all of us!"

I plant my hands to my waist, taking advantage of her emotionally induced stall. "Well, you won't at this pace, in this goddamned darkness."

Which, just like that, is no longer darkness.

Due to the fact that my wife, using her own terminology, goes full glowworm on me.

Yeah, the whole effect. Her pores are as blinding as Hollywood sky trackers. Her eyes are mixes of blazing blue and gleaming gold. Her hair is like strands of gilded sunlight.

In a word, under any other set of circumstances, fucking gorgeous.

All right, so that's two words—but I'm not counting the first because it's basically the modifier for every minute that passes now.

Fuck, fuck, fuck, fuck.

"Fuck." While it feels good to really pop one out, I refrain from succumbing to an adjoining rant. Just the growl is one word too many. I know it after a single flash of a glare from my gorgeous wife.

"Bright enough for you?" She fires it while spinning around and then continuing her possessed pace.

I follow, letting my own stress shatter the confines of my composure, turning my fingers into ten light batons. If she's that hell-bent on getting home, might as well turn it into a family affair. Focusing less on camouflaging my powers also means I can concentrate more on her. With just half a block until we get back to the safe house, I'm willing to take the risk—

"Holy crap!"

—of something exactly like this happening.

Emma joins me in whipping back around to confront the source of the exclamation.

While dread still pumps through my veins, it's diluted by at least a few drops of relief. "Cal," I whoosh out, pivoting toward the gawking guy. While there's nothing optimal about this intrusion, at least we're talking to someone with a rational head on his shoulders. Or so I hope. We weren't at the party long enough to get the details on what that saucy Juliet really is to him. Casual date for the night? We're in luck. But if they're at friends-with-benefits or more...

"She's not with me." Unsurprisingly, Calvin deciphers my

urgent expression. "Juliet," he clarifies nonetheless. "She's not with me."

I nod, instantly understanding, but Emma's already stomping up with one hand fisted at her side and the other splayed against her stomach. "What do you mean, 'not with you'? Where the hell did she go? Is she still at Maddie and Mel's, or did she completely—"

"Okay, whoa. *Shit*," Cal rushes out. "She's still there; I swear. She didn't poof or anything." The guy proves his wise mettle once more. Though our wedding reception concluded so bizarrely that many have written it off as a publicity stunt to expose Emma's superpowers to the world, Cal clearly believes differently—enough to respect Emma's trepidation and give his answer straight. "She's asleep in the guest bedroom. Passed out right after you two bugged."

"Thank God." Emma's voice is thick with solace despite her tightly contorted face. She looks down at her middle, which she now covers with both hands. "I know, Bean," she murmurs. "I *know*. Just a little while longer."

She finishes with such a wobbly sigh, I move in without thinking and sweep down to scoop her up. But before I get her knees secured, she's stepped clear—closer to Cal and his growing gawk.

"Holy crap," he reiterates, shaking his head. "I seriously can't—I mean, *wow*." His stare keeps raking down to Emma's bulge. "I—I was freaking out in there, thinking my instincts were all wrong. But my gut kept firing, right and left. The whole time, you two felt so familiar to me—"

"Familiar?" Emma cuts in a split second before I can. "Familiar *how*?"

Cal waves a hand. "Don't worry. I think I'm the only

one who noticed. Those Bolt-inis were doing their thing on everyone long before you walked in. Both RRO teams are staying at the Lido House hotel so they're ridesharing back, but Juliet lives in NoHo, and I wanted to stay clear to drive her home. Besides, there's—" He openly gapes at Emma's belly. "I mean, *how* the hell..."

"Same thing we said." Emma attempts a smile, though it's clear the stress is still clawing at her.

"Your wedding was just over three months ago."

"Same thing *we* said." I'm the one to restate it while wrapping a protective arm around my wife.

Cal nods again, indicating his commiseration. "So," he murmurs, still clearly awestricken. "A super baby for the Richards." He ticks a glance back toward the Makras' house. "But with super enemies who'd like nothing better than to know that, yeah?"

I clutch his shoulder with my free hand. "Which means we're now trusting you with some super-level secrecy." I don't diminish the force beneath the fingers I keep coiling, ensuring he'll feel their heat even through his thick wool jacket. All right, *now* I'm taking the biggest risk of my night. Of my *year*. There's no way of discerning how much time he's actually spent with Juliet before tonight, meaning Faline might have already gotten her paws on his psyche already. "We can do that, can't we, Cal?" I press. "Because you can probably tell what's at stake if we can't."

Despite the permanent burns I'm searing into his coat, Calvin straightens his shoulders with the pride they've always possessed. "I'm a father, man." In all the important ways, he speaks the truth. The only thing he hasn't done for his sisters was give them life in the first place. "And thanks to you and

RRO, I'm a damn good one."

He sweeps a hand across his torso before smacking it atop mine with fraternal-style affirmation. For a second, I actually envision Tyce or Chase making the same move and realize how intensely I miss them both. There's nothing to be done about the ache for Tyce, but I promise myself that Chase is going to get a phone call and a visit as soon as I'm not evading the world's most persistent mutant bitch.

"As a matter of fact, I wish I could do more for you guys than just keep secrets." Cal's comment, issued with sincerity I can practically touch, snaps me fully back to the moment. Not that I was really gone, with my wife still glowing like a Christmas tree topper along Ocean Boulevard. Thank God the weather is more East Coast gloomy than West Coast balmy tonight, resulting in sparse traffic along the road.

"Maybe there is," I reply, moving back in next to Emma. She's moving noticeably slower, every step now an unsteady wobble, but I don't dare go for the stupidity of fully picking her up. When my bunny's in her let-me-do-it-myself mode, all I can do is stand by and hope to help.

"Shield her from the right side," I instruct Cal. "If we're noticed, maybe it'll just look like we're walking with a flashlight."

"Yeah." Calvin repositions himself, flanking Emma to the right while I wrap an arm around her from the left. "Good idea."

"I have better ones," I grumble. "But Miss Tenacity wouldn't be fond of them."

"Where do you think I learned it from, *Mister* Tenacity?" But the second she's finished with the retort, she comes to a full stop. She groans and grabs my arm with the strength of twenty men.

"Velvet?" I lean over, all the way in her face, inside two seconds. "What is it, baby? Talk to me, damn it."

"Shut...*up*." She spits it back between wheezing breaths. The ferocious breaths keep racking her form as I fling a look to Calvin across her heaving back. The tightness across his burnished features confirms I've communicated clearly enough. While Emma's obstinance is typical behavior, this stall-out isn't.

"Okay," Emma finally rasps out. "Forward. But slowly."

While we start to shuffle again, I stay hunched over. "All right, can you talk to me now?" I prompt. "Please, baby?"

She rolls her head hard enough that I infer the negative answer on that. But a few steps later, she utters, "Just...get me... to the car."

"The car." I refrain—barely—from pitching it into a question. Not that the restraint does me any good. "Where the hell do you think we're going in the—"

"Home."

Her dictate makes *me* halt this time. Her inflection already implies the full meaning of her word, but I still try to explain, "We *are* home, Bunny. Well, nearly. You've got only half a block—"

"No." Emma tears so deeply into my forearm, I'm certain she'll hit bone and tendons. That doesn't seize my attention as much as the stark pain denting her features. "You know what I mean. I want to go *home*, Reece. To *our* home."

I gulp hard. And force myself to say it. "To the ridge."

"To the ridge." She gives it with the certainty of finality while continuing her hobble down the sidewalk. But she only gets two steps, because I still can't move. I'm assaulted by memories as clear as they are vicious. Standing in the command center at the ridge—until I had to sit, as Dad's voice filled my ear. *They've narrowed down the search. They're going to find you, Reece...*

"*No.*" I spew it violently enough to shatter the vision, though my payback is watching deeper pain cut into my wife's brow. "Velvet, you're not thinking clearly," I dictate. "I know that all that bullshit with Juliet was stressful—"

"No." She stops, wincing harder. "All that bullshit was a wakeup call."

I draw in a harsh breath. "But that doesn't mean anyone's got to pick up the line right away, okay?"

"*Yes,* Reece. That means they *do.*" She inhales too but takes in her air with chopped-up spurts. Her lips form a pale and taut twist before she amends, "That means *we* do. If she's put enough intel together to start activating the Newport Beach-bound Faliniacs for recon missions like Juliet's, then she's gotten just as close as her efforts to pinpoint the ridge."

"'Faliniacs?'" Calvin pushes in again, shooting a narrowed stare between the two of us. "What the hell does that—*whoa.*" Just as quickly, his gaze pops wide. "That whackball who runs the Consortium...isn't her name Faline? Is that what you're getting—oh, hold up *again.*" He stabs a hand through his well-pomaded black hair. "Do you think *Juliet* has something to do with that psycho? Holy *shit.*"

"We can't get into it all right now." An understatement of fact to match the mountain of stress I'm trying to hide with what feels like a hand towel of composure. Every second we linger out here is another opportunity for exposure—because, goddamnit, Emma's more right than I want to admit. "But cutting to the chase: Faline's found a way of expediting a mass brainwashing technique. Over the last few months, she's been quietly gathering more and more followers."

"The last few *months*?" Cal ripostes. "Are you serious?"

"As a world domination vendetta," I confirm.

"But why?" He jerks his head as if trying to shake dirt out of it. "What the hell is her issue?"

As antsy as I am to rush all three of us to safety, I take some extra seconds before replying. Not because I've never considered the question but because I *have*—at least a thousand times already. "Wish I had *that* answer too," I counter. "But it's not as easy as opening the cosmic coloring book and turning to the 'badly parented kid gone wrong' page."

Emma pushes out a little snort. "If it were only that easy."

I share a commiserating glance with her before going on. "The woman's a triple threat of enemy force. Obscenely smart, intensely driven, deeply damaged."

Calvin hikes both brows. "And well-funded."

Emma manages a short laugh. "Someone was taking notes during your press conference last spring."

I give the kid a nod of deference before clarifying, "We've learned a few things about that since then, though. The relationship with the Scorpios might be taking some... evolutions."

I'm deliberately sketchy because I have to be. The hunch is all I have to go on right now, but logic is leading me closer to the conclusion each day. The cartel, even with their global muscle, can't still be Faline's biggest fans right now. She hasn't sealed off *every* crack of the Consortium's secrets—nicks that we've been successfully widening.

"But she's still amassing a secret army-cult thing."

"Yeah." I nod—reluctantly—at Cal's observation. "There *is* that." *Goddamnit.*

"But why?" he presses then. "What's her end game?"

Here's the part where my thousand questions and just as many contemplative hours bear fruit. "She really believes in her ultimate purpose. To her, the human race is permanently broken—and to save it, she has to reboot it. Literally."

With a clouded gaze, Cal sucks in a harsh breath. "An evolution for the digital age."

I slowly shake my head. "Sounds like batshit nutso time..."

"Until it doesn't." Emma's the one who fills it in now, finishing with a hitched breath—as she drops her head toward her stomach. I press in over her, kissing tenderly into her hair, sharing as much of her pain as I possibly can—but there's so much more of it than I imagined.

Irony is a word with which I'm powerfully familiar— but never so much as right now. We've been fighting Faline about her mission to alter the human race—even as we've accomplished exactly that in creating our perfect bean.

So how do we justify our battle with her now?

Or *can* we?

And do those answers even matter if Faline finds out about our baby? If that happens...what then? Am I supposed to think the bitch will acknowledge our rights as his parents at all—or just tick out a notation as the kid's DNA contributors? She values human life so little that she *cataloged* us inside the Source. To her, in so many ways, I'll always just be Alpha Two.

So to what lengths will the woman go once she learns about our child? What extremes will she use in the name of creating more super babies?

But even worse: what will she do if those children don't reach the high bar she's already set?

But this is a brood meant for a different time and place.

And it'll be ready and waiting once I choose to revisit it.

For now, I have to refocus on a scowling Calvin, his mind clearly churning into a high gear of conclusions. "Okay, so the witch turned her troubled past into an alliance between the Consortium and the Scorpios and let her intellect carry that into dreams of grandeur—which got bigger when the Consortium's experiments were successful, using human subjects like you"—he stares at me but swiftly sweeps Emma into his regard too—"well, holy shit, now like *both* of you."

"Another story for another time." My rebuttal is in response to the blatant curiosity in his stare—which has probably been waiting to be set free since our wedding day, when he was part of the crowd who witnessed Emma outing herself during the reception that broke the internet. The connection amps my trust in the guy by another notch. As one of the most public faces of RRO, Cal's likely been approached for hundreds of interviews in the three months since then but hasn't accepted a single one. "A *much* different time," I repeat as soon as my wife stops to double over again. "With much different timing."

Emma twists her head, looking up to reconnect our stares while dragging her hand the opposite direction. As she pops off several buttons, she grits, "You mean the kind that doesn't suck ass like this?"

It takes every ounce of my self-control not to scoop her up here and now. Despite the fact that we can count the scales on our holiday-themed mermaid porch mat from here, the woman continues tossing me so much stubborn intention, I know I can only redress with words. "Nothing sucks anything," I assert. "And look, we're almost home."

"*No*," Emma retaliates, her lips still tight and her teeth

still clenched. "*Home* is two hours away." Without waiting for my retaliation, she whips her attention at Calvin. "You know how to drive an Audi Q8?"

The guy's eyes pop wide. "You want me to pay you for the chance?"

"Other way around," she counters. "We'll reimburse you for the overtime on your sitter."

"Jina and Tosca are at a sleepover tonight and then a birthday party tomorrow," he returns. "And I've prepaid for Juliet's Lyft." His composure stiffens. "Her roommate can help her get inside once she's home, because I'm not getting anywhere near that brand of crazy anymore."

"Smart...guy." But Emma's encouragement is more a pair of guttural grunts and then a bunch of heavy breaths. "The keys are hanging from the hook...next to the inside door of the garage." She bursts with some more winded gusts after we clear the crosswalk in front of the house. Her whole form is trembling from the strain of simply breathing.

"Okay, listen." The woman can continue to refuse the free ride in my arms, but she's sure as hell not going to ignore the logic from my lips. "I get that we've had some crazy-as-shit times lately, and that tonight was crazier than usual, but we can't just pick up and leave—"

"You mean the same way we didn't 'just pick up and leave' from the ridge in the first place?" And just like that, she's accomplished her normal one-two punch of enthralling me and maddening me in the space of one sentence.

"Point to Mrs. Richards," I concede. "But hardly the match." As I take a few seconds to enforce the claim by shoring my stance, my opened posture clears the way for more of the searing memories from Dad's last moments alive. And his desperate words to me...

Faline...she'll never fucking stop, Reece.

Words that became prophecy.

Because tonight, one of the woman's minions raised a glass full of Bolt-ini to us...before seeming to see right through us.

Thank fuck she'd passed out drunk a few minutes later. Which has given us the pause button we need to think this shit through.

If only I can get my headstrong wife to track with that program too.

"Look, we don't have to kneejerk this now," I go on. "Taking a second to go inside and talk strategy here is—"

"A second we *don't* have."

She's still all glowing fire and glorious impatience, tempting me to think about taking her inside to do *other* things, but I set my jaw and rebut, "All right; it's clear that you're still upset about all this—"

"Reece." Her lips press together and her nostrils flare. "I'm not upset."

"Okay." I pull in a breath, focusing on being the neutral factor here. "Fine. Not upset. Freaked out, then."

"Reece."

"Or spooked. Or whatever you want to call it—"

"*Reece.*"

"What?"

"What I *am* is in labor. And what I need—what your *son* needs—is to take his first breath in his real home."

So much for neutral.

Or pause buttons.

Or strategy.

Or thinking.

Or anything beyond the hot ball of pure terror that careens down my throat—before I finally manage to blurt, "Cal?"

"Yeah?"

"Grab the keys. Take the 405 to the 101." I coincide the command with my full body dip, sweeping my gorgeous Flare off her feet before she can so much as yelp half a protest. Remarkably, perhaps even gratefully, she finally sags into me. Her head is a welcome weight against my shoulder. Her surging belly is pressed tight to my ribcage.

Her belly...

Where our son's heartbeat throbs into me and through me...

Bringing a voice along with it.

A voice so steady and beautiful and pure, my entire breath leaves me as I listen to it. Recognizing it. Loving it beyond every human *and* superhuman sense in my being.

I'm ready, Dada.

Ready to see you at last.

I'm ready now.

⚡

For the world's most notable super mutant, I'm one hell of a clueless jackass.

I don't waste the breath to even admitting it aloud, though Emma's assuredly gotten my gist by the time Calvin speeds us through the transition onto the 405 north. We've managed to find the sole hour out of the year that the notorious freeway doesn't resemble strands of brake-light-colored Christmas bulbs, despite the typical slowdowns near the interchanges,

Long Beach Airport, and LAX. A second item for gratitude: sometime before tonight, my brain worked long enough to pack a hospital go-bag for the car as well as the house. For now, at least, we've got the essentials, and I attempt to haul every one of them out as fast as my trembling hands will allow. Blanket, timer, bottled water, saltines, cookies, lip balm, massage oil, slippers, fuzzy socks, rubbing alcohol, iPod and speakers, the latest Helen Hardt book, wipes in a battery-operated warmer...

"Screw it," I finally spit when the bag's narrow opening slows down progress. On a burst of agitation, I lightning-slice the top two inches off the bag. Cal extends his right hand, ready to assist, and flings the discarded piece back to the rear stow space. I nod my gratitude but hide my guilt. In less than an hour, the guy's become invaluable, though there's been no time to tell him what he's really signed up for. He's now officially down the rabbit hole—yeah, the same one that Wade, Fershan, and Neeta have also leaped down...and are now paying for it by facing every day as if it might be their last. That's not the kind of thing to spring on a guy without his knowledge. But like so many other chapters of this crazy story called my life, there's been no time to notate with the proper bullet points.

Hell. I'm pretty sure *I* still don't have the right bullet points.

As if those even exist for what's happening here. And now. *Right* now.

Whether I'm ready or not.

"Not" being the stronger candidate for the moment.

I've never been more terrified to wrap Emmalina in my arms—or been more driven to do so. I've never seen *her* look more frightened but brave, her skin alternating between summer gold and winter pale, her eyes lakeside peaceful in one moment and then fireside fierce the next. I do know I've never been more in awe of her graceful strength or more in love with her tenacious spirit.

But I'm utterly unable to describe the sensations that strike from the moment her first hard contraction sinks in.

"Oh! Ohhhh, *shit*! Reece!"

"Here, Bunny." I'm astonished I'm able to form the words, even more so that they're coherent. I sure as fuck don't feel coherent. I'm dumbfounded but dazzled, weak but wowed, joyous but utterly and scarily helpless. "I'm here. *I'm here.*"

"I heard you the first time," she snaps but doesn't elaborate. Breathing becomes her priority, and she pinches her lips to get in the zipping inhalations that Lydia and Neeta taught her. The actions are meant to settle her nerves, but I have no idea how. Every one of them is like dull razors scraping every inch of my tendons. I seriously wonder if I'm about to bleed to death from the inside out.

Good Christ. Really, asshole? You enjoying the hell out of that wuss bath, while your woman is trying to push a watermelon out of her womb? The melon grown from your seed?

But as she shrieks again, I'm not thinking about spoons anymore. Only knives, dipped in fire and then following the same path as the razors, sinking deeper into my physical fibers in direct proportion to the slice of her anguish into my spirit.

"Fuuuuck!"

We explode the word together, filling the car with the force of our torment. By the time the contraction is over, I've kicked the front passenger seat off its axis, folding the thing forward, with Emma prone along the whole back seat.

With her head in my lap, she's fully staring up at me. Her

eyes are sharp with pain, and her skin is dotted with sweat. Yet unbelievably, she tugs at my fingers and pulls them down to her mouth, capturing the tips in a pair of weak kisses.

"You okay, Zeus?"

I spurt an incredulous laugh. "You're stealing my lines, cheeky bunny."

One of the water bottles is jabbed into the space between our gazes. Cal, taking advantage of the slow-down before the 110 split, has yanked the bag onto the middle console and taken stock of the contents. "Drink up," he orders. "Both of you. This is probably just the start, and you need to stay hydrated."

I slant a grateful glance at him via the rearview but end it with a wry smirk. "You taking midwife classes in between the engineering curriculum, Neves?"

He chuffs. "Who do you think helped my mom push out Tosca and Jina? Not their asshole sperm donor, that's for sure." He shoots me a grin while checking behind us to switch lanes. "Only I'd just turned fourteen and had to figure all this shit out for myself. When I almost passed out because I hadn't done anything to take care of myself in ten hours, I finally got the clue."

So maybe the guy *can* handle the bullet points.

I only take half a second to indulge the thought before concentrating on my wife again. With a tender nudge, I urge her head up and coax the water bottle to her lips. "You heard the man, Mrs. Richards. Drink up."

I expect Emma to slip out some snarky one-liner, but my terrified grate seems to move her as if I've just whipped out roses and laid them at her feet. Right now, I wish I *could* handle all of this with nothing but a bunch of flowers. I'm as out of my element as the first few months of learning about my powers—

no, even more so because there's no room for margin here. I'm not out in the middle of nowhere with trees and boulders for target practice. If I make a mistake now, the woman I worship will pay the price.

As well as the miracle of a child we've created.

Shit.

Shit.

Shit!

"Hey." Her soft interjection prevents my panic from gaining root, though she's nearly out of breath due to chugging practically all the contents of the bottle. But the stuff works its magic, returning some normal color to her face between the glowing splotches due to her stress. "You heard the guy," she urges with a smile. "Take care of yourself too, you big ox."

I chug the final swallow of water she left behind. "There." Then crush the empty plastic and overhand it backward, to join the leather I torched away from the go-bag. "Happy?"

Her smile grows. "Never been happier." Emma guides my now-empty hand down to the rise of her belly. At once, even the sequins of her dress start vibrating, with the swell underneath seeming to dance to the same excited beat. "And I think Bean agrees."

Her statement hardly does the meaning justice. My Thor hammer of a heartbeat and my Firebird flame of a throat are solid confirmations—but neither of them eclipses the brilliance that swirls up through me from where my fingers join with Emma's. The happiness flames along my arm and across my chest, spreading out the rest of my extremities like a thousand racing, raucous comets.

All of them beginning to laugh out one joyous refrain.

Dada's here!

Dada's here!
Dada's here!

"Holy *shit*." At least I think that's what tumbles out of me, though comprehending anything in terms as basic as syllables and words is like asking a baby to comprehend chess.

Bad comparison.

Because in the case of *this* baby, that might damn well be a possibility.

"Holy shit," I repeat, twining my hold tighter with Emma's. As we roam our meshed fingers back and forth across her belly, we share a spellbound laugh when tiny hands and feet from within start following our route. "I—I mean, my *stars*," I stammer, grinning wide as her laughter intensifies—though we fall silent together when I'm joined by another voice again. *That* voice, so happy and innocent and absolute, ringing out from the center of her body...and resonating in the depths of my heart.

Stars, dada? What...are...stars?

"Oh, God," Emma rasps, and I press my lips into several of the salty rivulets down her cheeks as I funnel my energy inward and then direct that electricity into a silent, electric thought of response.

Stars are just like you, *son. Bright. Perfect. Magical. Original.*

There's a tearful gasp in my ear. I tilt toward it, kissing Emma on the lips this time. She's eavesdropping on our little chat, but I have a feeling it's not the first time. And dear God, I pray it won't be the last. We're a family now—and it hits me that we've been so for a while now, so much longer than what most families are blessed with. She and I aren't just about to "meet" our son. In so many ways, we already have.

I pull back a little from my wife so that my gaze can fully take hers in. Her face, still a sheen of gold-flecked sweat, has never sucked the breath from me harder. Her smile, shaky and still a little scared, has never made the world fade faster.

"A star," I whisper to her. "Woven to life inside a star."

She swallows hard. Squeezes my hand. "And given life by a beautiful bolt."

Our son kicks out his immediate approval on the assertion, followed by a new contraction of the walls around him. Our bean fights back at the bonds, doubling the intensity of Emma's pain... And, at once, my pain too.

"Holy *fuck*!" Okay, I'm not imagining this insanity. As my head drops and I bonk foreheads with Emma, I'm given a shred of comfort in the steadiness of her stare, validating I really haven't just signed up for a lifetime membership in the Worldwide Wuss Collective.

But it's only a shred.

Incinerated as soon as the contraction goes on.

And on.

And on.

And my hope for relief is incinerated along with the biological dynamite charges that explode everywhere through my body—but most horrifically, south of my navel. Yeah, including the TNT stick between my thighs, feeling clamped into a merciless medieval torture device. It's one of those cock cages with retractable spikes on the inside, except karma's decided to ignore the "retract" lever. How I wish I could write off the imagery as melodrama, but it's not. This shit is real. In the last three years, I've become an expert on pain, from the little smirk between level three and four up to whatever exists after the sobbing red guy at ten. This isn't my goddamned imagination.

A conclusion leading me to an inevitable, incredible recognition.

I'm connected to her. I mean *connected*.

No. Beyond that.

Not just feeling every beat of her heart, or absorbing the Fahrenheit of her blood, or savoring every word that emanates from our son's awakening spirit.

Beyond all of that.

Much further beyond.

Our baby hasn't just become a product of our DNA. He's the fusion of it, in every sense of the word. A product of the bond that's melded the two of us, in ways that have never been humanly possible. But because of this impossibility, never making me feel *more* human.

Yeah, right down to every damn birthing pain.

Pain I'm not about to trade away, despite how Cal locates the ibuprofen I keep in the center console and frantically passes the bottle back.

But after I bat it away, sending it flying into the front windshield, he slams on the right blinker and declares, "Just saw a sign for a hospital off the next exit. I don't know exactly which one—"

"And I don't care," I retort.

"But—"

"*No* hospital." With perfect timing, the contraction wanes. I'm able to bolt him with a commanding glare via the rearview. And I mean *bolt*. My irises are the color of liquid steel, my brows hunched into low thunderheads. "We can't afford a shred of unwanted attention, let alone what *this* might bring."

As if Bean is listening—and by now, I truly believe that's the case—he shoves hard enough at his confines to ignite a counter-protest from the skin he's stretching. Once more, every one of my pores groans and burns in alliance with Emma's, and I fantasize about being able to unzip my skin and then step out of the offensive stuff, leaving the burning husk behind.

Another thought my son is bizarrely in sync with...

As he kicks hard enough to turn Emma's stomach into an orb as blazing and hot as the sun she got her name from.

Which means the front of her dress is now a slice of toast.

All right, so *now* I'm exaggerating—unless "toast" suddenly got redefined as a few scraps of smoked stretch fabric and a handful of charred sequins.

"Oh, holy shit!" Cal's exclamation, spurted as soon as the smell of barbequed fabric has him swiveling a curious glance back, pretty much says it all. While I'm beyond tempted to add my echo of it to the air, I practically bite my own tongue off to abstain—an effort made easier as soon as I cast my own gaze back down to my wife's face. She's golden, glistening, gorgeous, and freaked the hell out. That's my cue to man the hell up.

"Velvet." I curl my grip tighter into hers. With my free hand, I caress the side of her face. My fingers slick through a layer of liquid gold. I'm unsurprised. If I had a creature inside me already capable of cognitive thought and the words that went with it, I'd probably be sweating a little too. "It's going to be all right, baby. I promise."

She swallows hard. Attempts an answering smile. "I know." As she rasps it, she guides our joined hands in a gentle circle over her bared belly. "And so does he."

No sooner does she finish saying it than her whisper is joined by another voice once more. The completion of our circuit. The new fire in our family.

Dada say all right. So we all right.

At once, I'm flooded with more feeling. Engulfed in emotions. Overtaken by such a cacophony of reactions, I'm shorted out before I can pick one to commit to. So what does that make me now? Nothing but a slack-jawed, mute-mouthed clod, forming my mouth around nothing but air and then releasing more of the same. But not completely. When Emma pushes her fingertips into my cheek, her fire combines with the wet tracks there, making me newly conscious of the amazement that's taken liquid form too. I don't make a single attempt to swipe the tears away or to hide the ones that spill out right on top of them. This moment is a miracle. This *child* is our miracle. He's already worth every ounce of the hell I had to pay to make him happen.

And, I learn with my next breath, the hell I'm still having to pay.

As the torture clamps us both again.

Except that this time, the spikes aren't just driving into my crotch.

My hips, my abdomen, my stomach, my ribs—anything and everything below my sternum is gashed into ribbons and then twisted into knots, only there's a goddamned burning coal cinched in the center of each one. My only lifeline back to sanity is the juncture of my hand with Emma's, though she's returning my desperate clutch with pressure that matches her excruciating wail.

"Ohhh, God! Ohhh, *Reece!*"

"Here, baby," I somehow choke out. "I'm—I'm right here. I'm not going anywhere."

"No shit," Cal mumbles from the front—though his sarcasm is short-lived once he dashes another look back at us.

"*Ohhh, shit,*" he's sputtering instead, putting the new refrain on repeat as he concentrates on weaving through the traffic sludge through Culver City and the west side. Silently, I beg him to be careful. The countdown to midnight is well over an hour away, but I'd bet my left nut—if the damn thing agrees to talk to me again—that half the west side has been screaming hello to the new year since Manhattan did. "Guess the hospital option is really off the table now," he utters, apparently really getting the point that the Richards Family light show is only just getting started.

"Just step on it," I get out in return, checking off just about every box for testy-asshole-billionaire in the process. But when I have to interject a bunch of wheezes that sound more like a constipated rhino, I feel Cal's empathy piling on top of his incredulity. "Over the Sepulveda Pass," I continue. "Then out the 101 to Las Virgenes."

He nods while trading glances with me again in the rearview. The motion is calm, but his dark eyes aren't. He's finally figuring out the scope of what's happening here—not that he's comfortable with it, which makes two of us. I'm not exactly down with being the poster boy for karma's retribution on behalf of every woman since Eve, but at least there's going to be a reward for this pain. A huge one.

Cal, seeming to read that thought from the resolve on my face, makes an attempt at levity. "Guess you drew the cosmic short straw, man."

I shove out a wry grunt. "Or the longest."

"Which makes you the world's wisest optimist or blindest idiot."

"Or both." With a sigh that's more weary than my years, I gaze out the window for a second. We've started up the rise into the pass, with the LA Cemetery sprawled to our right and the white Travertine beauty of the Getty perched atop the hill to our left. The two edifications to the past have me reflecting backward, resulting in my philosophical follow-up. "Sometimes, blindness *is* wisdom, buddy."

Cal looks ready to nod again—but in commiseration or confusion, I'm not certain—but before he gets his chance, my head is yanked back down by a hand at the roots of my hair. "Okay, Gandalf, save it for your son," Emma snaps, already writhing as her stomach really starts resembling the surface of the sun. "Who's hell-bent on hearing it sooner than later!"

All of that spews from her in a pained rush, and I'm positive she's yanked out a full hock of my hair as the next spasm fully hits. I brace myself for the same cutlass through my middle, hanging on to her tightly when it does. With my forehead pressed sideways across hers, I join her in breathing through the height of the jolt, though I'm not surprised to feel myself smiling at the same time. I'm no stranger to knowing how to handle extended pain, but I'm a giddy virgin at the thought of it actually yielding an amazing gift at the end.

The world's best gift.

The kid who's already stolen my heart, captivated my spirit, and worked his way into the depths of my soul.

The being with a vocabulary nearly better than mine—but likely doesn't recognize the word "ordinary."

And if I have anything to say or do about it, he never will.

As a matter of fact, I make a silent vow to the universe that I'll never crave ordinary again.

Even in this moment, with my bloodstream feeling like fried electrical lines.

Even in this moment, with my woman working to scalp

me with her fingertips.

Even in this moment, with my desperate bellows matched to her strident screams—and not in the let's-get-our-freaky-kink-on kind of way.

As a matter of fact, if I so much as breathed the words "freaky kink" right now, I'm sure Emma would work on rearranging my ball sack instead of my hair. And despite the rampant joy in all my senses, I make a new deal with the universe: to happily trade places with her, if only for a few minutes, to give her relief from the storm clearly raging through her whole system. It's worth a try, right? Before thirty minutes ago, who'd have ever predicted any man alive would know the torture of childbirth—or be grateful for it? But right now, I'm nothing *but* gratitude.

All right, not entirely true.

In between the awe and wonder, there are slices of pure pity for every member of my gender. And yeah, there's a little arrogance involved on that one. But even stripping my inner Tony Stark out of the equation, the feeling remains the same. How can any man say he truly understands this miracle without sharing in every stage of it? Yes, even in the pain. Perhaps *especially* in it.

Which is why, as Emma slams a foot against the door to gain traction for a new contortion, I let her yank my head down so hard that I'm getting a suntan from her stomach. Her other hand falls free from my hold and sweeps out to slam against the passenger seat headrest. She arches her torso up, and I indulge a few seconds of admiring how perfectly the move shows off every luscious curve of her pregnancy-ripened tits before guilt takes over on a bunch of different levels.

"Velvet." I let it vibrate with every husky note of my

emotion as I lift back up and then shift beneath her, hoping to cradle her head more comfortably. "God*damn*, you're amazing."

She tilts up enough to get down a new swig of water. As she settles back onto my lap, still breathing hard, she wobbles out a small smile. "Says the only man in history experiencing his kid's birth like this?"

"Says the guy who wouldn't have it any other way." I pull a towelette out of the plastic dispenser that Cal's managed to wedge between the two front seats. Each of the gentle swipes I give her cheeks causes a temporary swath of cyan through the pulsing gold of her skin, practically matching the brilliant gleam in her eyes. As soon as I stop, they darken once more to the color of midnight. Not the dreamy midsummer kind, either. Her irises are nearly indigo as she grabs the front of my shirt and twists hard.

"Hey." I toss aside the towelette and rub my hand atop hers. "Baby? What is it?"

"*Reece.*"

"What, Velvet?"

She gulps again. Licks her lips. "I'm—I'm scared."

I tuck my head, kissing her fingertips while keeping my stare locked to her face. "My brave little Flare. I'd be worried if you weren't."

She wants to be soothed by that—I can feel her spirit reaching for the comfort to the tips of my nerve endings—but her face remains taut. At last she mutters, "Like you've never faced anything more nerve-racking, right?"

I preface my answer with a quick kiss to her knuckles. "Oh, baby...I've never been more terrified in my life."

Her confused scowl is beyond adorable. "Huh?"

"Scout's honor."

And so is her quick eye roll. "You were never a Boy Scout, Richards."

"*Pfffft.* I'll bet Cal was."

The guy flings a laugh. "For a few years, yeah. Until my mom got sick."

"There," I quip. "I'm borrowing his cred."

Her features soften and her eyes brighten. "Fine. I believe you. You're officially terrified." She stretches her fingertips against my cheek. "But at least now you have company."

"More than 'company.'" I emphasize it by diving my gaze into the turquoise depths that give me so much of her soul. "I have my heart now." Another fervent brush of my lips, this time to the center of her palm. "My family. My *more.*"

Her eyes turn into liquid pools. "Me too," she whispers—but the words she's preparing as follow-up, with a huge inhalation, are plucked away by a startled gasp. She tags on a musical giggle, but it's the backing soundtrack to the next voice I hear in my head. That clear, joyous, excited little boy I've already been hearing in my heart for so long...

Me more too! Me more too, Dada!

I share a dazed smile with Emma as Bean proves his point with a happy gig against her navel. No way can I resist answering his happiness by pressing back down over that swell, alive with a million shades of shimmering gold. This time, I burrow my nose against that mesmeric heat, reveling in how she still smells like spice and summer even in the last few hours of December. Just like the effect of my fingers on her cheeks, my touch leaves a light-blue path. Suddenly feeling like a kid playing with the textures of a velvet pillow, I do it again. And again. Of course, the echoes of my child's delighted laughs have something to do with that—as well as the equally happy sounds that flow out of my wife, like tantalized little sighs mixed with ecstatic groans.

And unbelievably, this whole experience just got crazier.

While it gives me nothing but pleasure to be the cause of the exact same for my wife, I don't blame Calvin for hurling a startled gawk over his shoulder at us. If anyone called us right now and heard only the audio from the car, they'd swear Emma and I *weren't* back here getting ready to push out a new baby together.

Okay, not exactly together.

But, I'm damn sure, as close to that as two people can possibly be.

"All right," Cal ventures. "So no hospital. But do I—uhhh—need to be pulling over or someth—"

"Just *drive*, damn it." I try retracting the growl with as much of an apologetic look as I can manage and tack on, "Please."

Cal throws me an understanding glance before announcing, "Las Virgenes is the next exit."

"Take it south until you hit Mulholland. I'll give you the left-rights when we're closer."

He kicks up half a grin. "You mean without getting a video nondisclosure or anything?"

I cock a brow. "Do I have to worry about that?"

"No, sir." He clearly receives the message—good thing, since Emma has a broadcast of her own to order as soon as I let up the caresses on her belly.

"Reece!"

"Here, baby." I'm all about her and nothing but her again, pushing the force of my soul into the passion of my words.

"Right here. What do you need?"

"Don't...stop." While her words are both spurted on gasps, her clutch packs the strength of fifteen men. She uses that fury to haul my hand back down to her stomach. "Just...don't...stop." After just ten seconds of my renewed rubs, her eyes drift shut and her body again goes limpid. "Oh, *God*. So much better."

Like the man with half a brain that I've become, it takes me until now to snap all the logic together. The currents from my fingers...they're her Bolt-alized TENS unit. But while a hundred kinds of happiness suffuse me at giving her relief from the pain, I've researched enough about every pregnancy aid on the planet to know that this isn't exactly the right way to be approaching this. "Bunny, I should be doing this to your spine, not your—"

"Do. Not. Stop." Once more with the grip that carries the force of a small army. She secures her hand across mine, working it tighter against the rounded surface at her middle.

The surface that's now rolling like ocean swells.

And then lurching like the sea under a tsunami watch.

And then undulating as if every citizen in Atlantis has been awakened by that storm.

"Holy...*fuck*," I rasp, fighting to comprehend there's only *one* creature responsible for all that tumult. The most precious, powerful creation in the whole history of this planet...

The incredible little person who pushes so hard at his confines, I can count all ten of his fingers and all ten of his toes with one gawk at my wife's stomach.

And I mean a *gawk*.

A dazed, dorky, utterly dumbfounded version of the term—which intensifies as soon as Bean seems to rear back and then punch out as hard as he can. The strike is so zealous, it audibly strips away Emma's breath. But she gets in a tight laugh while inhaling once more. "Okay, Mighty Bambino, we get it. We get it."

I don't join her in the chuckle. Pure paralysis prevents me—from the moment a force takes over her body that has me wondering why I dared to toss around the word *terrified* with such cavalier ease. What I've declared to her as terror was a whisper of sensation compared to this. On the other hand, I've never had to sit by and witness something like this.

Her skin, glowing until the dazzling surface turns blinding white.

Her face and hair, ignited like some video-game fire fairy.

Her limbs, jerking out from her like splayed matchsticks—and then igniting the same way.

"Ahhhh!" Cal unhands the wheel long enough to deflect a flying kitten-heeled shoe. "That yeet's not cool, kids."

I attempt to work my mouth around an apology, but my throat still can't produce anything but lame chokes. The emerging sounds may or may not be vowels. I'd like to think the dude who just used "yeet" in a complete sentence will understand, but as Cal speeds us deeper into the canyon, his knuckles are as white as Emma's skin.

Emma—who's still giggling like we've simply gotten on a roller coaster.

Emma—who's radiating light as if that roller coaster has been erected on a beach in Tahiti.

Emma—who deepens my astonishment and adoration as *she* speaks up, offering to Cal, "Sorry, dude. The yeeting wasn't on purpose." She grins a little wider and bites the inside of her lip. "But I'm pretty damn sure my sweet son just broke my water."

"*Huh?*" Cal spurts along with his instant kneejerk. No, really. The whole car lurches as he instinctively goes for the brake. "Wh-What the *hell?*"

I layer the same demand over his, following it with a frantic burst at my wife. "*Now?*" I thunder as my pulse escalates to full thunder in my veins. I peer down and then around, petrified to venture my sights anywhere near her crotch. "And *here*? But I don't see any—errmmm, I mean why isn't there any—"

And the guy who used to spend his weekends playing between women's legs now can't form his lips around the words *amniotic fluid*. My man card just went up in flames. Appropriate metaphor, considering what's going on with the woman in my arms. Cradling her now feels like holding a kiln. Her hairline resembles a forest firebreak line. Her fingers and toes are feathers of flames.

And she's still smiling with the serenity of a damn Madonna.

"Ohhhh, Zeus," she chides, guiding my hand into broader sweeps across her belly. There's no time to marvel that her fire feathers aren't charring my skin, especially as she halts our twined fingers atop a spot where Bean has decided to pull a full *Riverdance*. "Feel that," she exhorts, though her voice cracks with impending tears. "*Feel your son*, Reece. Soak in everything he already is. That life. That magic. That drive." She swallows hard as we tangle our gazes, and I show her how thoroughly I'm obeying every syllable of her words. I do feel it all. I do feel all the brilliance of *him*. My *God*, he's amazing. "Now tell me," she finally murmurs, "do you really think he's going to be bothered with bullshit like spilling membranes all over the place?"

My breaths are threaded with lead now too. That doesn't

stop the lightning speed of the burn behind my own eyes as well as the quaver of my reply. "So...what now?" Or the desperation, as a full understanding decks me between the eyes. All the online classes, the procedure guides, the daddy workbooks... they all mean nothing now. I truly have no damn idea what I'm doing.

But that means nothing to this kid.

This is happening.

He is happening.

"Holy. Shit." I make a mental note to apologize to him for the profanity, in ten or so years. But at the rate he's already tackling life, that might be ten *minutes*.

Again, a factor I have no choice about.

Suck the hell up, buttercup. You've faced drug dealers on Skid Row, embezzlers in Century City, and pimps in NoHo back alleys. You are *prepared for this, just in different ways. A baby, even electrically enhanced, has to be easier than the collective lowlifes of LA—right?*

I don't let my instincts answer that. There's no time, anyway. Emma explodes with a sharp gasp as Bean changes up his beat, using her belly as his full-on mosh pit. As his kicks intensify, so does her exterior stress. The fire spreads out from her hairline, sizzling down her neck until the entire neckline of her dress is fried away. Through a jolt of divine grace, there are enough sequined tatters left to cover the essentials of her chest, as well as everything between her waist and knees.

And yeah, *divine grace* really is the right vernacular.

Since the woman still has flames for fingers and skin like gilded neon.

But that's my sole gift from grace—because then I notice the biggest change of all.

Her smile is gone. Completely.

Nibbled away by the pained winces that keep chomping at her serenity. With every new stab she endures, my gut is shredded into shark chum—especially with the comprehension that I'm no longer sharing the burden with her.

What the hell?

The circuit between us has been suddenly, inexplicably severed. And goddamnit, I have to accept it. Doesn't mean I'm going to fucking like it. *Now* is the time fate decides to give me a taste of impending fatherhood, normal guy style? *No thank you, asshole.* I'll take my mama-on-fire and my son-on-supercharge version any day of the week, along with every ounce of the physical pain that means. This worthless bystander shit isn't even for the birds. At least birds can gather twigs and chop up worms.

I'm worse than a worm right now.

Beyond mush.

A coiled ball of goo on the sidewalk, looking on as Emma wraps her fingers around my knuckles as if she's about to challenge me to an arm wrestle. With the way things have been going since we left the house tonight, I wouldn't be surprised if she did. Instead, with intent that's equally as vehement, she states, "I think we'll have to make this up as we go along, mister."

I roam my adoring gaze across every beloved curve of her gorgeous features. "I think you might be right, goddess."

She looks a little confused by my easy capitulation but issues just as firmly, "That also means you've got to listen to me, husband."

I pull her hand over and kiss her fingertips. "I'm hearing every beautiful syllable, wife."

She firms her features. "No. Not just hearing. *Listening*, okay? As in, complying."

I lift my head by an inch, arching my brows by an equal amount. Labor pains or not, she's tiptoeing through the delicate phrasing here—but "delicate" is a word as useful as "worm" to me. "Yes, Emmalina," I counter. "I *know* what that means."

It's not a lie; nor is it the truth I want to accept. But there's no time to debate the point. I'm not the one with the demanding creature in my stomach. So like it or not, I'm following her command—the exact same way *she's* taking her orders from the bean.

A modicum of solace comes when the car's weight noticeably shifts, and I look up as Cal completes the turn onto Mulholland. "Thank God," I mutter. "Less than thirty and we'll be home, Velvet."

But as the words are leaving my lips, she's lowered my hand back down across her stomach—and I nearly drop a shocked hiss as my own punctuation. But I'm too late. Emma beats me to the punch with a hoarse gasp that coincides with the massive heave of her midsection. At once, I'm joining her. No longer do I liken the swell to gentle ocean waves or a rowdy club dance pit. There's a raging alien in that cramped cavity, seemingly determined to take inspiration from his cinematic counterpart—by punching his way out of his mother.

Free. Free, Mama. Free, Dada. Now!

The look that takes over Emma's face is suffused with so much love and light, I finally understand why so many classic painters were inspired to create angels. But no masterpiece I've ever seen, even in all the galleries and cathedrals I've traveled to across the world, do justice to my wife's beauty in this moment.

"Baby, I don't think this kid will wait *three* more minutes, let alone thirty."

Yeah, even when she insists on saying that.

"Holy God." I seethe it out, realizing Disciplinary Dad Time starts right this second. When Bean kicks out again, his demand meets the plank of my restraining palm, backed by my decisive growl. "No you do *not*, young man."

"Reece." Emma's frustrated huff has me pinning her with my glare. Still, she charges, "Do you remember what you just agreed to? What you just swore that you understood?"

Gut-deep snarl. "That was different!"

"No." Faster and stronger than the golden bullet she's embodying, she whips a hand around my wrist. "It's no damned different." Her face softens, but her grip is still a solid-gold cuff. "This is the way it's going to happen, Zeus." As soon as she blinks back a new slew of tears, I comprehend the deeper gist of her shaky tone. *Shit.* She's known this all along. Has probably had several conversations with Bean about it already. She's known *all* of this but has waited this damn long to spring it on me...

Knowing exactly how I'd react.

Just like this.

With instincts igniting in horror. Then outrage. Then at last, disgusting coils of raw fear.

Nevertheless, this goddess remains my beacon of beauty, strength, courage, and tenacity—all even more so now, since there's a surge of a new element to her splendor as well. Maternal resolve.

"This is the way it *has* to happen, Reece." She openly winces as Bean high-kicks his approval of that. "Just...just tell me you understand. Okay?"

My heart howls to do just that—but the depths of my spirit and the fibers of my fortitude are still drenched in roars of protesting rebellion. "Understand *what*?" I snap. "That I'm supposed to watch while this child refuses to take the normal exit out?" *What the living fuck?*

Though I hold back from spewing that aloud, I refuse to school my face into the same obeisance—a call I regret as soon as her whole body tenses with pain. But this time, her suffering isn't due to a contraction or any of Bean's kicks. Her heart is bruised—and *I'm* her callous assailant.

Damn it.

"Bunny," I grate, sliding one of my hands to cradle the back of her neck. "Come on, now. Return the favor. You *and* him. Listen to *me*." I spread my fingers up and then in, tenderly scraping them along her scalp. "What's wrong with taking at least one part of this gig the *right* way?"

With a shaky exhalation, Emma lets her head rock back into my hold. With a gaze glittering as bright as abalone shells, she rasps back, "But what if it's the wrong way?"

Narrowed gaze. Then even tighter, until I'm nearly squinting. "What do you—"

"What if..." She frantically shoots her gaze downward, but the sight of her cavorting belly only pales her skin by three more shades. Despite the bizarre sight and the nerves it unhinges for her, she goes on. "What if...it's easier to get him out like this, than by forcing him down a dark and scary tunnel?" She raises her gaze and locks it to mine once more. "What if...he reacts to that fear by lashing out? By using any or all of the powers he's inherited but doesn't how to control yet?"

From the front, Cal busts out a sharp snarl. "Oh, *hell*!"

I twist my lips. "And now that *that's* been said..."

My wife digs her hand into the front of my vest again. The tremble in her hold matches the dread in her gaze. "D-Don't be mad."

Shit.

I'm officially certain she's not the only one flashing desperate fear right now—but I can do her one better. Guilt plugs so deeply into me, both my hands look tucked into dayglow-blue gloves. "Mad?" I blurt. "Velvet, does this kid have you high now?" I grab her hand and mesh our fingers back together. At any other time and in any other world, we'd be a special-effects department's dream, my isotope digits mashed against the mini tiki torches of hers, but right now, I look at the sight with nothing but desperation and contrition. "I'm not mad, Emmalina," I finally confess. "I'm...I'm sorry. And I'm terrified. And I'm feeling so goddamned helpless."

I give in to a heavy wash of the latter, unable to even complete my thought. Four months ago, we stood before God and our loved ones, making vows to always be real and open with each other—but this is honesty I never thought I'd have to face. An impotence that's worse than hell.

"Fuck!" I grate it as our bean shoves up again and Emma's face contorts in a dozen angles. I repeat it as her torso lifts off my lap, almost as if the life inside it is pulling at her in his need to be free.

"Reece."

Her sough interrupts my goal to invent a profanity better than the F-word. As soon as I fling my head back down, soaking up the magnificence of her beauty even in the throes of her distress, she speaks again.

"Y-You're not...helpless." As she speaks, she demonstrates the point—by sliding her hand to reposition mine.

Directly over the middle of her stomach.

With my forefinger straight and the rest curled in.

"I—I don't underst—" I fall silent, darting a quizzical scowl between her face and her belly. "Wh-What the hell?" But as the words tumble out of me, mortification clings to them. The dread thickens as I really start understanding what she's going to ask of me.

No.

What she'll demand I do to her.

"What the *hell*, Emma?"

As if *that's* going to hold her—or our irascible child—off.

"Reece." A new grimace lances her face.

"No." I jerk my hand up, twisting it into a tight fist. "*No*, goddamnit." I notice Calvin twitching, as if he's debating whether to pull over again. Wisely, the guy maintains most of his attention forward, gunning the car to an urgent but safe speed.

But not urgent enough.

"*Reece.*"

"No!"

"You need to do this, damn it!" I'm toast for resistance as she jerks my hand back down, forcing my forefinger back against her trembling skin. "He wants *out*, husband. He wants out *now*. And he'll do it, no matter what it takes."

"She's right." Though Cal mutters it with conviction, his shoulders are cliffs of tension and his knuckles are still coiled and pale against the wheel. "I don't want it to be true any more than you do, man. But if that kid's ready, he's *ready*." He finishes with a shared glance in the rearview, his eyes telling me what he doesn't dare voice aloud. That Emma may be rasping and shaking, but her will has never been forged of stronger iron—

her conviction never more focused or unfaltering. Because everything else, including me and even her own existence, pale to dim priorities behind the life that wants to break free now.

No.

That *will* break free.

That thought must be digitally scrawling across my forehead, because she speaks out as if following up to it. "So is he going to do this shit *his* way or yours?"

I wait for two seconds, hoping—in vain, I already know—that she has a third option. But I've got to gird my goddamned balls and accept those choices. Which aren't really choices. Am I going to let my infant son, brilliant as he is, go into random Hulk-smash mode on my wife's vital organs, or am I going to lead by example and show the little bugger that punches should only be a last resort?

And even then, with precision.

Precision.

Okay, yeah. That's going to have to be my keyword here.

And even as I think it, I can't believe it.

But I lock my teeth, square my jaw—and, most importantly, clear my mind of every last distraction except all the anatomy diagrams I've memorized over the last couple of months. If civilian study hours really counted toward anything, there's a damn good chance I could qualify for an OB-GYN residency by now, anyway. I'm just putting the knowledge to use in a way that turns my ears to bells and my stomach to rocks.

But I push past both. Hard.

Before pulling in a breath. Thoroughly.

Then shifting my finger on Emma's belly. Determinedly.

And then...freezing.

Completely.

Horrifyingly.

My vision clouds. My equilibrium careens. I zero in on the sight of my index finger, prepped and resembling a powered laser pointer, but activating it any further is a thought as foreign as slitting my own throat.

"Fuck," I choke. "No!" The mists in my vision thicken—but in the midst of them, clear as if it's happening again, I see Kane lying prone beneath me instead. Begging me to save Los Angeles—and his sanity—by killing him with my bare hands. I battle to tell myself this isn't the same shit at all, but the only answer from my senses isn't helping.

This isn't the same.

It's worse.

Even thinking of cutting into this woman—of purposely slicing her open—is a visceral rip in my soul. A violation of my existence. And while my logic swings back with swords of common sense, I furiously and methodically snap each one.

"I can't." It coils up from the sea of bile in my gut, a hateful gurgle. "Velvet," I rasp. "I—"

"Reece." But I'm torn off my mental moorings by the anguish of *her* whisper—and then the taut, tormented moan with which she finishes. The Kane memories vanish like smoke, torched by the distress that takes over her whole form. "*Reece*. Please!" She grabs at the middle of my chest, igniting my vest and shirt until her fingertips sear my skin. Vaguely, I'm aware of the cigar-sized scorches now connecting my pecs, but there's no time to acknowledge the pain—not when Emma's clearly enduring so much more of it. "Intestines aren't supposed to be trampolines, right?"

I gulp hard. "Holy fuck."

At once, her stare sharpens. A few seconds of hope

interrupt her misery. At once, I'm invaded by conflicting, wrenching emotions. There's raging fury about her pain but consuming elation that I can do something about it. Except that my heroic duty here is going to involve...

"Goddamnit."

It bears repeating, probably a hundred times more, but there's no time for that. *Doing the right thing doesn't mean doing the easy thing.* But Christ on a pogo stick, how many more times do I have to show the universe that I fucking get it?

Apparently—and clearly—one more.

"Hey." With her fingertips still lodged against my chest, at least Emma's mellowed her fingers into warm churros instead of blazing skewers. "You're not in this alone, Dark Knight." She lends herself a tiny smile because of the reference. "I'm right here."

Though I've been working on a return smile for her, I embrace my inner Bruce Wayne and let a growl take over my throat instead. "Not cool to steal my lines, baby—even if you *are* Wonder Woman."

"Nothing to steal," she volleys. "They're not lines."

The space over my heart grows warmer, coming alive with a sensation I've never experienced before. I don't move my stare from her gorgeous golden face, but I'm damn positive she's lighting up everything in my chest with a mixture of liquid sun and forty-carat flecks.

"They're simply the truth, my beautiful Zeus." She wraps her other hand back around mine, filling all of my fingers with that incredible golden power. "We're going to do this together, okay?" she presses. "We're going to greet our son, face-to-face, at last. We're going to be here with all of the same elation and connection and jubilation with which he was first created.

We're going to look at him, and kiss him, and hold him—"

"And love him." I declare it in a thick husk, already watching the intention in her eyes. Instantly, it's cut short by the sharp gasp on her lips. But as Bean starts up his dance party again, I soak up all of the tearful gratitude she musters across her face and pours into the pressure of her fingers. "And then we'll tell him that, each and every day," I go on. "The same way I'll never stop telling *you*, my incredible woman."

I stroke a hand through her hair, savoring its silky warmth. I glide that hand along the back of her neck, remembering each and every time I've cupped that honey-soft spot before kissing her. I do that now, brushing my lips across hers. At the same time, I inhale deeply, dousing my senses in her sunshine and summer-wind scent. I notice it all. I memorize it all.

I memorize *us*.

Because it's all about to change.

As soon as I turn my forefinger into an electric scalpel and lower it to her skin.

And then *through* her skin.

"Aaaaahhhh!"

And then, with her shriek in my ears and her agony in my soul, slicing even deeper.

"Don't stop. Damn it, *don't stop*, Reece!"

And then obeying her—despite how it's all but killing me. Despite how I register how she's following my path with her fingers, seeming to mitigate her pain with solar-level heat, which is fine and dandy unless one is the guy inflicting the torture in the first place.

Christ. And I really thought my months inside the Source had forever squared away my debt to karma? Being Faline's lab rat was barely the appetizer course for this entree of an ordeal.

Having to reach in past my wife's intestines, enduring the slosh of her body fluids as I do.

Having to swallow back my sick as Calvin can't, enduring his violent dry heaves and his get-me-a-bag breaths.

Having to keep going, pushing aside her bladder, to gain an unhindered view of her uterus.

And now, for the shittiest hell: having to haul in a huge breath while feeling my way along the swollen bulge.

Farther. Farther...

My hands quaver as my mind panics. Where the *hell* am I supposed to cut? What did all the guide books say about this? Why the *fuck* can't I remember any of it? And most importantly, how far are we from home? Is there any possibility of holding off so Neeta can do it?

"Shit!" Emma's scream coincides with a new punch from inside her uterus. The whole thing vibrates from the impact, setting off similar tremors up and down her body. "Oh, sh-sh-shit," she repeats from between her chattering teeth.

"Holy *crap*," Cal exclaims as we reach a crest with a view out to the ocean. In the distance, over the waters of the Pacific, there are bursts of red, gold, blue, and green—and I sincerely wish I could attribute the guy's astonishment to those fireworks displays, officially heralding the arrival of the new year. But he and I have a more astounding light show to be concerned with right now.

The one emanating from the center of my wife's body.

"Christ on fucking dynamite," I spit. So having to stress about *looking* at my woman's uterus isn't enough. Now I've got to figure out how to cut the damn thing open? With it looking like an oversize magic bean, complete with the ethereal blue glow? And as long as we've gotten to *that* subject: *what the living hell is going on with* this *shit? What does this even mean?*

I'm entitled to spew that one aloud too, and I do. Not that it helps with one shred of my roiling gut, one beat of my thundering pulse, or one degree of my scalding bloodstream. I'm a mess, sitting here like one of the assholes I used to corner in back alleys, existing on a mix of raw terror and blind uncertainty—and the catatonia that fucked-up alliance can bring on.

"Damn it!" Emma digs her grip into my wrist, nearly putting a permanent indent between the two bones. "It means you've got to get him *out*, Reece. *Do it*," she orders, her teeth fully bared. "Just—oh, *God*!"

"Oh, *God.*"

Our overlapping iterations are different spears on the air. Mine's a rough, stunned croak; hers is a high, desperate scream. Her pain threatens to wither me again, until I fully recognize this shit is on me. She's not just relying on the lightning in my fingertips. She needs the power that *her* love has infused into my character—and the strength it's given my will.

But not just her.

My son is counting on it too.

I feel that now. I feel *him*, five times more forceful than before. His energy is a palpable power in my senses. It hums stronger by the second, crackling like static through all my nerve endings, as I reach into the opening I've created.

And feel a smile breaching my lips.

As pure happiness fills my spirit.

It's impossible to keep out, this joy and wonder and fulfillment, shining like the amber light that emanates from every inch of my astonishing woman. Yes, from inside of her too—a glow that pulses stronger and stronger, illuminating my fingers as if I'm reaching for a comet inside a nebula. If that's the case, I'm more than ready to let this orb pulverize every cell of my being.

And the next moment, I'm pretty sure it does.

As I suck up my qualms and laser the new incision across her uterus.

As I stop for a second, wondering why there's no reacting scream from Emma.

As I stare at the smile that breaches her lips instead...

Just as one tiny, perfect hand reaches out of the incision...

Then another, stretching the opening back a little farther. And then even wider, as those hands spread out like an angel distributing the riches of heaven...

A comparison that really isn't one.

Because I'm damn sure I've just laid eyes on a piece of God himself.

The most perfect, effulgent, brilliant, magnificent piece.

It's all right there, in the divinity of that little face. In the high strength of his cheeks, the proud jut of his chin, the brave set of his lips. In the lush mop of his white-gold hair and in the amber seriousness of his brows.

But most of all, it's in the grand glory of his gaze. Those silver-gray depths that blink at me, already knowing me. Already seeing right through me...

Already loving me.

But not nearly as much as I love him.

Wholly. Utterly. Terrifyingly. With a capacity I never even knew I was capable of—until I met his mother. Only this is even more. An expansion of that fusion. New doors and windows flying open inside me, exposing the beauty and light of a daybreak I never imagined for myself. A purity I never thought I'd know again. A new start in my soul. A new perfection in my life.

A new light in my heart.

As I pull him all the way free and then lay him across Emma's chest, I see the same comprehension moving across her features. I *feel* the same bright wonder bursting wide in her soul. It explodes into more intense light through her entire body, translating into a healing power to the incisions I've made. We both look on, wrapped in wonder, as our son rolls over a bit, reaching and trailing one of his little hands across the gap in his mama's body. The moment his tiny fingers connect with Emma's abdomen, all of her organs rearrange themselves into proper order. And though I've got the best seat in the place for witnessing this miracle, I've barely blinked in gawking astonishment before the outside incision itself starts fusing back together, already healing with healthy pink skin.

"Holy...*Christ*," I husk out—and then add a silent *Thank you, Christ* upon realizing I won't be the one called upon to sew all that shit back up. One good visit with my wife's innards is more than enough for one day, thank you very much.

"Huh?" Calvin calls from the front seat. "What's that, boss?"

Emma catches my gaze as our boy latches on to one of her breasts and starts sucking. Though her eyes are brighter than supernova stars, they also dictate what I already know. Cal would never believe me if I told him.

"*Right*," I blurt instead. "I said take the next *right*." And I do it with burgeoning, blinding happiness. This is our last turn of the trip. At the top of this climb, we'll finally be at the ridge.

As soon as Cal stops the car in the front drive, Sawyer and Lydia do their typical pop-out-the-front-door routine.

They're both wearing dorky glittery party hats. As soon as Lydia clears the portal, she blows on one of those weird snake charmer party favors, leading me to one of the few occasions I'm glad not to have had a typical upbringing. While I love my mother, I'm damn sure she'd have a kitten if confronted with one of those things.

"Shit," I mutter then. *Mom.* I'll have to find a second to call her and tell her she's just become a grandmother—as soon as I overcome the shock that I'm now officially a father.

"Heeeeeyyy! You two are heeeeere! Happy New Y—" Lydia interrupts her celebration to crunch a puzzled frown. "Uh...where's your wife?" she demands as soon as I hoist myself up and then out, standing on the runner with one elbow braced to the car's roof, the other atop the open door. "Dude? Bolt Jolt? What the hell is going on?"

I actually manage to cock a brow. "I think you mean what the hell has *already* gone on." And then crack a smirk, suddenly and immensely proud of myself. "Or if we're getting technical, what I've already pulled out."

Foley, who's moved forward to hook his arm around 'Dia's neck, skids to a halt. "Oh, *hell.*"

"No, man." I smile wider. "More like complete heaven. At least now."

He doesn't let me down, going at least three shades paler. "That your way of giving me permission to sit this part out?"

"Probably a wise idea."

"That also your way of saying I need to break out the good whisky?"

"Another wise id—"

"Oh my God." Right on cue, Lydia's outcry is like a new firework in the night. It's a verbal representation of the pyrotechnics already bursting inside my entire being—and, as I sweep back down to be with my wife again, the same light show taking over her spirit from the inside out. "Oh my *God*. Baby girl!"

"Hmmm." Emma quirks a teasing grin. "In case you haven't noticed, it's more like baby *boy...*"

But 'Dia's already activated into holy-shit-the-world-is-detonating mode. "Boil hot water!" she yells at Foley. "And get Neeta! And— And—"

"*Dee Dee.*" Emma winces a little but manages to reach and grasp Lydia's fingertips. She falls back against my lap but doesn't let go of her sister. Yes, with our son still yawning and happy on her chest. Yes, with her dress in shreds and her abdomen likely feeling like a punched football. Yes, with the happiest smile I've ever seen across her exquisite, exhausted face. "Come and say hello to your new nephew."

Lydia leans in, her bright-green eyes thick with a tearful sheen. "The most beautiful nephew there ever was." As she reaches and dabs our son's nose, making him burst with a soft giggle, 'Dia's chin trembles. "You're already a flirty hunk, aren't you?"

The tenderness in her voice has me swallowing hard. "He's already a miracle," I rasp out. "Just like his mama."

As if needing to prove my point, our son bats his little hand up toward Emma's smiling lips—and then gurgles, "Mama. Yes! *Mama.*"

Lydia goes paler than Sawyer. "Holy...*shit.*"

"Holy shit!" Our son laughs it out, adding emphasis with a sound smack of his palms. The sound seems to stun him, but he giggles louder and repeats the action. "Holy shit. Holy shit!"

"Oh dear God." Lydia blurts it fast enough to make it one

word. She jerks her wide, astounded stare up at her sister and then me. "Miracle isn't the right word for this creature." She shakes her head. "But I seriously have no idea what *is*."

"Lux."

My wife's reply has both 'Dia and me throwing dazed looks at her. She returns the curiosity in our eyes with the turquoise surety of her own—a confidence that makes its way down to her serene smile. "Lux," she repeats. "It's Latin for 'light'—which is exactly what he is." She lovingly strokes our son's strong forehead. "Which is exactly what we're going to call him."

Lydia inches her lips up with an enchanted smile. "Lux," she echoes before dipping an approving nod. "Yeah."

I lower my head until my forehead is resting against the side of Emma's. Together, we gaze in gratitude and wonder at our amazing anomaly of a son. "Our light," I murmur, at once accepting how right it feels to speak it. "It's perfect."

"Just like him," Lydia concurs.

"Just like *us*," I correct her with a jubilant grin.

Emma joins our baby in a tender chuckle at that. "How right you are, beautiful husband," she assures—and never has it felt more awesome to dazzle her with one of my fast, cocky, you-just-made-my-day winks—before I whip out the comeback that makes perfect sense for this perfect moment.

"I usually am, gorgeous wife."

CHAPTER FOUR

EMMA

"Holy shit!"

Lux ends his delighted shriek with wild applause, the smacks echoing out from the den and through the house like comic-book gunfire—with all that pretend residue turning into bitter grit between my grinding teeth. *Not* a fun sensation when one is in the middle of trying to master farm animal cake pops. And *really* not fun when one's big sister is sitting across the kitchen counter, giggling about the fact that this has been a daily occurrence for the last ten months.

I glower while shoving a new tray of unfrosted pops at her, along with the bowl of yellow "chicken" frosting. "This is still all your fault, missy."

"Heeeyyy." She sticks out her tongue before sliding a new ball through the Big Bird-colored goo. "How was I supposed to know your 'miracle kid' already knew what words *were*, let alone the trick of connecting them to stuff?" As she lets the excess frosting drip back into the bowl, she goes on, "I was just the auntie who thought we'd get to do 'mama,' 'dada,' and 'the duck goes quack' first."

I purse my lips. "So I guess an apology is overdue."

She swipes up her free hand in a dismissive wave. "Let's leave the silliness to the boys in the next room." Then cocks her head and kicks up one side of her mouth. "No apologies—but perhaps a few explanations? Considering you have a kid in there who *looks* like a ten-month-old but is walking, talking, and nearly applying for college—and you're still all Zen World supermom, as if all of this is normal?" She frowns at the dripping ball, which has begun looking like a lemon instead of a baby chick head. "So what gives here, baby girl? You *do* know none of this normal, right? So where's the Easter Egg in this plot? Are you freaking out in private or..."

"No." I attempt a small smile between my measured breath in and my resigned exhalation. Lux's cognitive progress isn't the only factor around here that's running faster than it should. I owed this explanation to 'Dia a long time ago but have been taking advantage of her tactful distance from the subject. "Reece and I were well aware of his...errrmm...*uniqueness*... long before he turned himself into our New Year's present."

"And?" she prompts when my silence extends too long to be a simple pause. "You'll have work harder than that to drop my jaw, sister. You think I didn't figure this out after"—she laughs as a new spattering of claps and a fresh "holy shit" cut in on her from the den—"the first time he did *that*?" she concludes, giving up on the lemon-shaped pop and starting anew with another. "But I've been holding back on pressing you about it," she goes on, her expression softening. "It's one thing when you're a mere mortal with a new baby, dealing with every damn detail of life that changes. Gotta be a whole new level of stress when you've given birth to Sonic the Super Baby and can't tell your own mother about it."

I laugh because it's better than tears. "Yeah. Something like that."

'Dia growls and then palms her forehead. "Annnnd I

evidently am *not* thinking like a sane person today." And then lurches off her barstool and rushes to my side of the island, scooping me into a tight hug. "I'm sorry, baby girl. That had all the sensitivity of a floor full of Lego bricks."

"That mean you're volunteering to help my kid pick his up?" As soon as we share a good giggle at that, I tug her into a new hug. "Listen. It's fine. You can walk on Legos around here but not on eggshells, okay?" I shrug. "Things are what they are with Mom. Maybe one day, and hopefully soon, she'll have her sanity back." I force as much positivity into it as I can, despite the fact that Reece and the team—which now includes Calvin, who's faking his way through a continued relationship with Juliet in hopes of the girl giving up more details about Faline's location or plans—haven't gained a shred of new intel to act on. "Until then, at least Lux has the blessing of *one* grandmother, as well as—"

"Grandpy Todd!"

The volume of my son's shriek makes his previous cries sound like gentle rainfall. Sure enough, Lux is answered by the rhythmic rap with which 'Dia and I are all too familiar. For years, it was the tap that served every purpose from summoning us to dinner to reminding us to start homework. Because of that, we trade commiserating grins while listening to Sawyer challenge Lux to a race for the front door.

"Ahhhh, it really *is* our paternal unit, baby girl," my sister remarks, leaning over to cast a smile down the hall, toward the front foyer. "And oh my, does he look snazzy."

"'Snazzy'?" I tease. "Thank you *so* much for the red-carpet commentary, diva."

"Most welcome, daaahhhling." She giggles.

I plunk down the last of the white lamb pops to join her

in watching my little guy and her big guy slide onto the area rug inside the front door. We chuckle softly together as Sawyer and Lux go down in a raucous heap, flashing glimpses of gold hair, bluejeaned butts, and Aquaman T-shirts. "I just thank God *he* did a while ago."

Lydia folds her arms and rolls out a sardonic expression.

"Oh, hell," she quips past quirking lips. "I'm in love with a cheeky meatcake."

"Then thank God you're not a vegetarian."

She backhands my shoulder, but my answering giggles are chopped short by my son's gleeful squeal. "Mama, Mama. Look! Grandpy Todd—*and* Unca Chase!"

"Well, look what the cat dragged in." I laugh once more as my brother-in-law sweeps me into a full hug. Another affectionate hug for Joany, who's just finished with presenting Lux a little present. The action figure, complete with light-up wings, becomes his new fascination—the same way he captivates Chase and Joany with his little zooming and zapping sounds. Not that they can be blamed. The sight isn't instinctual for anyone—an infant mastering a toy meant for a kid three times his age—though everyone on the team has grown so used to the anomaly. It's just daily life for us.

"We hope you don't mind us dropping in," Chase offers. "It was a last-minute decision, and we figured we'd just surprise you guys."

I beam a smile at my handsome brother-in-law and his petite and pretty wife. "And what an awesome surprise it is." I break in on myself with a little laugh. "Though I'm sorry if my enthusiasm got either of you flour-dusted. We're in the middle of sugar-high barnyard pals for a playgroup field trip to the zoo tomorrow."

"Ooooo." Joany breaks out with goodie-goodie claps. "Sounds like fun! Dibs on the roosters."

Open wince. "Uhhhh...we have chickens..." And then a hopeful smile. Roosters are beyond my fondant-molding skills.

"But no roosters?" Joany pushes her purse and sweater into her husband's grasp. "Now what's a barnyard without roosters?"

As soon as she disappears around the corner into the kitchen, Chase and I trade good-natured chuckles. "Guess you're getting roosters now," he remarks.

"Guess I am." I grin.

"But that doesn't mean they come with houseguests too. If you've got a full headcount, Jo and I can head down and find an Airbnb." As soon as he states it, I peer around and realize all he's holding are his wife's things. There's no luggage behind him in the foyer or out on the front step. I *do* take note of their shiny rental parked between Sawyer's Ducati and the Q8, and I take a second to wish that Reece's new M850i would appear with him behind the wheel, flashing his most roguish smirk as he parks. But that moment is still hours away, and at least I'm not waiting all by myself now.

"Nonsense," I chide Chase. "Your mom was only in town last week for the RRO board meeting, but you probably already knew that. Anyway, her room is freshly made up and free."

"Awesome." He lifts a fresh smile, which puts deeper grooves into the crinkles at his temples but doesn't diminish his boyish good looks. After indulging a chuckle at Lux's antics with the action figure, he says, "Summer's already in full swing back in New York, and the heat was a bear to endure. We're happy to be here, back inside the blissful Bolt bubble."

At once, I break out an affirming smile—for myself as

well as him. *The blissful Bolt bubble.* There aren't many ways to express it better, and I'm aware of my soul's new plea to the universe that this glass ball stays intact for a little while longer. While Reece and I used the announcement of Lux's birth to convince the public we'd merely been "busy" and "preoccupied" instead of hiding from the harpy who's hell-bent on drafting all of humanity into her crazy cult, it was also our way of withdrawing from the limelight for a while. I have to admit, it was an excuse I welcomed—along with the epiphany it brought.

That "more" doesn't always have to be a grand adventure with my hair on fire.

It can exist right here, under my own roof.

Or in the breathtaking dawns just beyond that roof. And in the dazzling sunsets too.

But most especially, in the best light of every day: the carefree glitter that greets me from my son's magnificent gaze.

That same light that takes my breath away now, as Lux clears the corner between the foyer and the den. He's still got "Grandpy Todd" in tow, who's indulging Lux's enthusiasm with a proud, full smile.

"Hey, little light of mine." I lean down, interpreting his sprinting approach as an early request to be picked up, but Lux stops short and shoves me away. Since that's not a surprise, given my kid's fiercely independent spirit, I straighten and then ask, "What's up, bud? You and Grandpy Todd settling in for a movie? You want some snacks?"

Lux shakes his head with more vigor than a dog climbing out of a pond. "Come, Mama," he insists, yanking on my wrist. "Dada's already in the movie! Dada!"

"Huh? *Ow.*" I emphasize the latter with a frown, stopping

in my tracks and making my son do the same. "Lux Mitchell Tycin Richards. What are the rules about your special pow-pow? I'm waiting." I refrain from going full-on nag mom on him, keeping my stance neutral and my hands at my sides. Granted, I'm probably not that easy to take seriously in my Hello Kitty sweatshirt and pink polka-dot leggings, but even if he's on track to get his first PhD before he hits double-digit birthdays, I still make the rules around here.

"No pow-pow inside." He mumbles it while kicking the floor, clearly knowing what I'll do next. I don't disappoint him, turning my wrist over and thrusting it in front of his face.

"And what else?"

A harder kick to the carpet. "Only pow-pow with Dada, Unca Wade, or Unca Saw Saw."

Though Lydia visibly melts at his use of the special nickname for Sawyer, I stay the course with my discipline. "And what else?"

This time, hot color rushes up his face. He blinks back tears that turn his eyes into miniature storms—which makes this shit harder to maintain. When he starts looking this much like Reece, it's rough for me to do anything other than drop to my knees and hug the crap out of his sweet little form. "No hurt any human or animal."

Somehow, I find the fortitude to extend my arm out, wrist turned up. "So what's this red mark on my arm?"

The tears thicken. I'm seriously about to turn the texture of his crumbling little whisper. "Mama...hurt."

I can't resist any longer. I drop to my knees, bringing my face level with his sweet, serious one. Like his father, thick tendrils of his hair tumble against his temples. Also like his father, he makes my heart wrench and ache with the self-castigation in his eyes.

"Sorry, Mama," he husks out. "I love you!"

"And I love you too," I reply as he plops a penitent kiss to my "boo-boo." It's not easy to stay serious as he follows with a swipe of his thumb, which instantly flows healing heat across the area, but I tell myself to stand firm on the conviction. "And thank you for fixing it, honey—but one day, you won't be able to just walk over to someone and do this. You want to know why? Because people aren't used to people like you, Lux—and they'll run if you do something like this to them, even if you're just excited and trying to be friendly." I cup my hands around his shoulders, admitting the combination of his ten-month-old frame and his older, wiser gaze are sometimes jarring, even for me. "That's why we have the rules, okay?" I smile and give another reassuring squeeze. "You don't want to *really* hurt somebody, right?"

My heart already warms, preparing for the endearing grin he always has at the ready. Only it doesn't materialize. Instead, there's a furrow across his forehead with more hills than Angeles Crest, and his gaze is the somber shade of a Crusader's shield. "What if they bad people already, Mama?"

And there's my cue to snatch up a shield too. And a figurative dagger and sword to go along with it. And as long as I'm at it, a can of mace and a Taser pistol. "How do you know about bad people, son?"

So now he smiles. But only a misty version of the expression. "Because Dada."

I do my best to keep my expression neutral. It's easier than I thought, since I'm not sure whether to be enraged or alarmed. "Because Dada...what?" I charge, struggling to keep it light. If I've succeeded, Lux doesn't give it away. His composure settling once more into the realm of temperate and sober, he re-secures a gentle hold of my hand and leads the way back around the corner, into the other room.

We enter the den, where the spacious area rug is nearly invisible beneath the sea of crayons, Lego bricks and play toys—as well as a clearly uncomfortable "Unca Saw Saw" with the TV's remote control in his hand. Sawyer sends out a grimace-grin kind of look at me, while his grip visibly tightens around the remote stick.

"Lux wanted to watch the new episode of the Loki show with his grandfather." He reminds me of a kid attempting to explain why he line-drived a baseball through the window. "I was going to set it up for them. I had no idea the midday news was going to be on."

I trace a small nod on the air, though to be honest I barely hear the guy speaking. Not uncommon when I'm beholding my superhero husband in the midst of kicking some evil bastards' asses: a sight that stops the air in my body just as thoroughly as the first time I saw it, when he took down a whole crew of liquor store robbers while keeping two innocent civilians safe. This time, the illegal fuckery is a gang of horse thieves—I guess they really do still exist—who crammed five horses into a trailer only built for two. While I'm proud as hell of Reece for assisting the LAPD in the standoff with the abusive dickwads, my breath officially goes on strike watching him tear apart their old barn hideout, plank by lightning-bolted plank, while dodging shotgun blasts they're managing to rain down on him and the SWAT team.

Yes, *shotgun blasts*.

On him, clad only in battle leathers and shitkickers, and the SWAT guys, who look like walking tanks in their body armor.

"Holy f…" I extend the sound, walking a verbal balance beam between the dread I need to expel and the example I need to set. "Fartballs," I finally spit, at least staying with the theme by wadding my hands into round fists.

"Finely done," Sawyer mutters though nods back at the monitor. "To *both* of you, it seems."

"Yeah, well, that doesn't *seem* like the cushy dayshift calls he promised me he'd be assisting with." I turn my head when the news feed switches to a chopper shot, exposing the fact that Reece and the five SWAT guys are outnumbered by twice as many of the horse-stealing bastards. I hope every single one of them is slogging through piles of massive green horse shit—but more than that, I work on containing my anger at the main guy they're still shooting at. Yes, I know his battle leathers are reinforced. Yes, I know he has the reflexes of a cheetah and the predatory prowess of a panther. But I also know that he swore to never be in a situation where he'd have to use either. At least not right now, with Faline still out somewhere in the wind.

And our son at an age to be gazing at a TV feed like this, with exactly these kinds of stars in his eyes.

"Go, Dada!"

And exactly these kinds of words bursting from his lips.

"Bad guys, *no*. Dada, *yes*!"

And those.

"Lux…"

"Dada go save horsies. Go, Dada. Go, go, gooooo!"

"*Lux!*"

And this kind of reprimand ripping out of me, entirely too late, as our son's energy turns into his *energy*. Before I can warn him into restraining the fire, the blue-white comets that form in his palms turn into the double fireballs that shoot up to—and then *through*—the ceiling. This would be a great coincidence, if anyone was suddenly in the mood to smell like "Honeysuckle Heaven." Since the master bathroom is directly overhead, my son's found a shortcut into the caddy next to my bathtub. Everyone in the room is suddenly doused in my favorite bath salts, body talc, and skin lotion.

For a long second, I'm too stunned to react. During the next one, all my protective instincts surge, and I visually check my son from head to toe. Like the rest of us, Lux is covered in a sweet-smelling but totally gooey mush. Unlike the rest of us, his bottom lip is vibrating as if he's about to lose every speck of his composure.

A situation *not* helped when my sister totally does.

But while Lux looks ready to fill Malibu Creek with his tears, his Auntie 'Dia gives up the fight against a spurt of nonstop laughter. Crazily, even Dad joins her—and Sawyer looks ready to, until I quell him with a withering glance. With Sawyer down, I pivot back to fully face my irreverent sibling, with her hair full of talc and her face streaked with lotion.

"Oh, come *on*, baby girl," she chides at my glare. "You have to admit, *this* is way more epic than *that*." She nods toward the wide screen, which has come through the craziness with nothing more than a light talc dusting. Through that fragrant fuzz, we look on as the horse wranglers, suddenly realizing they're up against the superhero of LA as well as the SWAT team, actually come out with their hands high and their heads low. A full surrender. "Okay, maybe that *is* better." She pumps a fist. "Way to get that trash, Bolt Man!"

Lux sprints to join his auntie, a trail of talc and salts scattered in his wake. "Dada Bolt," he shrieks in joy. "Get 'em, Dada! Trash all gone. Trash all gone!"

"Oh, dear hell." I drop my head into a hand—as my sister breaks out into louder laughs.

"That's right, Lux-alicious," she praises, scooping him up and then spinning in a circle. "Dada's a regular badass. Yaaaayyy!"

"Badass Dada!" My son copies 'Dia by pumping his fist. "Bad guys gone!"

I turn away, giving my conflicted groan to the wall instead of unleashing my furious frustration on my sister. Thank God for Sawyer and the training of his drop-back-and-watch mode—from which he emerges to give me a brief shoulder squeeze before calmly walking over and taking Lux from Lydia.

"Hey, dude," he murmurs, setting Lux back down. He gently tweaks my son's rosy cheek. "Time for us to talk man-to-man, okay?"

Lux's shiny blond waves shimmer in the light from his vigorous nod. "'Kay, Unca Saw Saw."

At once, my sister changes from saucy to mushy, her face almost emulsifying as she watches her man's tender but firm expression. She lifts her head, finding my gaze quickly, before unleashing an "are you seeing this?" stare on me. As I wink out my affirmation, Sawyer starts his little pep talk.

"So, you see your dad up there, taking care of the bad guys?" He waits for Lux's new nod. "You want to know how he does that? Yeah, I know you do. Well, it's 'cause he ate everything your mama told him to eat, like even broccoli and beans." A smirk twists beneath his stubble in proportion to the scowl crunched by my son. "Dude, that stuff makes you mighty, okay? And you want to have big, strong muscles like your dad, right?" He flashes a you're-welcome wink at me before going on. "So, there's other stuff your dad did to get ready for kicking a—errrr, I mean beating the bad guys. Want to know what it was?"

"Yeah, Unca!"

The scene has me joining Lydia in the melt-me-now department, as Lux presses his tiny hands into Sawyer's stubble. I'm positive my sister and I are sharing more than outward swoons, as well. Her thoughts have to be chugging on the same track as mine. Our secret-agent-man-gone-chill-surfer-dude *needs* to have a new hyphenation on his descriptor. *Epic-awesome-baby-daddy*.

"Okay, so your dad has all those slick moves because he did something called *practice*. Do you know what that means, bud?" He endures the soft smacks of gold hair as Lux shakes his head in the negative. "Well, it means that he tried out all those things, over and over again, until he got it right." He leans his face in, ensuring he has Lux's full and locked attention. "If you want to practice too, then I'll help you. *But*"—his exhortation bites into Lux's squee of joy—"in order to be super good at practice, you really have to eat every bite Mom puts on your plate. And yeah, that means everything green, leafy, or smelly. Can you promise me you'll do that?"

I barely contain my jaw from dropping as my son nods in agreement—and with gusto. As soon as he's finished, he turns and runs for the kitchen, yelling at Anya that he'd like some grapes for a snack.

Before Sawyer's done rising back up, I state, "Unbelievably, I think I just fell in love with you a little more, dude."

"Heeeyyy." Lydia crowds into his side, smacking a possessive hand across his torso. "That's my job, missy."

"One that you accomplish very well, *missy*." Sawyer's rewarded for his declaration with a nibbling kiss along his jaw.

"Hmmm. *Very* well."

As the pair move together, finding each other with their mouths and then delving into an affectionate tongue tangle, I let a long groan tumble out. "All right, all *right*; we get it. And by 'we,' I mean the crowd including your *father*, Princess Purple Pants."

Lydia tilts her head and tightens her gaze to slits. "Well, just for *that*..." And then treats Dad and me with front-row seating as she yanks a fistful of Sawyer's hair and drags him into a kiss straight from a banned Tumblr feed.

"Aaggghhh!" I cry. "Seriously? I want to walk out of here, not wade through a puddle of your saliva!"

They break apart, taunting me with their mutual laughter, until Sawyer breaks his short by biting his lower lip. It's a sly rogue's move, one I'd expect more from Reece than him, making me do a double-take—even before he states, "Hate to break this to you, Em...but the lagoon might be getting worse."

"Why?" Lydia steps back, hands on her hips. "You got another kid to pull out of the woodwork, Chainsaw? Oh, wait. Hold the hell up." Her hands drop. "The Ducati...it was still rattling when you got home today..." And her gaze flares wide. "Holy *shit*. You didn't really go out and get that fixed this morning, did you?"

His eyes twinkle until they're the color of a damn Tinkerbell cartoon. "No, Fireball. I didn't go get the motorcycle fixed."

A distinct intuition niggles up my spine. I glance to Dad for confirmation of it—and he's ready with a knowing smile. Though a lightbulb of comprehension explodes to life in my mind, I keep a careful façade plastered across my face. Lydia still has no clue what's going on here, despite her delighted gasp and dazzling grin.

"Ohmigawd," she rushes out. "You went back and got the painting, didn't you?" She whips around toward Dad and me. "We hit the Roadium market on a whim the other day. It was a lot of the usual flea market stuff, but there was this one new guy there, and his paintings were out of this world. I fell in love with this one—*ohhhh*!"

Now I really do give in to the double-take, as Sawyer sweeps a framed painting out from behind the couch. While Lydia is right—the piece, depicting a windswept cliff overlooking a sunset-stained ocean, is beyond stunning—it's not the payoff I was expecting for the man's inscrutability.

"Errrmmm...wow," I stammer. "It's...uhhh...really pret..."

I trail off, realizing my sister isn't listening anyhow. "Thank you," she whispers fervently to her guy and kisses him with matching meaning. "Thank you, thank you, thank you!"

Sawyer smiles—still giving off that shit-eating mien that I can't figure out. "It's the one you liked the most, right? Is everything all right with it? You like the view and shit?"

"Of *course* I like the view and shit." She crunches two seconds' worth of a bemused frown. "And you *know* this one's my favorite. I only swooned over it for—" As her voice snags, her head slides back. "What the..." And then forward again.

I step over to where she's propped the painting on the couch, leaning it along the back cushions. "What is it, honey? It *is* a gorgeous piece. And hey, look; the artist even painted a bride and groom up on the cliff."

Lydia chuffs. "Oh yeah, he did."

"What's wrong with that?"

"Besides the fact that they *weren't* there when I looked at this on Sunday?"

I peer closer—and as I do, my heart beats faster. "And that they look like *you two*?" I say past a grin.

Lydia's answering stare conveys that I'm stating the obvious—though she doesn't get a chance to speak it.

"Well, would you look at that?" her guy drawls. "I suppose they do."

'Dia's breath snags hard. "Sawyer?"

She whips her head around, intent on impaling him with her stare—but encounters empty air instead.

Because Sawyer's already dropped to one knee.

"*Sawyer?*"

I rush to Dad's side, joining him in tearful silence as Sawyer Foley grabs my sister's quivering left hand. He's steady as steel, his spine straight and his gaze intent, while bringing her fingers up for a lingering connection with his lips. "I had him paint us there because that's what I want, Spitfire." At last his composure crumbles a little, but he hauls in a long breath and finds his fortitude once more. Damn good thing because nobody else in the room can keep our tears from flowing now. "No." The guy shakes his head. "Not what I want. What I *need*. What I told myself I'd never need or never have to need—but now can't imagine living without." He looks like a beggar being shown the realms of heaven as he gazes up at my sister, the tender smile on his lips widening. "Because I can't imagine living without *you*."

I choke out a sob. Fortunately, Lydia's is louder and fuller. "Sawyer Howard Foley, what the hell are you getting at?"

I'm grateful for the excuse to snicker through my tears. Holding it in after learning Sawyer's middle name was an ordeal and a half.

"Well, I'm sure as hell not down here to moisturize

my knees." He casts a rueful look around at the puddles of congealing lotion. Lydia does the same before casting down a watery smirk.

"Technically, you could..." she hedges.

"And technically, you could still say no to me," Sawyer volleys, yanking back her attention by taking the inside of her wrist beneath his pleading kiss. When he's done, he doesn't let her go. "But please don't, sweetheart." With her hand crushed against his forehead, he drops his sights down. "Damn it, even your *father* has said yes."

Lydia's jaw drops. "You asked my *dad* too?"

Dad harrumphs. "Bet your sweet ass he did."

More disbelieving tears from my sister. "That is...so. Freaking. Cool," she finally blurts.

Sawyer's lips twist. "So what the hell does *that* mean?"

"What do you mean, what does it mean?" she counters.

"Oh, Spitfire." He lets his head plummet. "Baby, can't you just say yes?" Then swallows hard and mumbles, "Or...no."

Fortunately, Lydia's ready with a chiding chuckle. "Impossible to answer a question I haven't been asked, buddy."

I shoulder-bump Dad, mirroring his good-natured glance. Poor Sawyer, falling in love with a Crist sister. 'Dia's not going to spare him an inch of leeway—though if I know Mr. Foley well enough, he'll give back as good as he gets.

Sure enough, in the very next second, the guy locks his free arm around the backs of my sister's knees and then yanks hard, destroying her balance. Lydia lets out a little shriek while toppling down—into the cradle of Sawyer's sizable arms.

Before she can scream again, he douses her in a long, wet kiss.

Then the heat of his adoring stare.

Then the sigh-worthiness of his rough, reverent words.

"Lydia Harlow Crist, I've been in love with you since the moment I first met you," he confesses. "It was a night you were meant to be celebrating, but instead you were kidnapped and trapped in a cargo net for hours..."

Despite the tears flowing from her eyes, Lydia rolls them. "And I looked hideous."

"You were the most beautiful thing I'd ever seen." Sawyer strokes a firm thumb across her cheek. "So full of courage and fire, even after what Faline had put you through...I'd never seen anyone with that kind of strength before. That kind of light." He pulls in another breath, the air shaking with his emotion. "I was already addicted to you, and I'd barely had a chance to speak to you. And as soon as *that* happened, I just got downright terrified."

"Terrified?" Lydia jerks up, her spine straightening and her brow crunching. "Huh? Of *me*?"

"Only of what I felt for you," Sawyer clarifies. "Of what I was certain you could never possibly feel in return."

I swipe heavy drops off my cheeks as my sister pulls the guy in for another mushy lip lock. Though Dad squirms a little, I'm nothing but a blubbery wet mess full of female understanding. Yeah, these Team Bolt guys are impossible to resist.

At last, she pulls up far enough to whisper, "It was never possible for me to stay away from you, mister. I've been just as consumed with the very idea of you. The perfect magic of you. Hell, a man who finally knew what to do with *me*."

Sawyer bursts with a gruff laugh. "All I've done is love you, sweetheart." At once, his features intensify. He focuses on my sister like he's holy fire readying to carve into some stone tablets. "All I ever long to do is love you."

'Dia presses a soft kiss to his lips. "As I love you, big guy."

He tightens his hold, compelling her face a few inches closer to his. "So that shit's already sticking," he murmurs. "Now let's just make sure the rest of the world knows it." He consumes the side of her face with his broad palm and long fingers. "Marry me, Spitfire. Let's do this for real now."

In typical Lydia fashion, my sister strings out her teasing silence. Nothing mars the air except my utterly messy sob. I'm not sorry, either. I'm too damn happy, already knowing what she's going to say.

"That wasn't really a question, Sawyer Howard."

All right, so it wasn't exactly that.

"You going to marry me or what, Lydia Harlow?"

I ding a finger into the air. "*That's* officially a question."

While jabbing a middle finger up at me, she lowers a tender kiss in at her grinning, gorgeous guy.

Before finally saying, "Yes." And then rasping, "*Yes*, I will marry you, magnificent god."

As Dad and I erupt into wild, rapid applause, Sawyer tunnels his hand back into 'Dia's hair, forcing her to accept the deep, burning delve of his groaning, rolling kiss. When they're still at it more than a couple of minutes later, I finally intercept with a tormented groan. "All right, you two need to get a damn room."

Dad grimaces. "How about a ring first?"

"You mean like this one?" Sawyer's the picture of cocky confidence while reaching behind the lamp on a side table, where he's hidden a distinctive blue suede ring box. At the same time, he offsets the weight between he and Lydia so my sister is standing again. With the box poised between both his hands and his gallant Prince Charming kneel, our secret agent surfer man isn't just taking 'Dia's breath away now. I get a second to flash him with a firm thumbs-up before he sweeps his attention completely back on my bawling sibling. "Come on, Spitfire," he growls quietly, nodding at her left hand. "Let me see it."

As Lydia holds out her quivering hand and Sawyer slides the dazzling rock on her finger, Dad snorts with hearty approval. "That's the way to treat my princess, Mr. Foley."

Sawyer flicks up half a grin. "No. This is the way to treat my *queen*."

I lift a new finger into the air. "Ding, ding, ding! And *that*, friends, was the superstud answer."

With her eyes still leaking a little, Lydia still summons enough composure to insert a saucy smile—along with the perfect way to seal the deal with the man of her dreams. "Up, up, and away, kids."

CHAPTER FIVE

REECE

I've never been picky about the extra decorating touches Emma's brought to the Brocade's penthouse over the last year. Necessity has dictated that we spend more time up here than even the condo we've kept over on the west side, and I've ordered her to revise things to feel more at home here. From new pictures on the walls to extra knickknacks on the shelves to new paint and fixtures in the bathrooms, I've enjoyed and approved of it all, freshly impressed each time by my wife's creative eye and sense of fun.

But this time, she's gone *Fun*.

Yes, with a capital *F*.

And yes—though I'll never admit it to the woman's face because I value my testicles—I'm damn glad *this* revamp is temporary.

The occasion is a worthy excuse. For Sawyer and Lydia's engagement party, the woman of my heart has pulled out all the stops on her imagination—including the gift-table centerpiece that's getting the brunt of my perturbed stare this second. The decoration features a huge red latex balloon holding up a miniature hot-air balloon basket—with a pair of dolls custom created to resemble the soon-to-be happy couple.

Emma had called the look "adorable."

Not exactly the word that came to *my* mind.

As I glower down through the red balloon and force out thoughts of Annabelle and Chucky, I nearly pulse myself through the ceiling when a pair of playful faces appear on the other side of the huge orb. "Holy ssshhh..."

"Dada!" Lux cuts me off in the nick of time. "Loooook! You're like Red Hulk, only not mean!"

A pair of full snickers from Lydia. "Give him props for the slightly better hair, kid."

I lean out from the balloon, reapplying my glare. "*Slightly* better?"

"Compared to what's between my thighs every night?" she mutters, taking advantage of Lux's fascination with the gifts to throw a lusty glance toward her fiancé. Like me, Foley's attempting to be a good sport about Emma and Lydia's party theme choice. He's dressed in a camel-colored suit with a brown silk tie and matching fedora, though the silky locks that have earned my sister-in-law's worship are pulled back into a proper queue.

But I don't care if the dude is Douglas Fairbanks reincarnated. "Not a visual I needed, sister."

"Meh," Lydia counters. "Just imagine the dolls doing it instead."

"Ohhhh, that does it. I'm adding that one to your column on the list."

"The *eff*?" While I'm grateful she's replaced her favorite swear word with its kid-safe substitute, no way is she getting completely off the hook in my book—a fact I make clear with my serene smirk and unflinching arrogance. "What the hell kind of list? And why the daylights do *I* already have a 'column'?"

I cock a brow. "Because I'm pretty sure Alex didn't decide Steve Sarsgard was going to be a UFO geek all on his own."

In situations like this, it's fun to notice the differences between the Crist girls. Where my Emma would blush, avert her gaze, and then make a stab for my good graces with angel eyes and a sweet apology, Lydia is completely comfortable in her devil woman's skin. "Well, if that's the charge, then drag me away in cuffs, Your Honor." She adjusts her long pearls and then winks. "Can you just make sure that Officer Foley gets to book me? And punish me?"

"And don't you have the imaginations of *other* party guests to be ripping apart now?" I scan the living room of the Brocade's penthouse, where Emma decided it'd be best to stage the party in light of the extensive guest list. Many of 'Dia's friends from the tennis world are here, as well as some new friends she's made since deciding to dive back into college, studying Kinesiology at USC. There are also a number of staff members from the Southern California offices of Richards Reaches Out, who know and love both Lydia and Foley.

As if the universe cued the coincidence, my remark precedes the arrival of yet another guest to the throng. But as soon as he walks in, catches sight of 'Dia and waves hello, she flings a stern side-eye back at me. "Don't *think* of repeating that with my father on incoming, dude."

"Repeat what?" I drawl. "The part about Sawyer putting you in handcuffs or the part about his dreamy locks nestled between your—"

"*Daddy.*"

She rushes forward to be crushed in Todd Crist's affectionate embrace. "My sweet Dee," he murmurs lightly against her pin-curled hair. "Well, don't you look like the bee's knees?"

Lydia bops his shoulder, laughing at his teasing reference to the party's theme. "And you're the cat's meow, Daddy-o!"

I saunter forward. "You know, technically 'Daddy-o' wasn't a thing until the fifties."

She narrows her eyes. "It's seriously creepy that you know that."

"Amazing what a guy will remember from bartop trivia."

Thankfully, Todd gives my comment a commiserating chuckle. "Mr. Richards." And then extends his hand for a solid handshake. "Great to see you again—and for obviously contributing to *both* my daughters' happiness."

"It's my pleasure," I reply, dipping a respectful nod. "Just glad the party's a success."

He follows the line of my gaze across the room, taking in all of Emma's unique changes for the party. The vintage prints and Tiffany-style lights that have replaced our modern wall art and fixtures. The larger picnic props, such as a twenties-style bicycle and the front end of a Ford jalopy. And of course, the miniature hot-air balloons with the dolls creepier than my trivia compendium. "And what a party," he finally states, his tone thick with wonder.

Lydia raises her hands, palms out. "This is all Emma," she qualifies. "I've been nuts with school and the ProKennex racket deal."

Todd slowly shakes his head. "I never knew she had this in her."

"Right?" Lydia says. "And you should see the stuff she has out on the terrace."

As if a higher source is listening in on us, my son's delighted shriek accents the end of her assertion. That's the fun part. The not-so-fun part? Lux is ready to tack on the expression that continues to be his favorite. "Holy shit!" And then again, as he barrels toward his grandfather with eyes and fingers ablaze.

"Crap!" Lydia exclaims.

"God*damn*," Todd utters at the same time.

I don't add to the dialogue. I'm too busy lunging out, using a minor pulse to do so, in order to snatch my kid up from the waist, spinning him around until my body is firmly shielding his from the rest of the partygoers. Once I plunk him back down on the hall credenza between the office and master bedroom, he's shaking all over—especially in his cherubic little face. But behind that angel's visage is the wild, devious brain of a kid twice as old. In short, I'm dealing with a kid who's dedicated himself wholeheartedly to the "threenager" phase.

And yeah, that means steeling myself against all the stops he's yanking out right now. The wide, watery eyes. The gulping sob. The mournful pouty lip joined by the trembling chin.

Fuck me in a Ford jalopy.

If I survive long enough to get across the room to the damn thing.

"Dada." He adds to the act with a heartbreaking sniffle. "I sorry. I *sorry*."

I shut my eyes—much more a measure for my sustenance than his. The Almighty had to go and recreate my wife's gorgeous eyes in *his* precious face, turning every disciplinary act of mine into a feat of self-control. "Okay," I finally say. "You're sorry...for what?" When Lux only rubs his teary eyes with one hand and points haphazardly toward Todd with the other, I press, "Lux Mitchell Tycin. *Use words*. Tell me *what* you are sorry for."

"Not thinkin' smart about my powers."

"And what else?"

"Almost hurtin' Grandpy Todd with 'em."

"And...?"

He thrusts the lip out farther. Holy crap. Only eighteen months old—or whatever—and already working the feels like a Shakespearean-trained actor.

"Lux?" I prod.

"And— And almost showin' all the strangers my powers too."

His sweet voice trembles and threatens to break. Though he's successful in keeping that shit together, he loses the battle with his tears—the same way I lose mine with the heat of my tender love for him. "Come here, buddy," I croak, yanking him tight. He wraps his little arms around my neck, soaking my shoulder inside two seconds with his sorrow. "I'm not mad at you, Lux. But dude, you *know* why Mama and I are so strict about you hiding your powers."

His soft hair brushes my ear as he nods in earnest. "Yeah. I know, Dada."

"You do?" I swivel back, resting on my haunches, so he can see my proud smile along with my encouraging tone. "So prove it."

He cracks a huge smile in return but yanks in a long breath, per the training he's been getting with Foley and me, to act as an erasure of the outward signs of his abilities. I want to whoop until the ceiling blows off—before whomping him with another proud hug. What he's doing is the equivalent of a toddler sitting still during...well...*Sesame Street*. "Powers make me special. And special powers shouldn't be wasted."

"Good job." I raise a hand and high-five him. "And what else?"

"If I show my powers to the wrong people, they might tell

the bad people about it. Then the bad people will come and take me away from you and Mama."

I invite him to another high-five. As soon as we're done with the first smack, we go in for another, though end up with our fingers meshed this time—sending subtle bright-blue pulses at each other. The jolts, like static charge on repeat, cause Lux to laugh as if I'm fully tickling his belly. But as soon as he pulls away, finally overloaded on the intensity of his laughter, he mellows into deep contemplation.

No. He's not contemplative.

He's pensive.

"Lux?" I query. "Hey. What is it now, buddy?"

He shifts a little closer. Frames my jaw with the flatness of his palms as he peers hard into my eyes, as if searching for an actual item he's left inside my head.

"Dada," he finally murmurs, his big blues piercing to the back of my skull. "How come there are bad people?"

Ladies and gentlemen, this concludes our flight through the light-and-fluffy portion of this evening's adventure. For those of you remaining with us for the what-the-fuck-am-I-doing-now bonus package, please remain seated, with both your heart and soul girded in lead.

"I'm not sure I know the whole answer to that, son." I tug him tight and kiss the top of his golden head as he squirms to settle in my lap. And of course, because fate really wants to jack with me tonight, it's the same moment I catch sight of Emma across the room, laughing at something one of her RRO staffers has said.

It astounds me that not a single member of the team ever connected "Steve and Sophie Sarsgard" back to the two of us. It's even crazier that nearly two years to this day, Emmalina

Crist brought those monthly reports to me up here, winding up in us doing a lot more than talking RevPAR and occupancy percentages—and I crave her just as fiercely as I did that night. Probably more. At the moment, it's tough to really call, since our son is wiggling across my crotch as if we're at Disneyland and the *Lion King* float is about to appear in the parade—a metaphor that at least helps with inspiration for my next words.

"You remember how sad Simba was after his dad died? So sad that he went away for a long time and was really angry at the world. Imagine what would have happened if Nala had given up on him."

Another crotch stampede from my kid, who squirms with restless energy. "He would prob'ly still be angry!" he cries, twisting wide eyes up at me. "And Scar would be king!"

"Exactly." I duck my head so our gazes are still in line. "But Simba didn't go back and fight Scar when he was just a cub, right? He had to wait for the right time. He had to learn things and make sure he knew how to be responsible with his strength. He listened to the wisdom of his friends, like Timon and Pumbaa."

"Like I do with Unca Sawyer and Unca Wade."

"And in your school lessons with Miss Angelique, Uncle Fershan, and Uncle Alex."

"But none of them are farty, like Pumbaa."

"Well, I'm sure one of them would be, if you ask super ni—" I interrupt myself with a new groan as soon as my son decides that this is now a matter upon which the fate of nations rests and bounds off my lap without a shred of regard for the equipment he's trampled in his wake.

"Unca Sawyer!" he shouts, running through the party in

search of Foley. "I have to talk to you *now*. It's about farts!"

Despite the agony in my balls, I croak out a laugh.

And quickly stagger down the hall, into the master bedroom.

Where the break I *think* I'm giving my system is snatched from the second I close the door, and there's a jump of reaction from near the full-length window across the room. At first, my own senses prickle—until they're hijacked by utter amazement. And then awe. And then gratitude.

Amazement—that I've managed to steal a moment alone with the woman I worship.

Awe—at the sight of the city lights stretching out behind her, illuminating her beauty in new shades of silver, pink, purple, and gold.

Gratitude—that the universe has seriously given her to me. That I receive the validation of that enduring truth with the sight of the diamond adorning her left hand.

Mine.

Bound by the best superpower on this planet.

The love that glows from her kohl-lined eyes, breaches the crimson perfection of her full lips...and answers from every crevice of my dazzled heart.

"Well, well, well. Tell me what ya know, Daddy-o."

As she concludes the tease by tugging the inside of her lip at the edge of her brilliant white grin, I stroll across the room, one hand in a front pocket, cocking my head in my best Sky Masterson impression. "What is with you Crist girls"—I *tsk* past my chastising smirk—"and insisting on borrowing words from the wrong centuries?"

Her gaze flares, but she recovers quick enough to pop her fingertips across her O-shaped lips. "Oh, oopsie," she blurts,

Betty Boop style. "Am I just bein' a ditzy dame here, mistah?"

My gaze grows heavy as I slide close to her, savoring how the sexy spice of her new nighttime perfume blends perfectly with the tropical scents of her hair products. Like 'Dia, she's got artful curls that tumble from the jeweled band around her forehead, with a spray of sparkly feathers attached to one side of the band. The adornment features the same turquoise and black color scheme of her whole costume, with her sparkly sheath designed to resemble peacock feathers. The dress hugs all the best curves of her figure, which has gotten a little more voluptuous since Lux's birth—in all the best fucking ways.

"Were you saying something, doll?" I growl back, nuzzling my lips to her ear. "Sorry. I was busy being distracted by the most beautiful person on this planet."

She hums with obvious skepticism. "The most? More than your son?"

"All right," I concede. "The most beautiful person who's old enough to drive."

Her hum trickles into a giggle. "Wait ten minutes. That might change."

I almost yank back to again channel my inner Masterson. She's struck a subject that really does need our sober attention. If Lux continues to develop at his current rate, it'll only be seven and a half years until we start worrying about his driver's license. Less than five years after that, he'll be wanting to drink. Then *date*. By the time he's chronologically twenty, he'll be talking about long-term care insurance and addressing items on his bucket list.

"Okay, the kid has already detonated my brain once tonight, thank you very much."

She grabs the wide lapels of my vintage suit, warming

my chest with her next laugh. Out in the living room, Lydia's cheer coincides with a defined crank of the sound system. The penthouse is flooded with Dua Lipa's soulful voice. A second later, Lux's scream joins his auntie's joy. At once, we know what's going on. The two of them are like Rogers and Astaire reincarnated when it comes to music and dancing.

As Emma raises her head, her smirk reconfirming that our son's shriek was one of joy and not distress, I take a second to soak up her beauty all over again.

"So," she ventures, centering her stare on me, "detonating your brain, hmmm? Now I *do* need to hear all about it."

"In a second." All right, maybe longer than that. "I need to just...drink you in. Like this. Right here. With the lights in your hair and your face looking all va-va-voom..." Not even her full laugh deters my intent. "Just a little while longer," I persist, skimming her creamy arm with my fingertips.

"Oh, hell." She rocks her head back. "Was the conversation that serious?"

I press tighter in, not visiting the real answer to that. "Maybe you're just that gorgeous, my sheba bunny."

My use of the twenties slang, referencing the classic film theme in which she chose to outfit the terrace and the bathrooms, spreads her lips into an adoring smile. "You are definitely slick tonight, my dashing sheikh."

"Only tonight?"

"Says the guy who swept me off my feet in the very next room, nearly two years ago?"

I'm the one with the exultant grin now. "You remembered."

"How could I ever forget?"

And just like that, the world falls away.

Not completely, but just enough that every sound and

vibration in the air—the thuds of the dance music, the honks and sirens of the city traffic, the gentle rushes of night winds against the window pane next to us—fade away, making the room silent but for a single buzz of sound.

The sizzle of our connection.

The call of our heartbeats, crashing together.

The energy of our bloodstreams, fusing together.

The force of our attraction, screaming out together.

Without hesitation, I obey that urgent insistence. In one second, I wrap an arm around her smooth, firm waist. At the same moment, I clutch her other hand within mine and then curl it against the center of my sternum. Neither of us says a word as our bodies give up to our heated pull, swaying and rolling in time to the newest track that's come on in the next room. Dua sings about a lot of perfect things, like floating and bending and breaking and dying. The main line of the song is another ideal affirmation of everything we have been and everything we are.

Getting lost in the light.

And yeah...everything we will be, as well.

Everything so vivid...vivid...

As our lips touch and then smash, and our tongues stretch and then twirl.

Everything reckless, tangled, suspended...

As she plunges her free hand into my hair, twisting until I snarl from the rush of urgent pain. As I drop my hand and dig my fingers into her ass with the same brutal intent.

Wanting it all, nothing wasted...

And I swear, her tonsils are the most delicious thing I've ever tasted in my life. And now her body, sweet and soft and electric and alive, is the most perfect pressure I've ever felt. My skin crackles and incinerates. My arms are aching but filled and thoroughly on fire. The very threads of my being have been transformed into glowing strands of fiber optics, ignited brighter than the damn lion float I was thinking of earlier. Funny, because a wildcat is feeling a lot like my spirit animal right now. I'm starving. Stalking. Every instinct is on alert, craving the second I can make my move and pounce...

And seduce...

And devour...

And mate...

Except the crafty woman beats me to every single one of those charges.

In the space of two seconds—one for her to plummet her hand across my fly, the other to clench into it as hard as she can—she's turned me into her stunned, gasping prey...her helpless, huffing possession.

"Urrrmmm. *Fuck!*" I grate them nearly as one word, forcing my tongue free from her mouth while ordering my body to stay standing. Barely. As soon as she skates her fingertips up and then over the prominence in my pants that betrays the location of my cockhead, I'm a goddamned goner. All right, as far as my mind, my logic, and half my equilibrium are concerned. "Jesus with a boner, woman!" I end it on a groan while hitching my hips with fierce demand, needing the hot cage of her fingers again.

"Ohhh, Mr. Richards," she rasps, tilting her mouth up and scraping her teeth along the edge of my jaw. "I don't think *that's* authentic twenties slang, either."

I let my face drop into the crook of her neck while sliding my other hand down and around, palming her gorgeous buttocks with savage intent. "Oh, I'm sure Al Capone would know exactly what I'm talking about."

She giggles softly. "You and Al would probably get along real well."

I nibble the shell of her ear. "You calling me a criminal, Mrs. Richards?"

"I'm calling you notorious, Mr. Richards." With moves that match her sleek volley, she unbuckles my belt and then opens my fly. The *chinks* and *zwips* of her actions are as potent parts of her seduction as her husky narrative. "And naughty. And arrogant. And slick."

"Slick?" I manage a rickety laugh while snaring her in my lust-fogged gaze. "Isn't that supposed to be *your* line, sheba?"

It's a corny comeback at best, but I bask in the glory of taking full credit for it—though tell myself to rev the reflexes as soon as she flings back an equally cocky smirk.

"Not anymore."

Oh, *hell.*

Revved reflexes, my ass—which at the moment has been stunned into fully flexed mode, courtesy of the temptress who's truly embraced her inner Greta Garbo to the max. On her knees in front of me—and wielding as much bold, irresistible desire as she did two years ago, damn near in this very spot— she parts her ruby lips, taking in the hard, heated length of my growing arousal.

And just like it's that first time again, I moan hard.

But unlike that first occasion, I don't have to worry about what she'll see or experience or feel.

She already tells me so much of that, in the brilliant blue gems of her huge, gorgeous gaze. She's hungry for me but starving for a bigger taste. Intoxicated but needing a deeper buzz. Filled but ready to take more.

More.

Every vein in my now-lengthened dick looks like a lightning-zapped stream, and her eyes start to water from the strain on her mouth. I want to come hard and far and deep down her throat. And when I do, I want to feel her swallowing every drop of my essence.

But I can't.

I won't.

Because now, I need more too.

I need to give her more than this—and feel all of her reactions as I do.

I need to watch her be transformed by her lust in all the same ways I am. In the radiant light beneath her skin. The Tesla coils of her muscles. The solar flares in her eyes. The energy through her body. And yes, the charged clench of her perfect cunt and the glowing gold honey it'll drip all over my cock.

I need to see it. To watch it. To witness all of that perfect, modern power take over every inch of her body...

As I fuck her like a primeval beast.

There's a rousing cheer from the living room as Dua becomes Rihanna, singing about light in the beautiful sea and diamonds shining bright in the sky. Perfect timing. The noise masks Emma's distressed cry as I pull on her hair to separate her mouth from my body. And the moan she follows it up with? I drown that out as well, stealing the carnal sound away from her swollen lips as soon as I drop to my knees and then replace my dick with my tongue. I scoop powerfully into her mouth, stroking into every wet cushion of the orifice I've just invaded. Everywhere I sweep, I taste...me. My flesh, my sweat, my possession.

You're mine.

The recognition, rocketing me into the stars that Rihanna sings about, turns my senses into a nebula of need...and my cock into a rod of raw lust. I fist the length, turned on more as my hand is streaked in glowing precome. I'm like a power station on meltdown alert. A circuit breaker with too many plugs jammed on full. A bomb about to blow.

A monster ready to rut.

"Turn around." I don't wait for her mind to register the order. I just help with the compliance, twisting my grip into her shoulders and then spinning her away from me. "I've got to fuck you so badly, beautiful." While the endearment rasps from my lips and brutality dictates my movements. As she gets into position on the floor in front of the window, I snarl in pleasure at the sight before me as soon as I hike up her dress.

With eager lust, I stroke her bare thighs and ass cheeks, framed for my pleasure by thigh-high stockings that are attached to a sexy-as-fuck garter belt with matching black lace panties. The lingerie is offset by the pink glow of the city lights across her skin, joined by the faint gold of her aroused blood. Except for the first sight I ever had of our newborn son, this has to be the most breathtaking thing I've ever seen in my life.

"Jesus *God*, Emmalina." I knead my way up the backs of her legs, stretching my thumbs into the peachy crevice of her ass before splaying my grip across the flawless flesh of her gorgeous rear. "You make me want to become a real animal." In every wild, snarling, savage sense of the word.

She absorbs my declaration with a lush toss of her head, leaning back to the point that her body forms a gorgeous arch. As she does, all my bestial instincts are heightened by the gleam of her vintage earrings against the smooth column of her neck. Then even more by the words that make their way out of it.

"So who's stopping you?"

Ohhhh, those audacious words.

Ohhhh, that brazen ass wiggle of punctuation.

Ohhhh, the little glance over her shoulder, openly taunting me.

Ohhhh, *her*.

Always her. Only, ever her.

The only one who'll ever be the white to my black. The dawn to my midnight. The beauty to my beast.

Who'll never stop making me this hard with her sigh as I tear away her panties.

Who'll never not complete my whole being as I drive into her with one merciless stroke.

Who'll never cease speaking to all of my soul as her body gloves me with her wet, wonderful light.

"Oh!"

Who'll never hold back the ferocious grin across my face as she screams in the first throes of her golden fulfillment.

"Oh, *Reece!*"

I growl deep while seizing her hips with my hands, securing her frame for my next barbaric thrust. I pause there, my dick embedded and my balls clamoring, just long enough to give her a few gifts from my mouth, as well. A ruthless bite at the back of her neck. And then commanding words, rumbled from the pounding depths of my chest.

"Brace yourself good, Bunny. This ride isn't going to get any gentler."

As I expect, she lets out a long, keening cry.

What I *don't* expect: her hard, crashing orgasm.

And no, I harbor absolutely no doubt about what it is. The rapid vibrations up and down her channel, along with her staccato breaths and the juices drenching my cock, have dropped me onto a precipice of conflict. Half of me crows at giving her such swift and perfect pleasure. But the other half examines the daunting challenge ahead.

To give her a hell of a lot more.

"You enjoying that, my sweet goddess?" My teasing drawl is a direct contrast to the repetitive punches of my body, filling the air with harsh slicks as I impale her tight tunnel over and over again. "You like coming that good as I tell you how much my swollen cock is going to conquer your gorgeous cunt? That I may really turn into a beast and lose myself in the glory of taking over your body? That it might even hurt, but you'll love every fucking second of the beautiful torment?"

"Yes." She drops her head but rolls it back up at once, as if her skin feels as tight as mine. As if the pressure of her pleasure is a force under her skin, demanding her full detonation from it...

And so she does.

"Yesssss!"

Screaming hard as her second climax pounds in, overwhelming her. Glowing so brightly that I can see every exquisite inch of her completion reflected by the window's dark glass. Her lips, parted with lust. Her cheeks, suffused with sensuality. But best of all, her eyes—which remain open. She wants to watch too. She wants to see every undulation of my hips and every dominant stab of my cock. She wants to witness how she endures it all, answering my light and lust and passion with equal amounts of her own.

She wants to acknowledge her power.

An understanding that already starts building toward her next orgasm. A perception I share as our gazes connect in the murky world of the glass.

"Good," I say to it—and her. "So good." As I grab her tighter and fuck her deeper. "Let it come," I command from between my locked teeth. "Let it *come*, beauty. Let me give it to you. All of it." I flow more energy into my fingers, letting her see my possessive grip across her skin. I change up the rhythm of my rutting, ensuring she gets an eyeful of my cobalt length before I shuttle it back into her tight, soaked walls. "All of *me*."

"All of me too," she whispers back, tears wobbling through her words. "I love you, Reece Andrew."

"And I worship you, Emmalina Paisley."

"I know." She punctuates it with a shudder, bucking her head because I'm gripping too hard for her to gain control of her hips. "Oh *fuck*, how I know. *Oh*. Ohhhh, God. Ohhhh, Reece! I'm—I'm going to—"

"I know." Not a shred of bullshit in it, either. "*I know*." My commiseration is beyond sweet syllables of seduction or the physical sync of my body. It's beyond the taut pressure in my balls, the telltale trembles in my thighs, the harsh ache in my ass. It's in the flames that take over my blood. The electrical storm that rages through my senses. The connection that zaps into my soul.

The light that races up my cock.

The completion that drenches every corner of my being.

I pour myself into her, letting the quicksilver flow as my vision dances with the diamonds they're all singing about in the next room. Holy God, even the horizon beyond the windows seems to burst to life, as if all the stars have detonated at once. And even as my orgasm wanes, the room itself seems to shake and roll...

Until I realize that it really *is* shaking and rolling.

And that the singing has stopped—because it's been replaced by startled shouts.

"Holy crap!" Emma blurts as soon as I lean over, grab her around the waist, and roll us both away from the huge window. At the same time, in the other room, Lux lets out nonstop shrieks of glee, repeating his favorite expression. Lydia's yelling the same thing, only with not so much joy. Like Emma, she's a born-and-raised Southern California girl—and knows to take earthquakes with dead seriousness.

Despite that knowledge, I leap to my feet, ready to sprint down the hall to ensure my son's safety. I'm yanked back down at once, slammed onto the bed by a forceful gold fireball. "Goddamnit, Emmalina," I bellow. "Lux is—"

"Not going to be a happy kid if his father is tossed out a seventy-story-high window because he lost his balance in a high roller," she volleys. "Especially if said father still has certain body parts swinging in the wind!"

I take advantage of my supine position to zip up with a grimace—though I'm unsure if the expression is the pain of stuffing myself back in at half an erection or the jolt of riding out my first major California shaker. I gawk wider while looking out the window to see the downtown skyline looking more eerie than the day Faline commanded Kane to destroy half of it. And the rolling keeps going on, at least for another thirty seconds. *Fuck.* It feels more like thirty hours. I've heard plenty of people say that before, but the truth is never more vivid than experiencing the phenomenon for oneself.

Finally, Mother Nature's wild ride comes to a full stop. I reach for Emma, who's been maintaining a strange, quixotic expression through the whole thing, and clutch her close to me. I'm beyond grateful when she sprawls a hand across the center of my chest. "Jesus on a Quinjet," I croak. "My heartrate's at warp speed."

"So's mine." But her drawl conveys the unnerving opposite. "But not because of the earthquake."

As I debate whether to shoot her a glare or a grin, I abandon both when realizing 'Dia's string of "holy shits" hasn't stopped in the living room. Weirder still, Foley has joined her. All right, so he's muttering something more along the lines of "fuck me five ways," but I'm more concerned about the total shock in his tone.

"What...on..." Emma, clearly discerning the same thing, uses my chest as leverage to push up and then off the bed. She rushes across the room and jerks open the door—as I straighten on the bed like a vampire being hauled out of his coffin at noon. The sight before me is just as surreal—and stupefying.

It's my son. Flying through the portal that Emma's just opened.

Not figuratively.

He's...flying.

At least six feet off the floor—though that figure changes if he decides to do a backflip or a belly roll. He seems to be fond of both already, judging by the gleeful laughs with which he keeps praising himself for the moves.

"Okay." Emma follows Lux's aeronautics by turning and shuffling back into the bedroom. "What's it called when the heartrate goes past warp speed?"

"Galactic demolition," I blurt out.

"Reece-man for the win," Lydia mutters. "I was just going to say 'cuckoo-ville.'"

"Cuckoo!" From over our heads, Lux repeats it like a joyful war cry. "I have cuckoo, Dada! Like a birdie!"

Foley moves to stand next to me. "Well, this is going to make training more interesting."

"It's going to make *everything* more interesting." As my wife utters it, she pins me with her stare. It's not necessary. I already peg a lot of what she means because it's everything racing for precedence in my mind too.

Racing *fast*.

Officially, our son's abilities have surpassed ours—not such a tough issue while he's obedient and adoring of us. But what will happen once he hits a rebellious stage? And since that's going to happen sooner rather than later...

"Shit," I mumble beneath my breath. *Shit, shit, shit.*

Yet right now, "sooner rather than later" has to be given another connotation. A *much* more pressing one—leading me to pivot back toward 'Dia and demand, "When exactly did this happen?"

"Just now," she supplies. "In the middle of the quake."

"Shit." I'm spitting it now—and longing to add some choice profanities, though there's no time for that luxury. "That means close to twenty people were up-close eyewitnesses to this kid going airborne down the hallway."

I expect Foley to join me in the growl I twist on the end of that. Instead, he's grunting in satisfaction while peering down at his phone. If the bastard actually expects me to approve of him taking or keeping any video footage of this shit...

But the guy beats me to the preparedness punch. By a really long shot.

"Text from Neeta," he explains. "Before the Lightning Kid decided to zip his way down the hall, I told her to yank up an e-version of a nondisclosure pact. Wade's helping her monitor the door, and they're having everyone sign off before they leave."

"Tell her thank you." Emma's expression already conveys how little the words really communicate on our behalf. But she doesn't cling at her thinning composure for too long. I watch, admiring and adoring her even more, as she slathers on another layer of fortitude from the inside out. It instantly shores her posture and steels her face, giving her enough strength to shout, "Lux Mitchell Tycin, put your feet on the floor this instant."

"But Mama!" Our kid's voice is part cackle and part whine. "Look what I can do. *Looooook!*"

The triple barrel roll with a donut-twisty finish yanks a couple of impressed rumbles from Foley and me before they're tromped by a glare from Emma so frosty, she really does resemble the iconic ice princess from the Disney cartoons.

"Well, shit," Foley grumbles.

"Stole that one out of my mouth," I return.

"She does that look as good as her sister."

"And you're surprised?"

"No." Foley shifts from foot to foot. "I'm scared."

As soon as the words are out of his mouth, a foot gets shoved into it—royally clocking his maw in a kids' size three and a half.

"Not sure *you're* the one who should be scared," I offer past a chuckle while reaching up and snatching the ankle attached to the canvas emblazoned with grinning Minions. "Okay, my dude," I charge to my petulant son. "Before you take out something more valuable than Uncle Sawyer's face, you're grounded."

Sawyer narrows his eyes. "What the hell is more valuable than my face?"

But his jest is wasted. Emma's tension remains ice-princess cold as soon as Lux squirms with open petulance. "But Dada! Whhhyyy?"

"It's not forever, son." I lower him to the floor but align myself to his level by taking a knee. "But you remember the *other* rule we have about superpowers, yeah?"

With the ease of experience, the kid juts out his lower lip. "Limits mean love."

I nod and then grit out a smile. His iteration, full of such concentration and sincerity, is like a fist to my heart—made of pure star fire. I swear, if I earned a dollar for every occasion, on every day, when this kid makes me want to burst into tears... inside a year, I'd be handing over enough liquid cash to buy three new Richards Resorts properties. On the beach. In Abu Dhabi.

"Yeah," I manage to rasp back, reassuringly rubbing Lux's back. "Good job, buddy. Limits mean love—because love should be our first goal, right?"

He pouts harder. I can see the conflicting wheels turning for him. Agree with me and accept the no-fly zone for now or push the limits and zoom back down the hall again.

In the end, he jabs a fist against one of his tired eyes and then reaches out his other hand to palm my face. "I love *you*, Dada."

I smack an affectionate kiss to the center of his precious little hand. "As I love you, son."

But I'm only given a couple of precious seconds to cherish the perfection of the moment. Both Lux and I start when everything rattles around us again, rolling through a sizable aftershock to the tremblor that's less than five minutes old. But the pulse spike is like a warm-up shot to the arrows of adrenaline that hit when my back pocket starts beeping. Loudly. Incessantly. The tonal alert is as shrill as a tsunami siren because it's meant to be heeded the same way. It's been assigned to one entity alone—the Brocade's executive offices—to notify me of one message alone.

Drop everything.
Come now.
We have an emergency.
A big *emergency.*

LIGHT

PART 17

CHAPTER ONE

EMMA

Three screaming orgasms.

Two rolling earthquakes.

One airborne son.

And that's just in the last ten minutes.

As I race to follow my husband to the Hotel Brocade's private penthouse elevator, the universe itself answers my mental gawk about the whole situation. *Welcome to being a superheroine, chica. You asked for this, remember?*

I'm damn sure I'll never forget. Becoming solar-powered Flare was never an easy road, from my first feelings of helplessness during Reece's "adventures" to the second I told the Team Bolt techs to hook their equipment to a giant bank of solar panels and then divert that power to my bloodstream. So now I've got everything I wished for. I'm my husband's equal, and we're responding to an urgent emergency hail as a team.

Except...

Except...

Well, *shit.* I may as well admit it.

There's a huge part of me that just wants to go back and be the charming engagement party hostess, superhero spouse, and doting mama to the world's most perfect little boy.

Doting mama.

Words I never thought would actually describe me have become *everything* to me.

Maybe that's why it feels fine to see my amazing son clamoring up my husband's back, wrapping his small but mighty arms around my husband's neck, and squealing in joy as the lift doors open. Despite the danger ahead, I've never felt more joyous hearing my son's laugh as he swoops to hang upside down from Reece's neck. I've never felt more at peace as we prepare to help right some kind of gigantic wrong.

At least that's what my instincts are blaring as we disembark from the elevator and then sprint through the executive office's glass doors. As we leave behind the last signs of our shiny, pristine, private world, the insight bellows even louder inside me.

That maybe our not-so-small shaker wasn't a gift from the Elysian Park Fault System, after all.

It's the same feeling I experienced the last time that distinct alarm beeped from Reece's pocket—when Kane Alighieri had become a human hurricane tearing across downtown Los Angeles. Everything bound by Pico Boulevard, the 110, and the river bed was in danger of being flattened— and a lot of it was. Now, two years later, structures have begun taking form from that rubble. Some went up fast and are nearly ready for occupation, their advance sales offices doing brisk business. Others proceed at slower paces, with underground infrastructure systems needing repair before they can go vertical.

"Dear God." I can't help spewing it as we're confronted full-force by the grim grit of the real world. Where I wonder if Godzilla might really be a thing. Or Rasputin. Or Thanos. Or maybe Kane has simply earned himself a posthumous copycat city wrecker.

Or...

Or this grisly scene is courtesy of a *new* city wrecker, controlled once again by Faline.

Faline.

Another concept my brain forces itself to grasp—all over again.

The woman. The witch. The enemy.

And no, the bitch hasn't been *that* far from my mind. She still haunts all of Reece's and my nightmares—and neither of us has succumbed to the mistake of assuming she's slunk away forever—but it *has* been a beautiful break not surrendering every moment of idle mental time worrying, wondering, and pondering where the hell she's gone to elude us.

Unless I see proof otherwise, that stress has no place in the here and now.

When reality is giving us a hotel lobby full of suffering people.

Deeply suffering.

The marble floor is smeared with tracked blood. People in various states of injury and shock fill the furniture. The check-in desk is stacked high with bandages, ointment tubes, clean blankets, boxes of gauze, miles of rolled tape, and electrolyte drinks. Next to the desk is a woman who was probably Florence Nightingale in another life. Her hair is twisted in a prim Victorian bun, but her face is fixed in don't-fuck-with-me firmness. There's a smartpad in her grasp, and she's dutifully notating every new arrival.

What we *do* know is this. Someone approved the Brocade as a rudimentary crisis command center, and first responders—who are here in just as many numbers as the victims—are bringing people with minor and surface injuries.

But injuries from what?

That's what we *don't* know yet—and might not anytime soon.

If it sounded like an earthquake and felt like an earthquake, chances are it *was* an earthquake. Yes, an earthquake is an earthquake, but this looks like *a lot* of collateral damage in an area where most buildings in the area have been quake retrofitted.

And if Mother Nature's not really to blame, then there's only one conclusion to be gleaned right now.

Faline's back in town.

Not just back in it but fucking with it.

Every new development of this situation feels like it. Stinks like it.

Reeks of *her* special brand of wickedness.

Before I can utter either the obvious question or the ones that send a massive ice storm through my nervous system, the main guest tower elevators open. Angelique and 'Dia step out, along with the party attendees who accompanied them down. As Lydia hugs her farewells to everyone in the throng, a few of them direct knowing winks at Lux. Thank God for Neeta and her fast thinking with the NDA forms. With all the blatant human suffering in here, people should be willing to forget a flying toddler. Sugar highs can be deceiving fuckery, after all— but I don't think a single one of them has forgotten the show they just got from my son. *Not one.*

They can't talk—and they won't. So now you need to forget them and move the hell on.

Though it's sheer hell, I accomplish just that. The curious whispers about my kid are pushed to a distant back burner as Fern Pettigrew, the Brocade's new night manager, hurries forward. "Mr. Richards!" The freckles across her nose, which have always made her look friendly and open, seem to emphasize her glaring inexperience with a mass dilemma like this. "Oh, thank God you're here. I—I mean they—well, they all started stumbling in, and we had no idea what to do."

"The right thing." I speak it at once while sweeping my stare across the lobby again. "That's what you did, Fern," I assure. "And what Neeta or I *would* have done if we were still in your shoes."

As Fern exhales in relief, another wave of the injured stumbles past our departing guests. And, thank God, the partygoers finally have concerned stares for what's going on around them instead of amused gawks at my son.

The only new arrivals not looking shell-shocked are the firemen, dressed in full uniforms, boots, and shield-covered helmets. One of them breaks away and sets a course toward Reece and me. As he gets closer, I'm able to discern the meaning of the gold medallion on the front of his helmet. He's the battalion chief.

He stops and drops a respectful nod. "Mr. Richards."

Since there are a thousand ways in which the man already knows who Reece is, neither of us interrupts his flow with so much as a blink, and I hold my breath, waiting for the fireman to continue.

"Chief...Davidson, I presume?" Reece returns the nod after reading the name on the chief's helmet. "It's good to meet you. Thank you for your service to our city."

Davidson's answering smile is more like a facial tick. "Looks like *I'm* the one who should be thanking *you*."

"Doubtful, but my building and its staff are at your service."

Reece sweeps a commanding stare across all the areas of our impromptu crisis center. "What do you need? Some ground floor guest rooms for triage? Access to the roof, fire escapes, or basement?"

Davidson props his hands on his hips, covered in thick yellow pants that have become nearly brown by dirt and soot. "Actually, none of the above."

As the man looks up and studies Reece with half of a grimace, the ice in my veins throbs more painfully. I flick a glance toward Angie, hoping her electronic Spidey senses have told her if Faline's really crept back into the area. My whole torso gets the popsicle treatment when Angelique winces and shrugs, giving the answer that isn't an answer. Her mental *Je ne sais pas* turns my nerve endings into complete stalactites.

"None of the above?" Reece gives Davidson's assertion a dark scowl. "I don't understand."

"Well." The chief purses his lips while tracking a glance around the lobby, cranking his neutral expression into a look of undisguised fury. "What we really need is...you."

Reece rocks back on one foot. Nods with reluctant understanding. "Oh. Now I do see."

I flick a puzzled glance between him and Davidson. "You do?" Only to feel myself stepping back as well, since I'm now the subject of the fire chief's urgent perusal.

"We'll need you too, Mrs. Richards."

"Huh?" Only then does my own comprehension kick in—which doesn't do a thing for easing my intuition about all of this tying back to Faline somehow. I hate that my mind automatically reverts to her in times like this—though with my eighteen-month-old son standing five feet away, I've never been more grateful for my mama-lion instincts. None of this is about simply saving Reece or myself anymore. It's all about the little boy with the skies in his eyes and the universe in his smile. "Let me clarify," I direct toward Davidson. "You mean that you're in need of Bolt and Flare, yes?"

Davidson actually exposes a full grin beneath his Tom Selleck-sized mustache. "Flare?" he barks. "That's the alter-ego moniker, eh?" And then jogs his chin at both of us. "Yeah. Flare. That's a good one. It fits."

While I'm elated about the fire chief's seal of approval—and even make a mental note to have him up to the penthouse to weigh in on logo designs—I assert past a tight smile, "This matter you need our help with... What is it? What's going on?"

Blurting out the words feels like asking a nurse to go ahead and draw blood. This could be either a tiny prick or the gouge of a rolling vein. A run-of-the-mill city emergency—if there are such things—or the grand resurgence of Faline freaking Garand.

"The quake—or whatever it was—occurred because of a fault directly under downtown," Davidson explains. "As you can probably tell."

Reece folds his arms. Motions me over so our conversation with the chief isn't so available to prying ears. "What the hell do you mean, 'whatever it was'?"

Another grunt from Davidson, more pronounced than before. "Exactly what I mean—at this point," he supplies. "Because until I know exactly what's happening down there, I'm not about to go out to the press and tell them all that the US Geological Service has only reported one *minor* quake in the last twelve hours across the Elysian Park grid."

The icicles in my veins just grew into a Superman-sized ice castle.

I'm stunned to watch Reece's face remain damn near neutral. "And that's why you've come looking for Emma and me."

Davidson's mustache slopes downward along with his scowling lips. "I'd sing you a fun version of 'Bingo,' but there's no time."

"Crap," I mutter.

"Damn," Reece spits at the same time.

"Can you tell us anything about what you *have* learned so far?" I go on. "Did something collapse or explode—or implode? Do they know how many victims and where?"

Davidson's mustache droops farther as he steps back, called by the squawk of his radio. He still has time to let us know one thing, though. "We've got a pretty crazy situation with the Biltmore."

"Oh, shit."

I whirl to see that the soft exclamation has come from my sister. I had no idea 'Dia was still standing there, but I'm glad she is. As this situation gets more twisted, I'm feeling further and further out of my element. Her face is my needed boost of strength at the most perfect moment, though I feel crappy that she overheard this news. Few others are as enraptured with the hotel, located two blocks away, than my sister—though there are few in the world who won't recognize it. The place, built in 1923, has been featured in nearly two hundred movies and television shows—though the ornate interiors for which it was widely popular took a ton of direct damage during Kane's famous rampage two years ago. The owners have committed to restoring the property's grandeur, but the age of the building has made the process a slow one.

Now, it sounds like they've hit another snag—for which

I should have more concerned emotions, damn it—but they'll have to wait until after I bathe in my flood of sheer relief. Judging by the continuation of Davidson's no-bullshit demeanor, what we're dealing with is normal helping-the-human-race stuff, not anything in the holy-crap-Faline's-back department.

I actually feel invigorated about it now—for which I am surely going to hell—but I can't help myself. For the first time, people are in honest-to-crap trouble, and I can honest-to-crap *help* them. And I'm not going to lie about how good that recognition feels. Really, *really* good.

"Fill us in," Reece demands when the chief returns from his radio exchange. Since Davidson stepped away, my husband has donned his battle leathers demeanor, despite still standing here in his crisp '20s-style pinstripes. The all-business tone plus his classy, romantic threads incites we-want-to-lick-him stares from the two policewomen stationed across the lobby—but I have no time to toss around my possessive wifey weight, especially when Davidson's ready to refocus at once.

"They've finally cleared enough debris to start working on the lower-level meeting spaces," the captain supplies, dropping his bushy brows. "When your friend did his fun little 'walkabout' two years ago, the hotel sustained most of its damage on those levels."

"The lower level," I echo. "That's where the bigger room is, right? The Biltmore Bowl, where a bunch of the Academy Awards were held?" In response to the man's scrutiny, I supply, "Had to learn the trivia when I started working here. Was there a lot of damage to it? And what about any personnel?"

"Holy *shit*," Lydia utters. The good *and* bad news here is that the quake hit on a Saturday night. Since the hotel's lower level is still under reconstruction, there shouldn't have been any guests in the affected area—and, hopefully, no members of the restoration teams either.

Before the chief can answer, my son launches into a bunch of boingy happy jumps. "Holy shit! Holy shit!" If the situation wasn't so dire, I'd likely be snort-laughing at my little dude. Yeah, the little genius already comprehends that grown-ups don't always communicate happy news with balloons, goodie bags, streamers, and cake—and now actually thinks Lydia's calling for a party. "Holy shit! Holy shit!"

"Lux Mitchell Tycin." Reece reprimands him with a gentle but firm look. "Hey, it's time to take a chill pill, buddy."

"Chill pill." Lux echoes the words, which are new to him, and obviously decides he likes them. A lot. "Chill pill," he giggles out. "Chillll Pilllll."

After indulging one more smile his son's way, Reece returns his focus to Davidson. "Lay it on us," he charges, his stance fully alert. His shoulders are thrown back, his hands coiled but not clenched at his sides. His jaw is strong and set—and, I have to admit even at a time like this, breathtaking. "What are we looking at, and how can we help?"

Davidson, like the man's man he is, re-braces his stance and meets Reece's gaze. Only at this second, when his mien switches up, do I realize the guy probably didn't come here seeking Reece by choice. Reece has told me before that police and fire personnel tend to think he's still the spoiled brat billionaire playing games with the superhero persona. In short, maybe one step up from a Hollywood star ride-along. "No offense, man, but if I knew what we were 'looking at,' I'd likely not be here asking for your enlightenment on the situation."

I hold back from smacking the man only because of Reece.

Though he tells me all the time that I'm his spiritual better, times like this *he* teaches *me* how to be the better person. "Are you able to share a fly-over of the deets, then?" Reece asks while punching in the code to Sawyer's number on his phone. As if the code is a summoning spell, Sawyer bursts out of the executive office double glass doors, hands full with what looks like our battle leathers and already dressed in similar attire.

"Get yourselves ready first," Davidson returns. "I can brief you on the way over."

I nod along with Reece, thankful for the brief—*very* brief—break to impart some fast instructions to 'Dia about Lux's bedtime care, reassure my brain that I'm ready and trained for this, and then swiftly climb into my brand-new battle leathers. The outfit, newly designed for me by Fershan and Alex, features gold-colored piping along the inner seams of the legs and arms. They've installed similar accents in a rich cobalt blue to Reece's gear. While both ensembles are still meant for slipping in and out of shadows undetected, the different colors help us keep track of each other.

Davidson's so eager to get back to the building with the Roman columns and its distinctive barrel-vaulted entrances, the two-block journey to the Biltmore becomes damn near a jog. We enter the hotel at the main floor level off Olive Street. Across the street, at Pershing Square, the large geometric sculptures are joined by command centers for the Red Cross, the police department, and several fire battalions of the LAFD. If just some of what the fire chief has told us is true, all of them may be needed.

During the trip, Davidson dropped a few hints as to why he specifically sought us out. When the Biltmore's security team made its initial sweep, nothing out of the ordinary was yielded—until the officers started hearing voices. *A lot* of voices. Not cries for help or anyone in pain but also not belonging to anyone they could *see*. The whisperings seemed to belong to the walls themselves. They'd come from everywhere and nowhere at once and were in a slurred, unidentifiable language.

"And I do mean nothing we could pinpoint," Davidson clarifies as we pause inside the hotel's entrance. "Nearly every man in my battalion is decently fluent in Spanish," the chief goes on. "And we also have guys who speak Filipino and Japanese. With some additional help, we were able to rule out Russian, Chinese, Hindi, and most of the European languages. We still have no pinpoint on the language or dialect, just as we still have no exact location on the exact source point of the voices." His face twists as if he's just smelled something rancid. "Between you and me, it's just a lot of fucking creepy."

Creepy. It's a decent descriptor for the hollow scuffs of our boots against the heavy tarps that have been laid out to protect what's left of the marble floor in the hotel's most famous public space. The last time I was here, marveling at the resplendence of the soaring Rendezvous Court, Mom and I met for high tea on a bright Sunday afternoon. I'm gutted as I look across the gloomy room now, still awe-inspiring despite being devoid of all chairs, tables, and even its polished grand piano. The famous Renaissance-style balcony, along with its intricate pillars, astrological-themed clock, and double-sided staircases are also shrouded, looking like a massive ghost preparing to grab us.

Reece and I share a meaningful glance. We both understand, with crystal clarity, the jaded fire chief sucked back his ego far enough to bring in the billionaire superhero and his "blondie" partner.

But while the atmosphere is eerie, it's not terrifying. I'm puzzled by that and sense the same dilemma is pounding at Reece too. While I'm not as sensitive as Angelique to the poison of Faline's nearness, I'd still take a legal oath that I don't sense her anywhere near. Yet I don't feel like this is a run-of-the-mill case of locating someone's lost cat.

So what the hell *is* going on?

Reece maintains the all-business mien while pivoting back toward Davidson. "I assume you checked all the back hallways and storage areas already? The pool and spa areas too?"

"All of which have been closed for the last two years," Davidson rebuts. "But yes, we searched them thoroughly, along with the basement storage space."

"And nothing?"

"Not unless you count some spooked rats and a storage closet stacked with old cash registers as 'something.'"

"No humans, then?" Like the focused professional—and gentleman—that he is, Reece doesn't flinch at Davidson's condescending tone. "Not even some sleeping transients?"

Davidson shores up his posture. Sweeps us both with a steeled stare. He almost looks insulted—and likely would be, if he wasn't so blatantly freaked out. "Nothing and nobody with two legs."

He overemphasizes the syllables into determined spits— though the remainder of his saliva chokes in his throat the second a giant crash resounds through the room. As the loud *bwwaamm* collides against the vaulted ceilings, Davidson and I visibly jolt. Reece looks more like we've just gone to an escape room for date night and been handed a new clue. "I take it that's a new sound?" he murmurs.

He doesn't wait for Davidson's answer, probably because it's already stamped across the fire chief's face. Instead, Reece cocks his head while jogging across the room, around the fountain, and then over to the elevator banks beneath the balcony. I don't hesitate to follow, easily keeping pace in my sturdy but light-soled boots, the beloved black Danner Acadias I've been using for training and running with Sawyer.

Once we're in the alcove, every one of my senses easily spikes to high alert. Not a surprise when all my pores pop open, allowing the glow of my bloodstream through. It's definitely an advantage in the dim space below the balcony, where the air isn't so ventilated. Everything smells like disuse and feels like a sepulcher.

I stop when Reece does. Our movements would likely cause chirps on a cleaner floor. I turn into a brighter glow worm because of my heightened instincts but ignore Davidson's stupefied gasp. There are much bigger issues to stress about than shattering this man's mental checkboxes.

Like how the interior of the elevator shaft continues to shudder and hum and vibrate.

Then faster.

And faster.

The slit between the lift doors begins pulsing with light. Rapid-flashing hues of silver, gold, and green.

Then brighter.

And stronger.

We look to the indicator numbers over those doors.

And gape because they're *all* ignited.

"Just an electrical issue," I blurt. "Yes?"

My husband, encased in the glowing, godlike arrogance

of his full Bolt mode, exhales a grunt that makes *really* unprofessional parts of me tingle. "You truly believe that, Velvet?"

I don't waste time with a verbal answer. Surely he already witnesses the answer in my gaze—as well as the other internal war I'm waging. My heartbeat is a mess of lightning bolts in my throat. My chest thumps and thrums, tight with fear and anticipation—and the full comprehension of what's going on in regions *south* of my waistline. *Dear God. Seriously?* I barely hold back from emphasizing with an eye roll.

But appropriate or not, I've returned to a repeat performance of my runaway senses on the very first night I ever laid eyes on the Bolt of Los Angeles, when gawking at the news channel footage from over Neeta's shoulder. Just like then, I'm breathless with apprehension but tingling with awareness. The man in the leathers, facing an unknown danger, will never stop turning me into a puddle of enthralled mush.

But unlike then, I can't just slump against my credenza and then count out Zen mantras until I'm clearheaded again.

He needs me coherent. *Now.*

Lucid. *Now.*

Focused. *Really* right now.

As the elevator shaft keeps tremoring.

As the lights inside it intensify.

As Reece looks back for one fervent second and commands, "Stand back!" before extending his hands and directing a narrow pulse at the split in the carved lift doors.

They begin to part. And then open wider. And at last, they succumb to the pressure of my husband's incredible power.

When they slam all the way open, the alcove is bathed in rays of surreal light. Davidson cusses as he hurries backward.

The profanity doesn't last long, replaced by his barked orders into his radio. "This is Battalion Chief Davidson. All units stand by! Possible detonation of incendiary device at the Rendezvous Court elevators. Possible *multiple* devices. Over!"

"Copy your request, Davidson. This is Battalion Chief Garza, Battalion Fifteen, and we're moving into position. ETA two minutes. We'll be standing by with your men at the Olive Street entrance, awaiting further instruction. Over."

As that exchange happens, I read my husband's body language. Reece is resolute, not shirking from his promise to learn the truth about what's happening here. We still have no way of knowing if the lightshow in the elevator shaft is related to the voices in the walls, but it's the best we've got to go on.

But that also means somebody's got to be the first to look.

And my stud husband, with his awe-inspiring *cajones*, has volunteered for the mission.

He leans over, his ruggedly beautiful profile bathed in a mix of sky and ocean blues, sucking the air out of my system once more.

In spite of my dorky fangirl reaction, I force myself to inch toward him. "What is it?" I prompt. "Zeus? What's going on?"

Reece shakes his head as if my query is nothing but a breeze on the air. He crunches in his eyebrows. Tightens his lips. The bold angle of his jaw juts against his taut skin. "Davidson!" he bellows.

"What? What is it?" The fire chief jogs over but halts a few feet back. His face is set with the grim resignation of a man who's done this before. His career is comprised of running toward crisis instead of away, even with the knowledge that he may not emerge alive. So yeah, no wonder he was a little grumpy about seeking us out for help—but over the last three years, the man I love has emerged from behind his mask in more ways than one. Reece has a right to be here. He's shattered the world's labels and expectations and proven they don't define the man—the hero—he was born to be.

Even when that means peering down an elevator shaft that's gone completely Old Faithful with torrents of blinding light.

"How far down does this shaft go?"

And gone totally creepy movie with its distant, urgent creaks and crashes.

"The basement under us, and then one, maybe two below that for city infrastructure access. Why, Richards? What've you got?"

And now, even its streams of disembodied voices.

Disconcerting shouts—that soon become disturbing screeches.

And desperate wails.

And frightening outcries.

In an incoherent language.

"Might be a better question for you." Reece stretches his arms out, bracing his grip on either side of the shaft's opening, while cocking his head around. "What have I got, Davidson—since this thing is coming up from a hole a hell of a lot deeper than that?"

"The hell?" The chief sprints forward before either of us can warn him back. But in truth—holding him back from *what*? His demand is valid, as is the follow-up query as soon as he has a chance to peer down the shaft, and whatever else Reece has discovered in it, for himself. "What the living, fucking hell?"

Reece yanks Davidson back up just before the fireman leans past the point of no return. "Good to know I'm not hallucinating."

"Would be better if we both were," Davidson snaps. "Where the tarnation did that chasm come from? And why?"

"More importantly," Reece prompts, "what about the voices? They the same you heard before?"

"No," the chief counters. "I— I mean yes, but no. Same gibberish but clearly a different party. Or whatever the hell these bastards have going on now."

Reece hauls in a heavy breath. "Well, something tells me it's not the world's most elaborate episode of *Punk'd*," he states as the elevator—or whatever is still in that chute—really revs to life. So far, I'm still betting on an elevator car, with its gears grinding, pulleys squeaking, and ropes whooshing. That doesn't stop my nerves from becoming metal spikes—and my composure the balloon that's hovering over them.

A torment worsened by my husband's next moves.

As he backs up by three wide steps, pacing off the space he'll need for a clean attack at the approaching enemy.

As he drops into a battle-ready pose: legs spread, knees bent, arms reaching around an imaginary beach ball.

As I fight not to picture the colors of that ball as the shades of his blood, bruises, and sliced-open vitals. And severed limbs. And dying eyes...

And I was feeling *triumphant* about getting to do this... *why*?

"Shit," I rasp. "Ohhhh shit-shit-shit-shit."

Even as I crouch next to my husband—and assume the same battle position.

Have I gone insane?

It feels like the only explainable excuse, despite how the word feels like a battle flail in my gut.

Yeah. I'm insane.

Despite how I know we've trained for this. How I remember every second of every plan we've devised and perfected, exploiting the combination of our powers to their fullest. Despite how I'm pretty damn sure Reece and I will likely kick major ass and succeed, even if an army of bloodthirsty zombies spills out of that lift.

All of it still feels like insanity.

Even though we're both completely primed. Balanced on our tiptoes. Fingers sizzling. Bloodstreams humming. Heads lifted. Stares set.

Bring it on, fate.

Show us your worst.

But while my brain and body resound with the challenge, all my soul can think about are two pieces of motivation. The safety of the city I love and the face of the world's most perfect little boy, getting ready to fall asleep in it this very moment.

And just like that, I'm clear again.

I'm *not* insane.

I volunteered for this out of unbearable, immeasurable love. The commitment to protect my son's hopes, dreams, heart, and future. And I already know it's the same fire for Reece's spirit. I'm drenched in a wave of the energy I usually only detect when he's with Lux. He's sending it on purpose, with one sole intent. To assure me that I'm right. To welcome me into a league bigger than both of us: the connection to every warrior who's been in our position before. Embracing the reality of possibly losing my life while embracing the things that truly *mean* life.

As if by doing that, I can camouflage myself *with* life.

So death will have no choice but to pass me up.

Not that I'm believing it anymore—as the ropes and

pulleys in the lift continue to roll and move.

As the painful whines of biological lifeforms now mix with the grinds and screeches—and drag the whole elevator car into view.

I hiss while baring my teeth.

I seethe golden fire into my gaze as I torch every cell of my bloodstream.

And I realize, inside a second, the man at my side is doing the same. We're a pair of rebel alliance members, anticipating Vader himself in that lift car. Reece has the light sabers; I have the blaster cannons.

And my fingers on the triggers.

"Holy. *Crap.*"

Until I back them off. With sudden, sickened swiftness.

"Stop. *No*, Reece. Stop!"

I catch his backward flick of both hands, his version of priming his lightning barrels, and I'm terrified that he's already too deep in his battle zone to hear my scream. Luckily, my downward blast gives me the boost to fly in front of the shaft.

At once, I block the aperture with my outstretched arms. Reece, finally getting the point, redirects his lightning tines to the side. They rip an impressive slice out of the wall to my left. I almost want to reward him with a fist pump, but the creatures in the elevator are sucking every molecule of my attention. And shock. And astonishment. And wonderment. And about a thousand other emotions that invade my senses in the same cavalcade, threatening to crush my chest.

I can't move.

I'm locked in place, hands still gripping the sides of the opening.

My breaths pump in and out of me in astonished, agonized heaves.

"For the love of fuck!" Reece roars. "Emmalina, what the—"

"Kids."

"What?" he barks.

"*Kids!*" The single word taxes my physical strength and emotional composure. My glow surges anew as the fierce lioness inside takes over, but I'm able to get in some normal inhalations at seeing Reece acknowledge them too. Sort of. While he's stood down with his arms and hands, his posture is still as threatening as a Sith's, and his stare is still as piercing as an Asgardian's.

"Kids." I give the word a third verbal stomp, already discerning my husband is hearing but not listening. The utter stillness from him can mean one of two things: he really doesn't understand yet, or he's dead. "As in *children!*" I challenge once more, figuring it's at least worth a try.

But there's still no change in his expression as I turn around. If anything, he's throwing up more mental shields as he scoots forward, watching my back literally as well as figuratively. Yeah, that *is* the best word for it. My own defenses have raised again, but I meet the confession with shame. Whether we're about to confront children or adults or an elevator full of frogs, it doesn't matter. Of the many truths Lux has proven since his birth, the one that impresses me now is this: what one sees isn't always what one gets.

I drop to my knees. Tears brim and then roll down my cheeks—as I struggle to vocalize what I'm really looking at.

"Angels."

My stud hero of a husband hunches behind me, wrapping his hand around the back of my neck. His fingers are trembling.

Because he feels it too. He *knows* it too.

"*Reece*. They're...they're angels."

CHAPTER TWO

REECE

I'm so ready to believe her.

Fuck, I hate admitting it...but I am.

The twin girls appear older than Lux—at least on the outside—by at least a year. They look like three-year-olds who should be modeling in clothing and toy ads after being discovered by an agent in the Brentwood Whole Foods. They're decked in the finest, trendiest toddler wear as if to prove it, with hair and coloring that look like Moana and Snow White had a pair of angel love children. I'm awestruck by their black curls, cinnamon skin, and expressive eyes.

No. Not expressive.

All-seeing.

All-knowing.

Not exaggerations.

At first, they seem fascinated by Emma—probably her light hair and eyes, the opposite of what they see in the mirror every day—but as soon as they refocus, peering at me, I almost fall off my haunches and back onto my ass. Nobody except the woman in front of me and the child she gave me have been able to stare so completely down to my soul.

Holy. God.

And this time, I mean it literally.

Where the hell else would two children this beautiful, this ethereal, this surreal just suddenly appear from?

My logic hurls the answer into my heart—which then bursts like shrapnel of adrenaline through my body. At once, I'm back on my feet. The next second, my fingertips are light-blaring homing beacons. I angle the beams at my sides, pointing them outward like Wolverine in strike-ready mode with his claws. Another fitting comparison. I step away from Emma, making sure the two cherubs—or whatever the damnation they are—can see that I've got ignition and I'm not afraid to use it.

The girls shrink back with matching sets of O-shaped lips and we've-seen-a-goblin eyes. And while I hate being that ogre, it's better than trusting their exterior just to find out they're actually demons on the interior.

"Hey. *Hey*. Whoa!"

Emma's protest coincides with the girls' frantic retreat, but she's not fast enough to stop them from scurrying backward. They disappear through the burned-out hole in the elevator's floor. Okay, not fully vanishing. Their little hands stay visible, their petite fingertips clinging to that angry black lip. But they aren't screaming, and their huge impish eyes reappear after just a couple of seconds. *What the living hell?*

"It's all right!" Emma cries. "We mean you no harm! *Reece*," she hisses, "put those damn things away."

I grunt, enduring her glare as I pull back on my fingers' intensity. But just by a little. I'm the guy who once believed everything at such face value, I thought a "fun ride" into the Barcelona suburbs was going to land me in a kink club with Angie LaSalle's throat around my cock. Instead, I wound up on the Consortium's lab table with a needle jammed down that unfortunate cock. Now that the cock's back where I want it, I'm not trusting anything about this situation. Not even the two innocent faces that reemerge from the hole and get propped atop their seriously strong hands, sizing up Emma and me with renewed concentration.

"Hi again, beauties." Emma's sweet murmur etches a new crack in my heart. The tenderness she's displaying for these littles, not knowing anything except that they belong on a designer kids-wear ad over Downtown Disney, is moving... mesmerizing. "Come out, come out. I'm not going to let the scary man hurt you, okay?"

Record scratch. So much for "mesmerizing."

"Scary?" I spit.

"*Zeus*," she admonishes. "Isn't it obvious?" She tilts her head, sending them an engaging smile. Past her upturned lips, she levels, "I'm not sure they know where they are—or if they've seen the real world before."

"What?" I snap. "What do you mean, 'the real world'? Like they've never been—"

The twins turn over my answer before it's fully formed. Warming to Emma's soft coaxes, the pair finally steps across the threshold of the elevator into the halogen glare from the first-responder staging area. As soon as the garish beams flow across their faces, they let out taut, tearful screeches and then collapse to their knees, burrowing their heads into their folded arms.

Emma whips up her head, her stunned stare likely a mirror of my own. Clearly that twist wasn't on her list of expectations. Her distress has me crumpling down to the floor too. I reach out for the girls, though the action is probably too little too late. I hate that they've flinched because of me. *Fuck*. As far as I've come as a human being, sometimes I'm still an unthinking moron.

The girls beat a frantic retreat back to their mysterious hole, but instead of dropping back into the opening, they skid to a screeching stop right in front of it. They look down, heads nearly melding into each other like conjoined twins, before emitting more of those otherworldly shrieks.

"Oh, my God," Emma rasps. "What are they...*why* are they..."

"It looks like they're...grieving," I stammer.

"Or just seriously stressing?" she conjectures. "Wait. *Now* what? Are they...talking? To each other?"

Her point is validated by rapid-fire sibilance from the girls, carrying the ups and downs of a conversation. But my ears confirm Davidson's assertion—they're not communicating in any recognizable language. Being a global playboy in my former life has guaranteed I know a bit of nearly every popular language.

"But who are they talking *to*?" Emma presses. "Just...each other? Or someone down there?"

"You mean several floors down an elevator shaft?" My snark isn't intentional, but hanging on to a modicum of logic makes it necessary—which has to be the oxymoron of the year. Am I really standing here with neon-blue fingers, watching a pair of perfect anime characters, worrying about hanging on to my logic?

But in this case, the rationality is justified—perhaps the key to maintaining my sanity. Because if what she's saying is true and something from down *there* helped the girls get up *here*...

But who?

And how?

And why now?

"Well, do you think those two children bore that hole through an elevator car by themselves?"

That astute question from my brilliant wife is only going to be answered in one way.

But as soon as I clear one footstep across the gap into the lift, the twins cut loose once more with their unearthly shrieks.

Then spin around with terrorized expressions to match.

Gone are the pair of skittish doll faces. In their place are two visages with peeled-back lips, green-veined skin—and eyes that shine out at me in that same zombie-bright shade. And this time, it's no metaphor. Their eyes are definitely *shining*— glowing as if the cosmos has taken the light sticks of my fingers, changed the shade to bright green, and then shoved them into these kids' heads.

The effect is so jarring, I freeze in place. And wait for their adorable little heads to start three-sixty spins atop their bodies.

"The fuck?" I spew, unable to edit the profanity past my shock. But I'm certain that if Emma was capable of speech, she'd be spilling something similar. For the moment, her air is stuck in her throat and emerges only as a few shocked chokes at a time. "What— What the hell is—" But my breath isn't coming any easier. I'm not sure I want it to. If I complete the question, I have to consider an answer.

I have to supply the obvious answer.

And I can't.

Emma's form stiffens. Her glow falters. Her breath shivers like a flow of unstable ions. "Wh-What do we do now?"

I'm pathetically silent. Not by choice. I keep hoping that a shaft of enlightenment will explode open on top of *this* shaft, bearing seraphs who play harps with songs of divine wisdom for us. My pride wards off arrows of uncertainty, creating a full war zone in my senses. For fuck's sake, I've fought nearly every category of lowlife Los Angeles has to offer—so why the hell are two little girls unraveling my fortitude like cheap socks?

But they are.

Even through the next long moment and then the next. And the two after that. Nothing's changing about our bizarre standoff with the winsome twosome. Well, winsome up until a minute ago, when I dared too close to their territory. Their reaction, still blatant across their faces, continues to validate the hopelessness beneath Emma's query.

What *do* we do now? How are we going to find that answer?

Unless it's the light we've had all along—and have simply refused to acknowledge.

The light...

In the form of our amazing, dazzling, whizzing, whirling son.

Who accomplishes every breathtaking bolt of that wizardry through the air over our heads.

Through the air.

Over our heads.

I shouldn't be witnessing his flight with my jaw dropped nearly to the floor. The kid already showed us his aerial abilities less than an hour ago, zooming his way into our bedroom in the Brocade's penthouse. I guess this is a little like a parent who's watched his kid rehearsing clarinet at home but not with everyone watching.

Only this isn't exactly the clarinet. And the people watching aren't my son's teachers and peers.

My son, Lux Mitchell Tycin Richards, is airborne in front

of a couple of fire battalions, their dumbfounded chiefs, and half a dozen SWAT guys.

With arrogant ease, I swing a smirk over my shoulder at all of them. *Fruit of my loins, motherfuckers. Watch and learn.*

Who the hell am I kidding?

I'm right here along with them. Watching. Learning.

Lux twists and straightens and then touches down in a perfect landing just a few inches from the terrified twins.

He breathes steadily, despite how they react as if a rattlesnake has flown in and landed.

He scoots forward, tilting his bright towhead to the left and then to the right. As he favors each side, the little girl corresponding to that direction undergoes a sudden—and eye-popping—transformation.

As if my kid has brought some kind of wand along with his flight, the twins have been transformed. While traces of the green light still linger in their eyes, I don't still suspect they're about to summon the hounds of hell to help them out. Though part of me—a prominent part—still wonders if hell is exactly what they're used to, considering their bizarre behavior of the last five minutes. If that's the case, it was likely a hell inflicted by adults, since even Lux's unorthodox arrival didn't elicit as much as an eye blink from the two.

Holy Christ.

What the hell have these girls been through? What kinds of atrocities have they truly endured?

Just contemplating those answers makes me yearn to slice open the wall again.

Stupidly, I let the rage roll right out of me in a turbulent flood. It hits the twins as if I've physically charged into the elevator and stabbed lightning bolts into them. I attempt a correction, backing away and roping back my aggression, but not before the girls slide down to their backsides in the corner, each attempting to curl into the lap of the other.

Which lands me in a puddle of self-recrimination.

But beyond that...self-congratulation.

Yeah, at the same time.

Because though Papa Richards has messed up, Lux Richards is there to show the old man how this "rescuing people" thing is really supposed to go.

By rolling up all two and a half feet of his posture and then gallantly extending a hand toward one of the girls. And then the other.

By waiting there, with the patience most men—let alone boys—don't have, as the twins openly debate his offer.

By letting them reach back out to him, finally slipping their small hands into the comforting embrace of his.

And at last, by showing me—showing us all—the real, true lesson we have to watch and learn from him here.

From all three of these incredible beings.

EMMA

"Oh...my God." I'm aware of the words leaving my lips, but my awed whisper is wrapped in a thousand clouds inside my mind. My eyes are seeing this, but my senses aren't understanding it. Or maybe they don't want to. Perhaps because they already know what I'll be forced to admit once they do.

A recognition not sitting well with the rest of me. My belly is a taut, tangled wad. My breaths are dull blades *shink*ing in and out through the sharpening stones of my lungs. My blood thunders in my ears. But I can't deny the facts I have to face, manifesting with such resplendence before me. Amazing me but daunting me. Moving me but paralyzing me. Brimming tears to my eyes that sting with both wonder and terror in the same heavy drops.

And then heavier, as the children wrap themselves tighter around each other. As soon as they do, each juncture of their hands becomes a conduit for their energies: Lux's blue and gold streams begin mixing with their bright-green ones, forming sizzling arcs that swiftly blend into crackling electric rainbows. But the visual is just the start of their impact on the air. There's a vibration they give off, happy as waves of sunshine heat on a summer beach. And then a music they play, sweet as a choir lifted in praise to the heavens. And then a pronounced leap of energy...

Like three children rejoicing in the discovery of a new friendship.

My tears roll down harder. I look up to my husband, smiling softly as his jaw juts from the pressure of holding his own shit together. He's as moved as I am—but he's also just as conflicted. Because he knows, just as I do, exactly what we're beholding.

Our son has never been happier...because he's found others like him.

Which makes this more than just a new friendship. More than just meeting "mortal" friends on the playground, exchanging contact information for playdates, and then lecturing Lux once more about the necessity of using his limits, hiding who and what he is.

In this moment, he no longer has to hide.

He's Lux the Incredible, in every form he wants to unleash

that brilliance. He's Lux the Miracle, full of power. He's Lux the Extraordinary, full of light. But best of all, he's no longer Lux the Only. Or Lux the Lonely.

A celebration for him—but the world's worst dilemma for his Dada and Mama. I see that realization across Reece's tense face, as well. This isn't a we-can-face-that-tomorrow kind of thing, either. This is the part where we summon all the mettle behind our superhero designations. The part where we prove, in the crucibles of our hearts and souls, why and how we can rise above the rest.

By confronting the slew of obvious questions because of all this. The questions that already turn our stomachs, despite the beautiful package in which they've been wrapped. The questions that make us think of ripping out our fingernails as a delightful alternative.

Who are these girls?
Where did they come from?
Why are they exactly like Lux?
And the shittiest queries of them all:
Who the hell sent them here? And why?

In the moment Reece and I join our stares, our eyes bleak, before we can start conjectures about those answers, there are a couple of new figures in our periphery. We tick our heads in tandem to see the small crowd of first responders has grown by two figures, their faces full of as much gawk factor as ours.

"*Desolée*," the first of them rasps, wisps of her white-blond wig tumbling into her face. "Lydia was ready to tie Lux down with the party centerpiece strings, but I insisted he be allowed to come over."

Sawyer nods in concurrence to Angelique's story. "And I insisted on being his chaperon," he explains between harsh, exhausted huffs. "But we might have to change that kid's name to X-15. Or Sonic."

I almost laugh. Lux definitely wouldn't object to the latter, since the famous hedgehog stars in one of the few video games we let him play, but any claim I have on mirth has been crushed by a massive wrecking ball called anxiety. "You insisted...why?" I demand to Angie, hoping that she's still listening. The woman hasn't been able to rip her eyes off the triumvirate of bliss taking place inside the elevator. "What did you feel, Angie?"

I don't bother with asking *if* she felt it. No way would she allow Lux to violate a directive from Reece and me unless her powered perception had kicked into high gear. Reece, with his face already etched in the same grim admission, scoots around to directly block Angelique's view of the kids.

"We need answers *now*, Angie." A massive tick stretches against his jaw, and bright-blue sparks start popping between his fingertips. "As you can see, the damage might already have begun."

"*Oui*." The woman's face crunches with deep emotions. "I...I *do* see." She runs a taut hand across the top of her head. "But...but how is this possible?" And then digs her fingers in and yanks off her wig completely, exposing the purple and gold veins that are pulsing brighter than the jumbotron at a Lakers game. "*How*...is..."

"What?" I stomp in, butting my shoulder to Reece's bicep in order to crowd in on my friend. *My friend.* Never did I ever suppose I'd use that phrase to qualify my relationship to Angelique LaSalle, but the woman has earned her second chance on Team Bolt—and in this moment is solidifying a permanent spot there, as well. Our fate—and more direly, that of our son's—might rest in the hidden truths she can share.

"How is *what* possible?" I order while wrapping my hands around her forearms. "Angie, you have to tell us what you're sensing." I get down a painful swallow before amending, "You have to tell us *who* you're sensing."

She lifts her glowing head. The electricity in her veins is racing. "I...do not know...if I can."

Reece lunges in. Looms over her like a medieval interrogator, complete with the I'm-going-to-chop-off-your-feet glare. "Not. Acceptable."

Angie trembles. I hate myself for being grateful for it, but I am. She possesses our only insight into all this. No time for squeamish hesitations, despite how the woman hasn't lost an inch of her contorted expression as she pulls in a huge breath.

And utters exactly what I prayed she wouldn't.

"This—this is Faline's energy. Both of those girls are drenched in it."

Then everything I didn't expect.

"But Faline...*she* is not here."

Reece jerks his head, channeling complete shock. "What the hell does that mean?" he dictates. "What's going on here?"

But they're not the questions he's really intending. Queries that *must* be vocalized if we expect them to be answered.

I suck it up, gripping Angelique tighter. "Is Lux in any danger from them? Can you tell? And...and what the hell do they want from him?"

Angie raises her gaze to fully meet mine. There's still a grimace across her mouth, but I now catch the glimmer of tiny magenta lights in the backs of her eyes. Glowing roses of...

Joy.

Happiness.

Hope.

Beaming at me with an energy I readily recognize. The same sweet, honest rapture I felt the moment Lux joined hands with the twins. An elation that has me releasing her and then transferring my hold to Reece, cupping my solar flares against his neon rods before yanking him back around to behold our celestial gift of a kid again.

Our kid, still fused with his two new friends. Who's now trading wide smiles with both of them, which light them all up from the inside out. If someone snapped a picture of this right now, they'd be accused of using the "fairy magic" filter, since all three of them remind me of every incarnation of the elusive *sidhe fae*. That analogy and the fear of Angie's revelation should have me shivering at biblical proportions, but all I can keep thinking is that this triumvirate of merriment is completely right. Totally destined. Utterly meant to be.

Fate backs up my instincts with a visual fist pump in the form of the new energy between the children. No more electric rainbows up and down their arms or giggly smiles across their lips. The arcs of multicolored light have flattened out, becoming the sizzling sides of an equilateral triangle. And the mixed colors? They've blended to the point of being a silver-gold mix, as radiant and magical as the gleam of dawn on the ocean.

But all of that's not the most wondrous aspect of this sight.

That's all inside the kids themselves—and what they're giving each other.

Thoughtful nods. Contemplative head tilts. Even a few eyebrow drops, as if needing to absorb every last drop of what they're experiencing.

Or...*hearing*?

"Holy Christ." Reece's rough blurt is the perfect

verbalization on behalf of us both. "What are they... Are those three...?"

"Communicating." Sawyer, as so many times before, to the rescue—though his statement is serrated with enough awe to match Reece's. "Sure as hell what it looks like, gang."

It's the ideal segue into a few solemn moments from the three of us witnessing the three of them take part in a language we're only able to see—but in a thousand ways are already feeling. Sensing. Experiencing.

No. This is crazy.

But my breath stops as my soul affirms it.

Crazier than falling in love with a superhero? Crazier than loving him so hard, you became an electric mutant yourself just to save him? Crazier than the endless, bottomless love you feel for the child you created with him?

This time, I have all the answers to the questions.

And confirm them by watching my beautiful son and holding his incredible father.

And acknowledging the triangle of love between the three of *us*: not as visible and not as blinding but there all the same. Binding us. Connecting us. For always. Existing in the same forever that Reece Andrew Richards will always consume in my soul—enabling him to gaze at me as he does right now, seeing the core of me and knowing exactly what's there. And loving exactly what's there.

The same way in which our son pivots to look at us both now...

And speaks to us without moving a single inch of his smiling lips.

My clutched breath leaves me on a tear-filled gasp.

I can hear him. *I can hear him.*

The same way I heard him when he was still inside me. Not in the faint whispers that I catch every once in a while when he's asleep. This is his full, conscious voice. The same pure energy of what he sent to me when we were physically connected but better now.

So much better.

Because one glance tells me that Reece hears him too.

Don't worry, Mama. Don't worry, Dada.

Reece chokes out a taut breath. Fully empathetic to his cacophony of emotions, I press closer against him. My tears plop onto his shirt and then slide down his arm, and I let them. They're his decorations of honor. And probably mine too.

"We're not worried, son." Reece, finally giving up on trying to tune his senses to Lux's freaky frequency, simply spurts the words aloud. The stunned stares from Davidson and the others are immediate, but I'm beyond caring. "We're just..."

"Concerned," I fill in, at once accepting Reece's grateful kiss atop my head. Sometimes, moms just do know the right words. "We're concerned, Lux." I form a full sentence for the payoff of getting to repeat it. "Honey, are you okay?"

I gasp in happiness as his adorable towhead swings up and down like a dashboard bobble and the twins let out shy giggles. "I fine, Mama," he says in full voice. Maybe he's noticed that Davidson, Garza, and all their men have started inching forward, led by the stealthy SWAT guys. I'm on the verge of ordering them to stand down, paranoid that the drawn guns will wig out the twins once more. But the girls take in the spectacle behind us with open curiosity, as if they've never seen men in black with instruments of violence at their fingertips.

Knowing what we know now, there's a damn good chance that's the truth.

This is Faline's energy. Both of those girls are drenched in it. But she *is not here.*

"Are...are you having fun?" I finally ask Lux. "Are you talking to your new friends?"

He's the world's most precious bobblehead again. "Yes, Mama. They are nice. They like me!"

"I know." I draw out the second word, eagerly latching on to the same tone I use when we go venturing into the canyon behind the ridge together. His fascination with everything creepy, crawly, squiggly, or slimy means I've got the emphasis down to an art. "What are you three talking about?"

"Worms. And beetles."

I half expected it, even in this situation, giving me a leg up on preparedness with the follow-up question. "Oh, yeah? Do they like worms and beetles like you do?"

"Sometimes," Lux babbles. "But only to play with when they bored. And if the critters no come around while they are sleeping."

Okay, I'm not ready for that one. Or the horrified bile it surges into my throat. Or the equally awful words that I force to my lips, trying to tell myself that asking the follow-up is going to be more palatable than imagining the possibilities. "Wh-While they're s-s-sleeping...where?"

As soon as the query leaves my lips, there's a distinct change in the energy between Lux and the girls. A new kind of thrumming and a new pitch of sound. The pulses are rapid and fierce, like war drums intensifying before a fight. The song has changed into a similar chant. If I heard it on the radio, I'd think it was the start of a new Fall Out Boy hit. But the twins are still as serene as seraphs. Their light continues to swirl through and around Lux as he remains facing us.

For all of two seconds.

Just enough time for him to issue one more sentence to us.

"They show me where...now."

Just enough time for us to bask in the delight of his excited grin.

Before he disappears down the elevator shaft with his two new friends.

CHAPTER THREE

REECE

I've heard my wife scream in a lot of different situations. In the grip of fear, the heights of passion, the throes of labor, the sobs of pure love.

No sound out of the woman's mouth has prepared me for the wail she lets out now. It resonates through the alcove and then out and up through all three stories of the courtyard, its agony shaking the chandeliers and forcing even the SWAT guys to stumble back by discernible steps.

It makes me want to tear apart the building. The block. The whole fucking city.

But I force myself to hone that shit in so I can rip open the only space that matters right now. The whole floor of the elevator beneath which Lux and the twins have dropped.

Ten seconds' worth of a focused lightning torch—a power I haven't switched on in full since fending off the group robbery attempt at the RRO fundraiser in New York—and the lift's floor is completely free of its moorings. Emma's right next to me, her power on full so she can melt the slab back onto the shaft walls, preventing it from taking someone's head off during a plummet of its own.

A horrific thought for a different day. A different set of circumstances.

Like ones not involving me running through every option for saving my son between one eye blink and the next.

Which get whittled down by one—a good-thing bad-thing mix—from the second Davidson charges in, flanked on all sides like he's the reincarnation of fucking Teddy Roosevelt and the Rough Riders. "Move back, Richards," he growls before bellowing back over his shoulder, "We need rope! Lots of it! Fiore and Pratt, front and center. You're our fastest rappellers. Find those kids!"

"Rappellers?" But as it spills out of me, every pore of my skin is zapped by the lightning of my instinct. The solution makes sense—to the real world. But half my days aren't lived in the real world anymore. "No," I mutter. "*No*," I emphasize, pizza-cutting the rope coils that have been brought forward and plunked on the floor between Davidson and me. "That's only going to make it worse."

The fire chief grunts. At once I'm back to being the rich-boy wannabe hero who was lucky enough to receive electric-blood infusions for six months. "Mr. Richards." He seethes the syllables with such vitriol, I'm shocked the dude's not fried off half his mustache. "I asked you to move back. I won't ask again."

I grind down three layers of tooth enamel in the same number of seconds. "Damn straight you won't."

"Huh?"

Annnnd another three layers—as I hook an arm around Emma's waist and then flip her backward and up until she lands squarely across my back. Only after she's locked her arms around my neck and her legs around my waist do I let my grin relax by a fraction. "Bolt rappelling team, reporting for duty, Chief."

I punctuate it by ticking my temple with two extended fingers, as Davidson attempts to form words. I'm fine with being the fall guy for every asshole billionaire showoff he's ever had to deal with, but not when my son's fate is on the line. Now, all egos are off.

And all limits as well.

And, as Emma and I learn as soon as we plunge into the shaft, all the lights too.

She screams again, but only at half her volume from ground level and only into my ear. Her reaction is more visceral than emotional, a sound even Davidson would be yelping if I subjected him to a drop into impenetrable blackness. The ink-black air surrounds us on all sides. We have only the light from her glow and my pulses, which act as brakes for our drop along the steel-lined chute.

But not for very long.

As I've suspected since we first arrived and met the twins, this chasm is about more than the Biltmore's elevator shaft. That much is evident as soon as the clangs and pongs resulting from my pulses are replaced by earthen thuds and the smell of damp dirt.

We're below Los Angeles.

Well below it.

The atmosphere gets heavy. Heavier still. I'm conscious of the weight of everything over our heads—buildings, roads, society, *life*—as we plunge into a world of thick, abject silence.

And suddenly, out of nowhere, glaring and explosive light.

"Aggghhh!"

My growl tangles with Emma's stunned cries. My instincts, now trained to the point of auto-reactions, manage to land us safely—but barely. As soon as my feet hit the white tile floor, I skid along the slick surface until bottoming out like a drunk ice skater. I go down face first but continue to be a human drift missile, stopping only when my head collides with a pristine white wall.

The pain is bearable only because I lift my face and see hers. With her gorgeous blues open. With tears brimming in them. With her body seemingly unharmed as she tumbles off my back and then plunks down onto the floor until we're both on our sides, facing each other. It'd be the best torment I ever endured for this woman—if only we were canoodling between sheets instead of sprawled across an antiseptic-smelling floor. And the light wasn't so goddamned bright.

And there weren't at least ten pairs of eyes watching us. Including those of our son.

I push upright, not ashamed of using the grips along the wall in order to regain my feet. *Wait a second.* Climbing grips? Along a hospital-white wall? *Wait another second.* Why does this place look like a hospital? All this way under downtown Los Angeles?

"What...the..."

My impressions are solidified as I straighten with a labored groan. Emma, who's already waiting for me, brings some solace as she rolls a palm along the side of my face. "My Zeus," she whispers.

"My *real* jumping bunny." I attempt a wry laugh along with my stupid humor, but everything hurts. *Fuck.*

"You all right?"

"Are *you*?"

"Yeah. Yeah, I'm fine."

"That's all that matters, then."

She's getting ready to give me the best wound care in the

world by rolling her eyes and calling me something like a sappy ox or a reckless rogue, but here comes Lux to my rescue.

"Dada!"

Or not.

"Oof!" I choke it out as my son flies into my knees, which feel like they just braved every black-diamond ski run in France—on the same day. "Heeeey, buddy. You're safe!" *Thank fuck.*

"Uh-huh. Yep."

He jabs a thumb up at me, easing the tension in my chest a little more. I complete our ritual by grabbing his gung-ho digit and then gently nibbling it. But unlike every other time we've done it, there's no ensuing giggle from my son. Instead, I respond to his insistent pull, descending to his level despite the black-diamond disasters still connecting my upper and lower legs. Once I'm there, Lux frames my face with his hands. Pulls at the hair along my temples, compelling me to keep taking in his handsome yet solemn face—as he pulls in a breath too damn serious for a kid of his *mental* age, much less what he appears to be on the outside.

"*Dada.*"

I purse my lips and hone my stare. "What do you need, son?"

His little mouth tightens, as well. "We need to help 'em."

I don't bother issuing the obvious follow-up. It's given to me already, in the form of the twins' reappearance. Emma flicks her confused glance between them and me, and I admit to sharing her mystification. Now that the girls have lured—if I can call it *that*—Lux down to their lair, they should be strutting like queens of the castle. Or whatever the hell this place is. But no, they're back to their fidgeting uncertainty from the elevator, as if we've dropped in unannounced to their home.

Have we?

If that's the case, why did they deliberately haul Lux down their goddamned rabbit hole? What's the wonder twins' game here?

Which, goddamnit, leads to my most eerie question of all.

Why the hell am I so sure there's a "game" here?

Christ. What kind of a cynic have I turned into? Have I gotten so used to Faline's hijinks that I'm instantly mounting the worst-case scenario here? About a pair of nervous little girls who clearly worship my son already?

Oh, fuck that mush.

I'm close to a mile beneath Los Angeles, standing in some pseudo-psych ward with no physical backup or method of contacting help—because I'm damn sure AT&T hasn't thought of reaching out and touching someone down *here*—meaning we're on our own in this stark white weirdo-land. Facing off, once again, with a pair of creatures that share too many traits with my son for any kind of decent comfort level. So yeah, as far as I'm concerned, this is all on the shiny-shiny girls. They've got to prove why my guard shouldn't be hiked higher than a Starfleet force field and why my suspicions don't have to stay pegged at a glaring level ten.

But I'm willing to take the first step—at least for Lux's sake. "We need to help who, buddy?" I prompt him.

He steps back but doesn't look away from me. At the same time, the girls shift forward, flanking him. It's a chore not to let my jaw plummet at the ethereal beauty of the sight. The two dark princesses are like heaven's perfect completion for Lux's gold gorgeousness. I have to fight all the instincts that keep telling me this is right, instincts that keep prodding me to be as protective of the girls as my boy. But for all we know, maybe they're a couple of fabricated automatons in Faline's fucked-up forces. It's disgustingly possible that they're not *real*. Has the witch perfected holograms along with every other sick trick up her demented sleeve? We don't even know their names!

"They are called Ira and Miseria."

And I had to go there.

But Lux's disclosure is like a thousand new nicks in my intuitions. I'm consoled but concerned to see the concurring glints in Emma's gaze—especially as I state the frightening obviousness here. "Those are Spanish words, aren't they?" I funnel the force of the question, and the electric accusation of my stare, at both the girls. "They mean..."

"Anger." The answer is supplied by a new arrival in the hallway: a woman as striking as the twins but with distinct differences. The girls are so beautiful, I keep wondering if they're computer generated, but this woman is definitely flesh and blood. She could nearly be a Kardashian, though her features bear the wideset eyes, classic nose, and lush lips of someone directly from Eastern Europe. "And misery." The four syllables bear out my hunch. She's definitely from someplace between Russia and Italy. "And I am Aliz."

A discomfiting pause drags by. What the hell now? I've only been uncomfortable about meeting a pretty girl one other time in my life, and I wound up marrying that one. But what the hell am I supposed to say at this point? *Great to meet you, Aliz. How's it hangin'? And while you're at it, care to enlighten me about what the hell you're doing down here, keeping a couple of little girls hostage in your bizarro bunker?*

Thank fuck Emma's got her act together more than me. "Hi, Aliz." She steps forward, right hand extended. "I'm

Emmalina. And this is Lux. And this is—"

"I know who you are." Aliz's statement is like her focus on me. Direct, determined, undaunted. But beneath the steel of her voice, there's a softer cushion. Something shielding the armor around her exterior from permeating the flesh of her heart. "Reece Richards. Oh, yes. I know exactly who you are."

I shift my weight and avert my gaze. Meeting hers has become a trip to what-the-hell central. It's not the fact that the woman recognizes me. That's happened to me everywhere from airports and traffic lights to beaches and bathrooms since I was sixteen. It's *how* she phrases the salutation. As if the lining I just imagined across her heart is frayed and thin and getting worse by the day.

A feeling I understand in abundance.

A comprehension that threatens to burst my own heart from the inside out. Yes, even now. Yes, *especially* now.

"Okay." I draw out the syllables, hoping the woman will pick up on my valiant try for levity. She doesn't. "A lot of people know who I am." I nod toward Emma. "And her too, actually."

Am I fond of the blatant confrontation to which I've switched? Of course not, but Princess Mysterious here isn't offering much of a choice. If humor won't loosen her up, maybe a direct throwdown will.

"I imagine they do." The queenly demeanor isn't fast enough to hide how she twists her fingers in front of her stomach and purses her lips as if she's being presented at court. I mean a *real* court, with judgmental rules and strict rituals. Lots and lots of those. "At least *she* says they do."

And just like that, I toss aside the need to compare her with all of Henry the Eighth's wives plus their handmaids. I throw out every assumption and impression I've gathered about the woman, with the exception of one thing. The one word she's uttered that gives away all the information I need to know about her.

And damn it, everything I don't want to know, as well.

She.

The *she* who's being invoked like a demon that won't go away. The *she* who's likely banished this woman to this cage as much as the twins. The monstress who's been invoked by a person regal and graceful enough to be her fucking queen. Who might have been just that to Faline, in another world. A reality far different from this.

Whatever the hell *this* is.

But don't I already know that answer?

No. *No.*

I turn away. Slam my eyes shut against the ensuing images in my mind. Bright-red blood. Searing, burning pain. The hopeless acceptance of captivity.

The same sad futility I recognize in Aliz's gaze.

Fuck. *Fuck.*

I force my eyes back open. Work my hands against themselves, furling and then unfurling my sparking fists. I force moisture down my throat, despite how the damn thing has closed to the width of a pinprick. Fitting comparison, since my senses have turned the same texture.

Still, I order myself to peer around again.

To really look this time...

But instantly damning myself for it. In at least a thousand different ways.

Stark walls. Antiseptic smells. Emotionless light. Empty echoes.

Nuclear blasts of memory.

Assaulting. Incinerating. Frying me. Trapping me.

Alpha Two. Alpha Two. Alpha Two...

No.

No.

I'm not him anymore.

I'm not there anymore.

Not him. Not there. Not him. Not there.

Easier said than done.

I force my mind back to this moment. Again, easier said than done, but I finally dive headfirst into the box in my brain labeled Detached Analysis. Four years of university-level business management didn't pound it into me, but after a few months of facing off with felons, it stuck. Right now, it's my salvation.

"How can we be of service to you, Aliz?" It's the safest alternative of all the demands hammering at my brain and the one that matters the most right now. "Your children were clearly rattled when we found them upstairs"—feels like the easiest descriptor, so I'm going with it—"and we assumed maybe—"

"They are not my children."

And there's my lesson for the day about assumptions. "All right. Do they *have* parents, then? Where are they? Were they hurt during the quake?" *Or whatever the fuck it was.* I scowl for a second, not certain how I feel about the alternative theories getting easier to accept by the second, before swinging my focus from Aliz to the twins. "Is that why they sent you to us?" I question, pointing a finger upward. "Are your parents lost? ¿Necesitas ayuda con tu familia?" When they keep staring as if I've asked them how to get to the fucking moon, I mentally dig in my heels. I've been a man-slut, a party god, an extreme-sports junkie, and an insane big spender, but I've never been a quitter. "¿Padre?" I prompt. "¿Madre?"

Zap.

I've sure as hell hit the button this time.

I'm just damn sure it's not the right one.

The girls detonate into shrieks that are worse than their fits in the elevator. They grip each other as if they intend to fuse permanently. Even Lux's attempt at comfort, struggling to encompass them both with his outstretched arms, doesn't ding their grief. If anything, as our son tries to console them with the basic Spanish Emma and I have taught him, their laments grow louder—all triggered by one definite word.

"*Madre!*"

"*Madre!*"

"*Madre!*"

Every time one of them enunciates between their sobs, my gut twists tighter. When the torque is bad enough to match the torment of gazing at Aliz, I suck it up and fix my sights back on her again. "Holy shit," I rumble. "Their mother...did they lose her in the quake?"

The woman's bite of a laugh is nowhere near my top ten—*twenty*—anticipated reactions. "No. Though I am certain that is what they wish."

And that one? Don't look for it in the top fifty.

"Excuse the crap out of me?" Sometimes, Emma has the perfect words and matching inflection for a moment. But before Aliz can give her a reply, the girls cry out twice as loud. Their pleas are worse to endure, carrying the scratchy pain of pure desperation.

"*Madre* no! *Madre* no!" They keep up the synched screams, each spinning around—until I'm wearing one of them around a leg and Emma's draped by the other. "*Por favor, madre* no more!"

That one word of an extension, provided by the little girl who turns her terrorized, tearstained face up at me, helps to clarify a shit ton. While the surge of their raw emotion in the air has made it impossible to stay totally inside the detachment box, I'm able to register *that* part loud and clear.

Madre no more.

And then to let in some of my ensuing fury because of it. Just some.

If I crank back the hatch, I'll let the entire storm fill up the cabin of the ship of my composure. The ship that has to stay afloat right now. The ship that's already pitching hard on the waves of my comprehension.

"No more *what*?" I spit at Aliz. "Of their own mother?" Guided by raw impulse, I shield the back of Ira's head with the wide spread of my hand. "Where the hell is this woman?"

"Not here," Aliz answers. "At least not now. Thank God."

"Then *who* the hell is she?" And does the heartless hag know that her own children are screaming and shivering and cowering at the simple mention of her?

Aliz jerks up one side of her mouth, channeling her mirthless chuckle into new form. "Reece Richards, savior of Los Angeles, leader of Team Bolt, the walking lightning strike... you know that you possess that answer already, yes?"

Her words are like defibrillator paddles to my chest—only not in the life-giving way. They're on reverse, punching the power *out* of me, forcing my mind and soul to grasp what she's said but hasn't said—because she doesn't have to.

Because she's right.

I already know the answer.

The same answer that resounds in Emma's stunned choke and carries through into her sandpaper utterance. "Oh, holy *shit.*"

Aliz rolls back her shoulders with the grace of a queen, despite the anguish still glittering in her large dark eyes. "I would not classify anything about this situation, or the woman who created these children, as *holy.*"

Another shock of the paddles. Twice as hard. Five times as torturous. Unbelievably, I still grit out one word.

"Faline."

But as soon as I do, the twins shriek louder. "Noooo!" Ira bawls against my thigh, making my leathers glow green with the intensity of her dread. She clutches both my quads, her fingertips searing ten holes through my leathers before doing the same to my skin. I lock my teeth, enduring the pain in hopes it'll ease her desolation. But deep inside, I already know the answer to that quandary too.

Hope gives a creature strength. Maybe even the kind that Faline Garand can't control.

And there's nothing the bitch loves more than control.

"No more *Madre* Faline." Miseria sobs into Emma's knee. "No more, no more, *no mas!*"

My wife gulps hard. Rubs her lips together, clearly battling against sobs of her own. Lux has already lost that clash. With a trembling chin and big blue eyes turned into oceans of sorrow, he openly begs me with every inch of his sweet, expressive face.

But begs me for *what*?

As I stare back at him with seared quads and burning eyes, I wait for the answer to manifest for that one too. Surely, like all the others, it must be ready to blast in at me any second.

My senses give me nothing but bewilderment, agitation,

and confusion. They tangle tighter together as I attempt to wrap my mind around every astounding event of the last hour— despite how I know, *I know*, we're nowhere near to being done with every jolt yet. I knew it as soon as I spoke Faline's name. As soon as my invocation turned the twins back into hysterical wraiths. As soon as it made Aliz look just as morbid but in ways that terrify me in equally visceral ways. Clearly the woman's hung out a bit with royalty. There's a good chance *she* carries such a rank. Queens don't show their weaknesses unless they've been soundly beaten. Aliz looks like she's three steps from being ordered to the guillotine.

Is that because she defied Faline?

Or was she brought down here to be specifically utilized as a pseudo-nanny for Miseria and Ira?

Or was she here already and simply drafted into this strange role?

I yearn to cut to the chase and restart the conversation with that part of the investigation, but there's too much to figure out first. All the parts that already make my gut feel like a brick of solid bile.

"All right, let's take this back to the starting blocks." I take a pull of as much air as my lungs will allow. "You're telling me... Faline Garand is the mother of these two girls?"

Aliz levels her gaze. "If that is what you choose to call it."

My nerves stand on edge. On a basic level, I understand the woman's elusiveness. If she *was* the girls' steward but has absconded with the twins while leaving Faline in the dark about it, she needs to extricate herself from any further liability at this point. I understand that. Sure as fuck doesn't mean I have to like it.

"So her DNA is dancing in their genetic code." I hold up

a hand, indicating I'm not making this one a question. Emma's guttural gasp backs me up.

"Dear God," she rasps and flows a hand over Miseria's thick black curls. "I— I didn't notice. Not like *this*. Their skin's darker, but the set of their eyes...and if their hair were cut differently..." She interjects on herself with a tangible shudder. Her features crunch into a taut wince. "Oh, dear God," she echoes.

I nod again, though the motion isn't so steady. Carefully, I pick apart Aliz's communication. "The woman who created these children," I reiterate, half my mind breaking off for some careful timeline math. "But...why?" The blurt is my immediate, and best, reaction to that ten-ton brick of shock. "What the hell kind of prize was she after?" I take it down to the growl I'm already feeling. "The woman didn't suddenly jones after the Gerber baby photo trophy. Not even in another dimension is *that* shit show possible."

"She's sold her soul to the dark side six times over," Emma injects. "And only craves one return on that investment."

"Oh, I am well aware of what she wants." Aliz rejoins her hands at the front of her waist. Her pause creeps to the edge of ominous, unfurling a foreboding chill through my system. "All of us."

They're the words I'm fully expecting, only without her unnerving emphasis. But before I can fully dissect my disconcertment, Emma ignites with a fresh flare of fury. "And after the witch is done with everyone on earth, she'll start on the rest of the solar system."

For a split second—yeah, even now—I'm derailed. Can I fucking help it that my wife is a bonfire of pure hotness when she's incensed? But the second after that, I'm pounding my hands together, stomping down my libido and refocusing the investigation in the same *whomp* of action. "So that lands us back at the starting blocks. Trying to figure out how two *children* got mixed up in that bitch's grand plan for world domination."

"But how?" Emma demands. "In what way?" She turns as green as the girls' bloodstreams while framing Miseria's tiny shoulders with her hands. "They're *children*. If they're equally as enhanced as Lux, they can't mentally be older than five or six. What possible use could that witch..."

She stops herself short again, her imagination clearly taking over from there—and rendering shitty results. With a soft sob, she drops to her knees in order to now embrace the girl. But she doesn't surrender the stare she's locked with mine. Heartache etches little waves into her forehead. *Fuck.* More than ever before, I yearn to scoop her up, along with the twins and Lux, and cast a spell to banish every shred of their collective despair.

Since I can't do that, I spear Aliz with a pleading stare. "What do you know, damn it?" And let my shoulders fall, gracing her with visible respect. "*Please.* If you *do* know anything..."

I trail off as Aliz adjusts her shoulders, hitching them back as if she's just issued an inner decree to do so. "The girls' names," she suggests with steady calm. "They are unique, yes?"

"One way of putting it," I reply.

"And most people call children names that they would have the child inspire in the world..."

"Unless that person is a bitch who's wired opposite from the rest of us," Emma spits.

Aliz dips her head at a practiced angle. "And she has

created two life forms for the purpose of *attracting* those energies instead."

"Attracting them?" I counter. I unfurl my fist to issue the contest with an upturned palm. "What the hell are you saying? That Ira and Miseria were conceived to be *magnets* for negative energies?"

Emma rises with careful intent. "Which would make them damn valuable to a woman searching for miserable, angry human beings."

"The most vulnerable ones of the race." Before I'm finished, I know every word to be true. Agonizing but true. "Who she's been screening, selecting, and then using her portal abilities to whisk down here..."

"Where she puts them in a room with the girls, who have been ordered to act like selective emotional vacuums." Aliz looks both relieved and sickened to be finally putting this shit into words. I feel lousy for making her do it, but I'm sure as hell not going to stop her. "They then extract all the psychic garbage of each recruit," she goes on. "Miseria for violence, anger, rage, frustration, and pain. Ira for sadness, loneliness, depression, anxiety, and grief."

Emma erupts with a pain-filled choke. "So they all become blissful blank slates for Faline's subliminal programming," she concludes, visibly shaking from head to toe. "And then they're returned back to the real world as shells of who they once were."

She's yearning to add one more part of that. Only three words' worth—but possessing more intent than the simple trio of syllables. Though she holds them back behind her pressed lips, I already see every drop of their anguish in the turquoise lakes of her eyes.

Like my mother.

For a long moment, I'm speechless. Motionless. Furious. Even when my limbs function again, I can't decide whether to add my roar to the girls' grief or drive my fists into the nearest wall. Eventually, I realize the futility of both. Indulging the former will rocket the twins' stress. Giving into the latter may bury us all alive. Most importantly, goddamnit, I'm the fucking "superhero" here. That means moving beyond my tears, my screams, my punches, my selfishness. It means refusing to dwell in my own hell at Faline's hands.

It means being more.

And in this exact moment, it means sinking to my knees.

To pull a frightened little girl into the firm fortitude of my embrace.

To murmur into her sweet, shiny curls, "Oh, little *mija*. No wonder you're shrieking for your ever-loving life."

Because her life has had everything in it but love.

Fuck.

Fuck.

Fuck.

I can't think of any words beyond that. Once more, Emma rescues me with the syllables I can barely comprehend, let alone form.

"Emotional vacuum cleaners," she grates. "Soaking up the world's sadness and rage because one bitch couldn't call a therapist and deal with hers."

I shoot my stare back up at Aliz, funneling my fury into my eyes instead of my voice. "What happens if they refuse?"

The woman's stance becomes a steel rod. For the first time, I witness a huge tear plummet down her cheek. "They do not refuse."

Now Emma's clearly the one with the comprehension difficulties. She's my gorgeous avenging angel, igniting like the sun in this world so far away from it while rising to a high kneel. One of her arms remains around Miseria; she drops the other into a fiery fist. "*Ever?*" she charges.

Aliz isn't fazed by her light show. "They. Do. Not. Refuse," the woman repeats, bringing the mettle of every monarch in history behind each word. Despite her emotion, the woman's volume doesn't lift above a throaty grit. She saves the truth of her feeling for the depths of her gaze, her irises ablaze with laser-force intensity—suddenly and solely aimed at me. "Just as none of us do in here. You already know that, Reece Richards."

My brain goes black.

My senses go numb.

My arms fall limp.

I'm conscious only of letting Lux yank Ira away from me because even he knows Dada's circuits have just been fried into the realm of beyond-fucked-up.

But in the same moment, I force my senses to weld back together—before blasting them back into the middle of the war zone. A battlefield I've been searching so long for. Built a whole command center to find. Pushed my team to their limits, over and over and over again, in a relentless push to locate.

On the other side of the world.

I lurch back up to my feet. Stumble forward, scanning Aliz's face for a shred of insecurity or dubiety. She's as certain about her words as if telling me the earth is round. No, worse. She's telling me the earth is round, and now I've got to tell the heathens about it.

I've got to be the fucking hero.

But I'm no goddamned hero.

Not right now.

Will I ever be again?

Was I ever to begin with?

In this moment, I can't comprehend those answers. It's a dark, lonely hell to simply remember who I am. *Who* I am, not *what*. Not the creature I became after Alpha Two was born. Not the unthinking specimen they turned me into. Because thinking made all of it too real. Because feeling made all of it too vivid.

Because resisting made all of it hell.

They do not refuse. Just as none of us do. But you already know that...

"Jesus." It tumbles from my barely moving lips. They're still practically numb, reacting to the match of horror that's touched off the poisoned awareness coursing through my blood. "I— I don't...I *can't*..."

But I have to.

No, my heart and soul blast back.

Proof. I need fucking proof!

I don't bother asking Aliz for it. I know she already sees the denial across my features and is ready with a smooth swivel as I storm past her, heading for the locked white door in the wall behind her.

But for all the speed of my charge, I'm a brick of paralyzed fear once I brace myself before the doorway. The intensity of my grip burns black scars into the tempered steel frame. I'm so goddamn freaked, my muscles bunch and push against the shoulders of my jacket.

I drop my head. I beg the Almighty and any of his celestial pals to lend me strength. It helps, but only a little. I can't stand how familiar this is. Too familiar. I can't count how many times I've seen doorways just like this, only from a much different point of view.

Because I was always looking at them from waist height.

Because I was being wheeled through them on a rolling lab table.

Right past the bright buttons and blinking lights of security keypads—like the one I short out now, using a single pulse from the middle of my right hand.

The heavy slab disappears into its thick slot in the wall. Steel scrapes steel, and the sound rips into my senses like starving lions tearing open a gazelle. I keep my head dipped, certain I'm about to watch my entrails spill all over the glaring tile, but it still only feels like my intestines are being dragged from me like a skein of human knitting yarn.

Human.

If that's what I am anymore.

As I order my feelings back and away, separating them from the horror of the memories.

As I command the rest of my senses to shut down, giving raw instinct its freedom to take over all of me.

Bracing for the impact of what I see.

Steeling for the realization of every disgusting detail.

The monitors. The electrodes. The test tubes. The video cameras.

The steel surface at the center of it all, awaiting a new subject. A new *mutant.*

The angled corner, just behind the headrest of that slab, where she used to stand. The voice without a body. The mistress without mercy. The bitch without a soul.

The corner where I could never see her...

Because the room is shaped like a hexagon.

Another cell in a huge hive of torture.

A massive center of experimentation.

A reality I impel myself to accept, no matter how shrill the screams in my senses, the gashes in my belly, or the protests in my soul. The truth I thrust to my lips, despite their stinging poison.

Back to the starting blocks.

All the fucking way back.

"The Source." I whip a burning glare back up to Aliz. "This is...we're inside...the Source?"

Her awful stretch of silence is all the answer I need.

All the truth I can take.

Before I wheel back around, slamming both hands against the lab cell wall. Searing ten holes into the tiles before letting my head fall again—and losing everything from my stomach all over the floor.

CHAPTER FOUR

EMMA

Reece can't speak.

And neither can I.

A million words barrage my stunned mind and shocked soul. None of them sound close to right when I fight to form them on my lips.

And so, the pall of our silence. The air around us clinging and weighing like fog over a graveyard. The echoes of our steps clinical and cold, like prisoners being delivered to a dungeon. And my husband, now looking like a blue-skinned zombie. No life in his gaze but the dark desire for just one normal breath. The desperate, shuffling quest for a meaning in his survival. A nobility in his endurance.

A way back to his humanity.

But he's shut that switch off. Purposely plunged himself back into the darkness. One more time. One *last* time.

The dive he has to take.

The journey he *must* make.

I see that now. I *know* it. I feel it in every arc of energy that still passes between us, fusing his faint fire to mine through the conduit of our joined hands. Though his light is dim, it's still there. Still calling out to me as it did the night we first met. Still pleading with me to stay by his side, no matter what kind of a glowing freak he appears to be on the outside.

I'm not going anywhere.

I send the message to him with every step we take down the hall, despite the Tesla coils my neck hairs have become during our progress through the warren of underground passages. We ordered Aliz to accompany our X-15 of a son back up the shaft with Mis and Ira, along with Reece's terse voice memo on his phone for Sawyer's ears only. Aliz ensured us she'd do just that, showing off her own electric parkour skills.

Fortunately, Reece seemed to believe her. Sometime between vomiting in the lab room and shutting his brain off, he'd explained that he didn't yet trust this revelation to anyone but Sawyer. A valid point, since we've already passed three partial cave-ins along the halls. Aliz alluded to more, including the massive tunnel collapse that trapped her and the twins in a remote section of the complex, with only a couple of video monitors to disable. By now, we can safely assume the Consortium never ascribed to the wisdom of building all of this to proper earthquake codes. Even if the jolt wasn't caused by a real quake—a truth we may never know at this point—the effect on these rudimentary tunnels has been the same.

Too bad, so sad. Your loss, assholes.

Or so we're furiously hoping.

In truth, we have no damn idea of what we're heading into. I try telling myself this is no different than the insanity of sneaking into the Consortium's Rancho Palos Verdes stronghold, taking nothing with me but Angelique, Wade, and a lot of guts. I also try justifying that this is no different than what I did a year before that, facing off to Angie in the courtyard of my apartment, back when *she* was still a Consortium henchwoman. No-go on either. This party is different, and it's not just about the sparse décor in this part of the underworld. Maybe that's why Reece is taking the journey at his zombie-plod pace instead of an urgent sprint.

But I don't think so.

I think it's about everything I'm not seeing here.

And everything he is.

The mists of his nightmares. The ghosts of his torturers. The pain of his prison.

The essence of what transformed him.

I hope he'll accept at least that affirmation, but no-go on that as well.

There are some nights the brightest lights aren't meant to penetrate. Memories the strongest love can't totally erase. And from the moment I learned my hunk-boss-lover was really the electric hero of my city, I knew I had to accept such darkness as part of him. I had to embrace his shadows along with his radiance, his black alleys along with his neon boulevards.

And the walks through underground hells like this— bearing dim but high torches of hope.

A hope that my brave, beautiful superhero actually summons the strength to vocalize...

As we stop in front of a wall made out of fresh-fallen earth, broken chunks of tile, and giant slabs of concrete.

"Holy God. If I can save just one of them..."

He trails off, exposing the hitch of his own air, lost to the inexpressible emotions that take over his face. But that's okay. I already have the extra match for his torch.

"You mean if *we* can save just one?"

He tightens his grip against mine. His touch zaps me with sharper force. A billion fireflies zoom up my arm, across my chest, and all the way down the other arm. It's nothing different than the effect the man has had on me so many other times, but it's also wholly new. There's extra depth to his electricity. A harmony to his thrumming melody. A song his heart has never played for me before—because, I sense, he's never played it for himself before.

"Do you know how much I love you?" The music resonates in every syllable of his declaration. It fills my soul with an answering song as his dazzling silver stare takes me in. His thick dark hair tumbles against his rugged temples and jawline, turning him into an electric rogue. I flash back a lady pirate grin, indulging just one moment of obnoxious bliss. The man's most slay-worthy gorgeous glance of his entire *life*, and I'm the sole creature who gets to bask in it. Though I'll smell like a dirt clod the rest of my life, which may only be for another few minutes if this tunnel decides to go Armageddon on us, I'll die with a shit-eating smirk on my face.

"With lines like that, mister, you have two choices." I practically punch myself for actually issuing the interruption here, but at this point, eye-fucking each other won't get us anywhere.

"And what exactly might those be, Mistress Flare?" he drawls.

"Fire up my lips, or fire up your diggin' lasers."

The hunk has the nerve to ponder the question for another couple of seconds, ensuring my dying smirk will now be a bit wider, before turning and extending his fingers. He flicks them as if tossing off water, which serves as the On switch for those ten bright new blazes. Another unforgettable moment only my eyes will be treated to. Never has the man's power been more awestriking. Even his fingernails are part of the effort, their edges outlined as if Lux went at him with a silver metallic Sharpie.

Silver metal—that soon turns gold.

Reflecting the sun-colored energy that I summon to my hands.

His gorgeous eyes are a similar mix as the man squares his shoulders, braces his stance, and looks to me for one last, love-filled second. We grab the treat selfishly, acknowledging that it really might be our last.

As in, ever.

But if this is how I'm going to go, this is how I want it to be. Buried beneath the city that I love, next to the man gifted to me by the wisdom of the cosmos, knowing that my son is safe, never to be exposed to any knowledge of this dark world. He was named after light, and I'm determined he'll always live in it.

As the truth of my heart fills every pore of my body, I affirm it all with one tick of a confident nod toward my surreal hotness of a husband. "Ready to crush this dogpile, Zeus Man?"

Reece lifts a lopsided grin. "When you are, goddess sun at the center of my world."

REECE

An hour later, I'm truly ready to crown her as that actual goddess.

The incredible creature who made it possible for me to be standing here, stunned beyond speech by the scene before me.

Because this experience is beyond what I ever thought to have. To accomplish. To finally realize. For so long, it's been my fucking Purgatory, Pandæmonium, and Diyu. A hell I must have imagined, living on only in the reality of my darkest nightmares. A place supported on paper only, despite Tyce's and Angie's attestations to the opposite. In the back of my mind, I've written off both their accounts as matches to mine. Ramblings from minds that were stripped of the ability to reason or remember—though through every minute of every hour of every day I was in here, I vowed to never forget.

I swore I'd come back for them.

I dreamed of saving them all.

But began to think it was a doomed dream.

But now, I'm living that dream.

Surrounded by more and more of them by the minute, working my hardest to embrace each one as they stumble free from their newly opened cells, all of them dressed in what look like oversize white potato sacks, steel hoof-like hand covers, and nothing else. On the upper back of each "gown," there's a classification label in a garish military font.

Alpha 37

Omega 142

Omega 8

Alpha 210

Every time I see the red ink, my memories rupture open and my throat closes shut. Images, buried beneath the insanity of my first hours of freedom, assault me from all sides. Clear as if it's happening again, I recall the first sight I ever had of my own designation: *Alpha Two*. I'd run far enough away to be certain I wouldn't get caught and then had finally given in to the need to get the sack off my body as fast as I could. Then the harsher need to burn every thread of the fucking thing. I'd shot a furious lightning jolt into the thing, turning it into a massive ball of blue flames.

Hit with every instant of the moment now, I'm stunned I suppressed it. It had been the first moment I'd ever utilized my powers for me instead of the Consortium.

For me instead of *her*.

But the memory doesn't stop there.

After frying my clothes, I'd been as naked as the day God made me. I hadn't cared. I'd sprinted through the Barcelona suburbs until finding some clothes in an unlocked car and made a mental note to send the family a new car for their loss. Another first that night: consciously putting others before myself.

It was the beginning of a lot of changes for me.

But as the flashbacks of that night keep filling back into my mind, there's also a glaring commonality to them. One detail I don't try to deny.

I was in Barcelona that night. And I'm pretty damn sure I didn't leave LA and then zip across the continental US and a major ocean to get there.

Recognitions that would have me shitting a pile of purple Ding Dongs right now if I didn't already have a damn strong theory about how that happened.

But that's bullshit for the back burner for the moment. Number-one priority: ensuring every single person here that they'll never have to return to their cell again. I fight to vow it to them with the force of my embrace, the commiseration in my eyes, the confidence in my steps. But despite my efforts, they're not biting on the cookie of hope yet. I don't begrudge them. If I were in their skin, being dangled the big Chips Ahoy of freedom, I'd also be looking at the baker with a shitload of suspicion.

Everyone does perk up as Emma takes her second round through the complex, making sure the digital lock box on every cell is turned into a blob of melted wall art. But they're all back to open cynicism the moment I dig into a supply closet, finding boxes of freshly laundered lab scrubs. I don't push anyone to accept them. It's all *I* can do not to behold the uniforms and liken them to Gestapo greens. Not a fair comparison by half, but as I start my mental action plan list for reacclimating everyone back to the world in which they're now free, the first item is contracting a topnotch post-trauma recovery team. Every single soul in this room has survived a fucking war.

The trauma counselors are already on top of a rapidly growing list, including my commitment that they'll all be housed at the Brocade until we help them find new homes of their own or paths back to the loved ones they knew. It's an amazing feeling—no, a miraculous recognition—to realize I won't be tackling the tasks alone. I grasp the recognition with all the certainty in my soul from the moment Emma reenters the main gathering area—an intake waiting room, from the looks of it—with stress stamped on her face but devotion shimmering in her eyes. Doesn't take me more than two seconds to read what she's telling me.

Team Richards, baby. All the way.

God in heaven, I love the fuck out of this woman.

I fight the craving to flash-pulse my way across the room and kiss her until her knees buckle. Damn, damn, *damn*, I don't deserve her. Clearly this experience has extracted its pound of emotional flesh from her, and I ache deeply about that. Yeah, despite knowing she would've speared my balls and chomped them for breakfast had I ordered her back up the elevator shaft with the others. But at least she'd still be spared from this tableau of suffering—a shock she's valiantly trying to play down but isn't succeeding at very well. In many ways, it's not fair. A huge part of me was ready for my hellhole homecoming from the second we started clearing the cave-in, but she's only been prepared with the few details I've recounted about this place—and I held back a lot of them on purpose.

A confession that leads to deeper truths.

Not ones I'm proud of admitting.

I kept glossing over the grittier details for Emma because secretly, I never thought she'd have to go through this. Because *very* secretly, I was letting my own cookie of hope crumble between my fingers. As month after month dragged by without any new intel about the Source's location, even with the Team Bolt command center churning nonstop, I'd started bracing my spirit for defeat. Telling my soul to accept that I got away and no one else did. Ordering my heart to honor the victims of the Consortium's torture by making at least one city safer and happier to live in.

I'd been preparing to let Faline win this round.

But this time, in this improbable place and this incredible moment, we've beaten the bitch. Soundly.

A triumph I share with my woman via the lingering look we lavish on each other.

Just before there's a commotion near the mound of quake rubble.

And the only person I want to share the victory with more than Emma comes tromping in like an amalgam of Chuck Norris, Chris Hemsworth, and Han Solo's long-lost blond bastard.

"Ballsy fucker." I chuckle while striding through the crowd, which has parted like a petrified Red Sea. Instead of attempting a litany of reassurance, I show them Foley's worth by hauling him into a hearty hug, not holding back on the fierce back slaps.

"Said the crazy-ass pot to the ballsy kettle?" But only Foley's words are flippant. There's a fragility to his aura as he looks around, putting on the same brave show as Emma but barely succeeding at keeping his shit tight. "Jesus crapped a fucking load," he finally rumbles. "This never gets easier."

"It's supposed to?"

"Valid point, lightning king." At once, to my relief, his profile tautens. The Chuck Norris chunk of him wins out for composure. "I just...don't. Fucking. Understand. It's here. *Right* here. How could we have been so off this whole time?"

"Because I told you all that I escaped and finally made it back to Barcelona on foot?"

A gaunt but striking woman, with a bald skull similar to Angelique's, inches toward us. "And I was taken from a modeling shoot near Milan."

A man—no, a *boy*, probably not out of his teens—steps from behind her. His gaze is gilded brilliance. His teeth are gleaming squares. His spun-gold hair stands up vertically from his head. "I was seduced at a rock music festival near Denver. My band had just opened for Arctic Monkeys."

Others come forward, adding their testaments to the story.

"...on vacation in Greece..."

"...in a field near Stonehenge..."

"...after seeing *Hamilton* in Puerto Rico..."

"...during BUDS training in Virginia..."

The Consortium hasn't missed a corner of the globe or a segment of society. Big and small, young and old, every color and ethnicity there is...and yet none of it matters. We're the mutant version of the Small World ride—except without the laughter, hopes, and smiles parts.

"So how is this all possible?" But there *is* a golden sun, brilliant and beautiful, tucking herself against my side after giving Foley a ferocious hug. "I'm assuming Faline doesn't have an actual X-15 conveniently tucked in her back pocket?"

"Which still wouldn't explain how I got lucky enough to make it out of here and immediately found myself in Sarrià-Sant Gervasi."

"Bolt-amatic makes a sound point," Foley comments.

There's a fresh frisson of tension through Emma's body. "Unless the witch mastered her portal powers much longer ago than we thought."

Foley narrows his gaze, shifting to government ghost-man mode. "Or someone else had them locked and loaded first."

I crunch my scowl tighter. "A partner? But who? And how could all our research have missed that?"

"Not a partner." The objection is inserted by the young musician with the gold porcupine hair. His gaze matches the radiance of his teeth as he steps over, despite at least three of the others attempting to hold him back. "A slave."

Just when I thought my gut couldn't be a worse ball of bile. "Who's still under her thumb? Now?" I almost issue it all as basic statements instead of questions. The answers are already evident in the fear-sharpened stares across the throng. I acknowledge them with an understanding nod, but it's truncated. Focusing on my rock-star friend, who seems to be the only one eager to hand over a new plate of Faline's evil shit pile, is more important at the moment. "And is he...down *here* somewhere?"

So much for the shit pile. The stuff starts flying, in the form of screams and roars and outcries, as soon as my query leaves my lips.

"Don't answer him, Alpha Eighty!"

"Don't you dare show it to him, you showy asswipe!"

"If you do it, we'll all pay!"

Alpha Eighty whirls around, throwing his arms wide. Webs of fiery energy spread up and down his eye-poppingly ripped arms. "And none of you think we won't be *paying* already?"

"Nobody's paying for anything." I twist so much vehemence into the command, I'm at risk of becoming the gruesome villain on this soundtrack. But the savagery serves its purpose. I've wrangled their attention again. "I swear this to you on my own son's life," I bellow. "*Nobody's* paying Faline Garand a drop more of their blood, their body, or their sanity, today or any other day. I'm not leaving this hell hive until every last one of you has—meaning if that harpy is stupid enough to return and stick around, her carotid is going to have a fun little visit from my stormy squad." I raise my right hand as if there's a baseball in it, which allows the bright-blue arcs in my tips to cavort with each other. "Snap crackle pop, motherfuckers."

I swear the walls tremble from the collective blare of triumph that answers me. I turn toward Alpha Eighty, who motions for me to follow him down a long side hall that stops at a dead end.

Or does it?

Eighty swipes his hand across part of the wall to his left, and I'm not as surprised as I should be when the panel before us comes alive, changing into the outline of an electric travel portal. The inside of the large square consists of nothing but mingling mists. I assume it's because there's no destination given for the portal right now.

For a long pause, I stand and stupidly stare at the thing. And I mean *stupid*. It's wasted time we don't have. *Tick tock*. My blood beats out the message, driven by an instinct that says our Faline-free time might be waning fast.

"Welcome to the Consortium's birthing channel." Eighty chuffs at his grim humor. "The bitch that pushed us all out into this new life."

I absorb his statement with a tightening jaw—matched by the tension in my stomach. "Pushed...out," I finally echo. "But there's no way to...go back *in*? To leap back thr—"

"You don't think any of us has tried?" He chuffs. "Especially after the news got out that it was even *here*."

"Which was when?"

"The day after you escaped through it."

As my brain shoots to the inevitable conclusion from that, my middle becomes a morass of pain. "And then she made it impossible for anyone else to do the same."

"Bitch locked down that shit faster than Jimi Hendrix nailing 'Machine Gun' at the Fillmore."

"Points for the metaphor," I growl, feeling like a million bucks when he grins gratefully for the praise. But neither of us dwells on the moment. I need the whole truth here, and he needs to know that not every compliment will end up in physical torture. "So what happens if someone tries it now?"

His smile fades. "They're transported directly to the retraining center."

So much for the million bucks. From the two pennies left in my spirit, I manage to mutter, "*Fuck*."

"Wh-What's the retraining center?" Emma's mumble is barely audible.

"No idea." My answer is sincere. "But I'm damn sure I don't want to know." In the world of Faline Garand, *retraining* could mean everything from running laps on a treadmill to electric worms feasting on one's brain for a day. Or a week. Or a month. And after that, getting assigned "missions" like morphing into a superhero's brother...or taking down half the LA skyline.

I toss back my head and squeeze my eyes closed, allowing my grief for Tyce and Kane—and Mitch and Dad, and even Laurel Crist, as we once knew her—to spear every cell of my senses for one terrible torch of a moment.

But only one.

Tick tock.

I realign my posture, but accomplishing the same for my thoughts isn't as simple. "Fuck," I grate once more. "*Fuck.*" And then jerk Eighty in close, using him as proxy for every soul in the unnerved throng down the hall. "I'm sorry," I mutter fervently. "I'm so damn sorry."

The guy shoves me away as if I'm trying to take responsibility for gravity. "You're also fucking weird. What the hell, man?"

I stare back as if he's the inventor of gravity. "If I hadn't broken out, everyone's lives would've been a hell of a lot easier."

He barks out a laugh. A loud one. "You really believe that, don't you?" Then rolls his gaze at the ceiling, which brings back a bit of my smile. The kid hasn't said goodbye to *all* of his teenage quirks. "You do know that if you hadn't broken out, we wouldn't be standing here having *this* conversation?"

I whoosh out a full breath, despite the anvil of guilt still parked on my chest. "Okay, slick. You get the point on that one too."

"Damn straight I do." He cocks his head, taking his own turn at channeling General Solo. "But I'm even sharper after a beer and a plate of wings." But his gaze widens as if he's blastered his foot off. "Shit. Please tell me wings are still a thing."

"In any flavor you want." I clap him on the shoulder. "As soon as we get every one of you out of here."

His face lights up as if I've told him there's a side of sexy cheerleaders with those wings—only to dive back into pessimism the very next second. "Just tell me your plan doesn't include hotwiring this fucker." He jabs a thumb over at the portal. "Because if this activation hasn't already revved Faline's broomstick, messing with the default settings will absolutely fire those cylinders."

I add my grip to his other shoulder. "Wave buh-bye to the spawn subway now, buddy. You're never going to look at it again."

Eighty hums with meaning before uttering, "Oh, I've said all I fucking want to that thing."

I don't make him elaborate on that. He doesn't have to. Something tells me the kid is well acquainted with the portal to nowhere, and not just from one attempt to clear it. "Good," I say instead. "Because I'll need a third lieutenant to make this exodus happen as fast as possible."

"Then I'm your solid."

Beneath my hands, the boulders of his shoulders emulate his determined expression.

"Out-fucking-standing." I issue my approval with my tighter grip, though end the move with half a wince. "But there *is* just one thing..."

"Huh?" Eighty retorts. "What?"

I turn the wince into a steady stare so he knows how serious I am now. "What's your *real* name, Eighty?"

He grins. It's radiant. The light spreads across his entire face. "It's Kainalu," he offers. "I'm an islander. Well, I was." An uncomfortable shrug. "But my friends call me Kain." And another. "You can just do that if you want."

"Yeah, that's cool."

No, it's way fucking better. It's like a message in the sky from the universe itself—and the big hulk up there somewhere, joining Mitch, Tyce, and Dad to look out for me in all these amazing ways. I flash a quick glance upward, giving the original Kane my heartfelt gratitude, before focusing on the one I can actually save this time.

"Hey, Kain?"

"Yeah?"

I lock down his stare with an extra strong dose of conviction. "They're going to be calling you that again. *Very* soon."

I finish it with a full smile of my own, which explodes into a dazzled laugh as the kid switches up his light yet again. No. He's *turning* it up. His eyes turn into gold and white rocket flames that rise through his irises and then stretch up over his forehead. Once the energy reaches his hairline, every stiff strand on his head ignites into a sight similar to a nuclear-charged fiber optic, transforming his whole head into a bursting firework. I don't share the comparison with him, though. Something tells me he'd prefer something like "charging bull of brightness" instead of "pretty pretty boom boom."

But even if the guy insisted I call him Lord High Ruler of Light, I wouldn't care. Nothing can change the fulfillment he deals to my spirit with his victorious haka pose and his I'm-all-in grin. "Ready to do this when you are, Lightning Man."

"Lead the way, Hundred-Watt Hedgehog."

His gaze narrows. "You know if you weren't saving my ass, I might have to kick yours, right?"

I snicker softly. "Yeah, man. I know."

"Then you also know that I'm probably going to steal that as the name of my new band, right?"

The elation of my heart scoots aside a little, welcoming the completion of my soul.

"I'm counting on it, kid."

CHAPTER FIVE

EMMA

"Uno!"

Lux's exuberant shout is followed by giggles in stereo. The sound has Lydia, Angie, and me trading huge grins and soft chuckles over our lunch plates, ordered from Lux's favorite Italian place up in Hollywood. Normally, we all go and enjoy a meal inside the restaurant, where Lux joins the waiters in singing Italian love ballads, but it's been only three days since Mis and Ira got their first-ever exposure to the world beyond their underground prison, and it's been clear we'll have to go slow in their introduction to everything outside the strictures of Faline Garand's rule.

Three days.

In which I feel like I've been to hell and back three dozen times.

Every time, one of those precious girls returns there too—in the horrors that have been fused into their minds and spirits.

Some of the incidents, we can predict—nightmares at two a.m., screams from passing sirens, duck-and-cover drills when we turn on the TV—but others are surprises that go from amusing to wrenching. I'll forever treasure the experience of singing them their first lullaby, despite how my gut churned as they clutched their stuffed animals like refugees with life rings. And it'll be tough to forget the trial-and-error process of discovering foods that won't send them into agonized screams. In the end, I distilled the freak-out factor to two main points. If it's in a bowl and remotely resembles gruel, it's on the blacklist. So popsicles, yes. But ice cream? A hard no. Same with french fries versus potato soup and a plate of pasta versus a bowl of SpaghettiOs.

And that leads back to the joy of now. Lux never met a plate of Miceli's rigatoni that he didn't like, proved by his hands-on approach with the stuff in this whimsical moment. I look down the dining table in time to watch my imp of a kid raising all ten fingers, dripping with sauce-drenched tubes, crooning a self-composed song about his "pasta paintbrushes."

As Ira and Mis laugh harder, clapping at his antics, I park my head in a hand and quietly groan. "You're *not* helping," I chastise Lydia and Angie, who join them. Lux, cranked by all the motivation, swirls his hands in and out of each other. "Great," I grumble. "He's got choreography now."

"Oh, *c'mon*," my sister protests. "He's also rhyming 'orangey tubes' with 'dorky poop.'"

At least Angie makes an effort to quell her roll, sticking to mildly quirking lips. "I am not sure that helps your cause," she reproves Lydia, only to be rewarded by a massive roll of my sister's eyes.

"And this is why poetry is dying," Lydia mutters.

Just as Angie looks ready to go with the pro-poetry argument like the good Frenchwoman she is, my phone buzzes incessantly atop the table. Lydia glances over since she's closer than me—and unleashes an instant groan. "Our maternal unit beckons."

Some occasions are really perfect for my Debbie Downer

wince. "Imagine *that*," I grumble.

'Dia scoops up my device. She knows as well as I do that a call from Mom, especially these days, is like a visit from the Borg. Resistance is futile. Still, she suggests, "Let it drop?"

The second I'm going to say yes, even knowing the damn thing will start with the Laurel Crist buzz barrage in less than a minute, the private elevator dings and there are hormone-raising bootsteps on the landing. I smile and reach for the phone. My knight in tight black leather is back with the perfect timing that ensures I'm in love with him now more than ever.

"Mother." I abandon the tender comfort I was using on Mis for what I call my "front desk" voice. I'm warm but distant, brisk but friendly. "To what do I owe this huge pleasure?" At the same time, I pray it's not because of anything she saw on the news about our adventures at the Biltmore. Granted, it's been nearly seventy-two hours since Lux flew the twins back up the elevator shaft, and we've been steadily resting easier about the possibility of any secret video coverage getting leaked, but technology is a crazy mistress. She loves getting in a good bite on the ass when one least expects it.

"Hmmm. Isn't *that* an interesting choice of words."

Her terse tone sets me on edge and soars me with elation at the same time. She's almost—*almost*—irritable enough to be the nitpicky socialite I once knew and loved as my mother. And while I'll always love her, I do *not* know her anymore. Even in this second, which will probably turn out to be a sham of normalcy again. Because any second now...

"Don't get me wrong, dear. Your words are *always* wonderful. And beyond interesting."

Everything will return to *this*.

Stepford wifey, Laurel Crist style. Created, directed, and

produced by Faline Garand.

"But...?" I supply the lead-in despite already knowing the follow-through. Seriously, I wish I was hedging bets on it with a Vegas bookie.

"*But* I haven't seen my grandson in three months, Emmalina."

I pull in a calming breath. Or at least what I attempt it to be. "Well..."

As if on cue, Lux's happy shout fills the penthouse. "Dadaaaaa!"

"Oh, my word. Now would you listen to *that*?"

"I don't have much choice about the matter." I fight to keep my voice loving but level, despite the tearful crack in hers. "Speaking of choices, Mom—"

"Oh, goodness!" she butts in as Ira and Mis join in with their elated shrieks—using the same name for Reece in their greetings. Once we got the girls settled in here, we were too tired to create appropriate names for ourselves in their eyes. Our proper assignations felt too casual; "Mr. and Mrs. Richards" was out from the start. "You've got quite the pitter-patter of little feet there, missy," she prods. "Has Troop Richards grown *again* without Grandmee Laurel getting invited to the fun?"

I allow myself a facepalm. It gives me the chance to swing the phone away from my mouth and then mutter, "Things were so much easier when you had the steel pole jammed up your ass, Mother."

"Excuse me?" A frothy sigh. Then an annoying singsong. "Speak up, buttercup; it's the way to have your say!"

Thankfully, she doesn't continue with the dorky song she once sang to 'Dia and me, often on a daily basis. We eventually were cured of our mumbling tendencies from the simple desire not to hear the song anymore. Too bad the ditty wasn't part of her visit to the Faline Garand Mental Realignment Spa. I wonder how much loopier Ira and Mis would be if it was.

"Luke is having a playdate," I declare directly into the phone. Yes, my mother is getting the same pseudonym for the offspring that we invented for the press and public's use— because no, I don't trust her as far as I can throw her with the truth.

Correction: I don't trust what parts of her mind Faline may have access to now.

So much we still don't know, even now.

So much we still can't see, though now we've seen so much.

So much we can't control, despite how much we've now destroyed.

I confirm that truth as my husband completes his affectionate greetings to the three children—a ritual that apparently consists of them all hanging on him like scree'ing monkeys—and casts a long look across the room at me. At once, I'm dazzled. *His electric silver eyes.* And liquefied. *His beautiful, bold smirk.* And ohhhh yes...beyond turned-on. *His roaming study of my whole body...igniting every surface he lays eyes on...*

"Uh...yeah," I manage to stammer, responding to whatever memory from Lydia and my playdates that she's dredged up.

"Excuse me?" Mom flings back. "Helllooo, earth to Emmalina Paisley."

"Huh?"

She laughs. "Darling, are you listening to me?"

"Of course. Yes...of *course.*" The words are so full of additional meaning, responding to so much of the sensual promise in Reece's sultry stare that they hop from double to triple definition. At least I hope so. Depends on where the man's drawing the line between his silent *I need to talk to you alone* and *I want to fuck you mindless.*

"That's still not an answer to my question," Mom mutters.

"Sorry," I return. "Reece just got in, and now the kids want to go to Two-Bit Circus."

"*Where?*"

"An arcade here in town." I deck myself inwardly for not remembering to simplify the explanation. No way am I going to try explaining VR gaming, escape rooms, laser tag, and a digital midway to her right now. "Look, I have to go." Not a lie. My poor husband is still trying to navigate across the living room as a walking monkey mount. "We'll talk soon about a visit for you and Lux."

"Who's Lux?"

"Errrmmm—" I wince, enduring the same look from Reece, as I swiftly backpedal from the slip. "Just a funny nickname he likes. But we'll set a date for you and Dad to come up and see him soon." With supervision. Lots of it. As in, every molecule of the air being monitored by Angie, Wade, Sawyer, Fershan, Reece, and me.

"Thank you, honey. I love you so much." Mom's voice is back to a vocal sachet, soaked in gratitude and love. While my nose scrunches because I can practically smell the *odeur* on *this* air, I also want to sob because of the lie I've just perpetuated—and will *keep* telling until I'm one-hundred-percent positive she's not being swept by the Faline Garand brain bots anymore.

"I love you too. I really gotta go."

I end the call with another pinched expression. *Damn it.* I can't stand that it has to be this way. I'm throwing her the grandma version of bread scraps, a raw deal she doesn't deserve—but that isn't changing anytime soon. A chunk of her mind has been hacked off and carved out by Faline. I desperately wish the situation were different, but it's not.

God.

I wish *a lot* of situations were different right now—but they're not.

I set down my phone and meet Reece under the archway between the living and dining rooms, I feel like Cruella de Flare for coming at him with all my leftover tension from the call with Mom—especially right now. If we were living in the Team Bolt video game, his fuel, water, and life force bubbles would all be near the ominous red empty level. His leathers are scuffed and dusty, his face is smudged and scruffy, and his gaze is dull and tired as pewter.

Yet the man is still grinning like a mindless dork.

The expression intensifies as he trudges closer, still dripping with kids, and scoops a hand around the back of my neck. And kisses me like he really, *really* means it.

From the second I mewl in ecstasy and he adds tongue to the clinch, Lux and the girls jump free as if their climbing tree is crawling with fire ants. Just fine by me. The man's glorious mouth and tantalizing tongue send a million of those figurative critters across my skin and through my body. I'm feverish from the fire skittering up and down my limbs and then diving into the flood of my bloodstream until it all funnels into the pressurized triangle at my aching core. Oh *shit*, even now. In front of the children and my sister and—

"Perhaps you two should take that to a different room, *oui*?"

And Angie, becoming my sweater-and-leggings version

242

of a rescue knight extraordinaire, swinging her mottled dome around with a worldly smile on her cosmopolitan lips.

"*Go*," the woman urges, her gaze sparkling brighter. "You have not taken a moment for each other in three days."

"Mademoiselle LaSalle is *très* right," Lydia pipes in. "Besides, your phone is now officially commandeered, baby girl." She scoops the device off the table and slips it into the back pocket of her denim capris. "You won't see it again until after I hear screams or snores from the bedroom. Preferably both."

Reece unfurls a savoring growl. "Did I ever tell you you're my favorite sister-in-law?"

Lydia snorts. "Just go and spoil my sister rotten, would you? Preferably in horizontal positions."

"Deal." Reece extends his fist, making an explosion noise as 'Dia returns the bump. I give in to a fresh faceplant, rolling my eyes at them from between my sprawled fingers.

"Jesus wept," I mutter.

"No, baby." Reece grins while curling a hand around my waist and yanking me close. "Save the tears for what I'm about to do to you."

Lydia snorts. "I'm not sure whether to cheer or barf right now."

"Perhaps...neither?" Though Angie's cagey expression conveys her approval of the same sentiment.

"Excellent plan." My sister hooks an elbow through hers, guiding Angie back toward the kids. "Hey, Lux baby!" she calls. "How about we introduce Mis and Ira to the goodness of Twister?" She casts one last teasing glance over her shoulder at us while adding, "Because sometimes, you just can't have too much screaming in the house."

REECE

Lydia will probably give me shit for this later, but I don't care.

Once I have Emma behind closed doors and all to myself, all thoughts of getting her naked and mindless are shoved to my psyche's furthest corners. Truth be told, after the last twelve hours, a lot of me is naked and mindless already. I might still be covered in leather on the outside, but inside I've been stripped down and torn apart.

Over and over and over again.

With every step I had to take through that staggering maze of abandoned halls, darkened laboratories, and forlorn five-sided cells. The hive that was once my world. The prison in which I'd resigned myself to die.

The hell I forced myself to traverse again.

Every last goddamned step.

Facing the pain and rage and desolation for one last time.

And in a fucked-up but necessary way, welcoming them.

Walking those rooms again...standing there, flooded in the horror and brutality of the memories, brought me to the strangest but clearest perception.

I'll never fully leave that place. It's part of me now, etched into the walls of my psyche.

But it's not all of me.

Not anymore.

It's not even the biggest thing that ever changed me. It's insignificant compared to the impact of true love on my heart, the sea change of fatherhood to every cell of my soul.

Fatherhood.

The word alone stirs echoes inside my head.

Dada! Dada! Dada!

And yes...they're in triplicate. In those three distinct voices that are inextricably woven through me. Yes, already. Yes, after just three days. And no, I really don't think they're going to change to anything different.

All epiphanies I have yet to share with the woman standing next to me.

All purposeful omissions—for which I'm not proud but wouldn't change. I haven't shared them because I've needed to be sure. Have had to double-check my psyche, confirming all of this isn't just passing caprice fed by the adrenaline of finding the Source. Or worse, a bout of misplaced survivor's guilt—or my superhero complex needing its next nobility fix. More nobly, I can't deny the fathomless joy of seeing Lux with a mini tribe of his own kind.

To cut to the chase, the reasons go on and on. My list of explanations is longer than a catalog of Team Bolt fanfics, meaning I could dawdle forever and ruminate about the result or simply face the music and involve my wife in talking through our next steps in fate's newest twist for us. Not that it's going to be easy—but we've got to start somewhere.

And we'd better start now.

"Hey." I tug Emma's hand, urging her to follow me to the long ottoman that takes up the wall between our panorama window and the master bathroom. "Come here."

"*Here?*" The light tease in her voice matches the gold glints in her eyes. "You sure about that, Zeus Man? The bed might be nicer, considering you've been stomping around in a bunch of tunnels for nearly twelve hours."

"Which is why I want to talk first."

A crinkle of confusion takes over her forehead. "Who are you, and what have you done with my lust factory of a husband?"

I capture the hand she presses between *my* temples and then lower it to press my lips against the inside of her wrist. "Oh, don't worry, baby. All those gears are still cranking." I nuzzle her again, this time closing my eyes and inhaling deep, welcoming her honey and sunshine scent into my senses. With slow languor, I lick little circles around her delicious pulse point. "And believe me, they're ready to get me inside you, as deep as I possibly can go." I soak up the quickening of her heartrate and the rush of her gasp. "But we have to talk first."

As if my declaration is his cue, Lux's shout pierces through the walls. "Left hand green!"

Annnnd Twister has officially kicked off. Fitting imagery, matching the new contortion of my wife's features.

"I'm guessing you don't need me to clarify the category either," I murmur.

"Right hand yellow!"

More appropriate analogy, since Emma's fingers glow the same color as she tightens her hold against mine. "Yeah," she rasps. "You're right; I'm pretty sure we're on the same track for this. But first"—she stretches her free hand up, framing the corresponding side of my face with the sun-bright warmth of her touch—"tell me how you are. Tell me...what's happening."

She's castigating herself for the small pause. I already feel the tension of her self-recrimination. More than that, I read it in the tightness around her eyes and mouth. With my attention directed there already, I take her lips softly beneath my own, hoping she feels every part of my reassurance. It's okay that she can't say any more than that. It's also okay that she doesn't want to hear about every detail of what I've seen over the last twelve hours. The equipment I've helped destroy. The cells I've searched, retrieving anything that seemed like a personal keepsake from the refugees, all of whom are now comfortably checked into rooms throughout the tower below us. But most importantly, the items I've bagged that may contain the tiniest traces of human DNA. They're the first small step toward identifying everyone who's survived the Consortium's clutches.

But more exigently...identifying everyone who didn't.

"Well, her highness of the mad mole-hell scientists hasn't made any appearances yet," I offer as soon as we pull back a little—but just a little. For the last twelve hours, my world has been about nothing but fluorescent lighting and dark caverns. Now that I'm holding a sunbeam, I'm not about to fucking let her go. "And that's one for the gratitude column."

Though her eyes remain serious, Emma allows a small laugh loose. "The mad mole-hell scientists, hmmm? Do I get to guess who coined that one?"

"As long as you guess Sawyer." I smirk. She chuckles again. "But at least it made things a little more bearable."

Yeah, I've gone deliberately teenage nonchalance with the remark, calling on my inner sixteen-year-old asshole to help me skate through the moment. Okay, so "things" are now designated as a visit to my former holding cell and torture chamber instead of who I'll ask to prom, but my brain's melded the circumstances close enough that I can lift a cocky shrug and mean it.

"We got through every part of it too, baby." I declare the words while nestling my face into her neck and then yanking her tight once more. "Every last cabinet and closet, corner and crevice." I breathe her in again. So warm. So bright. *My life.* "Davidson and the city's structural engineers swept our six and took notes about where to park their charges. As of five a.m. tomorrow morning, the entire Source will follow the fate of Faline's portal-on-demand."

Emma lets out a long exhale, blending it into a sublime sigh. "And the bad guys go boom."

She husks it with such a perfect blend of Sarah Connor and Jessica Rabbit, I'm nothing but a huge ball of boom-boom-shakalaka myself for a good thirty seconds. "Well, at least their butt-crack bat cave does."

There's no sweet bunny giggle at that one, but I'm not expecting one. Her tiny tremor, coming a few seconds later, is more what my instinct has prepared for. "You think Fa-Fa knows what's going on?" As well as those words, complete with our snide nickname for our bitch nemesis.

"If she doesn't, she's sure as hell about to."

Another angle from me toward sardonicism, answered by another predictable shiver from her whole body. I battle the urge to fantasize about other times I've made her quiver from head to toe like this and am only partially successful. Which, of course, is the universe's full justification for tossing me into the cad-with-a-side-of-crap bin. Like Bruce Banner, sometimes my monster roars out at the stupidest times.

"Which means she could show up on the damn doorstep at any time."

And sometimes, the beast is beaten into submission with some simple words from a beautiful woman. But unlike Banner, I'm not tamed with a message of calm and comfort. I'm rendered silent at thinking what's now our inevitability. A house call from Mistress Garand—and *not* in the name of peddling cosmetics or cookies. But while it's silence, it's not a helpless one—bolstered by facts that return to me not a second too soon.

"When she does, we'll be ready." The vow gets the backing of my steady baritone because I'm sure of every syllable. "Foley's been on the horn all day long," I explain. "As we speak, some of his most reliable badass buddies are on their way to bolster the Team Bolt forces for the next week."

Her eyes widen and her lips lift. "The same guys who backed you two up at Teterboro?"

Teterboro. Her recall of the incident at first has me tensing. No, not an "incident." It was much more. The first time I'd ever been truly and thoroughly terrified of losing her because we were separated by much more than a minor bump in the relationship. Faline had kidnapped her and Lydia from the back door of the RRO fundraiser in Manhattan—and thanks to Foley, Mitch, Kane, and the rest of their friends, who'd all dropped everything to help us, that night had concluded in all the right ways but one. I hadn't killed Fa-Fa Garand when presented with the chance. But Emma was returned to my arms instead of being turned into hamburger by a jet turbine, and that was—and still is—all that matters.

Which is why I didn't hesitate to agree when Foley offered to call as much of the "old gang" back around. I know Emma sees as much in the resolve on my face as I answer her question. "One of them is returning," I offer. "Ethan Archer. Do you remember him?"

She nods with confidence, though her gaze grows misty with memories. "Yeah," she says slowly. "The languages specialist. Spec Ops out of JBLM in Seattle but splits his time between there and down here. His wife is a stylist for several movie and TV stars. And he picks up minor acting gigs too... right?"

I nod. "He finished up a project today, over at the Sony lot.

Depending on traffic from Culver City, he could be downstairs being briefed by Foley as we speak."

"Good." As she closes her eyes, the ridges across her forehead start relaxing. "That's really, really good."

Her blatant relief is my inspiring prod. "By tomorrow morning, we'll have two more here. The Bommer brothers." A short chuff.

She opens her eyes with a new smile. "Ah, yes. Lydia's told me about them. The older one lives in Hawaii. He started out in Special Forces but apparently is on a black ops team now. His younger brother is Ethan's brother-in-law; they married sisters." She cocks her head, focusing harder on me. "And from the hints 'Dia's dropped, we might share a few commonalities with the guy."

"With Shay?" I dip my head, giving in to the weight of curiosity. "That would explain why Foley made a point of sharing the guy's military call sign with me."

"Which is what?"

"Ironman."

Her lips part on a tiny laugh. "Oh, yeah. That certainly *would* explain it." At once, she sobers again. "I really don't care if their call signs are Jessie, James, and Meowth; I'm just glad they're going to be here soon." She wriggles closer as Lux declares it's time for left foot yellow in the next room. "I can't stand the thought of that witch showing up when we can't fully protect the kids."

With her head pressed to the center of my chest, I wonder if she can hear the uptick of my heartbeat. And the rush of happiness to my blood. Yet still, the subtle uncertainty in my voice as I echo, "The *kids*." I wrap my hold all the way around her until I'm tenderly rubbing up and down her spine. "Not just 'the kid'?"

She runs her own touch along the stretch of my collarbone. Her glowing fingers cause a soft sizzle as she strokes the worn leather. "I know exactly what I said, mister. And I know exactly what its implications are as well."

I spread my hands and discernibly enforce my pressure. "Even if those girls might be mine and not yours?" And then press harder but for my own fortitude this time. "Even if their 'mother' is the most poisonous bitch to ever donate her DNA to a petri dish?"

"No." She straightens until our faces are aligned with each other. "Not their *mother*," she declares. "That half-baked hag might have parted with an egg or two to strike the spark, but no way is she their ultimate fire." She jabs her chin higher. "No way is she their *mother*. And no way will she *ever* be."

As she speaks, full of gorgeous husk and hellfire, all my reactions intensify. The gallop of my pulse is up to Triple Crown speed. The elation in my blood becomes a full-blown tsunami. But now more than ever, the apprehension in my mind refuses to remain at the level of baby badger chitters. This nasty-ass nag has grown up and now lunges for the pulp of my memories—in particular, *one* memory that won't quit its repeat loop. It won't back down, even after three days, because its existence blows apart the few puzzle pieces we've notched together so far. And the bridges we've finally started connecting to Mis and Ira. And the ways they already feel so much a part of us.

But the recollection keeps tormenting. Endlessly. Relentlessly.

You know, Alpha Two...we would have been beautiful together...but now you have openly admitted your insipid attachment to that blond peasant...so this is how it has to be.

Shall we get on with things, then? Because the sooner you give me your liquid gold, the sooner they will be able to put it inside me. The sooner I will be the mother of a god!

She'd crooned all that while priming my balls and pumping my cock. I had no doubt what she wanted at the end of the speech, and it wasn't my hearty applause. My jizz was going to be her key to bearing the god baby.

Except for one major glitch.

By that night, she'd already created that kid. Twice.

And the puzzle crumbles a little more.

And so does my decision about waiting until the "right moment" to relay all of that to Emma. My main deterrent has also been the most obvious: when it comes to Faline, first assumptions should never be counted as the most trustworthy. The twins may look like they were born five years ago by human standards—two and a half using mutant math—but those are only standards with which *we're* familiar. For all we know, they've been sentient for only a month. And what about the fact that despite what Faline *said* in my memory, she never got anything more from me than a few drops of precome.

So how *were* Mis and Ira really created?

And is that really the question that matters?

Because as things stand, we can't ignore that they exist. Yes, with the big Garand eyes and the unmistakable black curls—but also with those noble Richards noses, proud Richards shoulders, long Richards fingers...

And the connection that *this* Richards soul feels for them. *With* them...

Part of the magic I feel is from Emma's incredible heart as she continues the lock of our stares and the resolve of her proclamation. A tenacity that sucks out my breath with its beauty. A strength that turns my whole damn system into a boulevard of brighter adoration. It all swirls and curls and twists through me before blurting out of me in an amazed, dazed rasp.

"So what are you telling me here exactly, Velvet?"

The woman dips her head and sends out a cute glance, as if she's peering over the rims of Ray-Bans perched on her nose. "What you already know I'll say, mind-reader guy."

I blink hard. Get down a gulp of twice the weight. "Maybe I'm just having trouble believing it."

"Are you serious?"

She stands up fast enough to knock the pretend shades off. At once, she's standing in front of me with hands slammed to her waist. "Why?" Despite her casual outfit of plain leggings and a T-shirt with a smiley-faced lightning bolt on it, she evokes the same badassery as she would in her battle leathers—with the same searing effect on my cock.

She goes on, oblivious to my swelling physical frustration. "Do you really think I'm going to shun those girls for simply being brought into existence? For the genes that formed that existence? For the disgusting reasons they were told their lives had any significance at all? For all the things they could no more control than the breaths they took?"

Well, now that she puts it *that* way...

But nonetheless, I begin my reply with a callous shrug. Then an equally stern frown. "Some people would," I supply and mean it. More than she probably wants to know about and likely refuses to. Which triples my adoration of her before she even formulates a comeback. Oh, but it's coming. I already see it in the fires beneath her stunning blues and in the tearful shimmer that gives them such gorgeous depth.

"Well, I'm not some people."

I spread my arms, reaching out to snare her wrists in my no-nonsense grip. "And I'm not ever going to stop being grateful for it."

The prickles dissolve from her demeanor as I draw her closer, kissing her palms before laying them over my shoulders.

"Those girls are miracles, Reece," she whispers as another round of excited squeals breaks out from the other room. "And they deserve to be told and shown that, each and every day. In as many ways as possible."

I slide my hands down to her thighs. Coax her knees back up until she's straddling me on the narrow velvet couch. "You've already started that magic, woman," I whisper into the hollow of her throat. "You're showing them by example because you're the original miracle." I tilt my head, angling so that I suckle the side of that elegant, creamy column...now vibrating with her shallow sighs and quickening breaths. "*My* miracle," I murmur while licking along her carotid. "My superheroine. My goddess. My breath, my life...*fuck*."

I surrender to the mindless word because that's what I've finally become, swamped with stupidity hand-fed by my own frustration. How can so many words exist in this world, yet none to fully fit what I'm trying to tell her? To make sure she knows, beyond any doubt, that she's never dropped a bigger bomb of beguilement on my spirit. That she's never trapped my soul in a stronger cage of wonder. That she's never converted me faster to the church of Emmalina or had me dropping faster to my knees at her golden altar.

"Fuck!" I repeat it because it's still the only filler that fits— only it doesn't. Even my go-to word isn't sticking the damn landing here—which has me holding up the apple cart once again. Why am I fighting to make *anything* stick with words?

"Right hand greeeeennn!"

"Oh yeah, buddy," I mumble to my son, happy when there's no silent psychic volley in return. The action of the game is consuming him too fully. Thank fuck for that, because I assure fate that I've now gotten its subliminal message loud and clear.

Sometimes, words aren't enough.

Especially when a guy is sitting with a soft, sweet, squirming little bunny on his lap, feeling her getting more wet and pliant by the second—and *doing* nothing about it but feebly dry humping her.

You say she's your miracle?

Then show her.

Your life, your breath?

Show her.

Your ultimate goddess?

Show. Her!

Fortunately, I'm pretty good about hints once I'm clobbered over the head with them—especially when they command me to do more than grunt and rub on my wife like an eighth-grade dork during a school dance slow song.

There's no time to lose.

Other than the minutes I've wasted already.

I start at once—but as soon as I do, sending a calculated pulse over the mound of decorative pillows on our bed, Emma interprets my action differently. "You particularly fond of left hand green?" She thinks I'm commenting on Lux's shriek, but that's fine by me. That'll make my sexy surprise that much sweeter—for both of us.

"Hmmm. Not really." I keep up the flow from my outstretched hands, imagining I look like a kinky Dr. Strange utilizing my mystic arts to form the wildest sex bed. I smirk. Not arguing with that one at all. As a matter of fact, the concept lends me a new stroke of genius. With a swirl of fingers and a whoosh of energy, I stretch out a flash pulse beneath her perfect body, using it to lift her through the air and across the room. Within a few seconds, she's the centerpiece of my new bedding sculpture, with her head and knees propped up...and her legs beautifully spread.

Gorgeous.

Delectable.

Perfect.

Almost.

"Oh!" she yelps in tandem to my admiring growl. "My... my goodness." The stammers are infused with a little laughter, turning them into music I could listen to all day, but 'Dia and Angie will only be able to amuse the kids for so long with the spinner and the plastic mat in the next room. Before long, demands for the trip to Two-Bit Circus will once more threaten to punch out the wall between us. The sorcerer needs to get busy here.

"Ohhhh, Bunny...I promise you, *goodness* is definitely the goal here."

Emma peels back the restraint on more of her sweet laugh. Lifts a stare at me full of the same warmth, though now it's dipped in sultry sensuality as well. "Well, you know how I like goals, Mr. Richards."

"One of the things I worship the most about you, Mrs. Richards." With steps of defined intent, I move to stand between her parted legs. My nostrils flare. My mouth waters. Even now, with her leggings still on, I catch the sexy honey of her aroused pussy on the air. "Among hundreds," I qualify as

I rake my heated gaze across that erotic juncture of her body.

I don't stop there.

And she knows it.

With every new inch I cover with my stare, the woman's breaths pump in and out of her faster. And then faster. By the time I reach the stunning swells beneath her tee, that air has turned into hot-as-hell husks up her throat.

Still, she manages to rasp out, "I...I worship you too."

More magnificent music to my ears.

More mind-blowing fire to my blood.

More unbearable pressure in my cock.

But bear it I do, borrowing self-control from some inexplicable force of the cosmos, the entity gaining my lifelong loyalty simply because I get to enjoy the next awesome moment.

"Yeah? Then prove it."

In which I get to watch her pupils dilate from my ruthless warlock's growl.

"Take off the shirt. And anything that's underneath it."

And then the exquisite part of her lips before she complies with my conjurer's command.

For a second, I grin. Her rushed obedience reminds me of Mickey Mouse from *Fantasia*, eagerly seeking to please the dark sorcerer overlord. I like that analogy too—only I'm pretty sure that magician was never conjuring what I'm going to do to my lithe little apprentice.

My gorgeous disciple, glowing in pleasure as she reveals more of her golden skin for me. And then the perfection of her bared tits. Their puckered rosy centers. Their erect berry points. Their sweet, heaving fullness.

"Damn," I grate, battling the desire to lean over for some

lingering tastes. *Not yet.* I vowed to honor her with my most profound worship, in the most perfect way I know how. That means moving on...

"So flawless," I tell her, roaming my hot scrutiny across every creamy inch of her swollen mounds. "So fucking stunning."

"Reece..." She licks her lips and reaches for me, but I capture her wrists and return her hands back to her breasts.

"Lie back," I direct. "And play with them for me. Pluck them. Pull them." For a few seconds, I demonstrate the motions with my own fingertips. "Hurt them." Oh, *yeah*. And that one too.

"Ahhhh!"

"Now stay still."

She chokes. "Seriously?"

"Stay. Still." I slam enough thunder into the echo that she finally gets the message. I'm not asking for her feedback. I'm dictating her compliance. "Yessss." I draw it out in conjunction with the perfect views consuming my sights. First, as I carefully sear away the crotch and upper thighs from her leggings, exposing the succulent pink folds beneath. At the same time, she continues heeding my order for her hands, kneading and tweaking her chest until her nipples resemble twin cinnamon candies. The textures impact me like a perfect erotic dream. Pink and red...soft and hard...wet and full...

Waiting and ready.

So perfectly prepared for my worship.

I can't wait any longer.

I crouch next to the bed and then lean in to where her legs are bolstered on the pillows I prearranged.

"Ohhhh..." Her moan corresponds to the new force of my

hold, wrapped around her thighs from the outside. The grip helps me spread her wider, until her feet are dangling from the edges of the pillow hills and her ass is lifted an inch off the mattress. With her leggings cut off above her knees, she resembles a naughty schoolgirl about to be punished...and her juicy cunt the forbidden fruit she's brought to buy mercy.

But I'm in no mood to give her any.

My discipline and my veneration come as one deviant package.

As it should be.

As she'll be taking it from me.

"Ohhh! Ahhhh!" Emma's keen is a perfect blend of the same duality, hiking in pitch as I deliver the first long tongue stroke to her parted, pouting sex. Her cry is as much sinner as saint, equal parts contrition and absolution as I devour her but exalt her. As I take but then give back. As I taste but ensure she gets her sustenance too. As my reward, she gushes her intimate essence across my tongue and then down my throat. I groan and swallow, treasuring every delicious drop of her creamy ambrosia.

"Ohhhh, *God*!" she bursts out, and I repeat an inward thanks to the Big Guy that it corresponds perfectly with a fresh round of squeals from the other room.

"No, baby," I rumble into the tiny valley between her labia and thigh. "Not him this time." And then kiss her there. And then again. "Just me. Your forever slave, serving you. Your eternal apostle, worshiping you." I trail my tongue even deeper into the balmy mysteries of her feminine shadows until I'm licking the sensitive crack between her ass cheeks. "Your smitten lover...needing all of you."

As I emphasize the last three words, I suckle my way

back through the shivering folds protecting her most intimate button. I push my way through those layers, seeking out the stiff nub at the center of her pleasure...the juicy candy that all but beckons me to nibble and taste and treasure. And fuck, do I ever. First I lick, rejoicing in how she gasps and then shivers her thighs against my ears. After yanking on her legs and pulling her wider, I indulge a longer stay, tracing her sensitive ridge with the tip of my tongue before lavishing it with my lusty breaths. That results in every way I possibly dreamed and more. Emma turns into a writhing mess of arousal, dropping her hands to clutch at the comforter and beating the pillows with her heels.

"Sssshhh, baby," I chide with a heated chuckle. "Don't want the kids thinking we've got a fun game of our own going on in here."

But *oh God*, how we do.

I dip in, bestowing a teasing kiss to the middle of her trembling clit. I'm ready for her responding moan, electrically forming her T-shirt into a twisted rope and then swiping it between her lips as a soft gag. The sight is so mesmerizing, with her plump mouth clamped against the yellow-and-blue graphic of the tee, that I keep gazing up her body while raining light kisses across her glistening pussy. Not that I'm going to be capable of doing it for much longer. My dick has turned into a lead door knocker, ramming at the inside of my fly, unwilling to stand down. Not when I watch her wide, turbulent eyes and imagine them bugging even farther as I fuck her. Not when I think about the mewls she's capable of emitting around that gag with every new stab of my cock in her sweet, tight cunt. Not when I fantasize about pulling the fabric from her lips, only to claim the length of her scream as she...orgasms exactly like this.

"Unnnnhhh! Mmmmmm! Fuuuhhh!" Her muffled shrieks are like aural frosting on the cake of her climax, with her tissues weeping and undulating around my tongue. Greedily, I lap and gnosh and suck at her intimate entrance, proud as fuck of myself for the lusty, nasty mess she's become. I love the crap out of this horny little bunny. I worship the fuck out of this ripe, gleaming goddess.

My goddess.

My hot, passionate, powerful wife.

My ardent, generous, openhearted lover.

The woman I'll never get enough of. The sun flare I'll never give enough to.

Even now, as I unzip my fly, set free my cock, and slide the entire, throbbing length inside her soaked, welcoming sheath.

Even as I withdraw all the way, hovering my head near her slit and my face barely above hers, until surrendering again to the call of her heat.

Even as I lunge all the way back in, this time with one hand at the back of her head, torqueing the ends of her gag tighter. Watching her gaze punch out wider. And her nostrils work faster. And her saliva start to wet the T-shirt as she huffs and moans and lurches and quakes beneath me. As her body takes in more of me. As her energy surrounds me and heats me...

"Fuck." Seems to be my word of choice right now, though I'm stunned I still have one to use. The things this woman does to me...they're beyond words. She's beyond description. This miracle, every time I become one with her, beyond any tangible realm of existence. With her, I'm more than a man. More than a hero.

I'm just...more.

"Fuck. *Fuck*." I whisper it past a dazed smile before trailing kisses over her bound and whimpering lips. "What a sopping, sexy little mess you are. My gorgeous, wet little goddess."

I run my thumb along in the wake of my lips, fascinated by the mixture of textures I find in my extended study. Her plush lips invaded by the coiled fabric. Her stone-hard nipples and her satin-soft pussy. And the best contrast of all: her erotic little noises interspersed with the life that goes on around us. A world of such normalcy, oblivious to how she's altering every synapse in my head and every molecule of air I take in. The rush of traffic through the downtown streets below. A helicopter thudding by, monitoring that traffic. The *shoosh*es of the elevators up and down the tower below us. And yes, Lydia's continuing shouts from the room next to us.

"Spread your legs wider, Velvet." I whisper it against her ear...naughtiness for just the two of us. She responds with her sweet obedience...and an extended, sexy-as-fuck moan.

"Ohhhh...*mmmmm*."

"I'm going to fuck you harder, Emma."

"Ah. *Ahhhh*."

"You like my cock this deep in your cunt, baby?"

"Yeah," she sobs through the fabric. "Ohhhh...yeahhhh..."

"I love you, Emma."

And then I can't hear the rest of the world anymore. My existence is nothing but those words, issued from the farthest corners of my heart...

"I need you, Emma."

The deepest trenches of my soul...

"Take me, Emma. All of me. *Yesssss!*"

The hammering heat between my legs.

Building. Growing. Swelling. Shooting.

And then detonating.

I freeze, my cock buried as tight and deep as I can possibly get, every muscle taut as the come finally breaks free from my throbbing head. I drench her womb in thick, hot ropes of the electric, ecstatic bliss, exploding a rough groan into the sweat-drenched column of her neck. With her throat beneath my lips, I finally realize that her strident scream has joined my outcry; the racing flutters of her tight walls tell me the rest. Well, not all of it. There are things her body can't tell me—elements I can only feel through the union of our psyches and the magic of our love. The blazing pinnacle only our souls and spirits can take each other to. The sun storm of our consummation. The unmistakable light of our unbreakable connection.

The bond I'll never let go.

The love I'll always fight for.

The magic that's my life's eternal miracle.

Even with a crowd of caterwauling kids in the next room.

"Auntie 'Dia fall down! You out!"

I loosen the T-shirt in time to let Emma share in my reactionary snicker. "And she's supposed to be the flexible one," she adds, adding an adorable eye roll.

I release a contemplative hum into the valley between her breasts. The move gives my mouth an excuse to get into the same proximity as her delectable nipples. They're still the color of ripe raspberries, begging for my bites with equally juicy appeal. "I don't know about that." I make my move, licking my way up the side of one creamy swell. "I like her sister's flexibility just fine."

She giggles as I blend a sensual snarl into the last two words, drawing them out—and buying myself some time to reach her proud peak. The stiff bud tastes better than I imagined, with the honey of her skin spiced with the salt of her perspiration. I take my time enjoying the treat, half-kissing the top like a kid getting sloppy with an ice cream cone.

Ideal analogy.

Because *I'm* the mess now.

And in this perfect, better-than-words moment, I let myself be. After the events of the last three days, my heart, soul, mind, and spirit are a giant, gooey mud bath of emotions. I grin as they slog through my psyche, trailing the mud of exhaustion in their wake. Nevertheless, I greet each of them with the recognition they deserve after the surreal events of the last three days. Joy, sorrow, triumph, tears, elation, confusion, regret, restoration, strength, weakness, thankfulness, emptiness—each of them tromps in and pitches camp in my psychological swamp, knowing they'll likely be here for a while.

Not forever. Even now, some diligent note-taker in a back room of my mind is scribbling that reminder, but I order him to take a break for the night. This second, I'm just happy in the swamp. Without looking or asking, I know Emma is cool with trudging through it with me. Hmmm. *There's* a fantasy. The woman, naked except for muddy fishing waders. Smudges of dirt all over her bare, golden body...

Her silky giggle tugs me out of the reverie. "Must be a damn good thought, Mr. Richards." Her saucy tone implies the double entendre for "thought," especially as my fantasy-jolted cock gets some more encouragement from her hitching hips.

"Mmmm." I growl good-naturedly into her ear. "You wouldn't believe me if I told you."

"Says the guy who just freed every prisoner in the Consortium's hell hole, has given them all temporary housing and medical attention, and is lying here with his hot-as-hell wife while his three super-mutant kids are likely decimating the Twister mat in the next room?"

"All right." Hearty snort. "So you probably *would* believe it."

I finish it with a lopsided smirk—which fades from the second she raises her hand to the side of my face. Her touch, tender but earnest, matches the steady set of her new expression.

Equally as sober, with gaze glued to mine, she states, "I believe in *you*, Reece Richards."

The swamp expands as more emotions dive in. Humility and astonishment. How did I get lucky enough to lock down this amazing creature? It's a daily question for me—for which I always have the same answer.

Stop asking, damn it.

Just make it your mission to fucking keep *her.*

Especially when fate gives me the perfect words with which to do so. It doesn't always happen like this, but with inspiration like the loving lights in her eyes, the inspiring lift of her chin, and the golden glow flowing from the middle of her chest, I don't need to ask the universe twice about what wisdom to speak. It's just there—like my love for her always has been.

"I believe in *us*, Mrs. Richards."

A divine goddess smile stretches across the breathing curves of her lips. "Ohhhh, mister, you really knew *that* right answer."

I break out my most roguish wink, along with the smirk that brings out my deepest dimples. "I usually do, sweet bunny."

CHAPTER SIX

EMMA

As I watch the sun peek over the eastern foothills, its golden streams washing over the awakening metropolis below, a corresponding warmth stretches through me. A goofy grin and a happy tune aren't far behind, though I've really got to stop humming the same four lines from "A Million Dreams" sometime soon. Three hours is more than enough for a Pasek and Paul homage.

But it's the perfect fit for this amazing new day.

Between lines about bright colors in my head and visions of the world to be, I sip on my third cup of coffee, despite that it's not nearly six a.m. yet. I've already been up for two hours, rising with Reece as he excitedly prepared to go out and do what I've been humming about. Making the world a place that a child can dream about again.

That *our* children can dream about.

The phrase feels so right in my head and more so in my heart. And it feels damn good to acknowledge them there, as the truth of my spirit and not just noble phrases spoken to Reece just because of the swoony feels he gave me yesterday afternoon. Okay, so maybe they were a little more than swoony at the time—but the swoon factor was definitely an ongoing theme for the evening, when we borrowed our "Steven and

Sophie" getups to venture out with the kids for a few hours at Two-Bit Circus, followed by ramen at Daikokuya and dessert at Honeymee.

Ohhh, yes. Swoons were certainly this mom's mood of choice while watching "Steve" go a few rounds of virtual tank battles with Lux, followed by midway games with the girls. More of the same as he slurped noodles at dinner, pretending to "accidentally" hit himself in the face with them in the name of distracting Mis and Ira from their trepidation at the bustling Little Tokyo traffic. The final match to my killed-by-swoons fever was his walk through the Village Plaza with both girls hoisted on his shoulders, protecting them from the "lava rock" bricks lining the plaza's pretty pathways. Even Lux got into the act, pretending to be a marauding dragon with little "flights" aided by his unique new power, until one too many onlookers wondered if they were looking at reality or a product of their sake-soaked brains. Fortunately, it was easy to distract my son with a Yuzu Affogato, which he downed in roughly five and a half bites, before asking for extra corn flakes in his cup.

Needless to say, I spent part of the last two hours messaging Anya about stocking up on cornflakes at the ridge.

The ridge.

I exhale in contentment with just the thought of finally returning home. Our *real* home. Our little three-day stay in the city, first for simply hosting 'Dia and Sayer's engagement party, became a week-long roller coaster of life-changing events. As of this morning, the Source is officially erased from the planet and the roll call of our family has grown by two special names. Two amazing little girls. Two spirits I can't imagine our lives being without, even now.

Two special people who fill the penthouse with their

sleepy giggles and voices...

Before appearing together in the doorway to the office. And making my morning even brighter with the joy beneath their impish smiles.

"Well hello, you two." I set my coffee on the corner of the desk while crouching to their level and opening my arms. "And good morning!"

My bid for hugs is unsuccessful. Though they both scoot a little closer, their steps are timid and soft. I hide my slight letdown. It's only the start of their fourth day in the real world—which they still don't really understand as the *real* world. Hugs will come once their trust does. I have to be grateful for the little things, such as the fact that last night passed nightmare-free. Damn good thing too, since by the time we got home from our outing, Mama Richards was looking at Papa Richards with something far more than the swoons. The I-gotta-jump-yous had gotten their turn for attention after all.

"You girls hungry?" It's much safer than asking how they slept and earns me an instant pair of eager nods.

"Pop Tarts," Mis declares at once.

"Cornflakes," Ira chimes in—and barely flinches when I send her a quizzical look. More progress. A couple of days ago, even a show of mild curiosity would spark the girl's open panic. Slowly but surely, they're both realizing that even if I fully scowl, that won't equal their instant punishment. Though the girl's shoulders hunch in a little, still programmed by her lifetime of degradation and shame, she makes a clear effort to roll them back and then jog up her head. "Cornflakes," she repeats with bold ferocity, and I seriously crave to hug her again. "Like Luxie." And even more now.

"Well, okay," I chirp, adding in a cute little dance.

"Cornflakes it is." And then make up a little cornflakes song—kind of a Pasek and Paul-meets-classic Madonna thing—to go with my dorky moves. But their fairylike laughs are all I need for encouragement, along with the fact that I've somehow rhymed "best cereal" with "stellar material" to keep up the schtick all the way out into the hall.

Where the twins have definitely *not* followed me.

I rush back into the office, most likely overreacting, but I can't help being freaked that they might be the same. The distant booms, courtesy of the demolition teams that are turning the Source into a solid maze of destruction, have continued for the better part of an hour. Most of the city assumes the muffled noise is Water and Power Department servicing issues, but a few of us know the difference, and I'm damn sure that legion includes Ira and Mis. Oh, *damn*. Are they affected by the destruction? Are parts of their hearts mourning for the only place they've ever known as home, despite Faline's sick and twisted version of the word? Or are they afraid we're preparing to shove them back down into that darkness, even after wrecking it all?

I hit the entrance to the office at damn near full sprint.

And then hit my full stop lever, my feet chirping on the wood floor from the abruptness.

The silence I sensed from the girls is just as palpable now.

Except they're not using it to dissolve into tears.

They're strolling along the side of the room that overlooks the desk. More specifically, they're peering at the knickknacks and framed photos arranged on the built-in shelves along that wall.

My heart aches, watching them study the images of memories great and small for Reece and me. A snap of us kissing on the beach, with the sunset in the background. Another picture of Reece and the whole Team Bolt crew before they even called themselves that. To the right in the shot, Kane is cuddling Mitch from behind, his rugged face taking up a good chunk of Mitch's shoulder. There are a few fun pictures of Lydia in her slick advertising shots for tennis rackets and athletic shoes and another one of us in formal gowns for one of her awards ceremonies. Concurrently, there's a long set of shots featuring Reece and *his* siblings: one big oval with the three handsome Richards dudes together, grouped with small circles containing solo shots. It's one of my favorite pieces because the guys are all in stunning bespoke suits and ties—from the waist up. But since the shoot was a Mother's Day surprise for Trixie, they mixed things up with wild Hawaiian shorts on the bottoms.

A smile warms my lips when I observe Mis and Ira taking a liking to the shots too—though it wavers when watching their interest turn into obsessed stares and then perplexed glances at each other. By the time they pivot around to fix me with the same puzzled looks, I'm back to crunching a full bewildered frown at them both.

"Girls?" I query, taking care to keep my steps soft and my voice considerate. "What is it? Is there something troubling—"

"Father."

I'm not surprised when it's Ira issuing the interruption. Despite Mis busting out of her comfort zone for the Pop Tarts request, Ira's usually the one who speaks for both of them, especially when it's a matter seemingly this dire. I quickly nod her way, though include Miseria in my regard as well. "Yes," I ensure. "That's right. Father is in there. Right there." My stomach knots in a strange way as I tap at Reece's solo photo. I should consider it a good thing that they recognize the ties, but I feel a little like the new stepmother, wondering what kind of trash the ex-wife has already been spilling about my husband. And probably me.

"No."

Ira's declaration jerks my focus back up at her. "No?" I shake my head and lower my brows, attempting to convey my confusion. "No what, sweetie?"

"No Father."

"Huh?" I demand.

"No Father." Her dictate is determined but her touch is gentle—as she reaches up and pushes my hand away from Reece's picture. "*Father.*"

And then raises her little hand back up.

And points at the photo of Tyce.

⚡

"What is it?" Reece demands, charging into the office as if my text declared the penthouse had caught fire. In all fairness, he can't be blamed. Though I was finally able to process the breadth of Ira's assertion, all the while getting the kids set up with their desired breakfasts as well as some necessary fruit and milk, the end result was a rushed text that I barely remember. Unchecked shock will do that to a girl.

"What's going on? *Velvet?*" he presses, prompting me to look up from the surface of the desk—where I've put the framed Richards brothers photo set that sparked Ira's stunner of a morning news flash.

"Hey," I finally stammer, taking in his disheveled hair, polished silver gaze, and heightened color. It almost looks like he got here using a two-and-a-half-block pulse, winding up with a look that tempts me to jump him. To be honest, maybe that'll help. Some natural serotonin and endorphins might be the perfect ticket at this surreal moment.

"Hey?"

He spits it back as if I've really told him to close the door and then get naked. Yeah, even with Sawyer and three more guys spilling into the room behind him. I immediately recognize one of the huge hunks. Ethan Archer is still the epitome of dark vampire handsome, despite being outfitted in black and green battle attire instead of a velvet cape and fluffy shirt. The other two, clearly the brothers Reece told me about last night, are a little bigger than Archer and cute in a scruffy soldier way. They're dressed nearly identically, clearly ready for action—and even seem a little miffed when all they find in here is dazed little me.

"*Hey?*" Reece repeats, incredulous. "After a text saying"— he snaps out his phone and frantically swipes open the screen— "'we need to talk, how fast can you get here?'" He stabs the phone back into his pocket. "And now just...'hey'?"

I hold up both hands. "Okay, baby. Just breathe."

"And now 'just *breathe*'?"

I scoot around the desk and sprawl a hand to the middle of his chest. "You heard me, ox. Just do it."

I mean every syllable. The man is still in the mode of expecting a thousand boogey men to spring out of the woodwork any second and truly hasn't taken a breath during the last minute because of it. I don't see what's so amusing about that, but Sawyer and the other guys don't make even minor attempts to hold in their mild chuckles.

"Oh, I like her already," drawls one of the brothers, who

flashes a sly grin along with his café au lait gaze. "You two need to come for a visit out on Maui," he tells Reece. "Lani will fall in love with her in two seconds."

His brother chuffs. "Ditto for Zoe—not to mention my kid, who'd think your two girls are the coolest thing since Pinkie Pie learned a cloning spell."

"Dude." Brother One grimaces. "Did you just name a character from Equestria by first and last name?"

"Did you just admit you know what the fuck Equestria *is*?"

Sawyer wheels on them. "Are you two turning Bolt Man's code red into a debate about cartoon horses?"

"*Ponies.*" Ethan chimes in on the rebuttal, and I spit out a laugh despite my fight for dignity. Or formality. Or whatever I'm calling my composure after a full plate of my husband's rugged hotness chased by a four-part chug of military-grade testosterone. Oh, yes, Sawyer's mojo is definitely a part of that equation right now—finished by a debate about the pony who made "nervouscited" a functioning word.

And, handily enough, a perfect description for my mindset as Reece resets his stance. All right, it's not like I'm about to tell him I'm pregnant again—but strange inner instincts are still enforcing the importance of sharing this, right now and in person. There's part of me that just hopes he shrugs and wonders why I invoked the dreaded "we need to talk," before he invites all the guys out into the kitchen for some sugar-drenched breakfast.

"Oh, cool!" The new slice on the air comes from my still-pajama'ed sister, standing in the open doorway. Before I have the chance to hate her for being the only person on the planet who can look that cute in a raccoon kigurumi splotched with Pop Tart filling, she gives me a reason to be even more frustrated with her. "Looks like you already told him. So what about that, Bolt Jolt? Tyce Richards for the baby daddy win!"

I'm not sure what reaction to expect from Reece. His face is already fixed at high intensity. Though he finally obliged and took a few breaths for me, his stature looks ready for any crisis, from breaking up a fight between the kids to confronting a nuclear bomb. I'm banking more toward that side of the scale as he rolls his gape from her to me and finally blurts, "The... *baby daddy*? Tyce?"

I wobble through a nod while pointing to the photo collection on the desk. "Ira pointed him out in the lineup."

A tense pause.

"Tyce," he finally repeats.

"Tyce," I confirm.

"Ohhhh crap," Lydia mumbles.

"Well, damn," Sawyer adds.

As another silence stretches, longer than the first, I run a fidgety finger along the photograph frame. "I'm sorry for the kneejerk text. In the grand scheme of things, I know that it doesn't change anything or even bring Tyce back for you..."

I'm saved from having to form a lame conclusion for that when Reece vaults over the desk with one determined pulse. In the same fluid motion, he hauls me tight to his chest. His arms discernibly tremble as he holds me even closer. "You're wrong." His husk is warm and tender in my hair. "It brings him back in all the best ways, Bunny. And I'm so damn glad you didn't wait to tell me."

"So are all of us." Sawyer's voice is weary and dry. "I mean, there's only so many times a guy can watch underground rooms being imploded on themselves via remote cameras."

"As usual, Folic Acid has a solid point," cracks one of the brothers. "Especially because this place smells better than that fucking cave."

His sibling, the one I'm pegging as the younger one, pushes out a grunt. "You live in Hawaii. Aren't caves considered recreational fun there?"

"Yeah. Fun that stinks," the guy retorts. "Especially if you're comparing it to Pop Tarts." He shakes his head with a wry chuff. "Swear to God, someone at that company is making full pension from my stepson alone."

"And our girls." Though Reece's tone carries a chuckle, his face is all seriousness when I pull back and stare up at him. "Yeah," he ensures, his gaze as gentle as the hand he cups to my cheek. "*Our* girls, baby—no matter what anyone else says." He kisses me with awkward swiftness. "I—I only mean that if Mis and Ira are okay with it, and *you're* okay with it—"

I cut him off by leading the way on our next kiss. Forcefully. Ruthlessly. I breach his lips with passionate zeal, offering everything I am to him. All the emotion in my soul. The adoration in my spirit. And more than anything, the connection to him that's just grown in proportion to the expansion of our family. I guess what they say is true. Children don't consume what already exists in one's heart. They break down walls into new parts of a person...

And new depths of their love.

Like every new way I'm feeling the energy and essence of this man. Every new chamber of myself that's being opened to him in return. Every joyous pound of our pulses, ignition of our bloodstreams, and whisper of our souls. Every new synapse of connection, thrilling me as if I'm riding lightning—and judging from the gobsmacked gasps from all the guys, am probably looking like it too.

Sure enough, as soon as I find the self-control to extract my tongue from my husband's tonsils, I pull away from him on a self-conscious slide—to confront my fireball of a reflection in the office's window. With the right kind of squinted glance and expanded imagination, one would almost think earth had just gained itself a twin sun.

Before I can start the strange rumination about what that would mean for Daylight Savings Time, Ethan Archer saves us all from the awkward silence in the room. "Well, damn. Guess I'll only be retelling this one when I'm really shitfaced."

Sawyer grunts out a laugh. "Damn good reason to get shitfaced, though."

"Or maybe...*that* is."

Nobody misses how Brother Number One has gone from swaggering to stupefied with his new declaration—as the air before us suddenly sizzles and crackles and whirls and burns.

Tzzzzzzt.

And then thunders and roars and rips and screams.

Thwwaaarrr.

And then breaks open. Wider. Wider still.

"Holy shit." I sob it out as my blissful warmth jacks into terrified fire and my instincts flare into full awareness.

As the rift in the air spreads even wider.

And as Faline Garand, in all her high-heeled, catsuited, bow-to-the-bitch glory, strides through it.

As she bares her teeth, spreads her hands into electric claws, and sets a direct course toward us.

All right, not completely direct. Sawyer and all three of his friends spring into action, going for their concealed weapons. Ethan and his SIG get in a good shot to her chest, causing a two-step fumble before she whomps him to the floor with a ferocious power pulse. The younger Bommer brother lunges to do the same, but she's ready for him with a deflection shield. The bullet ricochets and lands solidly in the chest of his big brother. But on his way down, the guy still delivers wicked damage, wielding a gleaming Bowie knife in a hand mottled by old burn scars. One deft flick and three stunning seconds later, the blade impales Faline's left thigh with a sickening *thunk*.

The woman's scream is one of the most awesome sounds I've ever heard.

Despite knowing what will follow in its wake.

Another outcry—this time, channeling her pain into pure rage. It morphs into a growl thick with the viciousness of hell. And then a savoring laugh, channeling the hot mire of Styx itself.

"Do you really think you've *ended* me, Team Bolty-Bolt? Do you think your dynamite and your do-goody-gooding have actually put a single *dent* in me?"

She jerks the knife out of her flesh, brandishing its blood-covered length in her hand riddled with glowing green veins.

"Think."

And then stabs it back in, lower on her thigh.

"Again."

And then into her other thigh.

"Fuckers."

And then into the side of her neck, resulting in a grimace that takes care of any remaining outward beauty that might have been trying to persist on her face.

"You won't end me, you ungrateful miscreants. You won't end me because too many across the world are now *thanking* me. Too many have seen the light of what I'm going to do for their disgusting existences and have given me the proper title for it."

She exalts her stance, which widens the wound in her neck. The deep V of her black bodysuit has become a pool of bright-red gore.

"They call me *goddess* now—and soon you will too."

She approaches again, each footstep a vivid crimson print on the floor, as her skin turns paler and her sneer grows more malevolent.

"But first, you're going to give back what belongs to me."

LIGHT

PART 18

CHAPTER ONE

REECE

I'll admit it. Reluctantly.

I've been wrong about a few things in my life.

A few.

But at this moment, I admit my complete mistake in thinking I could never fall deeper in love with Emmalina Paisley Crist Richards. My best friend. My key ass-kicker. My kids' super mom. My hot-as-fuck lover. My cherished wife. My guiding light.

And now, the warrior braced in front of me, fireballs for fists and a disk of sizzling energy for a shield, standing off with the sorceress of skank who's wormholed her way into our home. Clarification: the invader who's likely already killed a member of our extra security team before securing everyone else beneath a web of lightning she fabricated as if flinging a handful of rice at a wedding.

Only she's not at a wedding today. And goddamnit, I refuse to let her zap out of here like she did at the last one, disappearing through her portal with a "special parting gift." At our wedding reception, that "trinket" was Laurel Crist. One look at the vehement set of Faline's features and I already know the bitch won't be settling for low-hanging fruit like that again.

She's here to take back the whole damn basket.

The prize we snatched from her.

The twins.

And if not them, then equal compensation for them.

Lux.

Or Emma.

Taken by the woman to God knows where. With the Source now decimated, we have no idea of knowing where her backup destination is—and the search for it will be tougher than finding a needle in a haystack. She's a psycho being shielded by thousands of crazy converts—who are all ready to perform her bidding in keeping nonbelievers in line.

Never.

I repeat it in a snarl for my ears alone, though I'm damn sure Emma's heard me anyway. She flinches back her shoulders, an unspoken signal for me to stand down. I comply but only for the moment. If Faline so much as twitches one hand in the direction of my woman, I won't hesitate to jump into the ball pit most men would call insanity: the fray of a girl fight.

I save myself from contemplating an electrically enhanced estrogen takedown by alerting one ear to the movements out in the kitchen. Thank fuck for Lydia, who took advantage of the cover fire from Archer and the Bommers to escape out the door, likely sprinting straight for the kids. Since I can't detect even a small whimper of fear from that direction now, I'm assuming—*praying*—she and Angelique took them out the back door and down the stairs.

Possible hitch number one? We've practiced this drill with Lux before but not the twins. If either of them has a freak-out on the way down, their flight to safety might be over before it's barely begun.

And hitch number two? The plan always entails them meeting Sawyer at the ground floor. He knows to drive them to one of several safe houses I've secured around the city, with the Newport Beach complex as a last-ditch option only.

Right now, all that matters is what I can effect right now.

The crisis before me.

"We haven't taken a thing that you didn't steal from the world in the first place, Faline."

Though my amazing wife addresses the whole issue as the furthest thing from a crisis.

Clearly Faline shares my bewilderment about Emma's easygoing tone. If I weren't so paranoid about watching every millimeter of movement from the woman, I'd join her in casting an openly curious glare around the room—blatantly wondering, as she is, how this luxury penthouse office has become a police interrogation room, with Emma turning into the conversational "good cop."

"You're wondering what the hell I'm talking about... yes?" More of the let's-shoot-the-shit banter, though Emma doesn't back off the intensity of her fireballs and their shield-sized extension. It's not her intention to give me a coronary yet, thank God. "Let's follow the logic, then. The hundred and forty-eight souls we dragged out of your underground prison, along with nearly that many who paid the price for your evil with their lives, is pretty self-explanatory."

She straightens her spine and juts her chin as I privately contemplate Faline's fall into complete silence—but then start to experiment with it. Strangely, the woman seems to shrink back farther every time I so much as lean in Emma's direction. There's nothing different about the result of our proximity—as usual, our pulses quicken as our energies communicate and connect with each other—but those factors have always been ours alone to know about and revel in, never a tangible force outside of our supercharged bubble. Until now...

"That gets us to the subject of the twins," Emma announces. "A pair of life forms that you created without the consent or knowledge of their father and then drafted into your service from the day they became half-sentient beings—in essence, turning them into your slaves."

I have no idea how she keeps up her casual demeanor, but I'm damn glad she somehow finds the fortitude. Her rundown helps me continue mine. With a step closer to Emma, I watch Faline's immediate fallback. When I shift away, the bitch is back to determined stealth, making me wonder where she's hiding the katanas and poisoned apples. The result is a combination of exhilaration and trepidation. I imagine this is what Van Helsing felt when discovering Dracula's issue with crucifixes. *Great*—a way to keep the monster at bay. *Shit*—now we have to face the concept of seriously confronting her.

Not that my badass miracle of a wife is comprehending any of that—or, for that matter, letting it hold her up. She's still facing off against Faline with the grace of an Amazonian queen. If she feels the air shifting with the vacillating balance of power, she doesn't show it—even when Faline moves to fight it, flexing and unflexing her hands as she moves her weight from one hip to the other and back again.

"What they are is of no concern to you, little Flare."

Emma's jaw visibly stiffens. Her shield blazes so strongly, it sounds like a rocket revving for takeoff. "When children are enslaved, it's *everyone's* concern," she spits.

Faline flashes her teeth again. "They are *not* yours, damn it!"

"Hmmm." Emma taps her chin. "Is that so? Because we did just kind of *find* them, you know? And they just sort of followed us, like hungry kittens, you know?"

"A lie!" Faline lunges. Well, tries to. As soon as I shift closer to Emma, Faline's thrown back as if she rammed into a glass slider that was cleaned too well. "You did not just find them. You *stole* them!"

Emma folds her arms. "That sounds cool too. I always *did* wonder why Robin Hood couldn't be a girl."

Faline's face turns the color of furious embers. "Damn you."

Faline rages again. This time with an amped volume button. "Damn you!"

"Screw *you*."

The parting shot is gasoline on Faline's coals, but Emma clearly doesn't care. My woman's mind is already made up. Faline isn't getting anywhere near her children or her man, and she's willing to give her life for that cause. I don't make the observation lightly. The woman is prepared to die for this.

Meaning there's only one thing for me to do about it.

I stomp forward, bringing myself shoulder-to-shoulder with her.

Standing with her.

Connecting with her.

Compelling her to hold me as tightly as I grab her. Showing her, as clearly as I'm dictating to Faline, exactly how clear I am about the discovery of the twins' paternity—and how it changes nothing in what I just declared to her. If Faline wants those girls back, she'll have to go through us first. Both of us. And right now, I'd almost like to see her try—if only to show the pathetic hag that her hate and fear don't stand a chance against the force of our bond, our family, *our love.*

A love that overrides so much. A power, greater than lightning blasts or solar punches or air erasures, that makes my heart slam screeching brakes on so many of my angry, violent instincts.

For a single moment.

The only second Faline needs.

To whirl and then dive back into the portal she's reopened on the air—leading to God only knows where.

Not that I fucking care. She's good and gone, at least for now—a fact that should have me back at square one of my usual teeth gnashing and self-raging but simply doesn't.

Because as thoroughly as I still want to wrap my hands around that woman's neck until I feel her windpipe snap, there are more important issues to handle right now.

No. More important *people.*

As Emma already comprehends.

We race across the room, dropping between the sprawled men on the floor. Since Emma's already checking on Foley, Archer, and Shay Bommer, I drop down beside Shay's brother, Tait—and steel myself for the chest blooming with blood, the stare focused on nothing.

And the guy's staring, all right—fixing two irises full of incredulous gold light up at me. Then blinking in wide confusion. "The hell-forsaken fuckity fuck?" And then swearing like he's training to go pro at it.

His brother spews a rough laugh. "And you didn't want to bring your Kevlar."

The guy hitches out a foot, clipping his little sib's calf. "Butthead. Never said I didn't *want* to bring it, only that I wondered if it'd be necessary."

Shay kicks him with equal ruthlessness. "Because you said this was going to be a basic babysitting job?"

Tait raises his hands, palms lifted, offering a blatant *mea culpa*. "Guilty as charged. And holy half-pipe of fuckery, was I wrong." Or maybe he's already gone pro and hasn't had the chance to share it over beer and pretzel bites.

Not that he's going to get the chance now. With my bloodstream already pumping with fresh jolts of fire, I pivot around to face Foley, Emma, and the others, spreading my glowing fingers across my tensed haunches. "Now that we're squared up on who came to the party prepared, I wish I could tell you all it's over. But if her highness of evil depravity is up to half her usual game, there's a good chance she Elphaba'ed herself out of here and straight to the ground floor of this building."

"Which means what?"

But before Tait's done with the query, my wife is on her feet and halfway to the door. "Holy *shit*. The kids!"

I'm already on her six. By the time she clears the kitchen, I'm shoulder-to-shoulder with her. Damn good thing because once we reach the private elevator landing and I pulse the doors open, I've got my other arm locked around her waist. Thank fuck for the woman's honed instincts, which prompt her to do the same to my waist with her leg. By the time I sear away the floor of the elevator car and then leap into the shaft below, she's my perfect electric spider monkey, hanging on across my back as I pulse-bounce us seventy stories down. Though she's filled with urgent silence, I'm still hyperaware of how thankful she is for my action. Seventy floors goes by a lot faster when one isn't waiting on an elevator's machinations.

When we reach the bottom floor, we have the option of

veering right toward the executive offices or hooking left for the hotel's back-of-house, which includes the catering loading dock and the private parking space in which I keep a new Range Rover parked at all times. It's my version of a Team Bolt disaster preparedness kit. The bullet-proof, heat-proof, extra horsepower car is also stocked with enough MRE meals and water to keep six adults alive for a week.

In short, it's been ready for a situation exactly like this one.

And as Emma swings off my back and leads the sprint to the dock, I pray like hell that it's gone.

She gets to the strip of raised concrete first. Skids to a stop along the polished steel lip of the dock.

And then erupts with a tear-infused whoosh of air.

Which tells me absolutely nothing.

But once I pound to my own halt, I commiserate completely with her outburst. I slam my hands to my knees as a mix of a bellow and a sob erupts from my own throat, weighted with a world of relief and a whole cosmos's worth of gratitude.

The Rover's gone.

After basking in my three seconds' worth of elation, I yank my phone out of its insulated pocket in my left thigh—and pray that Lydia and Angie have remembered to tune the car's radio channel for receiving my private frequency code.

Before my finger hits the first button, there's an incoming call to my device. The Brocade's front desk. *Shit.*

The tension in my gut surges into a terse repetition of the word as I stab at the screen to answer. "Neeta. Talk to me." For the last three days, the woman has been filling in as main manager for the night crews at my request. Wade's been pulling the same duty for the day shift, but we're still an hour away from the eight o'clock shift change. During the E-ticket ride that's been life since we discovered the Source and rescued its victims, I've felt safer about the Brocade as an extended home front with the two of them on guard in the exec offices. What might seem like "nothing" to a normal supervisor might be a smoking grenade in our expanded dimension of the world.

Though at the moment, Neeta doesn't sound like she's reporting a mere grenade. "You should probably come to the lobby." There's none of her usual musical lilt or fragment of lightness in the suggestion. "You should probably come *now*."

"What is it?" I charge. My stomach has balled up so bad, it's the gastrointestinal Death Star. "Neeta?"

After a pause that's too damn long for the planet destroyer in my gut, she finally replies, "It is not a *what*. It is a *who*."

"Fuck." Though this might actually be a *good* thing. If Faline's staring down my front desk staff, that means she's not out looking for Lydia, Angie, and the kids. The assurance lends the mettle I need to finally dictate, "All right. Okay. So don't talk to the bitch at all. You tell her that whatever she's fucking here for—"

"Mr. Richards."

"—she'll talk to *me* for that demand and nobody else. Just say I'm on my way—"

"*Mr. Richards.*"

"—and then tell her she can stand or sit while—*what*?" Her exigency finally sinks in, forcing me to interrupt myself. The full stop means a physical one as well. I endure Emma's baffled stare while refocusing my attention on Neeta instead of my diatribe.

"It—it is not a *she*," Neeta states quietly.

I blink and then shake my head. "The hell?"

"It would be prudent for you to get here sooner rather than later."

It's the Neeta Jain version of *get your ass here five minutes ago*, and I only need to hear it once. "On my way," I bark before ending the call, ramming my phone back into my pocket, and then taking the remaining distance of the service hall at a full run. Emma, not wasting any time on questions, keeps up with my pace.

Neither of us stops until we turn the corner, race past the coffee cart and the gift shop, and arrive in the main expanse of the lobby. The professional decorators have been at work since we cleaned up after being the post-earthquake triage center, and all of the accessories in the space are now decked out in a nautical/surfing culture theme for the summer rush ahead, but I hardly give it all a glance. No... Less than that.

My attention has already zoomed in on the reason beneath Neeta's forced politeness. Forced because she's probably been terrified, along with the rest of the wide-eyed night crew lined up behind the desk.

Now here's a reason to break the laser focus for a second. And thank fuck, it only takes a second to solidify that they all haven't been coerced into standing there *Rent the Musical* style, as if waiting for their cue to break into "Seasons of Love." They're there because this is a sight to behold.

Because it's not every day that the boss of the world's most notorious crime cartel just strolls into the middle of one's hotel lobby.

But here he is.

Atticus fucking Scorpio.

Turning to greet me and smiling as if we've been lifelong pals. "Reece Richards!" And shaking my hand with the same surreal gusto. "And look at this. You have come to greet me in your badass Bolt outfit, *sì*?" He releases me to box at the air, and I take careful note of his wicked, well-trained right hook. "I am honored, *mi amigo*. Thank you for taking the time to speak with me."

I rock back on one heel, carefully folding my arms. Not a great stance for a balancing act because I literally feel like I'm up on one right now. I should be as tense and terrified as Neeta and the gang, but instead I feel like I'm at a Hollywood event and have been assigned a handler who's just a fanboy in disguise. Any second now, I'm prepared for the Bolt T-shirts, posters, sunglasses, and lightning sticks to come out, along with an assortment of nifty-colored autograph Sharpies.

"We're not exactly 'speaking' yet, *amigo*," I counter. "And for that matter, we are *not amigos*." I doubt he needs elucidation on the subject, since his organization basically bankrolled my mutation, but if he doesn't want to drop the butt-hurt innocent act, I'll be more than happy to reeducate him about why we're not going to go get nine holes in at Terranea anytime soon.

Fortunately, Atticus Scorpio is a smart man. At once, he cuts the smiley photo-op bullshit and motions for his two guards to stay back as he steps over slowly. With every inch he moves in, there's more of the hardcore business demeanor that has me finally respecting—and fearing—him. "Very well, then," he offers. "We are two successful business leaders, *sì*? And I can speak to you in that spirit?"

I hold back from pointing out that "successful leaders" don't make their fortune on smuggling shit like drugs, guns, and people, but some conversations are best left in the shadows at a time like this. Besides, the guy's made the good faith move of meeting me on my turf, out in public, during the day. He's got no double motives and has already proven it.

"Of course," I reply to him at last. "What happens to be on your mind?"

Scorpio tugs at the lapels of his suit. For a second, I admire the bespoke craftmanship of the thing. The charcoal ensemble fits him to the iota and is a collection of the classiest current trends. "An arrangement," he states. "Arriving at a mutually beneficial goal for both of us."

I hardly blink at the man. I sure as hell don't waver the rivet of my stare on him, despite my curiosity about what Emma's reaction to this is. Naturally, I'm picking up wave after wave of impressions, ranging from trepidation and suspicion to marvel and bewilderment—but the raw, unfiltered force of her gut reaction is only possible with a shared glance. Not going to happen.

So I take the only action that makes sense.

"What goal could that possibly be?"

I take no care to hide a single nuance of my skepticism—or my rage. The man and his organization have been all but ducked between Faline's legs for years, servicing her every need while sawing off their dicks as sacrifices for her temple. And this bastard knows it. He *knows* exactly what that woman authorized to be done to me and all the ways she's fucked with my life ever since. I've earned every fucking drop of this bitterness, and I mentally bask in it despite the man's unchanging expression.

Until he twists up one side of his mouth. And impales me with a stare that's agleam with new glints—matching his new aura of predatory energy.

"You don't like Faline Garand," he finally says. "*I* don't like Faline Garand." The violent purpose in his mien turns into a tangible energy. "Let's take her out, Bolt Man. Together."

CHAPTER TWO

EMMA

"Holy. Shit."

At this moment, Lydia's outburst is better than the sun that's reflecting off our pool and the juicy sangria in my hand. It's everything I hoped for—perhaps even more because it's joined by Trixie's astounded gasp and Angie's light clappings. Neeta doesn't add to the fray but trades a glance with me that's worth her abstention. She knows exactly what I'm feeling right now.

Validation.

Commiseration.

Confirmation that what happened two days ago was an honest-to-God reality.

Atticus Scorpio really hadn't been an impeccably engineered hologram. The man, in all his Black Panther-meets-Luther grandeur, had really shown up at the Brocade in his fine, fine suit and approached Reece with his wild, wild idea.

I'm still wearing half a smile of disbelief as my sister leans in with spare-no-details zeal. "*Emmalina Paisley.*"

"Whaaaat?" I tease back, clearly driving her nuts. But it's an afternoon made for teasing. And happiness. And simply rejoicing in the moment. Oh, yes. Especially that part. If a moment is all we have, then that's what we'll damn well take.

We're finally back at the ridge after the insanity of last week. We've decided to bunk the girls with Lux for now, though Reece has already commissioned blueprints for a new wing on the house with exclusive bedrooms for all three of them. Sawyer's buddies are sprawled through all of the guest rooms and have had fun assisting "Folic Acid" in training Lux on his newfound abilities. The rest of the team are enjoying some well-deserved time off, and the girls of the "Bolt Bunny" squad have decided to do the same.

Which leads us right back to here. On an epic poolside day bed that fits all five of us—and the large tray to support our pitcher of sangria and glasses. In short, *perfection*.

"You are forbidden to leave us hanging *there*." Yep, even when Lydia backs up her charge by snatching away my full glass of cranberry-colored wine. "No more for you until we hear the rest, missy!"

"Heeeyyy," I cry. "There are laws against blackmail in this state, *missy*."

"Don't look at *me*." Trixie shoots up both hands though dips one back down to get in a sip of the crimson nectar in her glass. "I definitely vote for *your* version of this over Reece's. To him, three grunts and an 'it was fine, Mom' constitute filling me in about everything."

That has me breaking into a new laugh—mostly because it's true. My husband can light up a whole room with his charm and wit when he wants to, but *only* when he wants to. In business, whether it's running the Richards kingdom, driving the RRO vision, or pulsing Team Bolt to greater destinations of do-gooding grandeur, he's all about the mission goals and nothing but the mission goals.

Which circle my mind right back to the surreal scene from the Brocade's lobby. And yes, the place in the plot where I left them all hanging on a jaw-dropping cliffie. Not intentionally, per se—though I have to admit, stringing Princess Purple Pants along like this has been more fun than parsing out the details about Brady Chadwick.

"All right, all right." I even readjust my position, switching from my relaxed head-on-elbow lounge to a fully seated thing, my hands in my lap and my legs crossed at the ankle. "The bunnies deserve the whole hip-hoppity story."

"But if you end it with Mr. McGregor chasing you guys out of the garden, I will be one pissed-off little rabbit." Lydia adds an angry swig of sangria to her soft growl. I'm tempted to call her out for sangria abuse, but she's in a sassy mood, likely due to Sawyer taking her off to bed early last night. Anytime Sawyer drags my sister off to bed, I have no idea what the woman will feel emboldened to do the next day. I want my beverage hostage returned unharmed.

"No Mr. McGregors, I promise." I cant my head while watching a pair of hawks swoop over the hillside, riding the late-afternoon wind with their massive wingspans. "Though I have to admit, Atticus's offer did feel like a shovel to the brain."

"You don't say."

'Dia's deadpan earns her a worthy snicker from Trixie before the woman looks my way once more. "Please tell me Reece had the presence of mind to give the man a good laugh at first."

A smile warms my lips. "I'm pretty sure he was strongly tempted," I relay. "I think there was even a comment about hidden cameras and the Consortium taking up video punking now that their hideout's been wiped out." I let the smile wane.

"But Atticus was clearly serious about every word. He stuck to his standpoint."

"Which must have been worthy of Reece's admiration *and* irritation."

Angelique's remark has me abruptly looking away, only to confront Trixie's knowing nod of understanding. It's three seconds that makes a huge difference. As thoroughly as I've come to love Angie, there's a tiny box of resentment in my heart about the past she shares with Reece and the things she knows about him because of it.

"Yeah. That's about right." I barely strain the snip from my tone before murmuring it. "But he finally took the man at his word, at least long enough to ask him why the Scorpios are ready to place such a public offer on Faline's demise."

"Demise." Lydia only says it once out loud, though it's clear she's mentally rolling the word around several more times. "That's exactly what Atticus said? 'Demise'?"

"No," I reply. "His exact term was that the Scorpios want her taken out."

"So what does that mean?" Neeta inserts. "Do they want her killed or simply destroyed?"

"They likely don't care," Trixie states. "As long as the woman is fully separated from them and the Consortium."

"Which essentially doesn't exist any longer anyway," I fill in. "Especially after Reece and I had a chance to fill the man in on the full extent of the Consortium's experiments and procedures."

Lydia sits up higher while openly scoffing. She hangs on to her finishing grimace. "Okay, back up that drug-smuggling canoe, sparky. Are you honestly telling *me* that sexy boy Scorpio told both of *you* that he had no idea what those freaky

Frankensteins were doing down in that lab? Even after they A-okayed the procedures and then snuggled in their beds with visions of super soldiers dancing in their heads?"

"No back-rowing necessary," I state. "Believe me, every upper-level Scorpio boss, as well as his or her lieutenants, knew exactly what they agreed to let the Consortium do—at the beginning."

"And what the hell does that mean?" 'Dia demands.

"Exactly what it implies," I return. "That the Consortium's scientists laid out exactly what the protocol was going to be for their 'unconventional experimentation,' designed with the goal of 'expanding the possibilities of human DNA.'"

Trixie frowns before prompting, "And if superpowers were the outcome of all that..."

"Never occurred to anyone that they would be," I fill in.

"Ah." The new glow across Angelique's skull relays her emphatic agreement. "*Oui.* That explains much." She explains, as soon as we all pivot openly curious stares to her, "In the early days, there was little to no organization down in the hive. Most of the cells were set up with minimal security. The leaders of the project were biogenetics scientists who had been handpicked by Dr. Verriere, the mastermind behind the whole concept. They were beyond brilliant in their fields but, like many geniuses, had no idea how to cope with the rest of life. Several of them barely comprehended how to operate microwave ovens or television remotes, let alone things such as steel containment fields and neutralization cuffs."

"What about Verriere himself?" Lydia queries.

"He was...not there." Angie's face clouds during her distinct pause.

"In the lab?" My prompt is cautious because I'm halfway

to figuring out the gruesome answer anyway. "Or...at all?"

Her skull turns a melancholy blue. She turns, meeting my stare directly. "He was Test Subject Zero."

'Dia gives up a heartfelt sigh. "And like most patient zeros..."

"*Oui,*" Angie rasps. "*Dieu ait son âme.*"

God rest his soul.

"So Faline got hands-on about running the show—and ran full speed with the power rush too." Trixie's comment, while totally true, earns her a wry grimace from my sister.

"More times than not, history is about luck more than anything," Lydia grumbles.

"Never more true than with the Scorpios and their unwanted 'discovery,'" I reply.

"Is that what Atticus implied?" Angie asks.

"More or less." I stretch out my legs even more, pumping my ankles to get some much-needed stretches. Tromping back and forth between the Brocade and the Biltmore has given even my muscled stems some well-earned shin splints. "He was pretty tight-lipped about most of it, but I got the gist of it in his subtext. Long story short, while the Scorpios thought the superpowers were cool and all, *nobody* in their organization was interested in being the next Professor X or Tony Stark. They're in the business of *quietly* making money, not commandeering a battalion of electric mutants who are ready to tear down cities."

A hefty sniff from Angelique. "Which must have made Kane's stunt an interesting twist."

"Especially because it was just six weeks after Reece publicly called them out."

"Ohhhh, shit," Lydia follows up to my statement. "There *was* that..."

"After the one-two battering rams of those events, they put little Fa-Fa on their version of professional notice—and that was before they even knew *I'd* been transitioned."

"Which explains why she went to ground for the months before the wedding," Trixie puts in.

"Which apparently was fine by the Scorpios," I explain. "Atticus told us they all hoped she'd chosen to get the hint and skulk away in peace. They had the order they wanted back at the Source, where they *thought* the scientists were back to work on the issues they cared about, like what the electric advances were doing for human cardiac stamina, physical agility, disease immunity, and high-stress survival."

"Bingo." Lydia nods like a kid pointing out that Lucky Charms turn milk the color of barf. "Super soldiers."

"Yes," I concede. "But that was only a small part of their bigger picture."

Neeta jerks up a little. If there's really such a thing as a lightbulb over someone's head, I'm sure it'd be manifesting over her high ponytail this second. "Because the pharmaceutical applications for all of those advances is much more lucrative than any military contract."

"Bullseye to Miss Jain." I soothe Lydia's tiny pout with an affectionate wink. She takes the setback with stride, even handing back my sangria as she wraps her newly free arm around one of the bed bolsters.

"So when did they find out that Fa-Fa wasn't off working on her tan and half the hotties in Ibiza?" she poses.

I shoot her another wink. "Three guesses, and the first two don't count."

She's ready with an equally sassy grin. "When the footage from your reception went viral."

"Big gold star to the lass with the luscious rack." After reveling in her blush and dodging her bolster toss, I go on. "Long story short, they were just as floored as everyone else at the footage—especially when they did their version of digging into the whole thing and learned very quickly about the woman's not-so-secret plan of 'elevating' the human race with a worldwide army to do her bidding."

While I'm really only restating the truth everyone already knows, they all react to it like a fresh—and staggering—revelation. If we weren't already lazing here like lionesses on the veldt, I imagine they'd all be searching out chairs to sag into.

Neeta's the one who relocates her voice first. "That was probably not the best news for a group controlling most of the world's underbelly."

"And living better than most kings because of it," Lydia states.

"Straw, meet the camel's back," Trixie chimes in.

"And Atticus Scorpio, meet Reece Richards," Angelique concludes.

I let a good minute of silence pass, letting them all absorb that mass of holy-freaking-shit details, before speaking up again. "Once we heard all of that, Atticus's arrival, as well as his proposition, almost seemed like no-brainers."

"Combining resources for a common goal." Angelique finishes that with a small but indecipherable smile. It's a *smile*, but the attached sheen in her eyes is definitely not tears of happiness. "Simple elegance in theory; an utter bitch in execution."

And *now* full awareness clobbers me. She's thinking about the moment when that full idea struck her, as well: sometime during her incubus of heartbreak and horror, after being told that Tyce had been executed. She'd sucked it up and decided to come to us in secret, despite knowing her word would be mud and her promises trusted as much as quicksand.

"But not utterly impossible." I focus the assertion completely at her, praying she sees the deeper message I can only convey with my own smile—and all the assurance and friendship and gratitude I can possibly flow into it. While I'm not ever going to be happy about the pain she's caused Reece, I also have to accept that his unique path landed him in LA to begin with, with his heart and soul in the right place to see and feel mine. The two circumstances go hand-in-hand. Perhaps the stars would have aligned to make us meet that night in the Brocade, but he would've still been the same prince of arrogance as before, and I'd have never been able to feel the impact of the hero he was always meant to be.

"No." Angie utters her reply with soft meaning, at once conveying that she sees and feels my meaning. The light in her eyes warms to the shade of spring grass as she adds, "Not utterly impossible."

The others take quiet sips of their sangria, letting Angie and me have our meaningful moment—which gets its perfect relief in the form of my sister's snorting levity.

"So...Team Bolt and Team Scorpio, in bed together at last. Wouldn't Netflix have a blast with *this* orgy, yeah?"

Before we're all done with our requisite giggles at that, Trixie hikes herself up on an elbow, coyly teething her lower lip. "Speaking of kinky fun..."

"Definitely a great subject switch," 'Dia laughs out.

"Did your adventures with Mr. Scorpio include any discussion about whether he's single or not?"

"Oh my God," I manage to blurt.

"Oh *yasss*, Mama Bear." Lydia leans over to make a quick sign of the cross in front of Trixie's face. "Sister 'Dia approves. That boy is Godiva chocolate *fiiiine.*"

"And a boss for the world's biggest crime cartel? The bastard responsible for financing the Consortium in the first place?"

Thank every saint there is for Angelique and her level head—not that my sister is giving her protest a shred of credence. "*One* of the bosses," 'Dia elucidates. "The man didn't sign off on the decision all by himself. Sometimes bad boys just need to be shown that *good* can be just as sexy and fun."

"Okay, hold up on *that* canoe." Trixie flips a hand up, *bitch please* style. "Didn't say I wanted to convert the boy—just have a little fun during his vacation from the dark side. Who knows? Maybe he'll teach me a few things *I* don't know."

Neeta brightens. "Well, that *does* sound like fun!"

Fortunately, I find commiseration for my what-the-hell-is-happening glower across the entirety of Angie's face. "Have I fallen through one of those damn dimension portals?"

"If so, I'm on the same ride," I mutter.

"*Pssshhh*," Lydia volleys. "Don't listen to the damp laundry, T." And then gives Trixie's back some reassuring rubs. "You're a vital, sexy woman with needs. There's nothing wrong with scratching those itches."

"Who's scratching *what* itches now?"

All five of us start when Reece appears along with his soft, shrewd query. As one, we spew, "No one!" And then reward ourselves with a wild spray of laughter, inciting the requisite round of hysterical follow-ups.

"No scratching happening here, buddy."

"Not a single scratch in sight. Nopey-nope."

"Move along. Move along. Nothing to see here, pal."

"We're just sangria-sipping bunnies, shooting the shit about nothing at all."

"Well, in that case"—Reece leans in and then down, slipping his arms beneath my back and knees—"you all won't mind if I borrow *this* little bunny for a few minutes?"

My fellow bunnies, relieved they won't be questioned anymore by Mr. Persistent himself, chime out their wholehearted approval of him making off with me as the prize. I can't say that the plan sucks, wholly enjoying the feeling of being held safe and sound in his massive coils of muscle and sinew. After being required to put on my brave Flare face for so many days, it's a blissful change to be simply his treasured girl again.

Until we get inside.

And I behold the four new visitors to our home, waiting up on the landing of the main entrance foyer.

A group of hunks who all look like they should be in a designer spread for *GQ*. Or at the front line of a Wakanda battle scene. Or on the covers of four hot romance novels. I'd take any or all of the above.

As long as I was doing it on my own two feet.

"Shit, shit, shit, shit!" It gets a seething repetition as Reece crosses the living room without setting me down, though at last, my irritation pierces all the way into the stubborn ox. As the bastard finally sets me back on my feet, there's the hint of a shit-eating smirk across his face—though I have no time to smack it away before he grabs my hand and pulls me up the slate stone stairs.

Once we're at the top, Reece tightens his grip in proportion to the tension beneath his "charming" smile. At the same time, I'm glaringly aware of the same energy flowing off his steel-straight posture and stiff limbs, his protectiveness a tangible force as he offers his free hand to Atticus Scorpio.

"Reece Richards," the man says, bowing low. "Your home is beautiful. Thank you for entrusting us with the knowledge of its location and the use of your command center."

"You're welcome," Reece responds with the elegance of a king in his castle. My swoon-worthy comparison gets help from his sleeveless, royal-blue hoodie, skintight black running pants, and the Danners in which he does all his training. If Henry the Eighth were alive today, these would've been the sporty monarch's togs of choice. On the flip side, it's not hard to imagine my man astride a massive destrier with his helmet tucked under one arm and a lance beneath the other. "And I apologize that we're not able to offer any guest rooms for your use, but we're at a full house with all of Mr. Foley's Special Ops friends choosing to stay over."

Atticus nods, his smile matching Reece's for regality—beneath a gaze that's already calling bullshit on half of what was said. He knows it; we know it. One: Reece isn't sorry about the bedding situation at all. Two: he used the formality as a chance to remind Atticus that should they try anything beyond working side-by-side with us, he's got a contingent of trained warriors at *his* fingertips too.

"Oh, please," Atticus protests in a mild growl. "Do not waste a single worry about us. Our mobile housing unit made it up the grade fine. We will not be troubling you for accommodations."

"You're no trouble at all, Atticus."

But he's already telling another half-truth—at least from

where I'm standing. "No trouble" is a relative term when it comes to this whole arrangement, and no amount of Trixie's carefree flirting or Lydia's lighthearted ribbing is going to untangle the knot of apprehension refusing to leave my stomach. And my nerves. And damn near every instinct in my body. While I manage to mask it long enough to get through the introductions to Atticus's guys—named Athos, Porthos, and Aramis; I am *not* kidding—the uneasiness stays with me. None of my usual "shake it off" fixes are working, either.

After some downtime with the kids, forty-five minutes on the treadmill, and even some alone time with my favorite instrumental music and the newest Sierra Cartwright book, I finally give up and take an early evening bath. I pull out all the stops on the extras, as well. I soak for an extra-long time in the vanilla-scented bubbles, surrounded by my favorite patchouli-scented candles. Ariana Grande's on my phone, playing through the wireless speakers in the ceiling. Just for the moment, I tell myself to focus on the words she's singing. To just keep breathing.

In...

Out...

In...

Out...

"Bubble for your thoughts?"

I smile but don't open my eyes. His arrival was silent but not surprising. I began feeling his energy, powerful and potent, between each of my steady breaths. Again, not a surprising meeting—since the man is as natural, vital, and intimate to me as air. Perhaps, right now, even more than that. As he rests on the lip of the tub, I go ahead and acknowledge that truth. The simple certainty that *this* is what I've been after all afternoon.

The strength of him on the air. The force of him in my world. The connection to him in my heart.

I take another moment to savor the physical pleasure of his proximity, as well. The blend of his masculine spice with the earthy sensuality of the patchouli. The slide of his muscled thigh along the edge of the tub. And now, the gorgeous contrast of his deep growl against the backdrop of Ariana's soft soprano.

"Okay...*two* bubbles for your thoughts?"

I giggle softly while lifting my stare up his form—before silently claiming the Luckiest Woman Alive prize for the day. The sight is beyond better than I expected. He's ditched the hoodie and switched out the running pants for a pair of swim trunks. Random droplets cling to the ends of his hair, and pure joy inundates his stare. I drink in his naked torso as if it's the first time I've ever ogled him, since all of my body feels exactly the same way. I'm warm and alive, sensitive and stimulated, needing more but openly wondering if I've had too much already. *But more what?*

And am I really asking myself *that* stupid question?

It's all right in front of me. *He's* right in front of me. So stunning and carved. So etched and defined. So burnished and brawny.

Holy hell.

Why does the bath water feel hotter by the second? And why does every little ripple or wave feel like a deliberate taunt across my sensitized nipples, my tingling thighs...and my quivering, impatient clit?

Why does the man pick *now* to start watching the bubbles as if he can see through them...and knows all that?

Why has it never felt more utterly awesome to have him reading my mind?

Awesome.

And awkward.

And absolutely craptastic on timing.

It has to be well after four o'clock. That means an army of fifteen hungry stomachs, including three Spec Ops hunks and an equal number of bottomless pits known as our children will have to be fed soon. No time for caving in to carnality and yanking his sexy-as-hell ass in here with me.

On to option two. Changing the subject. Fast.

"Looks like you've been busy, Aquaman."

"Errrmm..." He cocks his head, causing some of that deliciously damp hair to fall against his forehead. "The name's Aqua *Bolt*, ma'am."

"Ahhh." I can't help another light laugh. "Yes, of course." I quirk a mischievous smirk. "And is that what you told the kids to call you too?"

"Right." He snorts. "And you think they'd listen if I did?"

I pop up a little straighter, not caring about the suds running down my bared breasts, as a semi truck of a thought slams my brain. "Shit. Ira and Mis—"

"Had a blast," he supplies. "Though we could have predicted that, based on how much they already enjoy bath time."

A smile blooms all the way up from my heart. "Well, I've seen them giving the pool some cautiously optimistic looks."

"And once I informed them that there was such a thing called 'water ballet'..."

I break out with a delighted chuckle—though my horrified gasp interrupts it as Mack truck number two barrels in. "Oh, but shit! I haven't thought to get them swimsuits yet!"

"*Hey.*" He scoops one of my hands into his. "Follow the

directions, lady. Keep breathin'. Don't worry. Angie bought them some cute suits during her dash into Malibu yesterday." My instant reaction to that, a mix of relief and bewilderment, doesn't slip by him for a second. I can tell because of the ruminative look that claims his own features. "I told her it was all right, Velvet." His assurance is firm but gentle. "She's been processing her reaction to the new intel about them."

"About Tyce being their true father." I return his grip with some pensive squeezes. Get a swallow down that's just as conflicted. "Of course," I mumble. "I sensed as much during our estrogen and sangria fest this afternoon, but I didn't want to pry, especially in front of the others."

Reece dips in to flow a tender kiss across my forehead. "Because your heart is that tender and your soul is that insightful," he whispers. "And I know she probably felt your concern anyway. Your magic is a tough thing for anyone to ignore, beautiful."

I rock my head back, making it impossible for him to ignore where I want him to re-aim his kisses. "You're being really gooey for a guy who probably spent the last hour being ruthlessly clobbered at Marco Polo," I get in before our lips meet in a slick, sweet smack. "And being the enchanted water ballet prince."

Another wet kiss. A beam of his wider smile. "See? You *are* magic."

"And *you're* full of a lot of mush talk." I frame his jaw with my fingers, using the grip as leverage to push him back by several inches. "But maybe you just need to rip off the bandage here, Dr. Bolt."

His obvious bemusement backs him up by another inch. "Rip off the *huh*?"

"*Reece.*" I roll my eyes. "Just *stop.*" Another roll, this time of my shoulders. More bubble residue dribbles down my chest, but I'm beyond caring about propriety at the moment. "And just give it to me straight. If Angelique wants to file for custody of the girls, then we have to agree that we won't stand in her way. She's just as entitled to—"

I'm cut short by more rolling, though none of it's my doing now. My husband moves in to consume my personal space with a push of his shoulders and then a plunge of his mouth, whirling his tongue deep inside me while working his grip around the back of my neck. A moan escapes my throat. Steamy heat invades my thoughts. Arousal drenches my blood. I'm assaulted by his passion, expressing itself in ever-changing sweeps and angles, enforced by the sensual lunges and turns of his jaw and lips...and soon, his shoulders and arms, as well. A savage sound curls up from the middle of his chest as he leans in more, engaging his body in as much of the ruthless invasion as he can. In return, I slide my slippery hands up his chest and then around his neck, clinging one around that beautifully muscled column while delving the other up and into his thick, luxurious hair.

I'm still holding him that way, and he grips me with matching fervor, when our mouths finally break free from their fiery fusion. His gaze is a hypnotizing whirl of silver heat. His responding words are a stamp of noble vow—and violent promise. "Those girls are *ours*, Emmalina." He clenches his jaw so hard, there's an earthquake-worthy tick that appears in it. "That's not my arrogance speaking—nor my selfishness or my righteousness or my belligerence." He moves a hand around mine. Guides it from his neck to the center of his chest. "That's my heart, declaring what I *know* is the right thing for them. *Our family.*"

A tear-weighted sigh leaves me—one of several that have broken out since he started talking, though I've kept them subdued so as to not interrupt him. So as to not stop the declaration that vibrates my soul more than any other magnificent thing he's ever declared to me. The love he's committing to with such trust and grace, I'm drowning in the force it. Overwhelmed by the beauty of it.

At last, I'm able to form my lips around words of my own. "I know all of that too, my love. And I believe all of it just as thoroughly." With a small wince, I press my fingertips harder into the valley between his massive pecs. "But we can't just dismiss Angie—"

"And nor should we." His dedication to the statement is as plain as his others. "And she already knows that too; I'm sure of it. She sees how Lux already looks after them and how caring for him in return is a source of comfort for them." A deeper solemnity takes over his gaze. "And I think she also knows that they'll thrive more with the stability of a family rather than being at the mercy of whatever her life holds for now." The seriousness flees as a curious chuckle takes hold of him, reacting to the sharper one I've already tossed out. "What?" he finally prods past his twitching lips.

My own mouth, still surrendering to humorous twitches, calms enough to volley, "You really went there, didn't you?"

"Went where?"

"Called our life *stable*?"

He submits to a full snort. "Well, at least I accomplished my mission."

I arch both brows. "There was a *mission*?"

He nods. "To finally rescue my fair damsel from her brood

over the Scorpio invasion."

My cheeks heat as I stare up at him in new awareness—and a hell of a lot of chagrin. *Oh, God.* I took the man's hospitality and cordiality toward Atticus as total acceptance of their presence here and then let my anxiety cloud my mind from thoroughly thinking it all through.

Like considering that maybe Reece was acting out his part as much as I was mine.

Like realizing he has just as many reasons—no, *more*—as me to be skeptical of the Scorpios' new "arrangement" with us.

Like trusting that he's instructed Wade, Alex, and Fershan to lock away certain aspects of our intel until we comprehend the full scope of what the cartel is willing to share with *us* in return.

Like anticipating that he's going to regard me exactly as he does now, staring through my eyes and right into all the fears of my heart and have just the right words to say to that anxiety.

"Concern isn't something you have to go through alone, Velvet."

Words exactly like that.

"We're in this together, baby—and we have an incredible team of support to help us out."

And yeah...that too.

"I know." I owe him at least those words in return—especially because all of my spirit gets poured into them. *"I know."* All of my trust, my fortitude, my faith—which I feel Reece absorbing and understanding, despite the subtle tightness that persists at the corners of his eyes.

At last, he murmurs back, "But..." And draws out the word until it lilts up, intimating a question.

I haul such a deep breath in, it makes the water slosh. "But what if it's not enough?" I finally rush out—and don't plan on stopping there, now that it's honest confessions time. "What if Atticus doesn't really want to get Faline? What if they're still cozier than a pair of drunk girls in a rideshare and this is their way of robbing the new driver? What if—"

He silences me with a kiss. This one's brief and brutal, but my heart skips for so many beats that I'm forced to listen as my breaths catch up to the rest of my system.

"Half-credit points for getting one word right," he tells me. "*Driver* is right—which means that no matter what the drunk chicks in the back are doing, *we're* still controlling the route and speed here." From his position, still looming forcefully over me, he dunks his hand into the water and scoops my own inside it. "And I'm not leaving any fucking part of that equation to chance, either."

My lips part in conjunction with the fresh ferocity in his gaze. "Meaning...what?" I manage to babble out.

The fierce silver fires get liquefied and then poured into blade molds. "Strength in numbers," he explains as they harden into truculent daggers. "As we speak, Sawyer and the Bommers are calling in a few more old friends. A guy named Zeke is flying down from Seattle, and Tait contacted someone named Kellan, whom he calls 'brother close.' Guess that guy's bringing a gal named Lani, who can hold her own with a knife and a gun. She's married to one of them, I think—or maybe both of them, if I was really listening right..."

His narrowed gaze of confusion has mine expanding the other direction. "Well, *this* should be interesting." I conclude with a little laugh because I can afford to. Because I know, without a shred of doubt, how seriously he's been taking all of this all along—and because I don't want to think about how ashamed I am for thinking he wasn't.

"Oh, that's just the *beginning* of interesting." He flashes his finest rogue's smile as soon as I tilt a curious glance that has me feeling like a cute puppy greeting card. "We've got even more enforcements on the way," he explains. "I called Aliz and Kain and asked if they'd be interested in trial positions with us, starting right away."

Screw the cute puppy dog card. I'm now the animated oh-hell-yes celebration card—albeit the not-safe-for-work kind, since I pop my chest and more out of the water to yank him into a wet, delirious kiss—in more ways than just the obvious. "You're right," I gush, my damp lips still on his. "That's interesting on crack. And I'm beyond in love with you for it."

I set myself up for one of his snarky Star-Lord lines, meant to charm me and disarm me at once. I am *not* ready for his adorably humble half smile and the dismissive dip of his head.

"Well, it kind of made sense, right?" he asks—making me wonder if he's also about to demand if his butt looks big in his black and gray board shorts. "Kainalu can put all that technical prowess to work and learn the ropes from Fersh and Alex. And did you know Aliz used to be an au pair for several Bavarian nobles?"

"I didn't," I offer with a widening smile. "But that fits."

Having taken advantage of my mermaid lunge out of the water and gotten a solid grip on my slick body, he secures his hold even tighter—before hoisting me all the way out of the water. I let out a startled *yeep* but don't fight his move. Secretly, I even revel in it. As enticing as he is with the gee-whiz version of Star-Lord, he's a straight-up ovary exploder as a seductive Star*fox*.

And freaking gawd, what a perfect evocation.

As he cradles me against his gleaming, rippled torso, both of us dripping with the water and bubbles that have escaped the tub with me.

As he wraps himself over and around me, turning my spine and ass into tingling lattices of sizzling sensation as he caresses them...pulses them...awakens them.

As he dips in to hover his face over mine, his wet waves and his dark stubble turning him into a dark and dangerous water god.

Dark, dangerous...and nearly naked.

A fact I fight to keep out of my mind—*so* unsuccessfully—as the man roams his face yet closer, his lips seeming to ride potent trade winds across the surface of mine, his breaths coating me in hotter, heavier heat. "Of course it fits," he husks, referencing my quip—though he's as far from giving a quip as we are from Antarctica. "Just like *we* fit, Bunny." He extends his sensual flight over my chin, across my cheeks, up the bridge of my nose, and all the way to my upper hairline. Once he reaches that point, he adds heart-halting nips of his lips... and his tongue. "Our souls. Our energies. Our passions," he whispers as he goes, following a different path on his way back down to my lips...causing me to tremble in new, nerve-opening ways. "And our bodies."

I whimper with consuming craving from the second he speaks those last words against the front of my neck. I arch back, knowing the blunt offering I'm making of my suds-covered nipples, but I can't help myself—just like I can never control myself once the man starts touching me. Awakening me. Worshiping me...

"I was *so* hoping you'd say that." My rasp, hoarse and

needy, comes from places I hardly recognize—from the person I was before a trip through the Source irrevocably changed me. Enforced in me that every day is a gift, filled with moments to seize and savor. Yes, even moments like this. *Especially* moments like this, which are about more than the carnal pleasure for the taking.

They're about the *giving* too.

Offering myself, bared in body *and* soul, for his full consummation and pleasure.

Opening myself, emotionally as well as physically, for the glowing completion of his touch.

Exposing myself, to the core of my sex and the center of my heart, for the full, hot penetration of his.

Oh dear God, I certainly hope so...

"I always know what you want to hear, my beautiful bunny." His rumble is so delicious and deep, my ovaries start splintering again—especially as he uses the pause to rearrange our positions. By the time I drag my senses out of their Bolty-growl stupor, my ass is parked where his just was, with my thighs spread and locked by his possessive grip. Reece is on his knees before me, as magnificent as a conquering gladiator, the mountainous muscles of his torso gleaming with humidity and lined by water drips...with his masculine V arrowing my sights down to his glorious erection.

I swear to every higher power there is...this man's penis alone qualifies him for superhero status.

I plan on saying as much after hungrily licking my lips, but my stunning husband cuts in once more with his decadent, dominant snarl. "Now I want you to tell me what *I* want to hear."

One tangle of my stare with his, and I'm the magical mind

reader now too. What I decipher brings a slow, sultry smile across the lips I've just shined with the tip of my tongue. "But you don't want me to *tell* you, Zeus." I murmur it while fitting my hands atop his...and urging his hold closer to the part of me that's thrumming, aching, and dripping already. "You want me to *beg* you."

A new roll of thunder from the darkest storms deep inside him. "Fuck," he grates. "*Yesssss*." And then again, both words rougher and needier, as he works his hands down and in, stretching his long blue digits toward the golden honey at my center...

"Em? *Em?*"

Crap, crap, crap. As dire as the shout is, it definitely doesn't belong to Reece. *He's* become the stunningly still hunk between my legs, even managing to go stealth with his chuckle as I muffle my moan in the meat of his shoulder.

"Baby girl, I'm sorry about this." Lydia's tone gets terser, though I don't detect any come-now-someone's-bleeding-or-dying notes in her call. "Reece told us you needed some alone time, and I really respect that, but unfortunately—*ohhhh, holy shit!*"

I should be screaming in mortification, but as soon as my sister swings open the bathroom door with the gusto of Maria Von Trapp in the middle of "My Favorite Things," only to be record-scratched into scented candles, dripping bubbles, and Ariana singing about dangerous living and rising temperatures, all I can do is explode in insane laughter. Luckily, Reece is right there with me. His chest is filled with hearty chuckles; his shoulders shake as he stuffs that exquisite erection back into his trunks. At the same time, I grab my après-bath robe and make haste about the decency factor, as well.

"Okay now, missy," I chide. "We promise no more seared retinas for Auntie 'Dia."

"For now."

Lydia rewards Reece for his cocky taunt by dousing him with my "Coconut Lime Breeze" body spray. "Dick," she mutters, earning *her* one of the warm, confident chuckles that always takes my breath away.

In moments like this, the effect is made even better by the halo of gold energy I watch around the damp waves on his head. He's my dark, beautiful angel. The hero who knows how to keep me safe and sane. The man who even shares my utterly twisted sense of humor—providing specific proof by looping an arm around 'Dia's neck and then murmuring, "Come now, sweet sister. No need to turn this into a praise service. It *is* one of my finer features, but your sister can take care of making sure I know it."

"When I'm not interrupted." I punctuate with a giggle, looking forward to 'Dia's zinger in return.

"That so?" She seesaws her accenting glower. "Maybe you'd better be glad it was me and not Mother."

Okay, any zinger but that.

"Why the hell would it be Mom?"

"Because she just called your cell—and like the good, decent sister I am, I picked up."

"And?"

She folds her arms. Taps one foot. And prompts, "'Annnnd, what did our beloved maternal unit tell you, oh honorable best little sister in the whole world?'"

"*Lydia!*"

She forgives me at once for the retaliation, which actually reverts my gut to its giant sewer ball of dread. Her instaabsolution can only mean she's about to relay one really disgusting piece of news.

"She and Dad have just cleared Malibu. They'll be up here in half an hour."

CHAPTER THREE

REECE

I never thought I'd ever hear a sound worse than Emma's screams after hours of Faline's torture. She'd already spent hours on the bitch's table by the time I found out where she was, and when I finally broke into that lab inside the Consortium's Rancho Palos Verdes complex, my woman's pain had turned into a tangible beast on the air—a beast that had devoured my soul like no other torment before—or, I was damn certain, like no agony would again.

Until right now.

The wails of my two little girls are like banshee cries inside a medieval dungeon—despite the fact that the ridge's underground bunker is outfitted better than most high-end apartments. But the state-of-the-art kitchen, loft-style bunk beds, fit-for-a-queen bathroom, gaming area with theater sound, and reading area with a full library of books can't diminish the bunker's biggest trait—and my twins' hugest trigger.

The fucking thing is underground.

A necessity I have no choice about.

Just like the fate I have to thrust upon them.

"Fuck my life." I've never been one for that trite piece of crap, but in this messed-up moment, nothing feels more fitting. For the rest of my life, those girls are going to hate the hell out of me. For the same time span, I'll be doing the exact same thing.

My gut roils like a toilet tank filled with bile—especially from my next thought. I actually think about my own father and every wrenching call he had to make for *my* own good. All the school transfers, the groundings, the disciplinary meetings...hell, even the jail bail-outs. And finally having to tell the biggest lie of them all—faking his own death—just for the chance to gain intel that would keep the whole family safer.

Fatherhood.

It's not for pussies.

If I survive this night with my heart and soul intact, that's going on a goddamned T-shirt.

But first, the survival thing.

Which, at this point, is going to be sketchy at best—a certainty that hits my gut like an anvil as the twins' shrieks cut into the rest of me like shrapnel. And let's just forget any metaphors for what it feels like to turn and actually look at them again, huddled together on one of the velvet bean bags in the gaming area, a bunch of Minecraft princesses bumping into each other on the screen behind them. We might as well be back in the Biltmore's elevator, with the two of them staring as if I'm one of the hotel's ghosts come to life, except this time, their panic has worsened fivefold.

Because I'm worse than a ghost.

I'm the monster responsible for ordering them underground again.

"Dada."

I don't turn, pretty certain I'm the only one who can hear the gentle summons. Yeah, bringing the girls back underground like it's no big deal is wishful thinking on my part. Lux is obsessively devoted to his new sisters, and he knows they don't like this. If they told him they wanted to fly to the moon just to protest earth altogether, the kid would find a way to make it happen.

On that note, I refocus on pulling two trays of fresh sugar cookies out of the oven. Yeah, they're a brazen peace offering. And yeah, I personally cut them into the shapes of tutus and toe shoes and then mixed pink and purple frosting for the tops. But I already know they'll go ignored.

I suck.

Hard.

But goddamnit, there's no other solution at this point. Not with Todd and Laurel climbing out of their Lexus up at ground level as we speak. Sending the girls away, even with Foley, Archer, and the Bommers in tow, would've meant they'd run into the Crists during the journey down the hill, a risk we couldn't take given Lux's devotion to his "grandpy." Hiding the kids somewhere else in the house likely would've yielded the same result. This was the fastest solution we could think of, though *fast* sure as hell didn't equate to *careful* or *sensitive.*

"*Dada.*"

I look down at the incessant little hand curled atop my wrist. I jerk my sights over, genuinely surprised. He's not my imagination—but all the best parts of my dreams. "Hey, buddy. What is it? You need more chocolate milk already?"

My son shakes his head until white-blond curls drop into his eyes. He pushes them away with a small grunt of impatience, his mouth set in a grim pout. "Mis 'n' Ira scared."

I crouch down and grip his proud little shoulders. They're as tense as if the weight of the world rests on them—because to his mind, his sisters' distress is the same thing. "I know," I concede with as much calm as possible. "They're having memories of when we first found them. Do you remember all that?"

A steady nod. The wisdom of the ages in his eyes. It's not fucking fair for a kid his age, even at his psychological maturity instead of his physical one, to be shouldering so much knowledge of the world's ugliness. He should be over in front of that monitor, telling his sisters he's going to create a few Minecraft monsters to eat their princesses, not pickling several jars with his stress over their wall-jostling fear. "They came out of the hole. I had to tell 'em it was okay not to be in there."

"And now, because the bunker is underneath the ground, they think we're putting them back in the hole."

His forehead gains some furrows. "But we're not!" he argues. "And the bunker is fun!"

A few drops of amusement spread their way into my pond of guilt and dread. "Well, *we* know that, buddy, but they don't. And it'll only be for a few hours, I promise."

"Bad people coming, Dada?"

The lines across his brow get some friends in the frissons across my heart.

"No, son. It's not like that." I slide my hands down, surrounding both of his with them. "Just some visitors we didn't expect, who might be confused about what Mis and Ira are doing here. They might ask some questions we can't answer right now—and until we can officially adopt your sisters, we want to make sure nobody tries to take them away from us."

His responding rage is palpable, his eyes glowing like caution lights and his veins pulsing a rich cobalt. "I'll beat 'em up, Dada. *Hard!*"

"Okay, nobody's getting beaten up tonight." It's an effort to punch my tone with rebuke instead of high-fiving my little stud with pride, but I give myself a mental back pat for doing the responsible adulting thing. "Right now, I need you to be my big helper hero, okay? Lead the girls by example."

"Example? What's that mean, Dada?"

"Well..." I give in to a full grin. "In this case, it's pretty easy. Just show them how we like to party down here, okay?"

"Yeah! Okay!"

At once, the kid launches into a flawless shoot dance, while singing "Don't Stop the Party" complete with hand motions and an "autotuned" voice. He's roused into more by hand claps that synch to his beat, and I swing a stunned stare to watch Foley—*Foley!*—join in on the freaky dance. The claps are coming from Lydia, who sidles up and finally elbows me enough times that I'm joining into the syncopated applause. Even the twins halt their screams long enough to watch the guys bang out a freaky-fly routine, though they return to the exact same spot they were in—somewhere between mild dread cookies and full-blown spazzcakes—as soon as Lux and Foley finish off the routine by parkouring into backflips and then sticking their landings with "ta-da" poses.

"What the hell, Folic Acid?" I demand at once. "You been sneaking out for nights at the raves with the cool kids?"

A snort from the surfer stud who's just danced as if auditioning for a Black-Eyed Peas video. "News flash, Bolt-a-zoid. Your son *is* a cool kid." He turns his hands out and shrugs, looking like a fifteen-year-old caught teaching the preacher's kid to smoke. "What? You think we spend all our training time just *training*?"

"Like you're *supposed* to be?"

My comeback gets another chuff from his direction, along with an eye roll. The combination is enough to garner a belly laugh from Lux, with the trickle-down effect of stopping Mis's and Ira's sobs. For the first time ever, I'm tempted to reward the bastard for his insolence with a crushing hug—but I don't dare tip the room's energy balance that way. Hopefully, the Sawyer and Lydia show is off to a positive start, especially when the girls finally peer over at the cookie assembly counter with interest.

"Bolt Jolt. Dude." Lydia looks ready to give my ribs another "love tap" from her elbow but sticks to a fun-filled shoulder bump instead. "We got this for now. Go turn on the charm for your guests."

Hefty snort. "Guests," I scoff. "Who had the 'manners' to give us a fifteen-minute warning on their approach?"

She beams a shit-eating grin. "Which is why you're called the Sultan of Smooth and I'm down here frosting cookies, baby."

Narrowed glare. "I've *never* been called that."

"Well, you are now."

"So that would make Emma the Sultana of..."

"Patience." She's ready with that answer, in all its sincere reverence, before any of us can blink twice. "Especially when it comes to our whacknut of a maternal creature."

"Who's unleashing the crazytown Kraken on my wife as we speak," I return.

"Which means you gotta bolt, lightning boy." She shoos me with a spoon overloaded by a gob of lavender frosting. When a chunk of the stuff drops off, spattering across her sweatshirt emblazoned with *Cute but Psycho*, it's enough to make me add a smug smirk to my reluctant departure.

"As you wish, Princess Purple Psycho."

I'm not sure if it's my comeback or 'Dia's growl that makes Lux and the twins bust out with new laughs, but I'm grateful no matter what as I back away from the happy scene—every cell in my body hating that I'm not a part of it while every neuron in my spirit prays the positive ju-ju will carry through for at least a couple of hours.

⚡

A couple of hours?

And just what kind of crack was I smoking, thinking Laurel would limit their cute little drop-in to a hundred and twenty silly minutes?

Even with our cover story that "Luke" has gone for a sleepover at Unca Saw Saw and Auntie 'Dia's place—not a lie, if it's stretched by just a little—Emma's mother has insisted on a full tour of the house, with special attention to the minor improvements we've made, as well as enjoying the sunset over drinks out on the terrace. During that time, both Kainalu and Aliz have arrived and been introduced, fortunately having already received my texts that they're to be as general as possible about sharing details of any kind with Laurel. Though I didn't disclose too many details why, I deduced that both of them would discover that for themselves after three minutes in the woman's presence—but shockingly, Laurel goes by for much longer stretches without invoking the almighty name of goddess Faline.

Soon, I recognize that the disparity is just as obvious to Emma as me—an observation she finally gets a chance to vocalize when her mother wanders off to the kitchen on a quest to ask Anya about the artichoke and feta bites that were brought out along with our twilight cocktails. As soon as the two women are busy discussing gluten-free chips and alternatives to sugared coffee creamer, Emma grabs her father by the elbow to guide him into the sanctuary of our home office. While the room isn't soundproof, it's in the middle of the wing that's separated from the rest of the house by a large chunk of the cliff, adding some natural privacy to the setting.

"All right, Grandpy Todd, *what's* the four-one-one here?" she presses. "*I* had to mention Faline first? And Mother actually looked constipated about it for a second?"

"And thank you for *that* perfect visual, darling." Todd's cocked brow and arid tone convey the man's own knowledge about being a Sultan of Smooth. "But even with the colorful help, I'm afraid I haven't got a clue about your mother's new frostbite about Fa-Fa."

"Is it?" I charge. "Frostbite, I mean? Is Laurel completely broken of the addiction?"

"No." Emma mutters it from twisted lips, clearly craving to be wrong. "When she was in my closet and admiring my new boots, I deliberately told her they were an impulse buy, perhaps to make Faline jealous. She smiled and muttered something about how the woman doesn't have time to be jealous."

"Of course not," I snarl. "The witch doesn't waste time with the petty stuff. She goes straight for the big flash stuff. Spitting spite. Shondaland-show nastiness."

Emma spurts out a soft laugh. "You know you just invoked Shonda Rhimes, mister. You also know I accept bribes for silence, right?"

Brief snort. "Oh, I might have a few...talents...with which

to work off my shame."

Emma indulges my flirty sarcasm with a fond smile but picks up her point where she left off. "Mother gave the assertion with a lot of obvious affection, as if she was speaking about an old friend she dearly missed."

I rock back on one foot, letting my head fall in the same direction. "But still, an *old* friend." I study the patterns of afternoon light reflecting off the pool onto our ceiling. Following the intersecting light trails makes it easier to re-envision those strange moments in which Laurel wasn't really herself—which means, of course, that she's actually *becoming* herself again. "Did you catch the moment where she almost forgot Fa-Fa's name completely? She wanted to say something else, I think."

"Perhaps Farrah?" Todd offers.

"Yeah." I snap my head back down, meeting his quiet but insightful gaze. "That really could've been it. She was dancing with an 'r' sound, for sure. What came out sounded like 'Farrine.'"

"Yep," he confirms. "Heard it just as clearly." And changes his expression to convey how he remembers the rest of the moment, as well. Laurel had fumed, openly mortified with herself...as if she was inwardly punishing herself.

As if she was petrified that Faline would show up and do it instead.

"Farrah." Emma's thoughtful repetition is the hook on my concentration, yanking me away from the startling hypothesis my mind's begun spinning to life. It's okay, since I *know* the theory isn't fading off anytime soon. "Mother has a friend named Farrah, doesn't she?" she asks her father. "From the club?"

Todd nods. "You have a good memory, kiddo. They bonded pretty tightly during your last year at college, so you only met her a few times. She and your mom enjoyed the same books and movies." His smile is soft and genuine. "That was a good thing for your mother, since she was trying to get used to you girls not being around all the time. Farrah even encouraged your mom to start painting again. They started taking some night classes together."

"Until our wedding reception."

I could have predicted Emma's ensuing words, down to the emotional wobble. What I'm less sure of is what Todd's going to do with that. While I understand the crazy fence he's been balancing since the second Laurel returned from her "field trip" with Faline after the wedding, there's nothing he can do about the forces controlling his wife. Not so with his daughter, who needs to be guided and loved now more than ever.

And thank fuck, he gets it too.

My chest surges with warmth as I watch him gather Emma close, wrapping a hand around the back of her head as she burrows against his shoulder. "It wasn't your fault, Lina-Bina," he husks, rubbing the top of her head with his cheek. The new angle helps him look over to me as well. "Nor yours," he affirms my way.

And while I have a long and valid list of reasons as to why he's wrong about the last part, now isn't the time to re-hash how his daughter could have married a lawyer, a doctor, or even a lion tamer and had just the loony drunk cousin to handle at the wedding reception instead of the lunatic bitch with a grand plan of taking over the world, one susceptible mind at a time.

Except that now...maybe she's not.

Or maybe...she *can't.*

I've never been happier in the conviction that Emma and I must sometimes share the same brain—and that this moment is absolutely one of those occasions. Just as the revelation stuns me like a high-voltage Taser, it zaps her as well. She stumbles back from her father, hands and jaw dropping, before swiveling to confirm all the same jolts of understanding are taking over me. One second's worth of a look, and I confirm it's so. We're on the same page, down to the same damn letter.

And she grins, silently telling me what she plans on doing with that page.

Fold. Fold. Fold.

Tweak. Tweak. Tweak.

I'm pretty damn sure I'm the only bastard alive to ever watch a woman prepare to fly a paper F-18. Big deal if it only exists in her head. Her eyes, the color of rockets at full throttle, have me ready to whoop as if six Gs of force have slammed me back into my own cockpit. *Rock and roll, my gorgeous Flare. Let me see what you've got cookin', goddess.*

She slides closer to Todd once more, gingerly toeing the floor. "So...Daddy?"

"Hmmm?"

She switches up her posture, leaning over to make sure that Laurel and Anya are still jabbering away about chick pea cookies and kale cupcakes. "How long has this stuff been happening? The...frostbite?"

Todd seesaws his head, bouncing from ear to ear as he considers the query. "Not that long," he hedges. "Why?"

"A few weeks?" Emma persists.

"Oh, no. Not that long."

"A few days?" Emma persists. "Three, four?"

"Yeah. No more than that." He levels his stare, at once driving it straight at her. "Again, dear one, *why*?"

Emma works her lips against each other. Works her fingertips against her palms with the same nervousness. But she's calmer as soon as she darts a glance at me and I'm ready with a reassuring nod. We're still sharing the same mind, and that's becoming a good thing.

"You...errrmmm...may want to sit down for this," she finally tells her father. "I'm serious, Dad. *Sit.*"

Todd complies, bracing himself against an arm of the sofa, but not without looking like he's preparing to hear something freaky. Can't say I blame the guy. But he's rapidly become an expert on freaky and shows it by handling Emma's hasty but thorough report of everything that's gone down since the earthquake. Well, almost everything. I'm relieved when she leaves out the part about Atticus Scorpio and his three musketeers being literally camped out in the front driveway. Since she still notes that Foley's been calling in favors from his Special Forces buddies, I assume—and hope—that Todd writes off the motorhomes as accommodations for the extra houseguests.

By the time she's finished, the man is pinging a careful frown between his daughter and me. At last he murmurs, slowly but steadily, "So, you're thinking that the twins' freedom from Faline's control also means the bitch's 'big spell' is starting to wane?"

"That her hold over all those minds is slipping," Emma summarizes. Her nod is vigorous, full of excited energy. "Yes, Dad. *Yes*, that's exactly what I'm thinking." She snaps her sparkling gaze my way, and I'm ready with another cocky smile. "Exactly what *we're* thinking."

Securing his hands on the sofa's arm, Todd leans forward. His jaw is jutted, but his stare is filled with commitment. "It makes sense," he finally concedes. "Or as much sense as any of this shit does." A full breath in, followed by his significant exhalation. "So...what now?"

It's as good a cue as any to reinsert myself into the exchange. "I think we all wait and observe."

"Closely," Emma adds.

"And carefully." I jog my chin toward my father-in-law. "Theoretically, you're even closer to the fray than we are at this point. Don't put yourself in any danger."

He dips an efficient nod. "Noted."

"Any danger over what?"

The interruption, as breezy as an entrance from Scarlett O'Hara, has the three of us visibly hiding spooked-cat jumps to the ceiling. I'm pleased but a little perplexed to observe that Todd's the most accomplished at the feat, as he glides to his feet with the roguish grace of her Rhett Butler.

"I was just telling them about the new chandelier we were looking at for the formal dining room, dear."

And lies to his wife with polished panache to match.

But the panache might not be enough, proved by Laurel's answering scowl.

A moment that takes my brain into a new skirmish of dread versus joy.

Her suspicions could lead to trouble for Todd. But her suspicions could also mark trouble for Faline.

Well, *shit*.

"We've got bigger things to worry about than the chandelier." It's more of the old Laurel—a lot more—as she concludes with a huff and impales her husband with a glare.

"Did you know that some plants are actually trying to *kill* us, Todd? Anya gave me a list. I'll need to go through the cupboards and toss some things out. And we need an Instant Pot. Immediately."

Todd blinks. Then again before trading another knowing glance with Emma and me. Through the last year, she and I have coped with Faline's mind control by coming up with ridiculous nicknames for it—everything from "Faline's magic mind shell" to "Fa-Fa's psychedelic submarine" to "the bitch's loony rave." Well, now the shell is cracking, the submarine is sinking, and the rave has lost its DJs. They've been given their lives back. The party's over.

Only now, we just have to worry if Faline's going to be the drunk girl who slinks home to sleep it off or comes at the cops with a couple of knives in hand.

I don't want to think about the option to which my mind naturally gravitates.

Fortunately, there's a real party wrap-up to keep me distracted for the next few minutes.

"Well." Laurel adjusts her light sweater and strokes a hand across her Fendi purse. The bag is obviously brand-new, since I don't recognize the line right away. I'm not as current about that shit now that there's not a woman in my life begging me for it. "Maybe next time, we'll be fortunate enough to catch our grandson when he's home."

I admire Emma for maintaining her sweet smile in the face of her mother's sly denunciation. On the other hand, it's an authentic dose of Laurel-style nastiness. Old times have never felt more awesome to embrace. "Well"—her heartfelt smash of a hug to Laurel communicates as much—"maybe *next* time you can give us a few hours' notice so we can really roll out the welcome wagon."

By the time they're done with the clinch, Laurel's back to wearing a dreamy Fa-Fa grin. She even fingers the bottom of Emma's messy ponytail and tinkles out a playful laugh. "Next time, my lovely girl, we'll do just that. Perhaps make a weekend out of it. I do hope Lukie still loves the beach?"

"More than ever. And yeah...that would be nice." Emma's reverted back to the full clench of her forced smile—though no superpower on earth can make her stow the conflict in her eyes. The vacillation continues as we walk Todd and Laurel out to the front drive, waving until their Lexus disappears around the curve of the road.

But even after they leave, Emmalina makes no moves to return to the house. Neither does she turn to head for the "power generator" that's actually the door to the bunker. She's quiet and still, lifting her shimmering gaze from the road until she's staring out into the sage and sienna layers of the canyon. I give her the moment, relating to how her spirit needs a second for a reset, using her beauty for the purposes of my own.

Yeah...she's my perfect meditation.

The *maitri* of her graceful profile, from the top of her strong forehead to the gentle curve of her gorgeous chin.

The *shamatha* of the air she takes in, her parted lips like rose petals, her rising chest like hills of heaven.

The *chakras* she aligns through every inch of me, just by being near...being here.

Namaste. Nirvana. Perfection.

She's all of that and more...

Which makes it so damn hard when I can't make the same happen for her. Not wholly. Not right now.

I can only try my best right now, hoping to make a little

of it more bearable by drawing her close to me as the twilight descends around us. As the cicadas start to sing and the canyon breezes blend with the ocean winds, I lean in until my lips meet her ear and rasp just one syllable to her.

"Hey."

She snuggles in, fitting her head beneath my jaw, before whispering, "Hey."

"You okay?"

"I will be," she supplies. "Eventually." A cheerless sigh. "Once Fa-Fa's submarine hits bottom, what'll come back up is the grouchy sea witch known as my mother."

I chuckle only because she does. "Funny how life's a trade-off that way."

"Whaaaat?" she rebuts, softly teasing. "You mean I *can't* have calorie-free cake?"

"Or fire-engine-red leathers."

An open glower—mostly because she really asked for, and was denied, the impractical outfit. "You're a killjoy." She pouts.

"And you're stunning in this sunset."

"And now you're just being impossibly perfect."

Cocky snort time. "Yeah, well. It's a dirty job, but somebody's—"

"Hey!"

Foley's bellow not only intercepts the kiss I'm getting ready to lay on my wife, it grabs and twists at the center of my gut like one of those medieval pole weapons with the blades that spring out once the lance is thrust forward. And goddamnit, has Foley stabbed in.

Because he doesn't sound right. At all.

He's...scared.

No. Beyond that.

As he rushes up to us, his face verifies the theory. His face—which would be as pale as his own ass if it wasn't covered in rivers of blood due to a nasty blow across his left temple.

"Sawyer?" Emma rakes a horrified gape over him. "Holy *shit*. What happened?"

Perturbingly, he returns her scrutiny. Drives a glare at her that seems full of accusation before surrendering to clear confusion. "Fuck," he growls.

"*Sawyer?*" Her echo is twice as acute as before.

"You really don't know, do you?" he counters.

"Know what?" she retorts. "Sawyer, what the hell?"

"Crap. *Emma*." He staggers back, stabbing a hand into his hair. "But—but she looked like you. She talked like you. Absolutely everything about her...was *you*."

"Wh-What?" Emma gasps. "Her *who*?"

"Shit," Foley spews. "Oh, holy fucking—"

Emma shoves him to the side and stumbles toward the bunker. "What's going on?" she demands. "Is Lydia all right? Are the *kids*?"

"The kids." Foley's repetition is the softest grate I've ever heard from him before—unleashing a thousand decibels of sensation through every cell I possess. And none of them are good. "The...kids."

He says nothing else before jerking his stare up at me. His face is claimed by such an intense twist of agony, I already know what he's going to say. And am already tempted to vomit.

"The kids...are gone."

No time for hurling. Sheer instinct takes over, and I rush to seize Emma by the elbow. I catch her right before she races down the entrance, my senses validating Foley's horrific truth. The energy I always feel when getting near my children...is gone. Chasing her down the steps is only going to torture us deeper with that truth.

Nothing.

There's nothing here. Not even a lingering warmth of their happiness.

I have a feeling we're about to hear the explanation behind *that* too.

I wheel back on Foley, knowing my eyes alone are about to erupt with real lightning spears. "What. The. *Fuck?*"

The guy looks ready to tear open his shirt and beg me to impale him with ten thousand volts. "You—I mean *she*—Emma—" He chokes to a stop, meeting Emma's horror-stricken stare. "It was you, Emma," he pushes on. "I swear to God, it was you."

Emma is back in front of him in three seconds. She grabs the front of his blood-spattered T-shirt. "*Stop* stammering and *start* talking."

Foley frantically nods. It's not in fear; I can tell that. The guy is drawing strength from my woman's anger. Battling to use it, to gun his own. "Jesus Christ." But even the formidable Foley is struck low by his mortified anguish. "I should've trusted him," he grates.

"Trusted who?" Emma's voice pitches high from controlling her exasperation.

"He—he knew," the guy blurts instead. "Fuck...*he knew.*"

"God*damn*it, Sawyer!" Emma twists his shirt so tightly, smoke starts curling from the wet cotton. "*Who* knew *what?*"

"Lux," he finally stammers. "He ran from you—I mean *her*—or it. *Lux.*" He forces harsh breaths up and down his throat, clearly ordering himself to remember as much as possible. "He ran. He said it wasn't you, and I didn't believe him—and then you—*she*—clipped me, and I was out. She took us *both* out. 'Dia and I. But it wasn't you. *Fuck*. It wasn't you."

"As we already know," she spits back.

"Then who—"

"Holy fuck." As it spews out of me, so does the strength in my legs. They crumple beneath me, and I'm down in two seconds, my hands trembling against my thighs, my stomach sending up a new ocean of bile. The shit burns as I choke it back down. I'm not so lucky with the despair claiming my senses. It spins me ruthlessly, subjecting me to every disgusting detail of one specific flashback.

A recall of the day that was supposed to be everything—and ended up changing everything.

The uninvited wedding reception guest. A stranger at first until her regal rise gave her away—even before she peeled back her morphed façade, exposing us to her true identity.

Her morphed façade.

"Holy *fuck*," I repeat.

"R-R-Reece?" Emma rasps, hurling Foley away and grabbing me by the forearms. "What is it?"

"She morphed," I finally grit out. "It...it was her, Emma. *Her*. And she—*Christ*."

"Oh God." Her sob is shaky and mournful. "Oh *God*."

"Huh?" Foley's fallen to his knees, his head wound spattering blood into the dirt. "She—*who* morphed? *Whoa*." His brain finally catches up with mine. He facepalms in spite of the agony it causes. "Shit on a goddamned stick. Are you saying that *Faline* turned into *Emma* and then—"

"That's exactly what I'm saying." I snarl it from a burning throat and lips gone dry with rage. The dread that fills me is so immense, I silently beg God to reverse time by four days.

This time, when we find the Source, I'll gladly give myself up again into captivity—if only to save my soul from having to endure this moment. If only to spare *Emma* from having to live through this agony.

And agony is exactly what it is.

Her long, heartbroken moan is drenched in nothing less.

Her skin, flaming beyond solar heat, vows to express it even more.

And I don't stop her. I don't even want to. My mind is a raging firestorm as well, clouding the edges of my vision with brilliant cobalt while the center of my focus turns pure crimson. My breathtaking solar flare has grieved herself into the hue—and heat—of Mars itself. I've never longed to hold her more. I've never known, down to every last cell in my being, that it's the last damn thing she wants.

And as a door across the driveway opens, I've never been more certain a sap could have crappier timing than Atticus fucking Scorpio.

Not that it changes one neuron in my mind about keeping the hell *out* of my wife's way. Especially when all of those synapses now light up with a thousand watts of epiphany—the same message Emma proclaims with seething clarity as she clears the twenty feet to the bastard in three and a half seconds. The same meal she force-feeds him like the demoness she now resembles—the avenging angel I've never been more proud to call mine.

"*You.*" She roars it using every open orifice in her face, snarling it from her nose as well her lips, burning it from the bloodred flares in her eyes as well as the blinding brilliance of her bared teeth. "*You!*"

"The fuuuu..." But the man's spiraling bellow is his self-interruption, hitting its peak as Emma hoists him off the ground—burning a hole into the crotch she's using as a leverage point. "What the—holy *Christ*!"

"Shut. Up," Emma snarls. "Just *shut up* and stop pretending you don't know exactly what you've just done!"

"For the love of—"

"And don't you *dare* use that word in my presence, either." Her shoulders clench and she contorts her lips, as if realizing she's actually got a cockroach by the bug balls. With a grimacing sob, she hurls Atticus away. He flies back, taking down his three musketeers with him. They've wisely stayed quiet and look determined to hang back. "Are you really talking to me about love? About *love*, when you've betrayed us like this? About *love*, when you've let that bitch with her coal-black heart come waltzing in here and—"

"Whoa." Atticus has the balls—or maybe just the stupidity—to fumble back to his feet and pin Emma with a wider gawk than an owl in a Spider-Man mask. "I let *who* in?"

"Stop!" she screams back at him. "Just fucking *stop it* with trying to talk me into your innocence, asshole." She emphasizes the last word by tossing Atticus back onto his, with the edges of his designer duds sizzling from the force of her wrath. "You told us you were done with Faline Garand. We trusted you were shooting straight!"

"Wh-What?" the guy sputters out. "For the love of—I, uhhh, mean—for fuck's bloody sake, we *were*. And we *are*. What in all of Lucifer's *hell* is going on?" He ditches the big-eyed mask for a pair of figurative magnifying glasses. His gape is so wide, I'm sure I can see to the back of his skull. "Holy *shit*. Was Faline *here*?"

"As if you didn't know?" The indictment spews from

Foley, looking ax-murderer lethal with his blood-streaked face and beard.

"We did *not*," Atticus retorts. "I swear to God, we—oh, *fuck me*." His glare has speared past us, to the mini luxury hotel on wheels they brought up the hill with them. "The motor home. It— It must have a tracking device attached!"

"That you *didn't* sweep for?" This time, Alex barks the words. He, Wade, and Fershan have exited the lab after Atticus and his crew—whom our guys regard like boys with slingshots in the middle of a big-guns battlefield.

"Oh my God," Emma spits.

"Fucking amateurs," Foley fumes.

"Blow it up."

And *there's* the line I *wasn't* predicting—especially from the individual it fires out of in a no-bullshit command.

"Ummm...boss?" mutters Athos. Or maybe it's Porthos. I paid someone to take that final for me in high school. "You want us to blow *what* up?"

"What the fuck *else*?" Atticus bellows. "Mr. Foley is right. That bitch planted a tracker on our vehicle, and we were the idiots who let it get up here undetected. Blow the damn thing to shreds."

Foley jabs his hands up, ready to plunge forward, but he's beaten to the punch by a grimacing Fershan, with Kain all but yipping at his heels. If I wasn't so fucking terrified right now, I'd be indulging some satisfaction about the instant camaraderie between those two.

Still, Foley pounds back up and approaches Atticus with a no-bullshit stride. "So even though she's found the compound already, you want to attract extra attention to our coordinates, plus possibly start a raging brush fire, because...why?"

"It. Doesn't. Matter." The new words from my wife are separated by brutal stabs on the *t*'s, which also spike her coloring from dark gold to raging red. But just as fast, she's whirling from them all and lunging back against me. "Doesn't anyone understand?" she blurts into my chest, her form stiffening beneath my hold. "It doesn't matter! They're gone! Th-They're...gone. She took them. She took them...disguised as me." With that, the grief takes over. Her shoulders start to shake. "I hate that bitch. I'm going to kill her, Reece. I'm going to kill her!"

I clutch her tighter. Lower my head until I can feel her desperate breaths against my neck. Squeeze my eyes against their own encroaching sting but am unsuccessful. I don't care. There's only one goal I *do* care about now, and I rasp it into my wife's waiting ear.

"And I'm going to help you."

I know it won't allay her agony. If anything, her tears intensify. But it's a promise that emanates from the fiery center of my soul, the very core of my fucking being. It's an oath I plan on keeping, no matter what filthy tricks Faline has waiting for us now. The bitch took my freedom, my hope, my body, my blood—and in a lot of ways, even my innocence. She's not getting my family. My children. I'll escort her to hell myself on a lightning bolt right through her beating heart if I have to.

I'm getting ready to repeat the vow to myself, ensuring it sticks to my psyche in all the right places, when another utterance breaks in on it.

"Dada?"

So soft. So innocent.

So perfect.

I gulp hard, my throat a shaft of fire and my gut a knot

of doom. *Shit.* I'm even hearing the kid as if he's really here, and my soul splitters into a million shards because of it. Six months of physical torture, another six of lonely solitude, and the insane ride of the last three and a half years have been nips of pain compared to the gouge of this grief.

"Mama, Dada. No cry. Please!"

Shit. Shit. Shit.

I'm ready to snarl it out loud before banishing the torturous taunt—but in the moment that I suck down air for the task, my lower thigh is brushed by a tangible touch. Then another.

"Dada?"

And then my knee is wrapped beneath five small fingers.

And then the discernible swipes again, compelling me to dare a tentative glance down...

To be slammed by the hugest tidal wave of joy in my life.

"Dear fuck!"

Yeah, I just dropped the F-bomb in front of my kid. And as I drop *myself* along with it, I don't fucking care. Every etiquette lesson on the planet can kiss my ass because I don't care about that either. All that matters is the human burrowing into my arms, and then the other one who joins him. The center of my world is suddenly complete again, as Emma and I clutch and kiss and bawl all over our perfect, incredible, remarkable son.

"Oh, thank fuck! Thank *God!*"

Emma's weeping burst has me laughing through my tears. Guess I'm off the hook for the profanity. At least this time. Maybe for the rest of time. None of it feels so important anymore. Lux is here. *Right here.* In our arms. In one piece. Alive. *Alive.*

But...alone?

The alarm slices through my jubilant haze, making me jolt back and whip my gaze around. "Lux?" I manage to query. "Are you—where did you come from, son?"

Our little dude bobs up his towhead and shoves a hock of the white-gold stuff out of his eyes. "I chase them, Dada." As he points toward the little valley of wild brush and trees between our memorial marker hill and the house, the hair tumbles back into his face. "Through the woods. Over there." As his voice cracks, my heart snaps in a thousand places. "I try. *I try*, Dada. The lady wasn't Mama. She not talk or smell or love like Mama."

This time, Emma's face crumples too. There's not time to tell her that I know how the kid feels. A love like his mama's is a rare and recognizable force of nature, easily discernible if one knows what their soul is searching for. It's not Sawyer's fault that he didn't recognize it, but it speaks volumes about Lux's soul that *he* did.

"I knew she was prob'ly the bad lady, coming to take back Mis and Ira."

Emma nestles him close again. The tips of her fingers are trembling and appear dipped in liquid gold. "Yes, buddy. She *was* the bad lady."

Despite Lux's testimony, the revelation looks frightening to him. He turns, gripping her with all the ferocity in his little body before declaring, "I ran from her, Mama."

"As you should have, sweetheart." She drops a tender kiss to the top of his head. "But Mis and Ira...they didn't?"

His face, so cherubic and perfect, seems to double in age from its infusion of dark memories. "She tricked them," he growls, and I damn near high-five him. Fuck *yes*, my kid just *growled*. "She had the foofy ballet dresses. One for each of them."

"Tutus?" Emma asks. Better her than me, because I would've used the same terminology Lux just did.

"Yeah." Though he still looks aged beyond his years, he tilts his head to the side and starts toying with the drawstrings of his hoodie. "She said they could wear them, but they had to wait to put them on."

"Wait until what, buddy?"

Lux's expression gains a fresh wave of tension.

"She told them she wanted to take them to the ballet dance." He sighs and rubs his eyes.

"Ballet? What ballet?" Emma asks.

He makes us wait while he adjusts the drawstrings, pulling until they extend out to the same length.

"Buddy?" I prompt, trying to clench back my impatience. "*What* ballet?"

"She said...it was the one about the swans."

Emma frowns. "*Swan Lake*?"

"Yeah!" The kid pumps his fist, nearly clocking his mother in the jaw. Luckily, Emma's used to dodging when the kid gets fond of the ninja act. As she sweeps her head to the side, she uses the motion to catch my gaze with her open curiosity. I respond with an adamant shrug. Does she expect *me* to know if, when, or where *Swan Lake* is playing around town?

"Curtain is at eight tonight."

On the other hand, maybe it's *my* turn to have my mind read now—except the woman I expect the clairvoyance from is still sitting there with our son, tight-lipped and confused.

Until she joins me in looking up at the source of the intel.

Who happens to be her sister, stumbling up next to Foley, the back of her head bathed in as much blood as his face.

"Oh, holy God!" Emma hands Lux off to me and then

bounds to her feet, running for Lydia. "Dee Dee. Oh, my sweet 'Dia. Are you—"

"Stop." Lydia bats her away. "By Peter, Paul, and Mary, sister. if you don't stop, I'll force you to!"

Emma's having none of the Dee Dee lip. "You're both bleeding like Tarantino characters. You need medical attention."

Fershan marches in closer, bringing his starship-captain persona with him. "Which is why we have a fully functioning lab, convertible into a medical bay, fifteen steps behind me."

"Ah!" His comment has Atticus pivoting around, an approving grin sparking across his face. "Your team continues to impress me, Richards."

"As they should be mitigating Miss Paranoid Pants over here." Lydia snorts before shoulder-butting her sister. "Who should be listening as I tell her that the Los Angeles Ballet is staging a gala performance of *Swan Lake* tonight benefiting downtown revitalization efforts at the Dorothy Chandler Pavilion."

Instead of launching into her own happy ninja moves, Emma appears perturbed. "At the Music Center?" she retorts. "But the ballet doesn't normally perform there."

"Did I mention *gala*?" Lydia counters. "Benefiting *downtown*—which just took another hit from that damn earthquake?"

"Which might or might not have *been* an earthquake," I mutter.

"Lots of shit under those streets we haven't been sure about." Foley tags a sweeping glance at the end of his gritted observation—right back at my wife. "Maybe even the fact that bitch-witch Garand has some secret storage rooms we *weren't* aware of."

By now, I'm exploding back to my feet too.

As my head confirms the terrifying logic of my friend's statement.

As my gut roils in violent protest of it.

As my senses shoot into wild hyperawareness—activating my body into action.

"Fershan," I bark, already stomping my way back toward the front stoop. "Take Foley and Lydia and get them stitched up. I'm leaving Aliz here as your nurse and Kain as your tech backup." As I come abreast of Atticus, I stop long enough to order him, "Get that monstrosity off my property. Park it as close to the Music Center as you can. Take one of the musketeers with you. The other two, along with everyone else, are with me."

To his credit, Atticus cranks out an encouraging nod. When he stills his head, it's to gift me with his direct stare, filled with the affirming respect of a peer. "What is your plan?" he queries.

"To get my girls back."

That's it. Nothing more, nothing less. But the man's second nod is a confirmation that right now, it's enough for him. A damn good thing because it's enough for me too.

I just pray, with every filament of fortitude in my body and soul, that it's not too late for Ira and Miseria.

CHAPTER FOUR

E M M A

I thought I knew what fear was.

I assumed the bastard and I understood each other plainly by now, after every corner of hell through which he's already escorted me in the last three years. Watching Reece nearly die an equal number times. In matching quantities, thinking my own mortality was staring me in the face—and wondering if I'd be adding to the number by giving birth to an electric super baby. The bastard's been along for the ride as I've stared down gang bangers, high-end thieves, jet turbines, and crime cartel thugs. He's even taken the wheel completely to give me a terrifying spin on Faline Garand's lab table, as well as an excruciating dance with Mother Sun and a front-row seat for my mother's kidnapping.

Yes, I've tithed to Friar Fear enough for a dozen lifetimes.

But the damn mendicant keeps demanding even more.

And right now, he's sure as hell getting it.

As in, slicing it directly out of my body as we cover each new mile into downtown LA. When he's done hacking off all the flesh, he starts siphoning it from the middle of my heart. I barely notice—or care. Like Reece—and I'm pretty damn sure like Lux too—my concentration is funneled on only one giant gouge in our world. The open wound in our family, healable only when we get back our missing members.

If we get them back.

"We're going to do this." And there he is, right on time. Inside of three seconds after turning his attention from the lights of Figueroa Street to my face, my husband sees the penance I'm still doling out to fear and the words I crave for him to say. "This isn't a *maybe* thing, Velvet. This is a *yes, this is happening* thing." He lays a solid kiss across my soft-smiling lips. "Got that memo now, Mrs. Richards?"

"Yes, Mr. Richards."

He keeps his head low and turned in, pressing even closer now. "Then why do your eyes still look like you're getting ready to run through a brick wall at Platform Nine and Three-Quarters?"

"Or entering the castle courtyard to confront she-who-shall-not-be-named?"

"Eh, why not? The elder wand ended up in the right hands." The cocky shrug he uses as punctuation makes him suddenly irresistible. *Suddenly?* All right, honesty time. In spite of my complete terror, he's been irresistible since emerging in his most stunning Prada tux, after ordering me to change into the vivid pink Scervino number I've had sitting in a bag, waiting for a special occasion for its debut.

This was *not* the occasion I had in mind.

"We're not talking about a magic wand here." I run an impatient hand over the multiple layers of the dress's dreamy skirt. All the panels are only four inches wide, creating an edgy-flowy look when I walk. I felt like a kicky, cool punk princess when I first tried the dress on. Now, I feel a little more than ridiculous. While Reece's thinking is sound—arriving in our battle leathers will have the impact of the *Matrix* gang impinging on a Hallmark movie set—I'm still thrown off by the theming conflict here. Reiterating the mission goal feels like a good idea, especially now. "Especially because we're not after a fictional nose-less wizard." I tug on his luxurious lapel, wishing more than anything that we were actually bound for a glam night at the ballet, maybe followed by drinks in the penthouse and then some electric sex in kinky places... "We may end up having to kill the bad guy here, Reece."

And just like that, even with his hardening jaw and knife-blade gaze, the man has to go and look even more like the towering, steel-clad knight that I crave to climb like a horny, pink-swathed princess. "Not a bad *guy*, my gorgeous Flare," he growls. "The scheming, treacherous, soulless bitchzilla who stole my brother's spunk and used it to create a pair of humans for the sole purpose of bending to her will." His irises have transformed into pure, livid lightning—but his rage doesn't prevent him from dragging in a breath on unsteady hitches. "The monster who wanted to steal the same shit from me."

My eyes pop wide before my shock catches up with my mouth. "Excuse the hell out of me?" I have to coil every muscle and grit my teeth until they ache to keep the exclamation to an enraged rasp. Though we're tucked back in the Rover's third row, everyone's nerves are already pumped full of high-octane tension, and there's no need to add to that vibe.

"It was when she had me trapped at the Rancho Palos Verdes compound." He reaches up, pressing his palm to my cheek. "I'm sorry I didn't ever tell you about it, but—"

"It's all right." I grab his hand and kiss his palm. "I understand." And pull him in for a seal of sincerity, tenderly meshing our lips. "Those aren't easy memories for me either."

Reece softly shakes his head. "Nothing worse than

recalling the sessions from the Source." The storms in his eyes diminish into slate-colored mists. He expels a baffled huff. "I didn't really talk about what happened, because frankly, I was confused by it. The nutcase went on and on about how my seed would create perfection and how she'd be the mother of a god." A guttural rumble rolls through his chest as he swivels to face fully forward again. A mixture of shadows and street lights flows across the beautiful cliffs of his face, making the next phase of his confession more of a surreal entity. "To be honest, I had no damn idea what she was talking about. And I figured she'd jacked my IV full of feel-good juice so I'd get hard without her having to work too much for it."

It's sheer hell to work my next gulp down my throat, let alone bring up the question I hate worse than "How long is *this* Droughtlander going to be?" Much, *much* worse.

"So...did she?" I finally blurt. "Get you...up to..." Another torturous swallow. Another round of ordering my lips to form awful words. "Performance level?"

"No." Reece is all too ready with the response. "Thanks to you, bounding into that lab like Annie Git Yer Sun Guns, the Bolt boner was saved from indentured servitude that day."

He's going for the humor with intentional gusto this time, and it works. In half a second, I'm kicking Brother Fear to the curb as a mass of snickering giggles have me feeling like we just brought a half-rack to an AA meeting. The awesomeness is all mine—for one full minute. At that point, dread hitches a full ride back onto my senses as I watch the back of Angie's head turn from a gentle nightlight of pink and turquoise to a fiery ball of gold and purple. She lurches in her seat, turning to grab the cushion behind Wade's head, and he slows the Rover even though we're in the middle of a block.

"Ang?" While keeping one hand on the steering wheel, he arches the other back to grab her fingers. "What is it, gorgeous? Talk to me."

"Talk to *us*." Reece's urgency nearly pushes it into the realm of an asshole snarl, but he checks himself as soon as I curl my arm beneath his elbow. We're not going to win this one by goat-hooking all of them into our vat of terror. They're all here to help. Patience feels impossible but has to be a necessity.

Angelique shivers. Lux, sitting next to her, enfolds her free hand between his tiny glowing ones. At once, her stress calms from all-over shaking to just the heavy breathing beneath her thrumming skull. It's hell to watch her thoughts and feelings— literally—chasing each other across her mind, but those neurons, boosted by her special power, are another part of the team effort that's going to give us an edge over Faline here.

"Sh-She is close," Angelique declares. "Very close." As that spills from her, we turn the corner onto First, and the glittering spectacle of the fully lit Music Center appears ahead.

Reece, leaning forward, peers at every pedestrian on the sidewalks. "Are the girls with her?" he demands.

"*Oui.* I—I think so. There is chaotic energy around her. So much static. That is unusual for her frequency. She is usually steady." She opens her eyes, but her dark-green orbs are still unfocused. If we were in a different time and place, I'd even say she was sleepwalking. "Steady," she repeats. "And dark. And determined...to get her way."

"Well, not this time."

Reece's words aren't just a proclamation.

They're a promise.

And I swear, a whole new channel of my heart is unlocked, at once flooding with adoration for this beautiful man. And this time, it has nothing to do with his tuxedo.

Though I have to admit—once Wade has hooked a left onto Hope Street and stopped the Rover in the limousine drop-off lane in front of the Music Center—that it's impossible to ignore the artwork that is this man's ass in custom-fitted Prada. I may be a mom on a mission tonight, but I'm also a woman with a pulse, and nobody leaps out of a Range Rover the way my man can. "Wait!" Fine backside or not, I scrutinize him now like the whackpot he's seriously become. "You want to get out right *here*? All of us?"

Reece finishes aligning his cufflinks before scraping his hands back through his hair. "You think Faline's going to sneak the girls in the *back* way? Ms. 'Look at me and tremble, you peasants'?"

"Dude's got a fine point," Wade comments from the driver's seat.

"Of course he does." Trixie smooths down the poufy skirt of her bronze tea-length formal while sliding out from the front seat. "Richards men are a lot of things, but moronic isn't one of them."

"Thanks, Mom." Reece flings her a sardonic side-eye. "I *think*." The move results in a thick chunk of inky hair to fall free despite his finger grooming. The shiny lock lands perfectly between the lightning storms of his eyes, like the damn cherry on his irresistibility sundae. The indolent bastard quirks one side of his mouth as I stay in the back seat, watching everyone else leave the car—while squirming to control what my crotch wants me to do about him looking like the planet's hottest superhero in disguise as history's hottest James Bond. I swear to God, if he reaches in for me and husks, "Let's go, *Sassenach*," I may concede to being the first casualty of the night.

Thankfully, the man is already invested in the mission before us. Every inch of his rigid posture says so. Every ion of his energy radiates with it. Even the halo around his head is a new color, pulsing with a captivating mix of blue, red, and purple. The violet lends a regal air to his superspy stature, making me envision him as a knight of old, instead. We're his chosen warriors, and he's guiding us to finally cross swords with the witch who's planning on taking the whole world hostage, starting with the slave children she'll use to do so.

Except now that I put it that way, the "old" story doesn't sound old at all. Or very much like a damn fairy tale.

Yes, even this part. With the "courtiers" all gathering at the "castle" in their finery, what better cover can there be for a hag wanting to stow a couple of kids down in the dungeon again?

Not. Going. To. Happen.

But for that pledge to be reality, we've got to find the selfish skank before she goes to ground.

We've got to find her *now*.

With my mind and heart surging a rush of new commitment to the pledge, I ignore the hand Reece reaches in to help me disembark the car. Instead, with the help of a pushing pulse, I practically fly out the opening, using my extra two seconds to crush my lips to his in a kiss that's filled with fire, fervor, conviction, dedication, consecration, and every ounce of consuming love I have for this incredible superhero knight of mine.

As soon as we part, me wearing a stupid grin and him looking like a full train has burst up from the purple line and struck him, I chuck him lightly on the chin. "Let's go get this hag, Sir Reece Richards."

"Uh...okay?"

But that's a hell of a lot easier said than done.

As if the paparazzi have special hearing devices coded for Reece's voice, we're suddenly bombarded by a huge flock of the buzzards. While it's never an easy thing to suddenly feel like one is in the middle of a fish bowl with two dozen tweaked fireflies, I do my best to join Reece in giving them all the charming smiles and poses they want. Anything to keep their prying lenses away from Lux, who's scooted up the steps to the plaza by a fast-acting Trixie. Thank God Reece didn't give her shit about wanting to come along on the mission. The strength in our numbers gains its best evidence when we have to deal with obstacles like this lens monkey—and twenty of his buddies.

"Hey, EmRee!" shouts one of the photogs. "These are great shots. You two look like a million bucks."

"*Two* million."

"Which might be the bonus my editor flips my way when she sees these. You two *do* have all the superpowers!"

"Our pleasure to help out, guys," Reece answers. "But if you don't mind, we're meeting some friends before the performance. We haven't been able to locate them yet, so—"

"Huh?" someone in the pack cuts in.

The guy already celebrating his bonus adds an adamant nod. "Didn't *you* already find them, Emma? Over by the Lipchitz fountain? Like, ten minutes ago?"

My heartbeat thuds in my throat. "M-Me?" I squeak—already slamming all the pieces together and trying not to betray the fury that's spouting inside me just like the spouts of the Center's iconic fountain.

"Yeah," he answers. "*You.* Over there. You must have

found your friends, right? Were those little girls theirs, then?"

"Little. Girls." I get the words out but aren't sure if they're even intelligible, considering my mouth is full of bile-filled marbles. That bitch is still parading around as *me*. Letting the paps take pictures of her, Mis, and Ira!

"Yes. Right." Thank God for Reece, who's a thousand times better than me at pulling together his shit in the middle of a media circus. "We just meant...*other* friends. It's, errrmmm, a big night for the city. *Everyone's* here tonight! Wow. Did Taylor Swift and Katy Perry *both* come dressed as the black swan?"

As soon as the pack races each other back toward the step-and-repeat backdrops, he scoops up my hand and sprints up the stairs. I'm right with him, not breaking pace as we get to the main plaza level. The towering Lipchitz sculpture, called "Peace on Earth"—too damn bad I don't have time to conjure some meme-worthy one-liners at the moment—is at the center of two hundred miniature water jets.

At least it *was*.

Until the second Reece and I skid to a stop in front of the thing, joined within seconds by our son and the rest of the team.

At once, everyone gasps—except Lux, who couldn't be more excited—as Reece blankets the water jets beneath a sizzling force field. And then pulls all two hundred of them out of the ground.

And then twists the whole grid until it's vertical.

And then turns all two hundred of those jets into actual *jets*. As in, vertical blue cylinders wrapped in sizzling blue electrical currents. As in, two hundred superpowered missiles primed and ready to launch.

Three, two, one...

"Time for the bitch to get bolted."

Reece growls it before pulsing into an arcing leap... and then hurling the glowing tubes down the walkway that leads to the Center's other two theaters. Both the Taper and the Ahmanson are dark tonight, meaning there's only a few landscaping and engineering employees over here.

Along with a woman who looks exactly like me.

Running like hell. Dragging two little girls dressed in tutus.

A freakish experience in its own right, though there's no time to dwell on it. I'm still focusing on my husband and how he's started spinning the tubes in midair. Along the way, he twists and turns and manipulates them to "borrow" pieces of the steel furniture and cement buildings that they pass. Heat-molding the extra ingredients—until he's strengthened the two hundred tubes into just ten large poles.

Just ten poles?

Correction. The columns would make Scottish caber tossers look like toothpick jugglers—though it's hard to believe they aren't just toothpicks by how Reece handles them. With more eye-popping strength and grace, my husband twirls the poles around in midair, repositioning them into a vertical circle. As we all watch with stupefied gapes, he lowers them back down to the terrace with deafening *whamps*...where they're transformed into a trap for a fleeing madwoman and the girls she's taken hostage.

Two innocents who, judging from the happy singing we can hear thanks to the breezeway's acoustics, are still thinking they're getting to see *Swan Lake* instead of their new holding cell. Probably not so much now, since their sweet song has been replaced by the pounds of the poles and the sizzles of the electric arcs between them—such a scary contrast, my protective instincts urge me to pulse-vault myself past Reece and then run toward the cage as fast as I can.

I almost stop when realizing every member of the team has followed me, but when Atticus and his guys storm in from the other end of the passage, I'm filled with a new—and likely false—sense of security. Nothing about guys in military-grade gear should be the automatic recipe for breathing easier, but I have a feeling the musketeers are capable of handling the hellfire on this skirmish if that's what it comes to.

This skirmish.

Dear God.

Have I already doomed us to one just by thinking it? Then again, I'm not the one who stole two children for the purpose of re-enslaving them. Once again turning them into the stress management cans for a pod people army—so every one of *them* can help out with giving human evolution a not-so-gentle nudge. *It'll be fun, gang. Like art class. If you don't like the picture, erase it and start over.*

Only this lunatic bitch wants to do it to the entire human race.

And she's started the war by going the wrong way.

By duplicating...me.

I'm still at least ten feet from the cage when she spins around, hands splayed on the girls' throats, a rabid snarl redefining her face.

My face.

"Oh, holy God." The exclamation belongs to Trixie, because my convulsing throat can't manage air, let alone words. The cutoff makes me dizzy until I have to gasp, but even that's nearly too much. Fresh oxygen means confronting full thoughts—and facing this bizarre reality.

Gaping at myself.

A seething, raging, degraded me. A desperate, driven, beaten me. A me who's been manifested through the filter of fear instead of the choice of love. Who shows me, with gut-twisting explicitness, the deformity of what I *could* be—in a world where I haven't chosen beauty. In a universe where I haven't trusted in love.

"Mama?"

I snap out of my transfixion, shooting a dazed stare at my airborne son. I'm beyond stressing about whether the paps see him or not. A superhero kid who can fly hardly feels like the big story when a real-life *Orphan Black* is playing out at ground level. If even one stranger barrels up on this scene and thinks the real me is the one *inside* the bars...

Yeah. This bullshit needed to be diffused five minutes ago.

"*Mama?*"

A truth expressed, in all its raw agony, by my sweet little Miseria. I know it's her, along with the hundred other ways I've learned to differentiate between the girls. Outwardly they're identical, but in the last week I've started to learn their souls as well. All the little things that make them unique people in their own right. All the special ways I've come to claim each of them as my dazzling, amazing, extraordinary daughters.

My daughters.

I'm already grasping the miracle of it with my mind, but beholding their faces, locked with wide eyes and O-shaped mouths as that bitch imprints her filthy fingers across the columns of their necks, I know my soul is suffused with that truth as well. Every corner of my heart sings with it. Every instinct in my body is ready to fight for it.

And yes...if I must...to kill for it.

Regrettably, this isn't going to be that simple.

To win the game against this witch, I've got to dance to a few bars of her tune. I already hate myself for it, but getting my children back is worth every agonizing second.

"Well."

Faline cocks her head, emitting a sardonic chuff. I have to admit, the look is one of my cutest. "Well, well, *well*." But she's instantly back to being ugly, her lips twisting and her nostrils widening as she rivets her cautious gaze fully on me. "I must admit, you've got a snappy bunch here. You all figured this out quicker than I thought."

I mirror her little look, likely to the letter, but am heartened to see the slices of recognition in both the girls' eyes. If Faline's neck-snapping grips didn't give her away, I know that this face-to-face has confirmed the truth to them, once and for all. They *know* me. They *feel* my energy. Most of all, they recognize my love.

"Don't underestimate yourself." I want to hurl after handing her even half a compliment. "The move was daring. Impressively so." Yep. The Taper's reflecting pool is about to have chunks of floating barf. I have to swallow several times to keep the bile from coaxing it all up my windpipe. "But as you already can see, we're *snappy*—and you're trapped."

The bitch tosses her head back, gushing out a laugh. But when she lowers her face, it's not fast enough to hide her truth. At the edges of her neck, along the outer undersides of her jaw, I watch the shell of my skin peeling away, exposing the porcelain flawlessness of hers again.

I'm getting to her. Maybe just a little—but it's a start, and I'll take it. Any edge right now is a weakness that can possibly be exploited...a fear that can be drawn out...

"Trapped," she echoes. "So *that's* what you're calling this?" She chuckles again, and I fight not to betray how it wigs me out. I didn't exactly wake up this morning and brace myself for the weirdness of hearing Faline Garand speak and laugh through my lips. But dealing with that chunk of *Freaky Friday* isn't as crazy as watching what's happening to her now. Our battle is clearly diverting her energy from maintaining the face morph, and she's losing her grip on *me* as if she's left a cosmetic mask on too long. Parts of my face are falling away from hers in growing flakes of faded color.

The freak show isn't easy to surmount—but after looking at my girls' terrified faces again, I'm willing to converse with a talking pig if I have to. At this point, I think I'd actually prefer the swine. "It's time to cut the shit, *cariña*," I spit. "Trapped is exactly what you are."

"Hmmm. Well." She attempts a breezy head flip, but the move loosens half my nose and the majority of my chin. "Perhaps that *is* how you say it in snappy land—but from where I am standing, it seems you have secured me inside a tiny little circle with my pretty, perfect treasures..."

"*Not* yours!" I go at her with furious steps and balled fists, though they're both already casting several inches worth of a dark-gold glow. I'm ready to freaking melt the rest of her skin off her disgusting bones if I have to.

"And who stole *what* from *who*, my little *querida*?" With her incensed snap, I'm on higher guard but also greater consolation. The peels on her neck have crept up both sides of her face. At this point, I'm beyond the creep factor of the sight. The sooner my visage isn't on top of her skanky little body, the better.

"So you want to go there with this?" I rebut. "Fine by me. You milked Tyce Richards for half these kids already. And sure, that still makes you their mother—but I'm not sure any court across the whole globe is going to sit well with learning a mother forced her children to live in an underground bunker, being used as emotion-suction machines so she could invade and then hijack human minds."

"Minds I would not be *able* to hijack if the human race were not so pathetically weak!"

"Not your call to make, bitch. *Ever.*" I take two more huge stomps forward before parting my stance into a forceful A-frame. I square my shoulders. Hike my chin. Bring my hands up, curling them into defined, fist-sized suns. Their intensity doubles with heat that bursts out in a six-foot-wide perimeter—all the way up to the edge of the cage. "Not a call you were ever *intended* to make!"

The witch cackles out another laugh. Her derision is longer and louder this time, making me grit back the craving to push forward, reach through the bars, and simply melt the rest of my face away from her. And as long as I'm at it, the real one underneath too. But Faline's already handling the first task for me. In bigger and faster sections, my features are falling away, and her own evil, odious features are emerging from beneath. Her thin lips, no longer plumped by all-day lipstick, are an angry line that looks drawn by a three-year-old. Her skin is taut and pasty. Her hair is a sweaty, dirty mop. Her eyes are couched in dark-gray circles. The only life in her face is the glitter of insanity still clinging to her dark irises—which shine even brighter as she looks out over all of us, laughing long and hard again. The bitch might be silently conceding the first battle, but she clearly still plans on winning the war.

And right now, I'm not certain she's completely wrong.

With my two girls still securely in her grasp, the woman cocks her leering gaze with renewed confidence. "Ohhh, sweet little Emmalina," she croons. "Still so full of all that righteousness, are you? Along with *him*?" She jabs her chin toward Reece, who steps up next to me at last. I have to admit that *I've* wondered where he's been, but the answer is clear after one glance—and it's not one I expected.

Holy shit.

He's exhausted.

Not just figuratively.

I even dare a surreptitious double-take just to be certain of it, because I don't think I can remember a single occasion over the last three years when I've seen his pallor this pale, his vigor so draggy, his steps so plodding. But fortunately, I think I'm the only one who sees all of it. He's making the plods look like stomps, and every one of his fingertips is still sparking with blue combustion. I just hope we don't need to really blast Faline to pieces. Or even to pulse a piece of paper her direction.

"Do you two really think *you* are changing the world?" At the moment, we're safe, since Faline is devoted to spouting the idiocy of her manifesto. If her ramblings keep her here in front of us, still with Mis and Ira scared but unhurt, then I'm willing to let her have it for a few catchy bars. "Do you think you are doing *anything* but being the glorified criminal clean-up crew?" She snorts at what's clearly her idea of a joke. "Team. Bolt." Both words get her official stamp of Fa-Fa scorn. "One day you will be able to even buy the billboard for yourselves." She rolls her head as if reading said billboard. "'Proudly tidying society's messes for twenty years.'" A new snort. "Or...you can choose to see it my way, *team*."

"Sure." Reece's retort is delivered on a full growl, and my chest is infused with hope. Maybe he's recovering faster than I first thought. "You mean the way that turns functioning *people* into your waggy-tailed *puppets*?"

"Puppets who are *happy*!" Her eyes gleam like she's about to morph into a damn bear. With matching wildness, she claws Mis and Ira backward until their heads are trapped in her armpits.

"But robbed of everything that makes them *people*." Reece grits the last word and maintains his vicious countenance while moving in front of me. If Faline is going for the bear angle, then he's set on fighting back at full dragon mode. His gaze crackles with lightning blasts. His hands are curled like reptilian claws, looking ready to send out sci-fi laser balls. But *can* he? Or is this all for show, to keep her here and talking? "Don't you get it, woman?" he finally growls, shaking his head. "If you do this, you're no better than your own parents."

Faline's fire completely drains from her.

But only for two seconds.

After that, her fury is back at double its force—twice its violent emotion.

"How. Dare. You." And with that triplicate of snarls, three times its destructive conviction.

"No, Faline." My husband holds fast to his position, both physically and figuratively. "How dare *you*." I struggle not to wince as he carefully balls his hands back together, one quivering finger at a time. He's still flirting with danger by feigning his force, but there's not a thing I can do about it. Not right now. Not from where I'm at. "You got short-changed in the decent moms department, woman. For that matter, the dads too. But their dissatisfaction with their lives had little to do with you—and even if you don't believe me and succeed in creating a super race of every perfection there is, there are going to be humans in that gene pool who aren't ever satisfied. They'll be that way because they're *human*, and we're all hardwired to seek more, to crave more, to want...*more*."

I pace over, stopping when I'm directly by his side. "He's right," I state softly. "And there are times when *I* wish it weren't so, either...but he's right. Frail or strong, curvy or skinny, doubtful or fearless, powerless or even able to fly"—I smile through my awestricken tears as my kid hovers in the air between Reece and me—"we're always going to want to go further, accomplish more, *be* more. And sometimes we'll succeed, but at others we'll fail. But that's not going to stop us. Even perfection—or whatever it is that *you* perceive as perfection—isn't going to be enough, Faline. Don't you see? None of it will *ever* be enough."

There's more, so *much* more that I can say, but the fullness of my heart indicates that for now, it's all right. Or maybe I know that because of Angie's and Trixie's affirming smiles. Or Reece's electric magic of a hand squeeze. Or the matching hug my head receives once my son parks his backside on my shoulder and then leans in for the kid-sized clinch. It's a moment I bask in because I know it can only be just that: a moment of a very minor celebration because we've still got so far to go. Faline still has both my daughters in ruthless chokeholds.

Until...she doesn't.

My breath snags as she relents on the noose grips around Mis and Ira. But just as swiftly, she's grabbing both of them by the hands, until I see their little fingertips glowing green from the pressure. Their stares have turned the same color, overflowing with moss-green terror. In so many ways, both of them have predicted what the bitch is going to attempt.

What I've been dreading since I got here.

"Well, bravo, Mistress Flare," Faline sneers. "You get the day's honor for the prettiest speech." She forces the girls' arms into victory pumps as she dips into a mocking bow. "Yet regrettably, it's also the most ineffective." Then rises up, a sinister smirk turning the weak scribble of her mouth into a swerving strand of spaghetti instead. "Because nothing from your pathetic little mouths have changed my mind—and now you'll all have to simply live with the consequences!"

Yep.

Exactly what I've been dreading.

Down to every last syllable she utters. Every grand gesture she makes. Every sickening swirl of her head as she prepares to open up a new portal into the darkness of the world beneath us.

And does.

"*No*," I rasp.

"Noooooo!" Mis wails.

"*Madre! Madre!* No!" Ira screams.

I yearn to shriek out with them. What's the sound of a sun screaming? There has to be one. There *has* to be. And that sound has to be so hot and hateful that it shatters the air—and destroys a witch. But my throat is too dry. My senses are too weak. Soon, even my body is, as well. It takes everything in my being to melt down just three of Reece's pillars and then to race forward, through the gap.

As Faline reopens her portal. The doorway into the dark world where she'll banish the girls forever.

But once the wide round threshold is open, my mouth drops open in a matching shape. "What...the..." I finally manage to stammer, attempting to peer deeper inside the circle—only there are no depths inside there to be seen. Unlike the first time Reece and I ventured under the city, there's no smell of earth, vibrations of traffic, or scurries of eternally nocturnal creatures. It's a void. Literally, a blank space of nothingness.

"Oh, my God!"

But the Big Guy isn't ready with any fast answers—and right now, that's exactly what I need. I whirl back around, quickly locating the closest thing in my world to a living, breathing version of the Almighty. Except that right now, Reece isn't looking all of anything or mighty in the least. He's down on the ground, on all fours, with our son parked in the middle of his back. I blink in pure astonishment. And then again. Unless our son has had another wild and crazy growth spurt during the last hour, he's now glowing with a lot more than just his light. There are defined streaks of blue in his energy streams.

Which are now aimed at the same hole that Faline sliced open in the atmosphere.

Or...*did she*?

I whip my focus back around, taking in the woman with new eyes. Okay, with the same eyes I beheld her with before but with a clearer jolt of understanding.

Her sunken eye sockets. The old mop hair. Her wan skin— which, now that I'm looking closer, seems to be the only thing besides her bones filling out her catsuit. She's gone from being a sleek black Siamese to one of those weird breeds with all the wrinkles. While her aura still radiates nothing but bloodred, her actual energy and vitality are...

Gone.

Completely.

"Oh, my God." I can't avoid the repetition, though this time it's twice as thick with my bewilderment. "Then wh-wh-what...or h-h-how..."

"Mama! Hey, *Mama*!"

I wheel around, frantic about locating my son now. I don't expect to find Lux in the same place, but I do. There he is, riding my fine but weary husband like a champion buckaroo. I clamp a hand over my mouth for a second, barely muffling my overwhelmed sob. Can it really be true? Are we truly on the brink of ending *this* wild ride, once and for all?

"Yes, my incredible light?" I'm finally able to answer him.

"Holy shit, Mama!" Lux points excitedly at the portal. The strange opening that leads...nowhere. Even Faline has caught on to the anomaly and scrambles backward from the opening through which she was eager to leap before. "You see, Mama?" he yells. "You see the magic door? The door that sissies and I made?"

The sissies.

Oh, God.

Mis and Ira!

"Emma!" Reece snaps together the same connection at exactly the same time. While he roars it, I'm already maximizing the moment. In one lunge forward, I whisk the twins away from the woman's distracted grip. In one sweep back, I funnel every ounce of my attention down my free arm and across the patch of terrace we've just crossed. I almost close my eyes, not able to fathom what will happen if my powers—pushed to perform at speeds and across spaces to which they've never been challenged—let me down.

"Mama!" The exclamation comes from one of the twins this time. Swaying as if I've just given three quarts of blood, I don't have the capacity to determine which one. All I know is that hearing her refer to me by that name, and with such joy, feels like my butt's just landed on a cloud in heaven instead of a cement sidewalk. "Mama, look at the magic of *you* now!"

Slowly, I peel open my gaze.

And look out over what appears to be the four-story drop into the bottom of the Music Center's parking garage.

A whoosh of breath escapes from me.

Holy crap. I did it. I made a huge chunk of the terrace disappear.

An illusion that, thank God, Faline believed enough to jump back from.

Stumbling, fumbling, and toppling.

Until losing her balance altogether.

And then falling sideways—into the big scoop of noiseless, odorless, bottomless black air.

Before I even know if she screamed on the way in, Reece shouts, "Now, kids! All together! *Now!*"

And before I can blink again, the huge circle—and its new occupant—have vanished.

Gone.

Completely gone.

Vaguely, I'm aware of Mis's and Ira's ecstatic leaps. I'm not as able to hold back my stunned *oof* as they come back down, piling over my chest until I'm the bottom layer of a Richards girls pile-up.

And this time, I can truly mean the expression.

The Richards girls.

Can I actually hope to mean it? For real this time?

Still flat on my back, with dust blowing up the chiffon layers of my skirt, I roll my head to the right when a distinctive chuckle rumbles the air there. Sure enough, the stunning sight of my husband fills my sights. Reece, having flipped onto his back and then slithered over, takes my shaking fingers inside his own. I squeeze back with as much strength as I can, which isn't much. I've had my powers "cranked to eleven" for close to an hour and a half with no breaks or rest stops. It's been the longest and most intense test of my strength. I desperately hope I passed, but a lot of me is too tired to care.

There are more important things for my concern right now. And my gratitude.

"Did anyone get the license plate on that cataclysm?" I summon enough vigor to actually laugh that one out. "Starsky? Hutch? Hondo?"

Reece snorts and rolls to face me. "Nobody here by that name, ma'am," he murmurs while propping his head in a hand. "But if you'll settle for a guy named Richards, who can't wait to get his wife off the ground and into a real bed..."

"Hmmmm." I get it out before he dips in past the kids, claiming my lips in a kiss that perfectly matches the swell of the *Swan Lake* overture, now drifting across the plaza. I sigh against his mouth, feeling as light and flimsy as a ballerina, surrendering myself to passion that's as new as it is familiar, as beautiful and blinding as it is comforting and safe. "If you completely insist, Mr. Richards."

"Oh, I insist. And a hell of a lot more." His growl curls through me like a mix of sawdust and fairy sprinkles. The roughness of his lust is more vibrant than ever but possess a new enchantment that I still can't figure out—and perhaps don't want to. Maybe with Faline finally absent, this is some of his old bad-boy side emerging. Or maybe I'm seeing a whole new Reece Richards. A man of unleashed confidence and unhindered joy.

A man of ultimate freedom.

Of untethered love.

"Okay, *wait*." I issue the command as the kids spring away and he moves in for a new kiss. I stress the point by pushing the man over, pinning him to the breezeway again. Reece gapes with mock outrage, but his pleading look to the kids only gets him another rousing round of "We Are Family" from them. I have no idea when or where they learned it, but the tune actually blends quite well with the ballet's overture. The three of them are now leaping and twirling to both melodies, though Lux interrupts his rhythm for his karate kicks and ninja moves.

"I guess...I'm waiting, then?" my man finally murmurs against the pad of my index finger. I run my adoring touch up and over his nose and then back down until I'm tracing the bold angles of his sexy, stubbled chin. "Or other things?" he suggests, cranking his smirk until his dimples are gorgeous craters. "Like blatantly worshiping? Endlessly Adoring? Eternally loving?"

I hold his face in place for my fierce stamp of a kiss. "Oh, that's my favorite one."

His grin spreads wider. "Mine too." He scoops a hand around the back of my neck. "It'll always be my greatest superpower, Bunny."

I give him another hard kiss, this time lingering to push my tongue between his lips. We both moan from the instant—and much-needed—charge the bond brings, along with the flow of other emotional energies. Connection. Inspiration. Completion.

But as we drag apart, I admit the difficulty of believing that last one. *Completion*. "Can it really be true?" I challenge in a fervent whisper. "Zeus? Are we really done with her now?

For good?"

Reece hitches up onto one elbow. "I'm torn between keeping it to a whisper and ordering a hundred skywriters to blast it across the sky."

I nod. "It feels...pretty weird," I confess. "Maybe *very* weird."

"But you know what would feel even weirder?" he returns.

I tilt my head, instantly mirroring the new gravity behind his gaze. While I'll never be able to translate his thoughts as he does mine, his new intent is pretty damn clear. "Watching Faline bust out of that hole and then go back with our daughters in her arms?"

"Nooooo!" Ira tears away from her sister and Lux and sprints back over with terror reclaiming her face. "Not back in ground! *Not* with *Madre* Faline!"

By the time the girl is done with her sobbing protest, Lux and Mis have joined to embrace her from behind. Reece pushes toward her, tenderly thumbing her tears away from her face. "Hey, hey, heeeyyy," he croons, finally drawing her in for a strong and comforting clutch. "Nothing like that is *ever* going to happen again, sweetness." He pulls back and ducks his head, securing her gaze with the soft strength of his own before shifting his hold to the side of her head instead. "But you already *know* that, don't you, Ira?" He grunts in satisfaction as she nods with skittish bobs. "Now tell me why you know it— because I think your mama wants to hear this part too."

Before I can voice my concurrence to that, or even before Ira can pull in a preparatory breath for *her* account, Lux stabs his arm into the air like he's practicing New York cab hailing. "Ohhhhh! I know, I know, I know!"

"Lux Mitchell Tycin." Reece wags a rebuking finger. "I

asked your sister this one, not you."

And I'm silently snickering, watching the man walk right into *that* one, as Ira bounds around and grabs my forearm with both of her steel-strong hands. "Luxie talked to us!" she chatters. "In our heads! Both of us at the same time! Even when *Madre* Faline had us in the trap, we could hear him. And he told us to stop sucking out her anger and her fear. He told us to push our powers at the big round door he opened up!"

She stops as soon as I jolt. With a whip of motion, I impale my son with a wide-eyed gawk. "Lux. Th-That portal was... *yours*?"

For a second, the poor kid looks worried. "I only wanted to do good, Mama. Honest."

"Oh, sweetheart." I ruffle his thick, soft hair. "I know that. I really do. But..."

"But what, Mama?"

"Son...where'd you make the portal lead *to*?"

Reece jabs a contemplative fist under his jaw. "Well, shit," he mumbles. "Didn't think to ask *that*."

I wink quickly his way before Lux takes a messy belly flop into his lap. "Well, well, well. This mere-mortal-husband stuff is kind of fun."

As I chuckle from the brunt of my man's irked scowl, Lux supplies, "The lady Faline was sad and angry. She even pretended to be you 'cause she didn't like her own self." Abruptly, he stops his absentminded kicks and the itsy-bitsy spiders of his fingers. "I just made her a place that's quiet and peaceful. Where she can rest now—and not be so mad and sad."

Ira drops to the ground at Reece's side. With a matching amount of innocent abandon, she burrows her head against Lux's tummy while her lavender-tights-covered legs dangle off to the side. "Being mad all the time makes you tired."

Not one to miss the cue on the cuddle fest, Mis crawls into my lap and then lolls with the same comfortable abandon. "And sad too."

"Well, nobody's going to be mad *or* sad around here for a long time." As I declare it, using every queenly inflection in my repertoire, Reece stretches a hand out for mine. "You amazing miracles saved the day because you used the power of love. No matter what you do or where you go with your powers from now on, the three of you have to promise me that you'll remember the lesson of this day forever."

Lux tilts his head, cracking a rogue's grin so similar to his father's that my heart flips over a couple of times. He knows this answer already, and he thoroughly plans on beating his sisters to the punch with it this time.

Proudly and clearly, my son calls the sentence out like the perfect truth it is. "Love is the greatest superpower!"

Mis and Ira scramble to join their hands with his. As the three of them form their bright, bold triangle again, the girls echo, "Love is the greatest superpower!"

They remain that way, watching with endless giggles, as Reece pulls my fingertips to his lips and then runs lingering kisses across my knuckles. Our gazes meet, and my belly pings in a million places, zapped by the silver lightning in his irises. My breath hitches. My blood turns to fire. My sex turns to magma. He'll never stop doing this to me...and I'll never stop thanking him for it.

We're snapped out of our seductive reverie once more by our son. "Dada?" he prompts with the soft uncertainty he gets when bringing up confusing subjects.

Reece leans in over Lux, conveying the kid has his full

attention. "What is it, buddy?" he murmurs.

"If love is the greatest superpower, why was the Faline lady so scared of it?"

I suck in a huge breath along with my husband—and shoot him half a grin along with the silent snark in my head. *Oooohhh, I'm so glad this one went to you and not me, Zeus.*

His answering glower, filled with a whole bunch of *thanks a fucking lot*, precedes his reply to Lux—and makes me really, *officially* glad that the man got to field the query instead of me.

"Well, buddy...a lot of times, love isn't always the easiest answer. It takes courage and bravery, especially if someone doesn't understand it and then uses it to hurt you instead of heal you. But when you decide to trust in its power..." He squeezes the juncture of our hands once more, sending heat through every inch of my body. The *good* kind of heat this time. For the very *first* time... "And when you find someone who believes in it the same way you do...there's nothing like the very real power of true love."

Lux lets out such a long and savoring laugh, it'd sound outright dirty on a man twenty years his senior. To us, it's just the perfect magic of our boy, living out loud in the beautiful freedom of his existence. "And *that's* what you and Mama have!"

Reece joins him—and now Ira and Mis too—in their joyous, full laughter. In the light that will always captivate me, electrify me...and bolt me into the stars with everlasting love.

"Always," he answers our boy in an adoring whisper. "And forever."

EPILOGUE

REECE

The sun disappears over the waters of Dana Point Harbor as my best friend kisses his new bride. The small crowd gathered on the island overlooking the breakwater claps like crazy as Sawyer and Lydia, the new Mr. and Mrs. Foley, turn beneath the little arbor that's dripping with too many fluffy white flower breeds for me to name. I simply take Emma's word that her mother has picked out the best stuff and leave it at that. Besides, the best part of the day is yet to come.

The party.

With that thought lifting my spirits, I lean over and give Foley a hearty clap on the back.

"Well done, man," I murmur, deciding to stay quiet about the fact that he's practically as pretty as 'Dia in this moment. With his dark-blond hair tamed into a stylish man bun and his tuxedo still miraculously white, the guy's a candidate for the "Eat Your Heart Out, Jason Momoa" Pinterest page.

Oops. Too late. I guess I said that last part aloud, since the guy brandishes a scowl vicious enough to peel off my skin. "Did you just invoke DC in a crowd of Marvel True Believers, man?" He cocks his head and clucks his tongue. "Hope you remembered to protect your junk with some Captain America Underoos."

I narrow my gaze but lift a clenched smile. The videographer is moving in fast. "Smartass."

"Prick monkey."

"Fanboy snob."

"DC whore."

"Would you two stop being dicks and get with the program here?" Lydia spits as she wheels back around on us. The woman looks incredible in a sparkly mermaid-style gown with a frothy veil that perfectly frames her angular face—except that this second, she's out for blood as bright as the strawberry tints in her long curls. "Holy *shit*," she adds in response to her mother's mortified gasp.

"Lydia Harlow!" Laurel rushes over in a cloud of expensive perfume and maternal indignity. The second she's done with the reprimand, she bears down on the video guy. "All of that *will* be edited out."

"Yes, ma'am." The guy ducks in, adding for our ears alone, "I'll make sure you guys get the blooper reel."

"Lydia!" Laurel beckons. "No dawdling. We're three minutes behind on the timeline."

Lydia lets out a girl growl. "Hey, Bolt Jolt. For a wedding gift, can't you just give me a couple of hours of brainwashed Laurel again?"

Emma impales her with a scowl while bending to straighten out her train. "You want to keep both your nipples, sister?"

"Heeeyyy," I chide. "We all know marriage is about compromise. Brainwashing, not doable. But lots of double-shot cosmos for my beautiful mother-in-law..."

"And thus, the reason why I'm proud to call you brother." Foley smirks, lifting his fist to bump with mine. "I'll even get the first round."

"From the open bar?" 'Dia volleys though descends into a new moan as Laurel barks for her again. If any of us needed any moment to confirm that the woman is thoroughly free from Faline's spell, this is definitely that time. Ever since our astounding "night at the ballet" five months ago, we'd been hoping that would be the case. There will always be some uncertainty about the limits and duration of the "black hole" we banished the bitch to that night, but with Faline effectively sealed away—and Mis and Ira free from her enslavement—it seems that the Garand Cult was also wiped from the planet. The process took about a week in total, though Laurel does notice there are sections from her year beneath Faline's rule that she's forgotten altogether. Though the memory gaps continue to disturb her, we're all in agreement that it's probably a *good* thing.

The more we *all* forget and move on, the better.

The resolve is foremost in my mind as I step in behind Foley and Lydia and offer my arm for my own stunning woman to take. As she does, I'm frozen solid for a long second. My legs can't move. My heart can't beat. With all due respect to the bride, my Emmalina is easily the most breathtaking woman here. Her silver-toned matron of honor dress is a flawless fit across her luscious figure, and the color plays up every sparkle of the turquoise magic in her dancing gaze. There's a joyous blush on her high cheeks and a love-filled smile lifting the stunning curves of her lips.

She'll never stop taking my breath away.

Never *ever* stop captivating my spirit and soul.

Always and forever, she'll turn every cell in my body into raw electricity.

Yeah, even now.

I'm still swooning like a sap from an Austen novel when a chorus of kid-style whoops fill the air from behind us, lilting with the distinct exuberance of an animated little boy and his two adoring sisters.

"Ho-lee shit! Ho-lee shit! Ho-lee shit!"

I snicker. Emma moans. With their parts in the ceremony officially finished, the kids dart past us. Lux tosses his little tuxedo jacket at Emma. Mis and Ira, in their fluffy white chiffon dresses, are already scraping the bows out of their curls.

"Yesssss," Lydia exclaims. "I knew my Luxie wouldn't let me down!"

"Emmalina Paisley." Laurel's back, more flustered than ever. Todd accompanies her this time, already rolling his eyes. "Your—Your *children* and those *words*—"

"Talk to your *other* child, maternal unit." Emma raises a fast and determined talk-to-the-hand. "When 'Luxie' and Dee Dee join forces, I'm not to be blamed."

"Speaking of things we can blame each other for later..." Foley addresses me as soon as we get to the head table, where our wives give each other more gushing hugs, tears, and permissions to sample the custom-imprinted wedding candies in the shell-shaped crystal bowls on the table. "You ready to hit the bar, dude?"

"I can already hear that first cosmo calling Laurel's name."

As Lydia tugs her sister toward the ladies' room, we make our way over to the bar, tucked in an alcove off the comfortable living room area that separates the dance floor from the venue's dock. As soon as we're clustered together, nursing lowballs of Macallan, Foley turns until he can hitch an elbow back on the bar and survey the entire scene while appearing like the two of us are casually shooting the shit.

"Damn," he drawls after savoring his first sip of the top-shelf booze. "I guess I really went and did it."

"Welcome to the club, my friend." A couple of beats pass, in which I let him bask in contentment, before getting out my *really* big harpoon. "So now it's time to get busy, buddy."

"Eh?" He arches a brow. "On what?"

"My kids need baby cousins, dude." I smack my hands together. "Chop, chop."

"Fuck you."

I chuckle hard, relishing one of the rare moments that *I've* managed to roast *his* weenie, before waving a placating hand. "I'd rather my wife do those honors, thank you very much. And seriously, you take all the time on the baby-making that you want. Atticus's twins are more than enough entertainment for Mis and Ira—though I'm not sure those boys will be so cool about things once they realize *they're* the ones always getting dusted by Thanos and getting saved by 'Captain Marvel' and 'Wasp.'"

"Goddesses after my own heart already." He chuffs. "So things are going well with Atticus still? He really does want to start making money in the right ways?"

I nod before explaining, "Fatherhood changes a guy. And once I showed the man that his business model is ridiculous with all the overhead from dodging the authorities, he began to see that he's working harder, not smarter."

Foley pushes out his glass, openly toasting me. "And who said Reece Richards couldn't be a superhero without a sexy cape?"

"We're not going there about the cape again, man."

"*Dude.*"

"Shut it."

"You need a goddamned cape."

"Am I going to be getting *you* the cosmo instead of Laurel? You want a pink umbrella in it too, sweetheart?"

As his silent *fuck you*, he downs the rest of his Macallan in one chug. The dude gets props for not choking, though his eyes are watering as he ducks closer, lowering his voice like we're plotting a *Survivor*-style immunity alliance. "Okay. 'Fess up, capeless wonder. Who do you think we'll get to sling the next nuptial shit at? Wade and Angelique? Neeta and Alex? Kain and Aliz?"

I whip my head up. "Kain and Aliz?" Then hunch over my whisky again, realizing how loud the assjerk made me rail it. "*Kain* and *Aliz*?" I challenge when he's copied my pose. "She's used to castles and royalty, man. And *he's* starting a new rock band!"

He flings a sardonic side-eye. "Uh, yeah. I know." Then nudges his head toward the bandstand out on the terrace, where there's already a drum kit set up. The logo on the bass is imprinted with *The Hundred-Watt Hedgehogs*. Sure enough, standing off to the side is our adorable Aliz, who just last week asked if she could stay on at the ridge and continue helping out with the kids. Emma and I eagerly agreed though had been baffled about the woman's reasoning. I may have the main clue now. The woman makes me smile with her Hundred-Watt Hedgehogs T-shirt draped over her formal dress and a huge plate of chicken wings in her hands.

My grin grows as I watch Joany join her, also dressed in one of the band's T-shirts. My brother Chase doesn't seem to mind, but that's not shocking either. When Kain and his buddies played some small New York venues a few weeks ago, I sent some tickets to Chase and Joany for one of the gigs. Looks like she became a fan, since Chase offered them representation with the Richards Group's new entertainment management division.

My stupid grin continues to grow. And why not? At last, the world is right—and not just for a few minutes at a time. Never has there been a better moment to acknowledge that fact. The air smells like sunshine, sea spray, and roses—and life seems to be smooth sailing and very rosy for everyone these days.

My satisfaction blooms into joy as I watch my kids scamper to the middle of the dance floor, pulling Tosca and Jina with them, and start bopping to the prerecorded wedding standards that are being pumped through speakers before Kain and his guys start up. As "Celebration" and "Brown-Eyed Girl" give way to "Havana" and "Cake by the Ocean," they also manage to get my mom on her feet—and for the first time today, my heart crumples a little.

I push out a rough sigh. "Damn. I wish our predictions had room for the lovely Mrs. Trixie Richards too."

Foley takes a contemplative drag on his drink before responding. "Maybe they do."

"Huh? What are you..." My voice fades off as I follow the invisible line he draws with his jutting head—at least until my view lands on the person he's tagging. "Wait. *What?* Fershan?" When I zip a stunned gape between him and the most brilliant but shyest member of Team Bolt, Foley cocks a confident eyebrow, confirming the detonation of his bombshell. Still, I spew, "Are you *fucking* kidding me? My *mother* and Fershan?"

Foley tilts his head, evoking a perturbing swami-psychotherapist combination. "You think he's just a kid, don't you?"

"He *is* just a kid."

"Yeah? You know that for a fact? Did you ever really look at his file?"

I down my whisky, signal the bartender for another, and then finally growl, "No."

"He's nine and a half years younger than her," Foley supplies.

"Thanks. That and Kim Basinger gets him a kinky-as-hell movie."

The guy has the nerve to chuff. And then smirk. "You know that's 'Nine and a Half *Weeks*,' right? And FYI, I don't think he wants Kim Basinger."

"You really didn't just go there."

"I really just *did*."

I snatch the refill that's just been brought but don't take the time to sip it. I'm already back on my feet, battling the force of my weird-ass trauma—all the while trying not to acknowledge the stare of complete worship in which Fershan is all but giving my mom right now.

The kind of look Dad *never* showered on the woman.

The kind of adoration, veneration, and all-around pussy-whipped worship the woman has always deserved.

Oh, hell. I just thought of my mom and the words "pussy-whipped" in the same train of thought.

And now, in the thought that comes after that, I actually put a brand-new conviction into a committed plan of action. An action I *cannot* believe I'm carrying through, as I march straight back toward the dance floor. All the way around the dance floor. Right up to one of the tables that's closest to the stretch of red-glowing plexiglass. And then right up to the man of the hour—at least *my* hour—himself.

"Bennett."

Fershan slams down his diet soda so hard, some of it sloshes across his hand. Not that he notices because he's already scrambling to his feet faster than a spider in a watering can. "Uhhh...yes, boss? Whatever can I do you for—I mean do *for you*? I—I—errrr—I mean—"

I cut him short by pushing up into his personal space. Then riveting my gaze to his as if we're a couple of boxers getting ready to go at it in Vegas—except that my chest is double the size of his and I'm a good six inches taller. "I think what you *mean* to say is that you don't plan on hurting my mother. At all. *Ever.*"

At once, all the tension in his face transforms into a different texture. Oh, the guy is still terrified, all right—but even with that trepidation crawling through his veins, he maintains his proud stance and determined gaze. "I am in love with her, Reece. I am not ashamed of it or sorry about it. She is an amazing woman."

I clench my jaw. "I'm well aware of that fact."

"I will treat her like my queen for the rest of our days."

I let him squirm beneath the electric storm of my stare for a few seconds longer. But at last, I drop a quick but approving nod. "Keep it that way and we have no issues, man."

"Yes, sir!"

I turn and walk back through the crowd, not exactly stress-free about the encounter but damn euphoric that Mom has found the happiness she deserves. I believe every word Fershan just said. He's an upright guy who's never let me down. And who the hell am I to be throwing rocks at glass houses when it comes to normalcy? One look back at my son, who's pushing the limits by jumping *way* higher than a "two-year-old" should, pounds in that one with solid meaning.

I keep walking.

Seeking out the one person who'll restore the calm to my bloodstream. Who'll re-center my careening thoughts as no one else can.

But Emma's not at the head table, at the bar, or in the ladies' room. I know this because Lydia's returned to Foley's side, but my wife hasn't reappeared with her.

I keep looking.

The wedding venue is filled with lots of patios, breezeways, and alcoves fit for chatting. She's not in any of those either— though at last I route her out, lingering on a little porch on the back side of the kitchen. Her light sweater is draped over her shoulders. There's a thoughtful, faraway look in her eyes...and an entrancing, ethereal beauty in her profile.

And just like that, all my air is gone again.

Along with every thought or care or concern in my head. Yeah, even the upheaval over imagining my mother and Fershan Bennett in ways I never anticipated.

In this quiet twilight moment, there's only the perfect force of her. The one who's given magic to my world, pure light to my existence.

Holy God, how I love this person.

I walk up quietly, though the little shiver down her form is a damn good indication that she's already aware of me. This knowledge we have of each other...this surreal awareness... it's only gotten stronger during our months of freedom from Faline and the Consortium, and I couldn't be happier.

It's so good. It's so perfect. It's so us.

As destiny has dictated.

As my soul newly promises.

"Wow," I finally deadpan. "Killer view you got here." Which is basically...a parking lot. Then a small strip of the lavender and aqua marina waters. Then...another parking lot.

"Right?" she snarks in return. "But it's quiet, at least."

"And you're feeling the need for quiet?" My gentle prompt is hardly necessary. No matter what we've been through together, secrets have never worked well for us. Even surprise birthday gifts, like the sex swing she bought me last month, have a tendency to do shit like take out half the ceiling when put into motion. That was the night we both almost ended up in traction...

I almost laugh out loud about that now but instead jump on the excuse to again suckle her nape. Filling my senses with the vanilla smoke from the tea lights along the rail, as well as my wife's honeysuckle sweetness, is the boost I need to utter *my* chunk of truth.

"So...I just told Fershan he could court my mom."

At once, Emma bursts into a long giggle. I put up with her mirth, simply happy I've given her a reason to be laughing so hard.

Okay, *really* hard.

At last, she settles enough to say, "Well, first of all, it's about freaking time. And secondly, dude...you said he could *court* her?"

I clear my throat. "Fine. I probably sounded like some crusty old king about it."

She laughs again—not as long or as loud, thank fuck—before leaning back to cuddle our bodies closer. "Well, you're my crusty old king, so that's all right."

I unfurl a savoring growl into her hair. "Crusty old kings are also known for protecting their own. With swords and guns and even lightning bolts."

"Oooooh." She feels so right, wiggling against my chest. "Swords and guns and bolts. That's way more fun than crusty."

I push her away, but only for the purpose of sweeping her around to face me. "And you *know* how I feel about giving you more."

She pushes in until there's no room left between our bodies. I groan against her forehead as everything between my thighs cheers in approval. She fans the flames of my erection even higher as soon as she says, so breathy and beautifully, "But you already have, Reece Richards." She surges up on tiptoes to take my mouth in a warm, wet, nerve-popping, tongue-tangling kiss. "And guess what? You've done it because of the magic and excitement and glory that is *you*. Because of all the ways you make me laugh and all the ways you make it okay when I cry. Because of your passion and your fire, your nobility and your loyalty, and your commitment to being the best man you can be, each and every day. You give my world all of its *more* just by being in it, my love—and I will never, ever stop being grateful for the gift of you."

I'm numb all over again. I can hardly think beyond the certainty of loving her back, in all those ways and a billion more. I can't feel anything beyond our mingled breaths on the night air and the sweet tugs of her fingers at the ends of my hair. But as her little pulls get more forceful, so do the turquoise fires in her eyes—and the fervent passion in her voice.

"You're my *more*, Reece Andrew Richards, because of the way you love me...and because of the way you complete me."

I'm finally able to haul in a huge breath. I gulp it down with emotion that turns my throat into a vise and my eyes into stinging heat. "As you complete me, Emmalina Paisley

Richards. Forever and always...and beyond." I drop my head until our foreheads meet. "Don't ever stop loving me. Don't ever stop being my *more*, as well."

Our lips find each other once again. We mesh and claim and adore each other with the phenomenal force that only our kisses can convey...only our passion can fully express. I clutch her closer, fusing my energy to hers...pledging my spirit to always cherish, honor, serve, and fulfill hers.

"You see?" she finally whispers, staring deep into my eyes. Her brilliant smile flips every neuron in my system. "Here's the *more*, baby. Right here. You and me. We don't need swords and pistols and duels and jousts."

I kiss her again, tasting the seam of her lips with the tip of my tongue before husking, "But how about a little lightning?"

An impish smile spreads across her gorgeous lips. It widens as she swings our joined hands upward until they're clasped in the space between our chests...

A mesh of my glaring neon-blue digits and her golden glowing ones.

"Only if a few solar flares are okay too?"

A long, loving laugh rumbles out of me—before I kiss her soundly, thoroughly, and passionately again. And again. And again. I race my hands up and down her body, making sure she's very aware of the way we're going to end this brilliant, jubilant day. Her answering moans affirm she's already on board with my plan—already connected to my every hot, full desire.

As she always will be.

The completion of my passion.

The connection of my soul.

The partner of my life.

The bolt of my world.

At last, I find the strength to speak again—but I'm sure the volume's possible only because of the lightning roaring through my senses, the fire surging my blood...and the love illuminating every fiber of my heart.

The love that's moved me.

The light that's powered me.

The woman who's challenged me, changed me, pushed me, startled me, ignited me, inspired me, moved me, rocked me, reduced me, rebuilt me, and raised me to heights of fulfillment and happiness I never knew could exist. The human who's shown me all the glory and power in my own humanity. The miracle who's proved to me that miracles *do* exist.

My wife. My sun. My goddess. My life.

My superhero.

"Lead the way, baby," I whisper as I hold her close with all the strength in my body, the love in my heart, the lightning in my soul. "I'm ready for the adventure."

ALSO BY ANGEL PAYNE

The Bolt Saga:
Bolt
Ignite
Pulse
Fuse
Surge
Light

Honor Bound:
Saved
Cuffed
Seduced
Wild
Wet
Hot
Masked
Mastered
Conquered
Ruled

Secrets of Stone Series:
(with Victoria Blue)
No Prince Charming
No More Masquerade
No Perfect Princess
No Magic Moment
No Lucky Number
No Simple Sacrifice
No Broken Bond
No White Knight
No Longer Lost
No Curtain Call

**For a full list of Angel's other titles,
visit her at AngelPayne.com**

ACKNOWLEDGMENTS

Dear Readers and all Team Bolters,

I absolutely can't believe I'm writing this letter—and wrapping up the very final piece of Reece and Emma's adventures. As you can well imagine, the act comes with an immense combination of so many crazy emotions, culminating from a year of pouring every shred of my heart and soul into this project. Those of you who know me well, or have followed the journey of the Bolt Saga, know that this was a passion project like no other for me, born from a deep love and appreciation of all things superhero blended with a craving to lend the genre something cool and new.

The idea of doing so was—and has been—daunting. A story of this scope was bigger and bolder than anything I'd tried before, especially because I was determined to honor everything cool about superhero fiction *and* passionate romance. I hope that most of the time you think we got it right!

I use the term "we" because there is no way these stories would have become everything they are without a seriously amazing Dream Team, helping me to finesse the words, the tone, the voices, and the vision into the six books you've enjoyed. It is my pleasure, honor, joy, and privilege to thank all of them now.

Actually, "thanks" seems a horrifically pathetic word

for expressing my unending gratitude—and unfathomable amazement—for the patience, fortitude, strength, and guidance of my *outstandingly* talented editing team. **Scott Saunders** and **Jeanne De Vita**, the two of you were the very original Team Bolt, and without you, these stories simply wouldn't be here. Thank you for the handholding through the tears, the listening ears through tricky plot points, the strokes of genius that helped make some of the books' best moments, and the cheerleading when I needed it most. But most importantly, thank you both for caring enough to give me your complete honesty and unflagging passion about this project. This thing was so much more than a paying gig for both of you, and I knew that without a doubt, every step of the way. I have no idea how I'll ever show you the scope of my gratitude.

Of course, a project that busts boundaries is nothing without a team who feels it can truly soar—and for that belief, I am eternally, euphorically grateful to every member of the **Waterhouse Press** publishing team. **Meredith Wild**: from the very first day you read this thing in its original form, you have been Bolt's biggest cheerleader, encouraging me to stretch for this unreal dream of mine. You took my insane little lightning bolt and turned it into an astounding star storm. I have no words for how to thank you for that unflagging belief and love. Additionally, thank you to **Jon McInerney**, **Robyn Lee**, *and* **Haley Byrd** for the phenomenal support on marketing efforts—and to **Yvonne Ellis**, **Amber Maxwell**, and **Kurt Vachon** for making everything look so gorgeous. Additionally, so much thanks to both **Jesse Kench** and **Jennifer Becker** for handling the nitty-gritty details and making my life so easy. I appreciate you all more than words can say!

I cannot begin to say how grateful I am for the artistic

genius of the amazing **Regina Wamba**, who turned twelve hours on a snowy Minnesota day into photographic gorgeousness for the Bolt Saga graphics. I continue to be indebted to **Anthony Kemper** and **Hannah Lundquist**, who put their all into becoming Reece and Emma! Thanks to **Peter Phungus** on hair and makeup, as well as beautiful **Yuli Xenexai** for your shoot styling skills.

Bringing up a book baby truly takes a village—and in mine, there have been some friends that have gone "above and beyond" during the year it took to birth this thing! **Victoria Blue**, I appreciate your understanding, flexibility, and constant support. *Thank you!* I couldn't have done this without all of our Maniacs sprints with **Meredith Wild**! Cyber high-fives! Gooo Maniacs! **Carey Sabala**: you have become so much more than a fellow fangirl. I am eternally, endlessly thankful for all the long chats and understanding—and even for your three-hour drive to help me out at my comic-con signing! You are *amazing*! **Tracy Roelle**, thank you for being there and for all the cyberhugs when I needed them. Love you so hard, lady! **Shayla Black**: if you had a dollar for every time I've asked you to drop everything and talk...well, just know I would gladly pay that and more. Your wisdom, insights, and compassion have been gold. Thank you, lady, from the bottom of my heart. I'm also grateful for my fellow superhero fangirl goddess writers, **Anissa Garcia** and **Joany Kane**, who were always there with the awesome Marvel memes when I needed them most. You two rock my world so hard!

I cannot begin to encompass how much I thank the Creator, on a daily basis, for **Martha Frantz**. Lady, you really *do* need a cape and a big "S" on your chest! You are my Superwoman, through and through—but more than anything, you are such a beautiful and trusted friend. I am so thankful for you, and I'll likely die trying to show you that.

The crazy-insane hours of writing, reaching deep, and stretching far for this story would have been excruciating torture without the unfaltering support of some diehard, core Team Bolt Bunnies. Please forgive me if I missed anyone, but I really want to acknowledge the girls who have literally *been there since the beginning* on this and have *never* hesitated to jump in with support and love for our beloved super mutants: *Linda Dunn*, *Bethany Bachman*, *Corinne Akers*, *Amy Bourne*, *Kika Medina*, *Shel Abshire*, *Kelly Wolford*, *Belle Torres*, *Sharon Wingo*, *Shelley Peake*, *Jessica Adams*, *Nicole Posey*, *Karen Aguilera*, *Lorraine Gibson*, *Angela Tyler*, *Phuong Richardson*, *Ceej Chargualaf*, *Toni Paul*, *Trenna Harris*, *Amanda McCalip*, *Dawn Massie*, *Ramona Stacey*, *Carol Ann*, and *Dorothy Sobota*.

And as I'm on the subject of fangirling: a shout of thanks heavenward to the late, great *Stan Lee*, who showed the world that being a great hero means being a great human first. *Excelsior*, sir. You are missed.

Last—but absolutely not least—thank you to every single fellow geek girl and guy who has reached out to encourage me about taking on something like Bolt. Thank you for understanding that at the heart of heroism, there is love— and that true love, when experienced in its fullness, can guide us and lift us to being the finest versions of ourselves. Thank you for opening your hearts to me and for sharing your stories and your souls. You have made it abundantly clear that I'm not alone in this thinking. Please don't ever stop celebrating all the good that is in you too—and reaching for the compassion, caring, kindness, and love that we can all access within ourselves.

    Love your lightning. It's what will make you a hero.

    Team Bolt Forever.

With Love and Light,

Angel

ABOUT ANGEL PAYNE

USA Today bestselling romance author Angel Payne loves to focus on high-heat romance starring memorable alpha men and the women who love them. She has numerous book series to her credit, including the action-packed Bolt Saga and Honor Bound series, Secrets of Stone series (with Victoria Blue), the intertwined Cimarron and Temptation Court series, the Suited for Sin series, and the Lords of Sin historicals, as well as several standalone titles.

Angel is a native Southern Californian, leading to her love of being in the outdoors, where she often reads and writes. She still lives in Southern California with her soul-mate husband and beautiful daughter, to whom she is a proud cosplay/culture con mom. Her passions also include whisky tasting, shoe shopping, and travel.

Visit her at AngelPayne.com